D0959232

Deep Background

Also by David Corn

Blond Ghost: Ted Shackley and the CIA's Crusades

Deep Background

David Corn

ST. MARTIN'S PRESS

NEW YORK

THOMAS DUNNE BOOKS.
An imprint of St. Martin's Press.

Design by Ellen R. Sasahara

ISBN: 0-312-20900-2

10 9 8 7 6 5 4 3 2

For Steven and Barry

"You spin it and it's over."

—Thomas Hale Boggs, Jr., a prominent
 Washington lobbyist, on how to handle
 political scandal

Deep
Background

1

He paused at the top of the moving stairs and looked down to where it was dark. That was the way home. Maybe tonight, if he arrived at a decent hour, it would be different. No arguments. No shouting about where he had been, about why he never was around, about the money for this, the money for that, about her loneliness, her disappointment. And none of the silence that followed, during which they realized there was nothing else to shout, say, or whisper.

Other commuters pushed past as he considered. He watched the steps appear out of nowhere. *Do it*, a voice said—a voice from an earlier day. Break the pattern. Put one foot forward. Descend to the train. Stride through the townhouse door sooner than expected, carrying flowers, wine—*do it*, he thought. Everything might change. He pictured her at home, fixed in anger, blaming him for all of it. Waiting for the moment when he crosses the threshold and becomes the available target.

He stared down the escalator. Tomorrow, he said to himself.

He opened his umbrella, walked up Connecticut Avenue in the sticky rain, entered the Mayflower Hotel, and headed straight to the bar.

The thick-necked bartender with a boxer's nose greeted him with a nod. The same bar, once again. Shit, last week, he had been quoted in a newspaper profile about the bartender—the guy had won some contest—and the story described him as a five-nights-a-week regular.

This was a spot to be left alone. But three nights ago a heavy-bearded fellow insisted on buying him drinks to celebrate some unspecified triumph and spent an hour trying to find a common link with him. Someone he knew who knew someone who knew someone who knew him. No such person was found.

The place was not crowded. Probably the rain, he thought. He took off his suit jacket, sat at the bar, and ordered a vodka and tonic.

His hands gripped the rail. It can't go on, he thought. He stared out the window at people rushing home. He watched a famous television reporter hail a cab. Can't go on, he repeated silently. The fights with his wife. The trouble at the office. They were threatening to force a new assignment on him after he had been in his current position for only three months. He had given years to the service and had been awarded with a prestigious posting. Now they were complaining. Your concentration is just not there, they said. Something at home? Something else? They didn't have the guts to say it: the drinking? They probably had seen that story in the paper. In any event, they said, there's this new man we want to try. They had wanted him out this week. He had managed to postpone any change until after the Fourth. Maybe in the next two weeks he could . . .

Spent, he thought. Spent. His gaze fixed on two old men in dark suits—they looked like brothers—at a table by the window. Another vodka and tonic. Perhaps it was time to push on. He was finishing his third drink.

She had been sitting next to him for several minutes before he noticed her. He turned when he saw the bartender's eye hold on her, and he caught her face dead-on.

"Don't," she said.

"Don't what?"

"Don't turn away and pretend you weren't looking."

He started to talk.

"No, no," she interrupted. "You don't have to say anything, no stupid excuses. I sat here because I wanted to meet you. There's practically no one down here, and I wanted company."

Twenty-four, he guessed. Maybe Twenty-five. Teenage to thirty all seemed the same to him. Her hair was long, straight—what they call chestnut brown?—her lips plump. Her eyes—he couldn't tell in this light. Something was off.

"They're different."

He waited for her to continue.

"My eyes. You probably can't see in here. One is blue, one is gray."

In front of her was a notebook with the logo of the Department of Justice. She moved it aside.

"In town for a conference," she said.

"A lawyer?"

"No work talk. I know this is Washington, but let's pretend it's not for a few minutes."

He lifted his drink in a silent toast.

The bartender placed a scotch before her and moved off. He watched where the glass met her lips. He had stopped thinking about leaving the bar. He signaled for a vodka and tonic. He decided not to wonder why

2

this was happening, not to worry that his hair was thinning and that he was developing a slump.

She talked about growing up in Michigan and fishing trips with her father in the Upper Peninsula. He told her he left college to be a jazz pianist. They ordered another round. She mentioned a brother who had died in a car crash. He told her about the time he had seen a ghost in a Vermont farmhouse. She did not believe him and laughed as he tried to convince her.

"Alexia," she said, holding out her hand. "Or Alex."

"Brady." He grasped her hand.

After two hours of talking, she asked if he would escort her to her room. He said yes. This was better, he thought, much better, than once again having to call a friend in search of a bed or couch where he could wait out another night.

In the elevator, his arm brushed against hers. He thought about the escalator to the Metro. Both looked straight ahead. When the door opened, she took his hand. They walked past a maid toward her room. At the door, she looked for her key in her bag and dropped her notebook. He picked it up and noticed the first page was blank.

"A boring conference?" he asked.

"Aren't they all?"

She opened the door. The room was dark. She leaned in front of him to reach the light switch. He smelled her hair. The light came on. She closed the door behind them.

"Alex," he started to say.

The door to the bathroom swung open. Neither of them saw the gun. Nor did they hear the shot that tore through Brady's head. And before she could scream, she was dead, too.

The assailant knelt over the dead man and emptied his pockets. From the pile, he selected one item. He then went through her bag and found the microcassette recorder he had given her. He pushed the rewind button, waited, and pressed the play button.

"Seriously, one time Monk came in when we were playing in this West Side dive, and he—"

He put out the "Do Not Disturb" sign, went to the bed, and lay down, his head against the pillows. He reached for the remote control and turned on CNN. He looked at what he had retrieved from the dead man—a laminated press pass on a chain. He hit the play button again and listened to the tape, fast-forwarding whenever the woman spoke. He watched the television, with the sound turned off.

2

The White House
West Wing—June 21

Another trip to New Orleans. Nick Addis was not looking forward to it. He pushed around the papers on his desk. He couldn't sort out the mess: checks, tax returns, land records. He read the memo again. Re-create the trail. Find anyone who knew anything. Go to New Orleans. Don't tell anyone. But if anybody asks, don't say you're not going.

He looked at the bare walls. Another reorganization, another shuffle of offices was under way. Too many people here, he thought, care more about where their desks are located than anything else. Next to his own desk was a stack of boxes and pile of books. On top of the books was a framed postcard from LaTeenah Williams, a student he had fifteen years ago when he taught American history in a East New York high school. After graduating from Harvard, Addis, the son of two Columbia University professors, had postponed his plan to attend Yale Law School and answered the call of the New York City public school system, which, facing a teacher shortfall, had instituted an emergency recruitment program. Addis was placed in a school where he was one of four white teachers. He spent two years riding the subway each morning and plotting how to engage his uncaring students in the history of the United States. The slavery trade—what happened to slaves who rebelled? The building of the transcontinental railroad—how many Chinese laborers were worked to death? The California gold rush—who in the class realized that it led to the most severe slaughter of Native Americans in the country's entire history? The Jim Crow era—who knew that Joshua Gibson, a star in the negro baseball league, hit more home runs in a season than Babe Ruth? Half the class had not been able to identify Babe Ruth.

Few students took his bait. Most were more concerned with avoiding the violence in the school's hallways or guessing who was the father of the baby being carried by this or that student. But LaTeenah Williams, a

4

short, slight girl with a long neck and large eyes, had been one of the few students who had listened and absorbed. Years later, Addis still remembered the report she had written on how President Johnson manuevered civil rights legislation through Congress, cutting deals to win a greater good. Addis had encouraged her to go to college and helped with her applications. She sent him the postcard when she started City University. "Teachers make us all," she had written. "Thank you." Last he had heard from Williams—and that was several years back—she had become a psychiatric social worker based at a hospital in the South Bronx. He stared at her deliberate handwriting and wondered how many people she had helped directly: a suicide prevented, an abused woman rescued from a personal hell, an addict placed into a treatment program. Could Addis claim a piece of these triumphs? Even a small one?

Shit, here I am advising the most powerful man in the world, and I'm thinking, maybe I should have stayed a teacher. . . .

Then he recalled the evening at law school when he and the professor who ran the low-income law clinic had pulled an all-nighter to finish a petition for several families tossed out of a housing project for nonpayment. Why'd you come to law school? she had asked Addis. All he could offer was a cliché: So I can take a swing or two at changing what I don't like in our world. Very noble, she had said, but remember, the smallest victories are the truest.

Addis thought about where he should place LaTeenah Williams's postcard. He picked up a mounted cartoon: a caricature of the previous President at a podium, frantically waving his arms and saying, "Enrico Fermi, I. M. Pei, Lee Ioccoca—what sort of American names are these?" Below the cartoon was an inscription: "Add Nicholai Addis to the list. Without you, none of this would have been possible." It was signed by Bob Hanover, the President of the United States, and dated the day of his inauguration.

The cartoon referred to an event early in the presidential campaign. A foreign reporter had asked the President about a statement made by an aide to Louisiana Governor Bob Hanover, who was competing in the presidential primaries of the other party. The reporter had used Addis's full first name—given to Addis to honor a grandfather from Russia—which nobody ever did. "Nicholai Addis?" the President had replied. "What kind of American name is that?" After days of unfavorable editorials, the President sent Addis a letter of apology and one of the shoes he had been wearing when he made the remark. "Finally got it out of my mouth," the President had written.

Addis then announced he was sending the shoe to a Washington goodwill store and called for the President to donate the other shoe. Days later, Addis checked with the thrift store. Nothing had arrived from the President. That evening when a network anchor was concluding a live interview with Hanover, he asked what was most on the candidate's mind those frantic days. Hanover grinned: "Well, Mike, I'm waiting for the other shoe."

Hanover's quip made the cover of the major newspapers the following morning. He repeated it for days. Finally, the President donated a case of new shoes to the thrift shop.

Addis's face-off with the President turned him into a political celebrity. Photographs of the most influential campaign aide of the political season appeared in newspapers and newsmagazines. One long piece in a gossipy weekly speculated that Hanover had embraced Addis as a replacement for Hanover's brother, a zookeeper and part-time evangelist in Orlando. A woman's magazine put Addis on its first male cover: "Tall, Skinny, Pale, Nerdy: A Sex Symbol for Now." His toothy, crooked smile stretched across a full page. That had been four years ago.

In his barren office—no window this time—Addis looked at the unpacked boxes. The latest staff shuffle had been prompted by his own suggestion. With Hanover drawing no competition from within the party, the primaries had gone too well. Hanover's reelection campaign, predictably, was attracting little attention from the media. Instead, the press was obsessed with the surprising rise of first-term Florida Governor Wesley Pratt, Hanover's likely opponent in the November election. A onetime country-western singer who had entered politics merely five years ago, the handsome, silver-haired Pratt had won the Iowa caucuses of his party, with the backing of religious activists, and had gone on to sweep most of the subsequent contests. To counter Pratt's momentum, Addis had in mid-spring proposed moving his party's suspense-free convention from the sleepy days of August to the weekend of July 4. Changing the date would bring more attention to the event, the party, and the President.

It was, Addis recognized, a tacky idea: a rip-roaring, red-white-and-blue convention on America's birthday. Satellite connections to Fourth of July celebrations across the country. Country singers—who were not for Pratt—rock stars, orchestras, marching bands. And fireworks, plenty of fireworks.

Hanover embraced it. The mayor of Chicago, the hotel owners, and others screamed about the hardships of moving the date. But Hanover said to do it. Several White House aides were transferred to the campaign office, replacements were appointed, and a series of office roulette had ensued since then. Somehow Addis had lost both his office window and his assistant in the most recent shift. Another assistant, the daughter of the ambassador to Portugal, was due to start tomorrow.

Addis reread the latest memo from Chief of Staff Brewster McGreer. A reporter from a second-rate newspaper in Pittsburgh had been calling the White House press office, asking about an old land deal in Louisiana involving the Hanovers. No one on the staff knew anything about it. The President had provided McGreer the basic details: It had been a straightforward property investment. We were in and out, he said. Picked up some money, declared it all. In his personal papers, Hanover had located some records. McGreer had forwarded the documents to Addis. Sort it all out, McGreer instructed Addis: "Probably not much, but I'm a worrier. Go to New Orleans. See who's saying what."

Shit, New Orleans. Addis thought about his two previous trips to New Orleans. Nearly five years ago, the phone in his cluttered one-bedroom Washington apartment had rung past midnight. Governor Bob Hanover of Louisiana was on the line with an invitation. Could Addis drop by his office in New Orleans tomorrow? A reservation already had been arranged for a morning flight, and Hanover had checked with Addis's boss, Hugh Palmer, the Senate majority leader. "He's all for it," Hanover said with a laugh.

Addis didn't have to ask what was on Hanover's mind. He said he would be there.

In Hanover's office, the two had discussed strategy, the current state of the political culture, the themes that would move voters, excite donors, and impress editorial writers. They talked for three hours. Hanover, fifty-one years old, was square-faced, with a nose that hooked slightly to his right, and the perfect, disciplined speckled hair of a politician. He was more handsome in person than on television.

Toward the end of the conversation, Addis asked if he could pose a frank question.

"I'm waiting," Hanover replied with a grin. "And nervous."

"Everyone who runs for president has his own personal motives for doing so. But, basically, they're all driven. They all want to run the world, and they all believe they are singularly equipped to do so—"

"Naturally," Hanover interrupted with a laugh. It was a solid laugh that came straight from his chest. "And a few of us are right."

"They all want to prove that," Addis continued. "But why else do you want to be president."

"The high-minded answer, right?" Hanover said. "How I want to help all Americans better their lives and that of their families, right? Now, who isn't going to say that? You're asking for my vision-thing."

Hanover placed his fingertips together. He's concentrating his sincerity, Addis thought.

"This country, and the world," Hanover said, "are entering new and uncertain times. The forces and institutions that are propelling and profiting from this transition do not, by design, have an interest in tempering the changes to ensure that we avoid the harsher consequences. After all, these consequences are born by those whose hands are far from the levers of power: blue-collar workers deindustrialized out of a job; suburban moms who feel they have less control of their children and their communities; minimum-wage workers in Silicon Valley blocked from joining a union; young adults whose first jobs come with no benefits and no security. The global and national changes we must wrestle with are nearly inevitable, and the distribution of power in this nation—and throughout the world—is mostly immutable. But there is room, there is space, for demanding that the concerns of those not at the table when the new order is arranged be considered and be taken into account. Nick, to be honest— and I'd never say this to a class of eighth graders—I doubt that one man can change the world. By that, I mean fundamentally transform it. Not even the President of the United States can stem certain tides. But he can do a helluva lot if he knows when and where to push. I think you and I, maybe with the help of one or two others"—Hanover laughed again— "can figure out where to push. Now, do I pass the audition?"

Hanover was smiling. He has deep eyes, Addis thought.

Before Addis replied, Hanover drew a full breath and said, "I am going to be the next President of the United States, and I want you to be there with me."

As with Addis's previous positions—special assistant to the chair of the Equal Employment Opportunity Commission, counsel to the chair of the House Judiciary Committee, and chief of staff for the majority leader of the U.S. Senate—he had not had to apply for the job Hanover was offering him. Since graduating from Yale Law School, one important person had always referred Addis to another: *There's this young man, the most capable, intelligent, young man I've met in years, who I think would be just right. . . .* The jobs had come.

Although Addis did not know who had recommended him to Hanover, he had prepared himself for this moment. He had plowed through piles of clips on Hanover and his potential rivals in the party. He knew all the details of the Hanover story: born to public school teachers in Baton Rouge, Harvard '66, recon patrol in Vietnam, returned home with a commendation and appeared on Buckley's show as a critic of the war, NYU Law, assistant professor at Tulane Law. Hanover ran for attorney general—practically on a dare—as a reform candidate. He attacked the machine hacks of his own party and was an unknown underdog written off by the political handicappers. Then a wing in a public hospital collapsed, killing seven children, the result of the shoddy work of a builder who had obtained the contract in the sort of sweetheart deal Hanover had campaigned against. The disaster brought him statewide and national notoriety. He won by fifteen points. As attorney general, Hanover successfully prosecuted those responsible for the hospital disaster and went on to become governor. It was a grand story, one of the best known in modern politics. Hanover even married the daughter of the businessman/fixer whose cronies had rigged the hospital contract. He was the only national political figure to be the subject of a made-for-television movie: *For the Children: The Bob Hanover Story*. Addis had watched it three times.

Weeks before his meeting with Hanover, Addis had pored over the results of the last presidential election, congressional district by congressional district. He had done the calculations: Louisiana had few electoral votes, but it was next to Texas. He had covered as many angles as he could imagine. The race would be close, he had concluded. Any one of several could claim the nomination. But the best chance, in his estimation, resided with Hanover. The call from Hanover was the one he had wanted.

Sitting behind his desk, Hanover had locked his gaze on Addis and passed his certainty to Addis. Yes, Addis thought, in a year-and-a-half, I'll be in the White House, helping this man lead a nation.

"I'd be honored," Addis told him.

He stood to leave. The two shook hands. But then Addis remembered. One other thing. He had promised his girlfriend, Holly Rudd, that they would go to the next New Orleans Jazz Festival. They had missed the past two—each time he had had to cancel due to work—and he had vowed that this time they would be there.

"It's when the western primaries are—"

Hanover interrupted: "If I am right—and I am—one weekend won't make a difference. Whenever you can, Nick, keep your promises."

In his White House office, Addis looked at the computer screen:

1407 POTUS/Residence.

The screen told him and other senior staff where the President of the United States was at any given moment. When the abbreviation *POTUS* flashed, it meant Hanover was moving. Now Addis could see the President was in the family residence of the East Wing. He imagined Hanover trying on different ties, preparing for the afternoon press conference. Addis opened the small refrigerator in the corner of his office and took out a can of Coke.

One weekend won't make a difference.

Hanover had been wrong about that.

Addis and Holly Rudd did make it to New Orleans for the music festival. They saw the shows at the fairgrounds; they dined at four-star restaurants. Wherever the couple went, well-wishers interrupted them. Local politicos and passersby urged Addis to send heartfelt messages to their campaigning governor. People asked to have their photograph taken with him. They all smelled a win. Hanover's rivals for the nomination were fading; he was on track to the nomination.

Rudd did not mind any of this, even though she and Addis had not seen each other in six weeks. He was working out of the campaign office in Washington, when not traveling with Hanover. She was at a labor law firm in New York City and spending time in Austin assisting with the appeal of a convict on death row. Ever since she and Addis had interned at the Death Penalty Legal Defense Fund during law school, she had worked pro bono for the outfit.

Then the weekend went bad. McGreer called Addis on Sunday morning. Donny Lee Mondreau, a twenty-six-year-old retarded black man sentenced to death for murdering a convenience store owner in Point Coupee Parish was going to be executed by lethal injection in two days. A reporter had asked if Hanover intended to be in his office during the execution. It had not been on Hanover's overflowing schedule. Instead, he was due to be in California for a series of fundraisers. A day of conference calls followed. While Addis was on the phone, Rudd went shopping. When she returned, he informed her of the decision: Hanover would interrupt his campaign to fly back to Louisiana.

Staring at the boxes next to his desk, Addis once again replayed the conversation they held while sitting on an unmade bed.

"Damnit, Nick, it's just for politics. A campaign ad in blood."

"You know, he's always been for it."

"Yeah, and you went to work for him."

"We've talked about this a dozen times, Holly."

"And it never made me feel any better."

"Well, I'm not willing to throw everything else away for a fight we can't win. The rest of the country is not us. You want to see him take a stand against executing convicted murderers, when seventy percent of voters are for it? Then you can watch the other side troop right in and rip up tax credits for the working poor, cut back school lunches for kids, slash away at old-growth forests, and, while they're at it, toss tax breaks to people facing the rough decision of whether to put in a pool or a tennis court at their country house. Shit, I've always been in this to do what I can, with what we have. You've got to figure out what matters the most, and how we can help the most."

"Everything matters. Especially what you throw away."

"And would it be better for him not to come? He's for it. He should be here and take responsibility."

"Takes a lot of courage to kill a retard whose lawyer was incompetent. . . . Did he ask you?"

"Yes."

10

"You know it's wrong, right?"

"Yes."

She got off the bed.

"That's what makes it worse."

And what New Orleans meant to him now was an airport where she looked at him and said "Don't lose," before passing through a metal detector. That had been the end of it. He had not seen her since.

Shit, New Orleans.

Addis didn't want to go. Especially not after that phone call he had received a month ago from—damnit, he didn't want to think about it any more. All this god-damn nostalgia. Put that call aside, he told himself.

Addis checked the screen. POTUS was flashing.

3

The White House
North Gate—June 21

Brady Sandlin, wearing a hat, walked through Lafayette Square. "Sandlin" was the name on the press pass; that is how he would think of himself today. He tugged on the beard. It held. He checked the putty on his nose. It was firm. The wig felt snug. He put on the sunglasses and crossed Pennsylvania Avenue. Control, he told himself.

At the guard booth, he waited. As the guard checked the credentials of a camera crew, he shifted back and forth on his feet. The drawer opened, and he placed the plastic card in it. The guard asked his birth date. He replied. The automatic lock clicked. He stepped into the booth. Another uniformed guard handed him an access pass on a chain.

"Walk through, please."

The metal detector whined.

"Step over here."

The guard waved a wand up and down his body. It screeched when it passed a jacket pocket.

"Empty it, please."

He handed the guard a cassette player. The guard pushed the play button. The machine whirred.

The guard returned the tape recorder. Another lock clicked open. He left the booth, entered the White House grounds, and headed toward the West Wing. His left arm twitched. Stop it, he muttered under his breath. Give me half-an-hour.

The pressroom in the West Wing was filling with reporters. He moved past the technicians working on the lines for the television lights. No one noticed him. Sandlin was new to the assignment; he worked for a small regional wire service. He was not the type to draw much attention from the rest of the press corps.

He asked a cameraman for directions and found the steps to the basement. He walked into the men's bathroom. It was empty. In one of the stalls, he sat on the toilet. Strapped to his leg was a plastic composite .45 caliber gun. He ripped off the tape and placed the weapon in his lap. With a dime, he loosened the screws on the back of the tape recorder. He removed two bullets and the metal firing pin for the pistol. He inserted the piece into the gun and loaded the Kevlar-coated bullets. He put the gun in his coat pocket. Before he stood up, he noisily grabbed several sheets of toilet paper, wrapped them into a ball, dropped the wad into the toilet, and flushed. He washed his hands and returned to the main room.

All the seats in the first few rows of the pressroom were occupied. He pushed his way to an open spot in the middle of the ninth row. Never get too close, he once had been instructed. In one hand, he held a notebook. He took off the hat and placed it beneath his seat.

"Two minutes," said a voice over the intercom.

Technicians hurried to their places. The lights went on. Television reporters stood with their backs to the podium, providing live introductions to their networks.

"In his weekly press conference, we expect the President will be asked questions about the China treaty, a possible Cabinet shuffle, and the use of the White House mess by a Hanover fund-raiser," a reporter was saying into a camera.

This room's much smaller than it appears on TV, he thought. Several aides entered the room. They passed out the written statement the President intended to read before taking questions. Five Secret Service agents positioned themselves near the platform, behind which hung a blue curtain bearing the White House emblem. He reached into his pocket.

Downstairs, in a room with no windows, Addis picked up the remote and turned on the television.

President Hanover strode into the press briefing room. The reporters stood. The man in the ninth row stood, too, feeling the weapon in his hand. He remembered the training: *It's an extension of you. Will the shot.*

Hanover smiled at the familiar faces in the first row. He nodded toward a reporter with a leg in a cast: "Your editor do that for writing that positive piece on our economic numbers?" The journalists chuckled. The President moved to the podium. "Now, remember, this is on deep background," he joked. The reporters laughed and began to sit.

Still standing in the ninth row, he kept his body stiff. He jerked up his arm. He fired twice. Two bullets slammed into the face of the President.

Done, the gunman thought. Done.

The room rushed toward him. Secret Service agents, weapons drawn, lunged into the crowd of reporters; others surrounded the President. The reporters to each side of the assailant pulled him to the floor. One grabbed the gun. He let it go. Other journalists had dropped to the ground, some shouting to their camera crews to keep filming. Aides ran to Hanover and were pushed back by Secret Service agents. "No, no, no, no," screamed the assistant press secretary. Blood spattered the blue curtain. The dead President was slumped over the podium.

A correspondent for a business wire service realized he was lying on top of the assassin. He felt Secret Service officers pulling at his back, trying to reach the shooter. In his hand he held the beard that had been attached to the assailant's face.

"Why?" the reporter shouted at him. "Why the fuck why?"

The man answered.

The correspondent was yanked away by a female Secret Service agent. The fake beard was snatched from his hand. The Secret Service detail descended on the gunman. They kept him on the ground. One agent dug a knee into his back.

Nothing matters now, he thought. Nothing.

Handcuffs snapped around his wrists. Hands moved across his body. There was nothing to find. The White House emergency medical team was in the room. The lead paramedic had his hands covered in blood. The face was gone. He could find no pulse. He barked instructions he knew were meaningless.

Downstairs in the Situation Room, three amber lights turned on. The watch officer punched in a coded signal to the Secret Service team traveling with the Vice President in Dallas. "Recall the football," he ordered an aide, "and activate the unit on Air Force Two."

"And immediately secure Nighthawk and Foxtrot," he said, referring to the First Lady and the Hanovers' thirteen-year-old son, Jack.

The Secret Service was hustling the shooter out of the pressroom. Television reporters were shouting voice-overs. Live feeds were being transmitted.

"I can't believe it, I can't believe it," a network correspondent was screaming into a handheld microphone. "The President's been shot. Been shot. In front of all of us, the entire world." He pushed his hair from in front of his face. "Not me," he yelled at the cameraman. "Him! Get the camera on him!"

One reporter tried to place a mike in front of the suspect. A Secret Service officer punched him in the eye. The CNN correspondent grabbed the business wire service man.

"Did he say anything to you? Did he?"

"You'll have to wait to read it." He hurried to his cubbyhole to call the bureau.

In his office, Addis shut off the television. He listened to the shouting in the hallway. He ignored the ringing of the phone. He picked up a yellow legal pad and went to find the chief of staff.

14

"Say something, you fuck."

Clarence Dunne stared at the assassin. In the thirty minutes since the murder of the President, the fellow in the chair had been silent. He wouldn't give his name, his address. Where did you come from? How did you get the gun. Did you make it yourself? Nothing. Who are you working for? Nothing. Who helped you? Nothing. Who else is targeted? Nothing.

And there had been nothing on him. Nothing in his pockets. Nothing up his ass. Every button was being examined. Every seam of his shirt, pants, and jacket was being ripped and probed. No legal niceties. They had thrown him into a pair of overalls. Fingerprints had been taken, and hair and blood samples collected. The putty had been scraped off his nose and saved for a laboratory examination. The wig placed into a plastic bag. It would all be traced—followed back as far as it could. What store sold such putty? Who worked there? Do you recall ever seeing a customer who resembles this fellow in the photograph? Did he say anything to you? Did you see anyone with him?

There was a tattoo on his chest—the letter *M* pierced by a dagger. He would not say what it stood for. There were scars, too. On his torso, on his stomach, on his thighs, on his arms. In each place the word *HAPPY* had been carved several times into the skin. With a razor blade or sharp knife, one of the White House doctors had told Dunne. Seventeen times. Jagged lines of scabs. The inscriptions on his abdomen were upside down. The man could look at himself and read the letters. Evidence, the doctor had said, that he had cut himself. Self-mutilation.

Why *HAPPY*? Dunne wondered. All over his body. What did it mean?

"Tell me, you sick fuck."

Nothing.

As he hurled questions at his captive, Dunne silently cursed his own damn luck. The first African American to head the Secret Service unit at the White House; the first Secret Service man to lose a President in over three decades. No matter what, no matter what he got the assassin to say now, Dunne's life was set forever: the man in charge on that day. Remember how you used to see this chunky black guy next to the President all the time? He had that weird gray patch on the side of his head. That was the guy who screwed up. No one was supposed to be able to waltz into the White House and on live around-the-world television plug the President of the United States. The three assassination attempts they had stopped this past year and kept secret—who would ever talk about those? Not even he would.

And the question: Why? This man in front of him, cuffed and restrained thirty feet below the ground in the high-security White House crisis center, would not say.

"We're going to find out your name. We're going to find out every damn thing about your pathetic life. We're going to interview every blue-assed grade-school teacher who ever had to look at your miserable mug. We'll find everything."

He sat stone-faced. He knew all the routines. He knew none would work. He had been trained. And these guys couldn't use the most persuasive tactics. He could teach them.

"Waiting for a lawyer?"

Waiting, yes. His leg twitched, his foot tingled, as if it were going numb.

The other agents sat in the room watching Dunne. A vein on the side of his head throbbed. This was his only chance. He could not put the bullets back into the gun. He could only explain.

An agent entered the room.

"The Bureau is here," he whispered to Dunne.

"Give me more time."

"Can't."

Dunne looked at the assassin. The man in the overalls was in his mid-thirties. He had a strong build. A tooth was chipped. His hair was closely cropped, his face oddly shaped, angular. He sat stiffly. He was disciplined. Dunne could tell this fellow was silently talking to himself. Telling himself something over and over.

"Damnit, say something. Don't you want the whole damn world to know why you did this?"

For the first time, the killer gazed directly at Dunne, not through him. "No," he said.

"Sir . . . ," the agent said to Dunne.

That's it. The pooch was screwed. Dunne waved his arms and nodded to the other agents in the room. They moved to undo the restraints and pulled the suspect out of the chair. The door opened and several men entered.

"Nothing?" one asked Dunne.

Dunne did not reply.

"Maybe we'll do a little better."

The assassin stopped as he passed Dunne. He wiggled his tongue over a rear molar and then bit down hard. He felt a spurt of liquid—then convulsions seized him. He fell to the floor. An agent ran for a medic. Dunne dropped to his knees and grabbed the shaking body. The man's eyes were rolling upward. Dunne reached into the man's mouth to keep it clear. The FBI agents shouted at each other. Someone pounded on his chest.

"Damnit!" Dunne yelled. "Don't do this, you fucker!"

A medic pushed Dunne aside. The shaking was slowing down. The pulse was slipping. The medic grabbed for a hypodermic. He jabbed a needle into an arm. He sought a pulse. There was none.

"Gone," he said.

They stood over the still body.

Dunne looked at the Bureau man.

"You won't do any better," Dunne said.

"Mr. Dunne, that's two today."

4

The White House
Roosevelt Room—June 21

Brewster McGreer paced around the oak conference table.

" 'She knows.' She knows?" he said. "What the fuck does that fucking mean?"

He was trying to make sense of the only two words the assassin had said to the business wire service reporter sixty minutes ago. "Any fucking ideas?"

The senior staff was there. No one answered.

"And *HAPPY?* Is this a fucking joke?"

Addis sat at the table and stared at the Nobel Peace Prize medal in the glass case, sitting on the mantel at the far end of the room. Teddy Roosevelt had won the award for brokering an end to the Russo-Japanese War.

Addis was in shock. They all were. His mind drifted to his first tour of the West Wing during the transition. A Navy officer who worked in the mess was showing him about. In this room, he pointed out the medal display. You've heard about San Juan Hill? he asked Addis. Without waiting for an answer, the officer disclosed that he had studied that Spanish-American War battle. His speech quickened: It was, you probably don't know, not actually a heroic contest, as depicted in Roosevelt legend, with T. R. valiantly leading the Rough Riders in the fight for the ridge overlooking Santiago. Addis began to feel trapped. The officer continued his well-rehearsed lecture. Roosevelt's force, he explained, engaged in desperate maneuvers, reckless and bloody attacks, and took many needless casualties. When the Navy man started diagraming the battle on a piece of scrap paper, Addis requested they push on. The fellow was disappointed. He handed Addis the drawing, and Addis had placed it in his pocket.

Addis raised himself from his reverie. McGreer was proceeding with a situation report, the word *fuck* punctuating almost every sentence. Yesterday—yesterday?—an intern had asked Addis if McGreer suffered from Tourette's syndrome. For what else would account for the amount of *fucks* in his speech?

Addis concentrated on the chief of staff: the kinky red hair that resembled an industrial product, the bushy eyebrows. In his early fifties, McGreer walked with a bow-legged gait. He was tall, nearly Addis's height. None of Hanover's main advisers, Addis thought, were short.

McGreer raced through the list. The Vice President was flying back from Dallas—again it had to be Dallas—and a federal judge had been located to administer the oath of office. White House security had been tightened to the maximum; the nearby streets were closed. The military, at the Vice President's command, had been placed on alert, to Defcon Four. The Cabinet was to meet in a few hours. The National Security Council was sending messages to Russia, China, and the allies: the President is dead, the succession is transpiring in an orderly fashion, the chain of command is intact, the U.S. government is in complete control of its nuclear arsenal. The First Lady and Jack were being brought back to the White House from the young boy's physical therapy session.

"The Vice President's speech?" Addis asked.

"At nine," McGreer said.

Ken Byrd, the press secretary, nodded. It was his second week on the job. His predecessor had resigned after a tabloid television news show aired video footage of her smoking marijuana at a celebration in Berlin the night the Wall fell.

"I'll tell the nets," Byrd said.

"What exactly will the Vice President say?" Addis asked.

"The President—"

Margaret Mason Hanover, the widowed First Lady, had entered the room. Half of the staff at the table stood. The others looked uncomfortable. Her gray hair was in its customary bun. Her eyes were red, her face ashen.

"If I understand correctly," she continued, "now he is the President."

No one spoke for a moment.

Only a week ago—or was it less?—she had passed through this room while Addis was chairing a planning meeting for a White House conference featuring former Cabinet members who were supporting Hanover's decision to sign a controversial trade accord with China. Several of these past officials had helped run the Vietnam War. "Great," Margaret Mason Hanover had whispered to Hanover, "we can call this event, 'War Criminals for Free Trade.' "

McGreer kept his eyes on her. "We do not know what he's planning to say," he said. "He insisted on writing his own draft. Something reassuring, he said."

19

No *fucks* now, Addis thought.

At the doorway, Lem Jordan stood with his arms crossed. He was the unofficial bodyguard and man-Friday to the First Lady. As a state trooper in Louisiana, Jordan had been part of Governor Hanover's security detail. He came with the Hanover's to Washington. He was a constant presence, always within yards of her or Jack. Addis stared at Jordan, a short, barrel-chested fellow with chipmunk cheeks. Addis always thought of him as a fire hydrant topped by a pie plate.

"Any explanations, Brew?" she asked.

"No, we have none," McGreer answered.

"And 'She knows'? It's all over the news . . ."

"No, Maggie, we—"

That was odd, Addis thought. McGreer had known her for years, ever since NYU Law. He always addressed her as Margaret. Only the President called her Maggie.

She looked at Dunne.

"Not yet, Mrs. Hanover," Dunne said. Maybe never, he thought.

"You know what people will say?"

Everyone in the room realized what she meant. That she was the one who knew, the *she* in *she knows*.

Is anyone going to ask her? Addis thought. The room was quiet.

"I have no idea. No idea. And *HAPPY*? Where do such crazy people come from? Where?"

It was as if she expected an answer. No one said anything.

"Well, you'll excuse me. I have a son to tend to, and a husband to bury."

She started to leave the room. At the door, she paused and without turning said, "Nick, please see me when you have a moment."

Byrd waited a few seconds and then returned to the plans. The ceremony at the National Cathedral—who would preside? The Hanovers' local pastor in New Orleans or a national religious figure? Hanover's brother, the part-time evangelist, had already told CNN that he wanted to officiate.

"Let's ignore the fuck," McGreer said.

The route from the cathedral to Arlington. A riderless horse? Or would it be too reminiscent of the last time? A private burial for the immediate family or a larger affair for the public? What if the turnout was not overwhelming? someone asked. What about music? What pieces will be performed? And by whom? How do we handle the invitations? someone else asked. Which world leaders? Addis floated away from the details.

"We have to be true to him," McGreer was saying. "The images of this day will fucking outlast everyone in this room. We must send him off with something better than the footage of his face being fucking . . ."

McGreer issued assignments. Addis was to meet the new President at Andrews Air Force Base and then assist—"gently," McGreer said—in the preparation of the speech that Sam Mumfries would deliver that night.

Before adjourning the session, McGreer turned to Dunne.

"What are the prospects? Will you have anything for the speech?"

"Not unless we get lucky."

McGreer started to curse.

"But," Dunne continued, "we—the Bureau is trying to locate the reporter whose credentials he used. Maybe they'll have something soon."

"Can we have a closed chapter the day after next?" McGreer asked, referring to the day of the funeral.

"I don't know," Dunne said. "As of now, no name. No known address. No known history. No known associates."

"Just a fucking unknown psycho," McGreer said "Try, try very hard. That's the fucking least we can do."

Dunne knew what McGreer was saying. He knew everyone in the room was watching to see how he would react. "Yes, sir," he said.

"Let's go," McGreer said to end the meeting. "We will have years to mourn. We have only hours to act."

Addis left without talking to anyone else. He wanted to avoid questions about the First Lady's request. He returned to his office, sat down at his desk, and shoved all the land deal papers into an accordion file. And he cried for the first time that day.

5

Rosslyn, Virginia
June 21

The scene played over and over. There were no ambiguities. Dozens of cameras had captured the truth. Julia Lancette sat at her desk, switching channels. With the obligatory warnings, news broadcasters introduced those three seconds again and again. There were different angles, but they all showed the same. She felt sick. She also felt sad, knowing that eventually—and likely soon—the nation would become inured to this image.

She had to concentrate. She had a professional interest in the variety of shots—and she hated that. Which one best showed his face? She had seen profiles, three-quarters, and a jerky head-on. One shot for an instant showed him after a reporter had pulled off the beard. But then he was smothered by a mob of journalists and Secret Service agents. One cameraman had captured his dazed look as he was hauled out of the room. Everything was on tape. She would do a second-by-second analysis and select the clearest pictures.

She already had what she needed most—the mug shots taken by the Secret Service in the bunker. She had fed a digital set of those images into the computer and had tried to run the DUO-SHOTS program. But a glitch had occurred, and she sent for a computer jock. Not until he arrived and tended to the problem would she have the alternative identity pictures. With a beard. Without a beard. With a mustache. Without. Twenty pounds heavier. Fifteen pounds lighter. Five years ago. Ten years ago. Large glasses. Small ones. And so on. She was putting together a file.

The phone rang.

"I didn't want to bother you earlier, dear. Thought you'd be swamped."

She looked at the empty desks in her office.

"We are, mother," she said. "It's very busy here."

"Isn't it terrible?" She was crying.

"Yes, it is."

"Your father won't talk, and he hated him."

"I know."

She flipped through the photographs of the scars—rough lines forming capital letters. How much had it hurt? she wondered.

"Are you okay?"

"Work is a good diversion."

"What do they have you doing?"

"Just standard background research. You know, the usual."

"I should let you go."

"Thanks, I'll call you later."

She turned off the television and picked up the sports section. An hour passed, and the buzzer sounded. She checked the surveillance screen: white male, age twenty-four, just shy of six feet, 140 pounds, scruffy beard. She reviewed the photograph on record and let him in.

"What a day," the computer repairman said as a greeting. She agreed and described the problem to him. "No problema," he replied and went to work. She made calls to dead lines.

"Yes, sir," she said into the phone. "We can get you five hundred words on that right away." She scribbled a note.

"Hey, Myra," she said. "Not enough time for an assignment like that." She shook her head after hanging up and punched in another number.

"Can you scoot over to the Capitol," she said, "and get reactions as to how this might affect passage of the China accord?" She closed a folder and placed it in a pile.

No one was on the other side of any of these conversations. But the rules called for it. When a noncleared individual was on the premises, you played the part all the way.

"I guess everyone is out covering something," he said, as he worked on the computer.

"You can imagine."

"But you're not getting any incoming calls?"

That's a sharp observation, she thought.

"They'll come later, when people start filing."

"Yeah, guess so. . . . So, where were you when—"

"Right here," she said. "Staring out the window, daydreaming, when a colleague called." She was glad she could tell the truth.

"I was across the river. There's this boathouse thing for one of the schools. Not much happening there in the middle of the day. Sometimes I chill there, take a break from the hurly-burly of competitive computer repairs. Go down to the rocks and light a . . . that is, just hang, you know. And this guy's going by in this kayak thing. Got on headphones, listening to a radio. And he starts shouting at me. 'They killed him. They killed Hanover.' I was freaked. But it's funny how they always say 'they.' "

When she didn't say anything, he continued talking: "So what does Inter-Business Media do? Funny, it's like IBM, right?"

"We're a news service for business periodicals—mainly overseas."

"Just wondering. You know, we have only a few private firms that use this program. Usually it's law enforcement. I have to go to Quantico all the time. . . . And, here we are."

He hit a command; the program began to whir. "You just had to re-configure the preferences. No biggie." He asked her to sign the bill.

"That says Janet—"

"Lang." She hated using this alias. A playmate struck and killed by a mail truck when they were both five years old.

"Yeah, got it. So what did you say you guys do with this program?"

She wondered why he was asking.

"Not much. I told the home office that we didn't need it. But some vice president there insisted. You know how it is. So I have to run monthly checks of all the programs and send in a report saying all's well."

"Funny thing to be doing today."

"Bureaucracies like their schedules."

"The way of the world," he said. "This sad world."

And then he left.

Now she could begin. The assignment was an obvious one—the most obvious one since her unit had been established.

The office had been set up by the director of the Central Intelligence Agency. He had tired of the constant stream of problems created by past CIA employees. The former Agency accountant caught managing shady currency transactions for an African dictator. The onetime Soviet affairs analyst now advising a Russian mafia chief. The weapons dealer busted in Peshawar for selling missile parts to China—he had handled the CIA's arms transfers to the *mujhadeen* in Afghanistan. Most of the "problem children," as the director called them, were former paramilitary agents arrested on drug charges. They hired lawyers who politely noted that pros-ecution would lead to the disclosure of secrets certain to embarrass the U.S. government in general, and the Central Intelligence Agency in par-ticular.

The director had become fed up with clearing the trash of his prede-cessors. He could not will away the crap. What was fucked, he once told Lancette, always remained fucked. But his motto was, *stay ahead of the curve*. And now, because of that, Julia Lancette was feeding digital imagery data into a computer.

A simple job—that's how Director Timothy Wenner had described this posting to her. He had plucked her out of the East European division of the intelligence directorate, where she had become an unwanted woman. Lancette had refused to revise a report on the Balkans to reflect her supervisor's bias in favor of a particular Serbian faction. In retaliation, the supervisor instigated a disciplinary action against her, claiming she had mishandled classified records. Rather than accept this punishment, she took the matter to the agency's inspector general. The IG concluded that the supervisor had tried to cook the report. The supervisor was demoted, and Lancette was cleared. But none of this helped her career. The story leaked to the press, and she had to testify before the Senate intelligence committee in a secret session. After that, no branch chief would touch her. Three years out of graduate school, she was undone professionally. The word was out: not a team player.

But she had impressed Wenner, and he asked Lancette to create an office to monitor news reports and law enforcement cables in order to determine whether any scumbag-in-the-news had Agency connections. She accepted what for most CIA officers would be a nightmare assignment.

There was no prestige to be gained by reviewing newspapers, wire reports, foreign periodicals, and then trying to pry sensitive information out of the bureaucracy to determine if the Agency might be in for an embarrassment. Most Agency people preferred to keep the past underground. And that meant keeping it far from the seventh floor of Langley. Who knows what Wenner might do with their secrets, their tales of old? Be ahead of the curve? Not in this regard. If you start digging, you can stir up all sorts of muck.

The Directorate of Administration located the new unit in a satellite office in Rosslyn, a long five miles from headquarters. The cryptonym assigned to the operation was ICEMAN. All code names were chosen by a computer at random. But Lancette had wondered if someone was sending her a message.

On the television, a network was replaying the footage once more. She typed in a series of commands. The DUO-SHOTS program was working fine. It kicked out a series of photographs of the assassin. As an overweight hippie ten years ago. As a fit-and-trim business executive six months ago. She prepared the packages for the relevant offices throughout the Agency. Old and current files would be checked. Under the director's orders, an ICEMAN request had to be responded to within twenty-four to forty-eight hours. But the project depended on the individual bureaucrats who conducted the review in each office. Any of them, Lancette realized, could miss that one relevant file—for whatever reason.

She began transmitting the material to the communications center at Langley. From there, her request would fan out through the innards of the Agency. She hoped there would be no matches.

25

6

Memorial Bridge
June 21

The armored, black limousine crossed Memorial Bridge into the District. In the long rays of the setting sun, the Lincoln Memorial took on a reddish tint. Addis felt weird; he was riding alone with the new President. There was a small army of Secret Service agents in the cars and vans accompanying them, with Washington police officers at the front and rear of the motorcade. But except for Addis and the two plain-clothed, armed men in the front seat, Sam Mumfries was on his own during his first trip to the White House as President.

Earlier that day Mumfries had flown to his home state for a party fundraiser with the businesspeople who had supported him for decades. A stiff man of patrician bearing, Mumfries four years ago had been bested in the primaries by Hanover. Then Hanover named him to the ticket, giving Mumfries and his Lone Star friends hope for the future. Four more years—then eight for *us*, Mumfries had been saying at a private club in Dallas that afternoon, when an advance person whispered the news.

Mumfries's chief of staff, Hamilton Kelly, had stayed in Washington to attend to convention plans. With Kelly and Brewster McGreer now dealing with the transition, Addis had rushed to Andrews Air Force Base to meet Mumfries and discuss the speech Mumfries was to deliver that night.

"Nick, you know, we—Bob and I, that is—we didn't like each other much," Mumfries said.

"I know."

"But never in a thousand years did I—"

"I know, Mr. President."

Addis had used the title to see how awful it would feel to say it.

"Any more word on the asshole who—"

"No, sir."

26

"But a lone gunman, right? Nutcase, right? No signs of a wider plot?"

"No evidence either way, not yet."

The car drove past the Vietnam Memorial and turned on to Constitution Avenue. The police had cleared the route. Tourists lined the street and stared, trying to see the forms behind the darkened windows.

"How's Margaret doing?"

"Busy with the plans, with Jack."

"You know, she and I never got along, even when we were kids. When I was growing up in Louisiana, our families were close. Did some business—my uncle and her pop. And then years later, me and her are. . . . I remember this one time, I came home from Iran—that's when I was in the Air Force and flying these secret missions we couldn't talk about. She must have been sixteen. There was a party. Junior League or a coming-out—something like that. Had on my uniform. She was a pistol. Kept asking where'd I been. I wouldn't tell her. But she kept at it. I said I couldn't say. And she near about threw a fit. Everyone looked at us—like we were having a lover's quarrel. Then I moved to Houston and didn't see much more of her."

Mumfries looked at his thick, stubby hands and let the story drift off. Addis studied Mumfries's face: wide fleshy nose, a furrowed brow, and jowly cheeks. He remembered a columnist observing that Mumfries was disappearing further and further into his own visage.

"And Brew wants you to talk to me about the speech, right?"

"Yes."

"Thinks I'll fuck it up somehow. Not do justice to Bob."

Addis said nothing.

"We know each other several years, right?"

"Yes, sir."

"When you were working for Palmer in the Senate you tried to fuck me a few times. And I tried to fuck you—or him, that is. We're a party that eats its own. Even if we don't fancy the taste."

"Well, I'm not sure—"

"Don't bother with the manure. The Honduras business—your boss Palmer didn't have the votes to shut down the operation in committee, so you gave it to the *Post*. Had to have hearings. And we had those damn nuns protesting. Even at my house. Know what it's like to come home to a bunch of nuns calling you a murderer?"

Addis started to protest, but Mumfries put up his beefy hands.

"No need. That was ages ago. You know, Nick, I can't tell you how much I really helped them—both of them. And not just delivering Texas. Biggest mistake you can ever make, my grandfather told me, is to think you have something all figured out."

Addis did not follow Mumfries, but he did not care.

27

"You tell Brew," Mumfries said, "that I'll get this right. Not to worry. No politics over a dead body. It will be all about healing, coming together, as a nation. Writes itself . . . I'm sorry to say."

Mumfries pulled out a piece of paper with scribbling on it.

"Jotted down a few lines on the flight. And I'll be happy to show you and Brew a draft. I'll show it to Margaret, if she wants to see it. All in the family. Just like old times. The Masons and the Mumfries."

The parade of vehicles was turning on to Pennsylvania. A crowd had gathered in front of the White House. Addis could see people holding up photographs of Hanover. One man was waving an American flag. Flowers were piling up by the front gate. Police officers and SWAT team members surrounded the block. Newspeople and camera operators jostled with each other for the best shot of the motorcade.

"So you don't have to hold my hand. But there is one thing."

"Anything, sir."

"I've never been much for poetry. Grew up reading Westerns, Zane Grey, Louis L'Amour."

Addis wondered if Mumfries knew that L'Amour had been a radical in Oklahoma in the 1930s.

"But I thought a touch of poetry might be appropriate tonight. If you have anything to suggest, drop it off with Kelly, okay?"

Addis nodded, as the White House gates closed behind them. The limousine stopped at the front of the executive mansion. The Secret Service agents would not allow the President to leave the vehicle until extra security men were in place. Then Addis followed Mumfries out.

The White House grounds were an armed camp. Uniformed officers patrolled everywhere, brandishing weapons: .9 mm Glock pistols, Uzis. Government snipers were visible on the rooftops of the surrounding buildings. Mumfries was looking about. Addis guessed that the new President had expected to be greeted by the White House press corps. But there were no reporters, no microphones, no cameras. The media had been banished, with an exception. One camera crew had been permitted to remain on the premises and obtain footage for all news outlets. But under the new rules, the crew was kept far from the President.

Standing on the front steps, Mumfries spotted the camera crew two hundred feet away. He moved a closed fist across his chest in a sort of somber half-wave. He then strode through the White House front door and into a cloud of waiting aides.

Addis headed to the West Wing. Inside, he passed the Oval Office. Ann Herson, Hanover's secretary for thirteen years, was not at her desk. The door was open. No one was there, and Addis walked in. The President's desk was clean of all papers. Two empty cardboard boxes were on the floor.

Addis entered the small, private room to the side of the Oval Office. Here Hanover had placed a reclining chair. The room had a small stereo system. It was where Hanover did much of his reading. On the wall were his favorite photographs. His first day as attorney general. Jack running on a beach—before the car accident that had paralyzed the Hanovers' only child. Hanover in a college production of *Our Town*. Margaret wearing his army jacket. Both of them at Graceland. Few aides and no reporters or visitors were allowed in this room. Herson did not permit it. "The most powerful man in the world," she once remarked to Addis, "and all he gets is ninety-six square feet of his own."

Addis left the Oval Office and shut the door. In the hallway, M. T. O'Connor, the President's scheduler, was waiting for him. The two hugged; he bent his knees sharply so his cheek would be at the same height as hers. O'Connor's hair fell in front of him. He noticed a few gray strands among the straight black lines. As scheduler, O'Connor held an important position in the White House; she arbitrated all the requests for the President's time. Did he attend a nurses' convention, appear at a fund-raiser, call a foreign leader? She juggled, battled with demanding aides, and oversaw how Hanover spent his waking hours.

O'Connor and Addis were usually allies in the political battles fought within the Hanover camp. "The long and short of it," Hanover had once said of them. Rarely had they disagreed. A few months back, he had argued for abandoning a Secretary of Labor nominee after a network revealed the man had not disclosed his previous treatment for manic depression. O'Connor had urged Hanover to stand by his old college chum. The President dumped the nominee—and his popularity dipped a few points in the polls. Addis sent O'Connor a single black feather, with a card that read, "I've eaten the rest of the damn bird." A few weeks ago, the two had worked together to stage a meeting where union officials, human rights activists, and environmentalists could share with Hanover their criticisms of the proposed China trade accord. But that session had not won over the President. After months of consideration, Hanover had sided with those Cabinet members, aides, and fund-raisers pushing for the treaty, under which U.S. corporations would gain more access to Chinese labor, consumer, and financial markets and China's trade status would not be subject to those painful yearly reviews.

"Saw you go in," O'Connor said. "Thought I'd give you a few minutes."

"Feels like a tomb."

"The whole friggin' building feels like a tomb—or would, if there weren't so many security freaks running around. Like being in the embassy in Lagos, when the friggin' Nigerians were about to storm in."

O'Connor had been in the Peace Corps in Africa. After that, she founded what she called a "health-care empowerment center" for low-income women in rural Minnesota. At a conference on health care services, she met Margaret Mason Hanover, then the First Lady of Louisiana, and immediately became a friend and adviser.

"They're just overcompensating," he said. "They lost him and can't do anything about it. This is how they grieve."

"And how do we?"

"I haven't gotten to that item on the agenda yet."

O'Connor guided Addis around the corner. A security detail with attack dogs passed by.

"You rode back with Mumfries?" she asked.

He nodded.

"You think the changes will come soon? Or will he sit on them?"

"He didn't say."

"Brew's going to try to stay on."

"Probably."

"Prove after all these years he's not just a Hanover appendage."

"Maybe."

"What should we do? Yeah, I know, it's ghoulish to be talking like this. But we're just going to turn the whole store over to Mumfries? Imagine what happens to the President's program when he gets done with it. He reamed us on the tax bill, telling the committee what we were going to do. Man, he pushed for *their* environmental cuts. Remember that lovely interlude? And you can forget China—he'll make it worse. And in two weeks he'll waltz into Chicago, grab the nomination, and he'll—"

"M. T., he's the President now."

He noticed her eyes were puffy.

"But just hand him the friggin' keys?" She waved her gangly arms. "So he can toss them to his scummy cronies? There'll be no legacy. Zippo. Didn't you want a second term?"

I wish I could say, "More than anything."

But he couldn't. The past three years had been filled with too many political dogfights that ended in bland compromise. Hanover had not hollered when his proposed political reforms were ignored by Congress. Want your budget passed? the party leaders told him, Then keep out of how we raise money. The bombing raid in Lebanon—that had been pointless and it killed several civilians, including a prominent Jordanian journalist. But Mike Finn, the political director, had pushed Hanover to order the air assault after the press reported on a terrorist scheme to assassinate a U.S. ambassador. Otherwise, Finn said, the media would brand Hanover with one word: wimp.

Brew McGreer was always waving poll results, living in fear of the slightest downward tick. He said no to a top-to-bottom review of military spending. Don't want to get the generals too pissed, he argued. He nixed proposals to bolster the antitrust division at Justice and to strengthen the collection of corporate taxes. Could hurt with fund-raising, he explained. Let's not scare the business community: "Gotta keep the fucking markets fucking happy." And Mumfries constantly chimed in about the need to respect political realities.

It was easy, Addis knew, to blame McGreer or sneer at Mumfries. It was harder to admit that Hanover shared McGreer's belief that the guiding principle was, avoid providing the slightest opening to the opposition— for imagine how much worse it would be if *they* were in the White House. There would be one measurement of success: reelection. But that meant steering clear of the tougher fights.

Addis had agreed that the priority was reelection, but in his mind that did not require all the caution counseled by others. And until recently, he had wanted, above all else, a second term. One in which Hanover might be less receptive to the cries of his risk-averse advisers. One in which Hanover could wage the right battle or two. Addis was certain that neither Hanover nor McGreer would worry about what the polls said about Mumfries's future prospects. Only weeks ago, Addis had hoped that the next term would prove that he had made the right decision years ago in New Orleans.

That hope was gone. For Addis, it had slipped away before the assassination. But he wasn't going to tell O'Connor about the phone call. Not now. It no longer mattered. Like so much, it was moot.

"What's to be done?" he asked.

"There's something. There always is. We get everyone on the same page: continuity. Our few buddies in the press. Your friend Palmer in the Senate. Margaret, too. Continuity. If he keeps the same staff, the same Cabinet, the potential for damage will be less."

"For a few months, and then after he's elected on his own?"

"That's in months. You think I like being the bitch-from-hell right now? But it's really for *him*. If we don't get out in front, we'll . . ."

"Have you talked to anyone about this?"

O'Connor shook her head.

"Not Margaret."

"She's a little busy."

"Let me think about it."

"Don't think too long," she said. "You know Mumfries has a plan already. And if he doesn't, it's only because Kelly hasn't laid it out for him yet."

"Sam and Ham."

"The Sham Twins." It was a phrase they only used with each other. The two embraced once more.

31

In Addis's office, his computer was beeping, signaling his message bank was full. He scanned the list. His parents. Assorted journalists. Addis returned one call: the one from the woman who was to start tomorrow as his assistant. Let's wait and see, he told her message machine. And Holly Rudd had called. Six months ago, she had moved to Washington to join a labor law firm downtown. But she had not tried to contact him until today.

He checked the internal email. McGreer had sent a note requesting a report on Addis's ride with Mumfries. There was a postscript: "You don't have to worry any more about New Orleans." Addis tapped out a reply: "All's well with our friend. He says he is happy to share. No surprises." He hit the enter button. Then he realized that he had nothing official to do.

7

White House
Office of Clarence Dunne—June 21

"**I** said no, Clarence."

Jake Grayton, the deputy director of the FBI, pressed his palms together, Buddha-like, to signal the discussion was over. He stood behind the chair in front of Dunne's desk.

"I just want to tag along and hear what the wife has to say," Dunne said, sitting at his desk.

The two were in Dunne's office in the underground Secret Service bunker below the West Wing.

"This is our job. And, to be frank, Clarence, I don't want you or your crew even stepping on our shadow."

Crew? Dunne thought. Did he use street language when he talked to his white colleagues?

Dunne knew Grayton well. In his late forties, Grayton was a riser in the security establishment. The FBI director, a former senator, cared more for tennis and Georgetown parties than briefings and task forces. So Grayton got to call the shots. Last year, Grayton had organized a special interagency SWAT team to counter threats against government targets. When a few skeptical House members raised questions about its budget, a story suddenly appeared in the *Washington Post*: "New Unit Thwarts Drug Cartel Bomb Plot in D.C." The source was obvious: Grayton. His outfit won an extra $13 million from Congress. Slick, smooth, he played the game well. He was ever up-to-date on current developments in the security world: computers, advance weapon technology, the latest in terrorism neutralization. In various meetings, Dunne had watched Grayton hail one "new era" after another—in interagency cooperation, in internal communications, in international liaison. Dozens of times, Dunne had heard Grayton mouth the motto, "Drive the change; don't be pushed by it." He knew the younger agents mocked Grayton's can-do-ism: Dry the rain; don't be sussed by it.

Dunne stood up. Grayton was taller. He had electric blue eyes, jet black hair combed straight back, and utterly straight teeth. He spoke in bursts, as if his words were coming out of a teletype.

"Listen, Jake," Dunne said. "We fucked up, and I want to know how that happened. You're looking to solve a case. But we also need to figure out what went wrong security-wise. So I'd like to know what she can tell us about her husband."

Dunne knew he was bullshitting. This wasn't about security. It was about finding a way in.

"Listen, my friend," Grayton said, "in the prelim, a very upset Mrs. Sandlin told us she doesn't know where the fuck her husband is anyway. So why do you want to go over to J. Edgar and sit in on the three-oh-two?"

Grayton glanced at a photograph on the wall that showed Dunne, as a young man, being sworn in as a police officer in Atlanta.

"Because that's all there is right now."

In a gesture of compromise, Grayton sat down and waved his hand toward the chair behind Dunne's desk. Dunne accepted the invitation to sit and looked hard at Grayton. The man never blinked. And he kept his line of vision at a perfect ninety-degree angle to his erect, perfect-posture torso. Grayton was one of the Game Boys. That's what Dunne called them. They loved the covert game. They relished concocting schemes. They got off knowing they possessed grand secrets. In the security-intelligence world, there were those who enthusiastically embraced secret-keeping and clandestine actions. They might occasionally concede that it was just too bad that god-awful means had to be used to protect free society. But they were in it as much for the means—if not more so—than the ends. Then there were the reluctant ones who considered the dirty work necessary but who pondered the consequences of official lies and secrecy-by-bureaucracy. Grayton and Dunne were in different camps.

"Okay, sure," Grayton said. "Sit in. Enjoy. But I want your agreement."

Dunne tried to keep his face expressionless.

"I know the inclination here. You feel like shit. And you should. After all, you did let someone place two bullets into the face of the most powerful man on the planet."

Don't react, Dunne told himself.

"Now, you want to do something," Grayton continued. "Because you think that will keep you from feeling like shit. So you want to keep busy. And think about what you're doing, not what you didn't do. So here's the promise you're making to me right now: You will do nothing without letting me know. You will not take one breath of *our* air—without first telling me about it."

Dunne nodded. "You're the man."

"And once an agent always, right?"

Grayton was referring to Dunne's seventeen-month stint in Hoover's FBI. After six years on the police force, he had joined the feds. Dunne's career in the Bureau ended when he punched a fellow agent who had thought it was amusing to call him a nigger during a training session. He subsequently found a job with the Secret Service and now was into his twenty-eighth year.

"Oh, by the way, let me tell you," Grayton said, an accommodating smile on his face. "Our missing Mr. Sandlin said nothing unusual in his office before he left. In fact, so far—nothing unusual about him. Just covering the White House for a crummy, dying Midwest chain of small-town, asswipe papers. And not doing such a hot job, his boss said. Drinking. Problems at home. No oddball friends anyone knows of. No Arabs, no kooks—right-wing or otherwise. We're still waiting on the phone calls. Damn phone company. They made us go to a judge."

Grayton leaned forward in his chair.

"I've spent enough time on this. I have to go."

Dunne escorted him out. In the elevator, Dunne asked if Mumfries had made any decisions about the assassination investigation.

"Not yet," Grayton said. "But I expect I'll be in charge. The President and I get along well."

"Good." Dunne felt stupid for saying that.

"On the intell committee, he always backed us. Has respect for the professionals. Lets them do the job. One of the few guys in his party who believes in us. I like that. He understands."

The door opened.

"Glad we settled everything," Grayton said. "We are, after all, on the same squad. If you have any ideas for the investigation, do bring them to my attention."

Grayton spotted the national security adviser passing by and headed off to catch him. This is a man who does not walk, Dunne thought; he strides.

Outside the West Wing, Dunne paused to watch the the limousines dropping off Cabinet members for a meeting with Mumfries. In his earpiece, he heard the watch command tracking Mumfries's movements. Dunne somberly greeted passing Cabinet officials. The Defense Secretary bit his lip and shook his head. Out of sympathy or out of blame? Only Louis Alter, the septuagenarian Treasury Secretary, stopped to talk.

"I've already heard from Mumfries," he said. "That is, Hamilton Kelly. He wants a replacement for the White House security unit."

35

"That's understandable."

"And an investigation of how—"

"Of course. I've begun to—"

"An *outside* investigation. We'll figure out all these details later."

Alter placed a thin, withered hand on Dunne's shoulder.

"It's a heavy load to bear, Clarence."

"Yes, sir."

"Plenty of people will be looking for heads. There'll be hearings, commissions, Monday-morning media harrumphing. I'll do my best."

"Thank you, sir."

"But I'm no miracle worker. Remember that."

Alter drew back his hand. He signaled to an aide, who brought him a cane, and he slowly shuffled into the White House.

Dunne's car was waiting. As he got in, a message came from the watch commander: Brady Sandlin had been found.

"Up the street, to the Mayflower," Dunne told the driver.

8

White House
East Wing Residence—June 21

Lem Jordan was sitting outside the private office of the First Lady. The door was closed. He rose abruptly when Addis appeared.

"How is she?" Addis asked.

"Fine. Going through papers." His usual stammer was absent.

"And you, Lem?"

Jordan raised a finger in the air. It was an odd pose for him, Addis thought, as if he were imitating a politician.

"Well, I keep thinking that if I had been there . . ."

"There were a dozen Secret Service agents in the room. I don't think you could have done anything. And your job has always been her, not him."

"Yeah, I know. But I keep thinking . . . You know those g-g-g-guys h-h-h-hate me. They do."

Addis knew; this was Jordan's constant complaint.

"We were at the hospital with Ja-Ja-Jack, and when they got the news, they tried to pu-pu-pu-pu—"

Jordan paused to catch up to the stutter.

"—push me aside, and take her away."

"They were upset."

"Guess they d-d-don't remember Cincinnati."

There it was, the sentence used whenever anyone in the White House wanted to mimic Jordan. Among the more mean-hearted of the White House, these words had become a catchphrase to end a conversation. *Guess they don't remember Cincinnati*—a threat that the discussion would go on and on, unless it finished then and there.

Heroism to mockery, Addis thought, can be a short journey. In Cincinnati during the first presidential campaign, Jordan was by the side of Margaret as she shook hands in a busy mall. He spotted a fellow wearing an unbuttoned overcoat, and Jordan positioned himself next to the man. When the man went for the gun he was carrying in a back holster, Jordan tackled him before a shot could be fired. Jordan had realized that the image on the man's T-shirt was a photograph of Squeaky Fromme, the woman who had tried to kill a previous president. None of the Secret Service agents had noticed that. Only Lem Jordan.

His speech impediment, his habit of repeating stories ad nauseam, and his seemingly bottomless devotion to Margaret Hanover prompted most White House people to regard him as a near-buffoon—though the sentiment never was expressed in his presence or before Margaret Hanover. She was as loyal to him as he was to her. He did more for her than most White House staffers realized, Addis suspected. On those occasions when Margaret seemed particularly well informed about a meeting or conversation to which she had not been privy, Addis uttered a one-word explanation to himself: Lem. So Addis listened patiently to Jordan's stories. He even enjoyed a few of the tales, especially those from the years when Jordan had been a prison guard. "You d-d-don't know p-p-people 'til you seen 'em in jail," Jordan liked to say.

"They'll always remember Cincinnati," Addis said to him, "especially now. Okay if I go in?"

"Sure," Jordan said.

"Thanks, Lem."

"P-p-p-people ought to not underestimate p-p-people. You know that, N-n-nick?"

"Yes, I do," Addis said, and opened the door. He patted Jordan on the arm. Then, as he entered the office and left Jordan at his post, Addis wondered if that gesture had been condescending.

"Not eavesdropping on the new regime?" Margaret Hanover asked. "Missing out on the first meeting of the Mumfries administration?"

She was at a desk in what had once been a dressing room. When the Hanovers had moved into the White House, she had turned a portion of the residence into a personal office, one more private than the space reserved for her in the Old Executive Office Building. The move—which coincided with Hanover's announcement that Margaret would attend Cabinet meetings—had prompted criticism, with her predecessor as First Lady pronouncing it "unseemly."

The widow Hanover was alone. She had dispatched her aides to the West Wing with various instructions on whom to invite to the funeral, a seating chart for the cathedral, a list of foundations to be designated as the recipients of donations in lieu of flowers. Her face was pearl white. It looked as if it would be cold to the touch. Addis felt uneasy. Was he here to grieve with her or to plan?

"Not interested right now," Addis said in reply to her questions.

"He didn't even ask me to come," she said. "But Kelly came by a few minutes ago to explain. Merely an oversight. That Sam—I mean, the President—assumed that I was busy and not available. And that, of course, I was invited."

"Not interested, either?"

"Not ready to see him in that chair. Or to be stared at. To have my mourning judged. . . ."

She pulled a tissue from the box on her desk.

"You know what Mumfries is going to do?" she asked.

Addis shook his head. Was the question rhetorical? Years ago he had trained himself to follow the advice of his father, a professor of music history and the author of the definitive biography of Woody Guthrie: When you do not know what to say, *listen.* Later on, at law school, a negotiations expert had told his class that one should always let the person across the table speak first. Addis had developed his habits. Waiting was one of them. Margaret looked at the papers and folders on her desk.

"You know," she complained. "I asked for storage boxes over an hour ago."

Addis wondered if anyone had put their arms around Margaret since the . . . the event. Her focus returned.

"I don't think Sam knows what he's going to do. But I'm sure Kelly does. And I doubt we loom large in the picture."

"They certainly don't need to move quickly," Addis said.

"I am thinking of the grander scheme."

Whose grander scheme?

She paused before continuing. "When we were at the Cape, that first summer, we were on the beach, alone—except for the usual pack of watchers. But they were giving us our space. Jack was in his wheelchair on the deck. He could see us, and we waved at him. Bob took my hand. He held it tight. It almost hurt, but I didn't say anything. He said, 'if anything ever happens to . . .' I wouldn't let him go on. But he insisted. 'You'll have to finish,' he said."

She was crying now. Addis felt the moisture forming in his eyes; his throat was tightening.

"Imagine Sam in his place. Brings in his hacks. Undoes the little we've been able to do—what he and his idiot pals on the Hill weren't able to stop. Or that Brew didn't water down. We will have to . . . But Sam—ever notice how he smells? Moldy. I can't bear it. Never could."

Addis didn't want to consider where she was leading. Her husband's

39

body was still in pieces at Walter Reed Hospital, and she was thinking of. . . . Of what? Where was her invalid son, Jack, now? Who was watching him?

"The funeral will be the day after tomorrow," she said. "Taking calls, receiving visitors, accepting sympathy and pity—I'm not very good at that. Then, then, after that I . . ."

Addis did not ask what she meant. If he did not ask, he would never have to lie about his first conversation with Margaret Hanover after the assassination of her husband—in which she was thinking of politics. But of what precisely? Succession? The election? She had said "I."

This is too much. Mind if I just slip out, and . . .

But perhaps this was her manner of dealing with the shock and pain. Fixate on a concrete future.

"Nick, will you do a favor for me?"

"Anything." He clenched a fist behind his back.

"I know you were planning a trip to Louisiana, to sort things out. After the funeral is done, will you still go? I'd like to have that business cleared up. Find the missing pieces—we all have our missing pieces, don't we? Make certain."

I'd rather the fuck not.

"I'm sure no one will bother with it now," he said.

"You're right, but just to be sure. Will you see what you can do?"

As Addis nodded, the questions began. Would this be an official trip? Would he have to explain his absence? Should he tell McGreer? Or anyone else? It felt wrong, he thought. But he couldn't do anything but agree. He didn't have the heart—or was it the strength?—to say no.

Damn. I've become a floater. . . . Call a press conference. Time to rewrite all those magazine profiles about Nick Addis.

He took a step toward her. She got up and paced about the room. Her hair had fallen out of the bun. She held her shoulders up. She stared at a point on the far side of the room.

"You were his—" she began to say.

She walked past him to the entrance to the room. She opened the door. Jordan peered into the office.

"There's still much to do," she said.

"Yes," Addis said, and left.

In his office, more messages, more email. A note from McGreer: Hamilton Kelly had promised that a draft of Mumfries's speech would be ready soon.

Addis pulled a book from one of the cartons scattered throughout the office. He thumbed through the pages. There was no notepad on his desk, so he reached into the trash can and found a plain white envelope. On the back, he wrote down a passage:

> *We never know what we have lost, or what we have found.*
> *We are only ourselves, and that promise.*
> *Continue to walk in the world.*
>
> —*Robert Penn Warren*

A light rain had just begun as Addis walked from the West Wing to the Old Executive Office Building. Inside, his wet heels squeaked against the tile floor of the hallway. He entered the suite; the secretary was gone. He pushed open the door to Kelly's office. It was empty. He placed the envelope on the desk. He noticed that the rain had caused the ink to run.

9

Rosslyn
June 23

Julia Lancette watched the funeral on television. The closed, flag-draped casket lay beneath a too-bright sky. Margaret Mason Hanover stood in the front. Next to her was thirteen-year-old Jack in a wheelchair. Behind them was President Mumfries, his wife, Sally, Bob Hanover's brother, and the senior White House staff. Addis was grasping the arm of the sobbing woman next to him. Wesley Pratt, the presumptive presidential nominee of the other party, stood off to the side. A crowd of thousands flowed down the hill at Arlington Cemetery. A minister was talking about unfinished work and the never-ending task of redemption. A flock of crows was squawking. A Marine bugler played. Two members of the honor guard stepped forward. They lifted the flag and, with precise, crisp motions, folded it. One handed the triangle to the widow. She clutched it to her chest and then passed it to Sally Mumfries. Next, Margaret Hanover wheeled Jack to the casket. She knelt beside her son. She leaned forward and placed her lips against the polished wood. The television pool camera zoomed in. She whispered a word or two toward the casket. The microphones caught only the sound of the wind and the birds.

As was usual, Lancette was alone in her office. She had arrived early, knowing that the responses to the ICEMAN inquiry she had dispatched after the assassination awaited her. Through the day, Lancette had been plowing through the material. But the televised images had pulled her away: The noon remembrance, when all traffic ceased and church bells rang across the city and the nation. The service at the National Cathedral. The slow procession through Washington and across the water into Virginia. The mourners lining the route.

Now the President's family and friends were filing out behind Margaret and Jack. Carefully, they descended the hill, with Lem Jordan wheeling Jack down the incline. As the wife and son were helped into a black van, a news anchor asked a correspondent what was on Margaret Hanover's schedule for the rest of the day.

"Nothing," said the correspondent.

The network rolled background footage: Margaret Hanover by the side of her husband-to-be the night he was elected attorney general of Louisiana. Margaret Hanover introducing her husband and declaring victory the night he was elected governor. Margaret Hanover coming out of the hospital to announce to the world that their only child, Jack, had survived the car crash that had occurred when Bob drove the family truck off the road while returning from a father-and-son fishing trip. But, she said between tears, Jack was paralyzed and brain damaged. The accident—Hanover said he had swerved to miss a deer—had left the father uninjured.

Another correspondent reviewed the familiar tale of the Hanovers. When she was a girl, her father, Robert Charles Mason, a prominent financier and political kingpin in Louisiana known as "Chasie," packed her off to boarding school in Vermont. Her best friend there, a fellow Louisianan, was forever talking about this boy back in Baton Rouge: handsome, she gushed, "smart as paint," and going places. Years later, Margaret, then a student at Yale, was visiting a friend at Radcliffe. She attended a Harvard production of *Romeo and Juliet,* and there he was—Romeo—the fellow her girlfriend had raved about. After the show, she waited by the stage door. She introduced herself. They went out for coffee. A romance began. When Hanover was in Vietnam, she wrote every day. When he returned, they both enrolled in law school at New York University.

Then they went home to Louisiana. He found the better job, teaching at Tulane; she rejected her father's offer to join the family business and took a position at a community college in New Orleans. During the campaign for attorney general, Hanover attacked the influence peddlers and corrupt contractors, and she cheered him on. When he assailed her father by name—after the hospital built by one of Mason's many business partners collapsed—Chasie Mason issued a public ultimatum. His daughter would have to choose: him or Hanover. She stayed with Hanover; her father announced that he had written her out of his will. The media embraced the story of the woman who gave up millions of dollars for love. The father and daughter were never seen together in public. All three network news shows ran reports on Bob Hanover and Margaret Mason's wedding.

On the screen was a scene from the television movie. An actress playing Margaret was confronting an actor playing Chasie. Lancette pushed the mute button on the remote.

From the window in her office, she could see the crowd lining Memorial Bridge. She chastised herself for having forgotten once again to pick up the plants she had ordered for the office. Then she tried to focus on the papers before her. Responses to her high-priority inquiry had come in from dozens of offices.

One by one, she pulled reports from the stack on her desk and examined the documents—to make sure that the mandatory computer-photo comparisons had been conducted, that agent files had been checked, that potential agent files had been scrutinized, that all employee records had been located and screened, that the task had been overseen and reviewed by the unit chief, that cooperation had been full.

It was methodical work. She began with the replies from the Directorate of Operations. These were the records she always reviewed first. The DO was the home of the case officers, the covert operators, the agents, the contract agents, the clandestine warriors—the troublemakers. Nine out of ten Agency embarrassments emanated from these quarters. All their reports came back negative, with no one fitting the known details.

She began to relax. Nothing from the DO probably meant there was nothing at all. Next came the Directorate of Intelligence: the egghead wing of the Agency, where analysts pored over reams of data to determine the rate of soybean production in this or that country, or whether some maniacal colonel might be considering a coup in some backwater capital. The DI had been her home base. Again, nothing.

Then the Science and Technology Directorate—no hits here.

Next, the Directorate of Administration—the bureaucrats who ran the Agency. Payroll, personnel, promotions, the physical plant—these people could be working for any major corporation. They cut the checks, balanced the books, made the trains run. They could tell you how much a division spent but not what it did. Her rule was to turn to the paper-pushers last. Department by department, she read the notices they had sent her—nothing, nothing, nothing.

But one response was missing: DA/MA/P.

She looked up the bureaucratic designation: Directorate of Administration, Medical Administration, Psychiatric. She reviewed the transmission of her original memo. It had been received. She looked at the clock on her computer screen. The report was now one hour and seven minutes overdue.

The television showed people gathering in Lafayette Park, across from the White House. A wild-eyed fellow holding a Bible was standing on a chair and shouting into the crowd. She kept the sound off. Flags waved slowly. A series of teary mourners talked into a microphone thrust in front of their faces, saying something for posterity. An old Latino man wearing an Army uniform—World War II vintage—and bedecked with medals held a framed portrait of Hanover that was covered by a thin black veil.

Lancette picked up the phone. She punched in an extension.

"73653," a voice said.

"Hello," she said. "I'm trying to trace a report that I should have received from your office."

The woman on the other end did not reply.

"Oh, this is DCI/SS/E&IR," Lancette said. "If you check the SecNet transmissions, confirmation number 576392, you'll see—"

"Hold a moment."

She looked at the TV screen. Two days ago, the killer had walked through this square. She knew that from the news reports. The preliminary investigation had found that he had booked a room at the Mayflower under what appeared to be a false name: Max Bridge. That he had shot the reporter he later impersonated and a Georgetown University student. That he then spent the entire night in the room with the two corpses. The next day, he put on his disguise, left the hotel, strolled through this park now full of mourners. And . . . according to the official reports, his true identity still had not been established.

"This is Dr. Stan Blum," a new voice said. "I must apologize. I knew you'd be calling. You see, I just took over the office. Just a few days ago. Did you know Dr. Killigren?"

"No," she said.

"That's probably a good thing. People don't get to know us until they're in a . . . Anyways, after forty-two years here, he finally left us. Down to Orlando. DisneyWorld and all that. Good man. Snatched long ago from Johns Hopkins. God knows what he would have done in the private sector. Helped pioneer the profiling of overseas leaders before he took over our shop. You can imagine what it's like to take the reins from someone who's been holding them for three decades. A bit overwhelming. And, I must say, a bit of a disaster. His secretary left with him. It's as if they had devised their own system for everything in and everything out. Quite frankly, I'm drowning. But everyone knew this would happen, so I'm not worried. We'll catch up."

"I just wanted to see what—"

"Was happening with our response to your priority inquiry. We had to pull out a few memos, dust them off, to familiarize ourselves with SOP. I want to go by the numbers. And we have. Just completing our review as we speak. And we'll be zipping off the report to you any minute now. Wonderful what they do with computer communications these days. Here, I can even give you the transmission number, right now."

She scribbled it down.

A line of police officers ringed the White House. They wore helmets.

"I hope you'll tell whoever you tell these things, Miss—or is it Ms.? Don't mean to insult—that we made a good-faith effort to be on time. Would probably do better next week. Once the feet are wetter."

"No, that's fine," she said. "I was just finishing up."

"Very kind of you."

"And what does your office do?"

"Good for you—that you don't know. We're the psychiatric wing of the Meds. One of our colleagues needs help. They come to us, not some outsider. Easier to talk to one who knows this world then one who doesn't. People throughout the building think we tend to a bunch of crack-ups. But, mainly it's routine. Marriage counseling. Stress relief. The occasional bout of depression. Some substance abuse. But there's an entirely separate outfit for that. We couldn't handle all of that. But I'm not asking for any special consideration. We play by the rules. If you must, report our late filing. Our defense is an easy one: a guide through the office that Dr. Killigren—an otherwise fine man and administrator—bequeathed us."

"Okay, okay," Lancette said into the phone. "Let me hang up and look for it."

"Certainly. And though I've checked the regulations and know that an oral report is not deemed sufficient in these instances, I can give you a sneak preview: *nada.* But you'll see."

Lancette rolled her eyes. She thanked him for his help and got off the phone. She logged on and saw the report had arrived. As she sent it to the printer, she again gazed at the television. One shot after another of flags at half-mast, throughout the capital, across the country. Then a picture of Nick Addis in the Oval Office holding an empty box and looking at the empty chair behind the desk. Then a slow-motion replay of Margaret Hanover and son moving toward the coffin.

She left her seat to grab the document from the printer. She noticed no one was standing on Memorial Bridge any longer. Regular traffic was moving across it. She returned to her desk to finish the report. Never has it been truer, she thought: No news is good news.

10

The White House
Situation Room—June 24

Clarence Dunne tried to recall the kiss his wife gave him when he left the house that morning. This was his last day as chief of the White House security detail. Almost three decades with the Secret Service—and all was gone. Nothing—certainly not the kiss and the words "Honey, I love you"—would ever cover up that damn moment. Maybe his three sons—a doctor, an advertising copywriter, and a bookstore owner—could balance the ledger. But that was fanciful thinking. It would be a challenge for the rest of his life to keep the love, the kisses, the children out of a mountainous shadow. *Where were you when . . . ?* He would never be able to answer the question. Already the truth had become a sad joke: poor bastard was in the can wiping his ass when a lunatic waltzed into the White House and drilled the President. At the training lectures he was now set to deliver, the greenhorns would be watching him closely, looking for the toll taken and wondering why the hell they were being taught by the guy who blew it.

In the wood-paneled conference room next to the Situation Room, Hamilton Kelly was explaining that, per President Mumfries's instructions, Jake Grayton, who was already in charge of the assassination investigation, would also be overseeing White House security.

"First step, a top-to-bottom evaluation of what the procedures have been," said Grayton, who was sitting next to Kelly. He turned toward Dunne: "I'd like you to be in constant touch with the reviewers. You won't be in on the writing of the final report, but—"

Of course not, Dunne thought. I'm the target. I'll be blamed for failing to have foreseen the possibility.

"—your insights certainly will be invaluable."

Dunne nodded.

"Not too much to be in charge of the investigation *and* security?" Brewster McGreer asked.

"The President is well acquainted with my abilities," Grayton replied. "I used to spend more time with him and the committee than with my wife. That's why"—he held up his left hand—"I lost the golden band. At least I still have a good relationship with one of them."

"You made the right choice, Jake," Kelly quipped. He rubbed his hairless head with one hand. The other hand pulled at the suspenders that arced across his paunch. Thirty-eight, Dunne guessed, staring at Kelly's round, pink face—a premature middle-aged man. You should slow down, Mr. Kelly, Dunne wanted to say.

"Wasn't really mine to make," Grayton asked with half a chuckle.

"Enough banter," Kelly said. "The NATO ambassadors are due here in an hour. And I don't have all their fucking names memorized."

Dunne could see who was running the meeting. On paper, McGreer was chief of staff. But Kelly was the big-foot in the room: "Jake, the latest, please."

Grayton nodded toward an assistant who was standing by the door. The young man stepped forward, opened the file folder he was holding, and began the briefing. Nothing, still, on the identity of the assassin. The Bureau had received over twenty-three thousand phone calls from people who thought they possessed some knowledge of the fellow or the deed.

"Only a third mentioned Elvis," Grayton interrupted.

The assistant waited to see if Grayton had anything else to add. Then he proceeded: The hotel room was clean. No prints. A few strands of fiber and hair. A shaving razor was found, and the condition of the blade's edge indicated that it had been used recently to shave off a beard. No phone calls in or out. Paid in cash. No credit cards found on him. No cash cards. No driver's license. The local theater supply stores had been checked; no one remembered him. The wig, the nose putty, the false beard—commonly available.

The autopsy had produced leads. His face had experienced serious trauma at some point within the past several years. The nose had been broken, the cheek bones and jaw smashed. Probably an accident. Perhaps a car crash had sent him through a windshield. He had undergone reconstructive surgery. It would make it harder for people who knew him before the surgery to recognize him. A full genetic screening was underway at the NIH.

"Look for the psycho-killer gene," Kelly said. "And those scars? Any fucking idea what he was so *happy* about?"

Nothing solid, the aide replied. A team of psychiatrists was working on it. The medical unit had determined the scars were all carved recently. Within the past few weeks.

The aide continued: The woman was a Georgetown University junior, majoring in mechanical engineering. Allison Meade. No criminal record. No known political affiliations. No known past association with the reporter. The bartender says he had never seen her before. Her friends and family are stunned. Her roommate says nothing unusual had happened recently, that she had no idea where Allison was off to that night. No known boyfriend—or girlfriend. No one has an explanation for her presence at the hotel or for any connection she may have had with the shooter. There were five $100 bills in her purse. Her phone records are being checked.

The aide turned a page in the folder and kept reading: Brady Sandlin was a regular at the bar. According to the bartender, she came in, they talked a long time. They left together. He was a drinker, several a night, most nights of the week. Sometimes didn't make it home. Not doing well at work. A transfer was pending. A neighbor often heard fighting. The wife denies this, but not convincingly. Knows nothing of the girl or the shooter. The gun—apparently handmade, composite plastics, highest of tech. Except, that is, for the metal firing pin. Agents are working through a list of known experts in this field.

"Inside and outside?" Dunne asked.

"Excuse me, Clarence?" Grayton asked.

"Inside and outside the government. I assume that somewhere we have our own people coming up with these sort of devices."

"We will check everyone we know of," Grayton said. "Wherever."

"But—"

Grayton rapped his knuckles on the table. The aide returned to his report: Nothing on the fingerprints registry. The hotel workers—nothing there. His clothes—standard Caldor's, trying to trace, but not likely. His boots—a knock-off brand popular at Wal-Marts everywhere. No pocket litter. No room litter.

"This fellow was good," the aide said and closed the folder.

Kelly was twirling a pen in his hand. He started to speak but McGreer interrupted him.

"Fucking bullshit," he said. "You're saying, we've got nothing. We know nothing. All we know is that this madman was a fucking genius? We can't do any better? Seems to me he had to be fucking working with someone. Where'd he get a gun like that?"

"Been to a gun show lately?" Grayton asked. "You'll see shit that most governments don't have. Hell, last week my secretary showed me an ad for cyanide pills from some mercenary Internet site her son had found."

"Why can't we dig up one fucking thing on his identity?" McGreer said.

"Mister Happy," Grayton said, "obviously was a few eggs short of a dozen. Probably a schizo-paranoid. We'll get something on him."

"And you got everyone working on it?" McGreer asked. "CIA? DIA? NSA? Anybody else we don't fucking know about? Any strange intercepts your boys picked up before or after?"

Grayton assured McGreer that the NSA had gone through all its intercepts. Twice. Nothing of any bearing had been found.

"The President of the United States needs an answer," Kelly said, taking charge again. "An answer he can share with the world. Last night he was on the phone with the President of Russia, and Vlad asked, 'So why did this asshole shoot Hanover?' The President had to lie: 'Got some good leads, Vlad. We're gonna get to the bottom of this. Don't worry.' Jake, find him a god-damn answer."

Grayton nodded.

"Any ideas, Clarence?" McGreer asked.

"When you have trouble with the *who*," Dunne said, "you got to focus on the *why*."

"Sheer brilliance," Kelly responded. "Got any other guesses? Who should we be after about the *why*?"

Dunne shook his head. Then he thought, why the hell not?

"Actually, yes. There's the First Lady. Their friends. His brother. Associates in Louisiana. President Mumfries. Anyone might know of something that we in this room"—he looked at Grayton—"don't."

Kelly checked his beeper. "Speaking for the current President, he has no clue why that clown decided to evade *your* security and shoot up the leader of the god-damn Free World."

"And I think," McGreer interrupted, "that we have to proceed carefully, if we're going to start officially questioning friends, family, and . . . associates of President Hanover."

Kelly looked at his watch and stood up.

"Time for another CIA briefing." He headed toward the door. "On Asia, I think. Let's hope none of the assholes over there think now's a good time for a nuclear test. We'll bust their balls."

"Let me walk you there," Grayton said. "See who's doing the briefing. Still got some friends there. And . . ."

The pair left the room. Without Kelly, there was no reason for the conversation to continue. The others filed out. No one said a word to Dunne.

11

Adams Morgan
June 24

Addis dropped his car keys and knelt down to find them. The accordion file slipped and fell to the wet cobblestones. Several pages slid out. Damnit, he cursed silently. He needed a light in the alley behind his house, where he parked the sensible Honda he had been driving for six years. He scooped up the papers and grabbed the keys.

He considered dropping by Havana Village, a bar around the corner. Rolando, the owner, always was a good host. A plate of rice and beans. A beer or two. But Addis was tired—the day after the funeral had been full of meetings on transition plans, on convention plans—and he had brought work home.

"Mr. Addis—"

Had he heard something? He didn't see anyone. He peered into the shadows, between the parked cars, beneath the fire escapes. No one. The glasses he wore for driving at night were askew. He straightened them. Across the alley—he thought he saw a figure. Using a finger, he tried to wipe the mist from the lenses. Nothing there. But be sure, he told himself.

"Hello, hello?" he half-whispered. No reply. After a long wait, he opened the gate to the garden behind his brownstone. The clicks of footsteps? He could not tell. He recalled the security briefing held for the White House staff two days ago. Or was it three? The previous days held no fine distinctions. One of Dunne's assistants had warned all White House personnel to be cautious. Make sure to inform the duty officer where you will be at all times. Report anything unusual at home or work immediately. Use common sense. Don't take risks. Addis was sure that looking for a stranger in a wet, dark alley fell into the don't-do category.

A clear footstep. Addis looked in its direction. A woman stepped out from behind a parked van. A ray of light fell across her face. Addis squinted to see through his glasses. She had long hair—dark red?—and a pointy chin. She was wearing sunglasses.

"Mr. Addis?" she said.

"Yes," he said and started to walk toward her.

She stopped abruptly, and, as a reflex, he did too. They were still fifteen feet apart. Her face was now in the dark.

"I think, that is, I . . . I have some information that might be useful."

She was nervous. He stood still.

"About what?" he asked.

"The, the . . ."

He thought she was crying.

"Why don't you come in and we can talk," he said, realizing he was further violating White House security guidelines.

She stepped in his direction—hesitantly.

A beeping sound went off. And Addis heard the rush of a car racing through the alley. He fumbled for the cellular phone in his jacket pocket and again dropped the file. The beams from the car's headlights flooded the alley. Addis looked for the woman. All he saw was glare. The car—a dark-color sedan—drove by, missing him by inches. He fell and landed on his side. The car moved through the alley. Addis hurried to his feet, while pulling the phone out of his pocket. It was still ringing.

She was gone.

"Hold on a minute," he said into the phone.

He ran through the alley and to the street. He did not see her. He did not see the car. Was there a connection between her disappearance and the sedan? Too many people desperate for parking in his neighborhood sped through the alley in the evenings. Might have been merely another diplo-trash club crawler.

"Sorry, sorry," he said into the phone, catching his breath. "You still there?"

It was Dunne. He asked Addis if he could stop by.

"Sure, Clarence," he said, "whenever you like."

Addis entered his house through the kitchen and ignored the tower of dishes in the sink. As he reached for the light switch in the dining room, he felt something against his leg. He spun around and knocked a lamp to the ground.

Shit, I'm too jumpy.

He turned on the overhead fixture. Eric, his cat, was on the floor in front of him. The cat cried in Addis's direction and then trotted out of the room. Addis put down the soaked file and followed the cat to the kitchen.

The food dish was empty. He checked a cupboard. He was out of cat food.

He poked around until he found a small jar of caviar. The prime minister of Russia had given Addis the caviar in Moscow while guiding Hanover and Addis on a late-evening tour of the Kremlin during the first summit. We read much of you here, he had said to Addis, when they were in the kitchen facilities. "Do you have a brother?" And he placed a jar of caviar—"the best," he remarked—in Addis's pocket.

Addis opened the caviar and fed it to the cat.

He knew her voice would be there—Holly Rudd's, on the answering machine—so he disregarded the blinking light. He sat down at the desk in the corner of the living room, opened the file, and laid out the damp documents. When he ran out of desk space, he used the floor.

Earlier that day, Margaret Hanover had stopped by the office. "Remember," she had said, "the loose ends. Give them a good tying." Addis had tried to make a start by going over the documents. But concentrating in the office had been impossible, especially after M. T. O'Connor had burst in, waving a sheet of paper.

"From Kelly's office," she had declared. He could see the page had once been crumpled.

"From the garbage?"

"Does it matter?" she shouted. It was a first draft of the initial policy initiatives of the Mumfries administration: tax cuts; deregulation; enhanced business subsidies, particularly for energy companies. "He took two bullets so Mumfries could reward the home-state shits who have greased him ever since he was a numskull bootlicker in the state legislature?"

She wanted to leak the document to the *Post*. Addis talked her out of it. Any leaks, and Kelly would clean house and clear out the Hanover holdovers. Piss inside the tent for a while, he counseled.

At his home desk, he again looked at the financial records, as they dried. Pages were missing, some were torn. He hated doing cleanup work and cursed Evan Hynes-Pierce, a British reporter who wrote for a Pittsburgh newspaper owned by an arch-conservative millionaire. It had been Hynes-Pierce who had put the inquiry to the press office: Had the Hanovers many years back invested in a land deal in Rapides Parish and received preferential treatment due to the intervention of Margaret's father, even though Chasie Mason and his daughter were notoriously estranged? The press office had ignored his request for information. Friends in Louisiana subsequently informed the White House that a seedy Brit was skulking about, asking about the old days, about Chasie Mason and the Hanovers. But, so far, no story had materialized.

"Give it a good tying-up," Margaret Hanover had asked Addis.

Before the convention? Was that the point? Clear the way?

The front door buzzer sounded. Addis let in Dunne. He cleared the living room couch of two weeks' worth of newspapers, and Dunne sat down.

"Ever see this?" Dunne asked and handed Addis a fax.

It was a memo from Hamilton Kelly to Bruce Harpold, who had been the White House director of administration, until a heart attack killed him while he was eating lunch in the White House mess. The memo carried a date from the transition period:

> *Vice President-elect Mumfries, whose work on the intelligence committee has convinced him that security safeguards are not sufficient throughout federal facilities in Washington, has asked me to convey to you his concern on this front and his suggestion that, following the inauguration, the White House implement a full review of all security, especially all rules and regulations governing the entrance of non-White House personnel into the White House/OEOB complex.*

It was cc'ed to Dunne.

"Never saw it," said Dunne. "But a bunch of reporters have now. One sent me this copy. Wouldn't say how she got it. And Kelly's not commenting. At least, that's what I'm told."

"Shit," Addis said.

"Did you ever see it? You were staff director for the transition, right? Working with Bruce?"

"Yeah, but you know how much paper flew across my desk then. I don't remember this. Can we check Bruce's papers?"

"Yeah, go digging through the archives. Like there's time for that. I wouldn't put it past that Kelly to have—"

"But why?"

"Make himself look better. You know the type. He can only smell good, if someone else stinks like shit. And Grayton wants me far out to pasture. This makes me even more radioactive."

Addis offered Dunne a drink and then realized he was out of everything but tap water. Not even Coke. Dunne declined.

"You think they want one lone nut?" Dunne asked.

"Who?"

"Grayton, I don't know, whoever. Like last time. One head case. The Bureau and everyone else are working their butts off, trying to figure out Mr. Max Bridge. But. . . ."

"Why are you asking, Clarence?"

"Makes it easier, I suppose. . . . Don't know. I have lots of time to wonder about lots of things. And then this." He held up the fax.

"Got one thing," Dunne said, "and I don't feel like sharing it with them. They don't seem to like my input so far. . . . Maybe I'll take a drink. Have any Scotch?"

Addis explained the house was dry and went to get a glass of water for Dunne. There wasn't even ice in the freezer. As Addis cleaned two glasses, Dunne kept talking.

"Got a friend on the local force, a sergeant. Last night, two of his guys answer a call. Someone in an apartment building on New Hampshire hears a guy beating the crap out of a woman in the apartment next door. Cops show up. Bang on the door. The guy opens it. Inside there's a woman. Messed-up, a little bloody. But not too bad. Crying. Guy's drunk. Starts blabbering about being a diplomat. And then this other fellow shows up. Turns out the guy's right. They're both low-level schmucks at the Moroccan embassy. Cops ask the woman what happened. She keeps saying, she's all right. Says she just got mugged outside the building, roughed up by some black guys. Happened too fast to identify them. Cops ask her for I.D. She's got none. The black guys—always black, right?—took her purse. Gives them a name and address. Turns out it's false. The second Moroccan tries to smooth everything over. The officers aren't buying this. But she won't press charges. Then the drunken Moroccan says something like, 'Hey, I can help you out. That girl in the paper, the one in the hotel room, I saw her.' But then he starts blabbing about how he's related to the prime minister. Next he vomits over one of the cops."

Dunne took the glass of water from Addis.

"Cops got their names. Didn't bother bringing him in. Diplomatic immunity's always a pain. And the woman won't say what really happened. The cops make her as a professional. They insist on seeing her leave, and she gets into a cab. When they go back to the station, they tell my friend what the drunk said. He rips them a new backdoor and sends them back to get more information. Dumb-ass cops. You know it, the Moroccans are gone. And today, when my friend went down to the embassy, they tell him the drunken asshole has so embarrassed his wonderful nation that he was sent home."

"So," Addis asked, "should the Bureau chase this guy back to Morocco?"

"What I might do. But I'm neck-deep—or going to be—in Kelly's shit."

"You going to tell them?"

"Maybe. My suggestions don't make the top of the list these days."

Dunne gulped down the water.

"Wife will be worried. We'll keep in touch, okay?"

"Sure," Addis said. "If I can be—"

"I don't think anyone can be."

After Addis locked the door, the phone rang. Go away, he said to himself. Everyone. Please.

After the fourth ring, the answering machine took the call.

"Nick, hi, it's me. Just calling to say hello. Just wanted to see how you are . . . Nick, I'm so sorry. I won't bother you again. I just want to . . ." She hung up.

Eric jumped on the desk. Addis pushed the cat off the papers. Why bother with all this now? he asked himself. But he knew why Margaret wanted to, and he wished he didn't. He took out his pocket calendar and looked at the days ahead.

12

"It could be a problem," Julia Lancette said.

She looked for a response from Timothy Wenner, the CIA director. Instead of speaking, he bit down on his pipe. It was unlit. Doctor's orders. She could hear him wheeze.

"Justice is proceeding with it," she continued. "Judge won't post bail, so he's still in Dade County lockup. Hasn't said anything yet about his past. Maybe he's just waiting."

Wenner tapped the folder on his desk. Today's headache. The President had been assassinated. The country was still mourning. But all the other shit didn't stop flowing.

He stood up. His shirttail hung behind him, his tie was crooked. He walked—actually, it was more of a shuffle that moved his large figure— toward the window of his seventh-floor office. Lancette recalled a joke well known through the ranks at Langley. What's the difference between Director Wenner and a sack of potatoes? Sorry, our satellite imaging is not that sophisticated.

"And you're sure?" He coughed.

She nodded. It was all in the file. Subject had been retained in the early 1980s as an information source on the internal decision making of a right-wing party in El Salvador. While on the Agency payroll, he became a leader of *La Fabrica*, a death squad. His unit tortured, raped, and assassinated. But the CIA station did not drop him. Years later, after the civil war had ended, a State Department human rights officer in the embassy was investigating the murder of an American hotelier. He called on this fellow—the subject. The Salvadoran declared his innocence but referred, as a warning, to his connection to *La Fabrica* and his "mucho close" relationship to the "hombres con cajones" at the embassy. The human rights officer dispatched a cable that rang bells at Foggy Bottom and then at the

57

CIA. An internal CIA review ended up questioning the station's relation with this source. But no reprimands were issued, not a word was mentioned in public. Another mess was locked away in a filing cabinet—until Lancette read a story in the *Miami Herald* about a Salvadoran businessman arrested in Coral Gables for smuggling Mexican heroin into the United States. She called for an ICEMAN trace. The file appeared: The businessman was the same death squad leader who had been on the CIA payroll. Another potential flap.

"It's god-damn endless," Wenner said. "Enough bad history to keep us on our knees forever. When do the sins of the past end? At least you have job security."

She tried to smile.

"What do you think we should do?" he asked.

This was the first time Wenner had asked her this question. During her eleven months running the ICEMAN office, she had brought him ten problem cases. He had not solicited her advice before.

"Take the hit," she said. They both knew what that meant. Forget business as usual: leaning on the Justice Department to drop the case. Let it proceed. Let the thug try to raise his past association with the CIA to escape the jam. Let some headline-seeking member of Congress noisily inquire about his allegations. And then tell the truth. Blame it on the zealots of the bad old days. Tell the media that all that nonsense was still echoing and it's not our fault what the cowboys did in the Cold War years. And allow those people who already think that the Agency routinely pays off murderers and scumbags in all corners of this dark, nasty world to say, "told you so." Accept all the bother because this murderous, drug-peddling asshole did not deserve a pass.

"Easy for you to say. You don't have to take the spitballs from the windbags on the committees."

Wenner coughed and kept talking: "Well, nothing so far from him. Maybe he forgot his old friends." He chuckled uneasily.

They never do, Lancette thought.

As she left the office, the director asked, "And nothing came up on Max Bridge, right?"

"Nothing, sir."

"Thank God for small favors."

In the outer office, Wenner's secretary, Viv Novek, winked at Lancette and gently touched the top button of her own blouse. Lancette looked down; her shirt had slipped open. She noticed a man sitting on the couch. She recognized him from the news reports: Jake Grayton. She blushed slightly, and he paid her the courtesy of turning away. She fumbled with the button. As she left the suite, Lancette whispered to Novek, "Shopping time."

The elevator carried her to the basement. She walked down a corridor painted pale green and entered the gift shop. On the back wall hung T-shirts, jogging shorts, windbreakers, all bearing the CIA insignia. There were ashtrays, lighters, Swiss army knives, and miniature cameras emblazed with the emblem. The oversized shot glasses always amused her. Had the irony escaped the manager of the shop? She picked up a coffee mug and looked at the bottom: Made in China. A sign by the apparel read: "All CIA personnel should ensure that none of the merchandise sold here is used in a manner that would be considered inappropriate." In other words, no posing for *Playboy* in a sweatshirt with a CIA logo. She selected a baseball jacket with the CIA seal on the back. Her brother's birthday was coming up.

What a change from the old days, she thought as she moved through the shop. When anyone can wear CIA clothing, the mystique was long gone. She remembered how people had reacted when she told them she was working at the CIA's Directorate of Intelligence. Some eyes widened. Some people muttered, "how interesting." But mostly this news was met with a sympathetic, oh-poor-you look, proof the citizenry shared her own belief that the Agency's biggest sin—and there were many—was that it had become another sclerotic Washington bureaucracy, full of the mediocre. Screwing up the big calls. Missing moles. Protecting misdeeds so promotions were not threatened. Not much prestige came from working at Langley.

Now she told friends and family she had left the CIA for Inter-Business Media. Wenner had wanted to keep ICEMAN out of the Agency mainstream, so he had a front corporation established to house the operation. But Lancette retained access to the CIA caps, paperweights, and notepads everyone enjoyed receiving as gifts, and she explained this to her relatives and friends by noting she still had pals at the Agency who could get her into the gift shop. She disliked lying, but she had developed her own justification for keeping true to her cover story. Suppose you lie to someone out of necessity. If you are certain that when you eventually reveal the lie, that person will say, "Oh, I understand and that's okay," then you do not have to fret about it now. Everyone would understand this lie. Perhaps a husband or a boyfriend would not. But she did not have to worry about that.

On the way to the register, Lancette picked up a shaving kit with the CIA logo. Maybe she'd give it to her father, she thought, and she got in line.

"Stuff makes great gifts, eh?"

The man behind her was talking. Fortyish, receding hair, glasses. A seersucker jacket.

"Yeah, uh, everyone loves it."

"Wonder if the money goes into operations," he joked. "Look."

He was holding a cap bearing the seals of the CIA and the KGB. "On sale," he said. "Could be a collector's item. There's one more left."

"No thanks," she muttered and turned toward the cashier. She dug her purse out of her handbag and dropped the jacket and shaving kit. He rushed to pick up the items.

"Walters, Dr. Charlie Walters," he said. "In the DA."

"Julia," she said, and took the jacket and shaving kit from him. "Thanks a lot." She paid and left the shop.

He caught up to her in the lobby. They walked past the stars on the wall—each representing an unidentified CIA officer killed on duty—and across the large CIA emblem on the tile floor.

"Truth be told, I still get a little rush when I walk in and out of the building," he said. "Feel like that fellow in the movies. What's his name? He did all that space stuff before those CIA movies?"

She knew the name but did not offer it.

"Nice to meet you," she said brusquely, outside the front entrance. A downpour was underway. His umbrella was open and up.

"Been raining for days—except for the funeral. That was something wasn't it? How it cleared up. Need an escort to your car?"

"No thanks. I'm right there." She pointed to her 1965 Dodge Dart. It was, she joked to friends, the only frivolous item in her life.

"Cool car. A Valiant, right?"

"Yeah," she said. "Something like that."

"And what an important person you must be, with parking so close. I'm in the far lot. Are you over here much?"

"Nice to meet you," she said again and skipped down the steps.

Her key stuck in the lock. Only an anal obsessive, she said to herself, would lock her car in the parking lot of the CIA. She jiggled the key and opened the door. She tossed her CIA merchandise on the passenger seat. Her blouse was soaked. Clumps of dirty blond hair stuck to her face. Just what I need, she thought, a lonely CIA man.

She drove past the guard booth and made a left on Chain Bridge Road. The rain was worsening, a typical wet Washington summer. She cursed her wiper blades. Both were old; one was torn.

Close to the parkway, a dog—it looked like a dog—darted across the road. Lancette pounded the brakes. The dog cleared the car. And then she felt the impact, as a car slammed into the rear of the Dodge.

She waited—no fucking way I'm getting out in this rain, she thought—and the other driver, a young man in a dark suit, came over, carrying an umbrella.

"You hurt?" he asked.

60

"No, but you should have paid more attention during surveillance training."

He did not react.

"It's a joke. I saw you turn out of the Agency after I did," she said. "And you were way too close to me."

"Sorry."

He held the umbrella over her as she inspected the damage. The rear bumper was dented, the lights smashed, and the back corner crushed. But the car would still drive. She got back in her car and invited him to sit in the passenger seat. He declined and talked to her through the opened window.

"Well, all in the family, right?" she said. "What office are you in?"

He ignored the question.

"Should we trade insurance information and all that, or—"

"It will be taken care of," he said. "Executive Insurance."

She knew what he meant. That was the name of the Agency's own insurance company. It covered employees who had to live or work under assumed names. It provided insurance for Agency cars and those registered to fronts.

"This isn't a company car, so there better not be any problem."

"Won't be," he said. "If there is, call this number." He handed her a business card: no individual name, no company name—only a post office box address in suburban Virginia and a phone number.

"And your name?"

"Ask for Dell. But I'll have Executive call you."

"Then you're going to need my number, right?"

"Yes."

She gave him the information and he returned to his car. Fucking Agency, Lancette thought, too many weirdos who think all this is the real world. She saw that the collision had thrown her CIA gifts to the floor of the car. She gathered them and spotted a piece of paper sticking out of the shaving kit. It was a note folded in half. She opened it. On the top was a logo: "From the secret files of the KGB." The message read, "We have to talk. LOC/Genealogy room, tonight 2030. Please."

One message was on her voice mail when she returned to the office. Viv Novek, Wenner's secretary, had called. Lancette rang her back.

"Nothing important, dear," Novek said. "Just thought that you'd want to know. After Mr. Grayton finished his meeting with the director, he asked me a few questions about you. Must have been quite taken. That old popped button routine—"

"Mrs. Novek, I—"

"Don't be so shy."

"What did you tell him?"

"The usual. Who you were. Where you worked. I know I'm not supposed to say—but he is the deputy director of the FBI, after all—but just a little, not much. Said you were a former analyst the director had taken a fancy to, I said, and—"

"Thanks a lot."

"And your number. That was it. I only wanted to help. He is a catch. And the director is so keen on you, and others have made inquiries. You're more popular than you think, and I'm only trying to—"

How does she know how popular I think I am? Lancette wondered.

"I know, I know. But please don't give out—"

"Okay, dear, I was only—"

Lancette said good-bye and hung up.

Two men in one day, she thought. Now she would have something to tell her mother the next time she called. At her desk, she looked at the note. Charlie Walters must have placed it in the shaving kit. The genealogy room at the Library of Congress was an odd place for a romantic encounter. Damn strange bunch, she thought, people who spend their lives in secrecy.

13

White House
June 25

A memo from McGreer was on Addis's desk.

> *Hamilton Kelly informs me that President Mumfries—President damnit—wants to invite prominent historians to the White House to discuss transitions and periods of national tragedy. Please compile a list of those who should be invited.*

The resident son of eggheads. He would call his mother, a European history professor at Columbia, and gather names. This was the sort of action Hanover would have taken in a similar circumstance. Reach out, bear the symbolic burdens. For Mumfries this cut against his public image as a drawling, backroom patrician who above all else cares about the deal, whatever the deal is. This is *presidential*. Kelly may be learning, Addis thought.

Addis picked up today's pack of newspaper clippings. He had avoided looking at the newspapers at home. Now he forced himself to read. "Mumfries Request for Better Security Ignored." "White House Security Chief Neglected Veep-Elect Concern." Addis felt sorry for Dunne. He flipped through the other clips. Mumfries had granted an interview to the Associated Press, during which he discussed his feelings about assuming office due to tragedy. He talked about healing. He said that a staffer had suggested the lines of poetry he had placed in his first presidential address. "Not my strong suit," he explained. When the reporter asked if he intended to seek the party's nomination, Mumfries took her by the hand and said, "Young lady, let's just get through the next few days. I'm still thinking about him—and Margaret and Jack."

Addis threw the stack into the trash. He looked at the boxes still scattered throughout the office. Well, that's convenient, he thought.

There was a rapping at the door. Addis turned to see Mike Finn. The White House political director was banging his cane against the doorjamb.

"Mind taking a walk with me to Brew's office?" Finn asked. "Are you busy?"

"Not much. Hard to tell."

"Know the feeling. Come on."

Addis knew better than to take Finn's arm and guide him. Finn had memorized every foot of the West Wing. Wearing his usual wrap-around sunglasses, he steadily tapped his cane and did not brush against Addis.

"These office shuffles are murder on me," Finn said. "Just when I know where everyone is, they up and change it all. Almost went into your old office. Heard M. T. in there. Think she was talking to a reporter. Don't know about what."

"Wouldn't know, Mike," Addis said.

"Not the time for hotheads."

"M. T.'s fine."

"That's good to hear."

Finn walked into McGreer's suite, nodded at McGreer's secretary, and entered McGreer's office; Addis followed. McGreer was at his desk. Dan Carey, the consultant, was on the couch.

"Glad you could join us, Nick," McGreer said. "Don't want those historians to keep you too busy."

"Not a problem," Addis answered.

He said hello to Carey. The two did not like each other. Addis did not trust Carey. The consultant was always urging that more money be spent on polling, that more money be spent on television ads, that more money be spent on focus groups, all expenditures from which he received a sizeable cut. Carey daily tested the appeal of words and phrases and had vetted all speeches prepared for Hanover. He had worked for candidates across the political spectrum. He had advised corporations and foreign leaders, including a few whose devotion to democratic principles was weak. McGreer had brought Carey aboard in the last weeks of the first presidential campaign. Insurance, McGreer told the skeptics, including Addis. And Carey had stayed. He lived in Virginia's horse country and commuted by limousine, sometimes by helicopter. In the first book on the administration—four had been published so far—Carey had been quoted remarking, "Nick is a waterboy who thinks he's the President's conscience."

"How you doing, Nick?" Carey asked. He was wearing his customary black, Italian suit. He had a rack of them at home. Addis remembered the picture from a newsmagazine. Each one cost three thousand dollars. Is that a new wig? Addis wondered, as he looked at the matted brown hair lying above Carey's large, sloping forehead. Like paint on a breadbox, he thought.

"Been better," Addis replied. He turned to McGreer. "Did you know about that memo?"

"No," McGreer said. "Too bad for Clarence. Mumfries never mentioned it to me."

"Didn't think so—"

McGreer held up his hand to signal, Enough, this is not on the agenda.

"We're discussing the future not the fucking past," McGreer said. "What to do with the Hanover Re-elect."

"A campaign without a candidate," Finn remarked.

"I suppose the question is, who inherits?" Carey said. The conversation paused.

"We've been thinking, talking informally," Finn said, addressing Addis. "Do we swing it behind Mumfries? He refuses to say anything publicly about his intentions. And he and Kelly haven't said anything to any of us, right?"

Carey and McGreer nodded, and they all looked at Addis.

"I don't know anything," Addis muttered. "Isn't this a bit too—"

"And—who knows?—there might be someone else out there with a plan," Finn went on. "Nick, hear anything from your friend, Senator Palmer?"

Addis shook his head. He had spoken briefly to the senator at the funeral. Anything I can do to help, I will, Palmer had said.

"Dickerson?" McGreer asked. The previous year the black congressman had threatened to challenge Hanover in the primaries, but he had not entered the race.

"I don't think so," Addis said. "It will look a bit opportunistic. And his son is in trouble for a cable business deal in Oakland. The U.S. attorney is looking into it. Dickerson thinks we started that rolling. We didn't, and I told his people that. But he still believes—which probably will keep him out."

"And do we want him out?" Carey asked.

No one replied.

"I suppose that depends on who we want in," Carey said, answering his own question.

The discussion was beginning to anger Addis. He wondered if perhaps he was too sensitive. The number of days to the election was finite and growing shorter. Didn't they have a responsibility—maybe even a responsibility to *him*—to plot instead of mourn? That might be so, but did it have to seem so enjoyable?

Damn, I am out of it.

"Isn't the first move up to the V-Vi . . . the President?" he asked.

"Sounded like Lem there, Nick," Carey said quickly.

"Fuck yes," McGreer said to Addis. "He'd be the easiest, maybe the best. Continuity and all that. Probably what Bob''—he hesitated—''would have even wanted. Mumfries helped him get here and was on the team.''

Addis let it pass.

''Not sure Margaret would agree with that,'' Carey said.

''But we're not committed,'' Finn interjected.

''Not yet,'' Carey added.

Addis had it figured. McGreer was pushing Mumfries. Carey was worried he would be cut out of Mumfries's campaign—and its spending. He had never gotten along with Kelly. Finn was doing what he always did: calculating, extrapolating, gaming it all out. And each was worried that a loop existed that he was not in.

''Mumfries will have to say something in the next few days,'' McGreer said. ''Everyone in Chicago is in a fucking panic. Every state chair, too. Every fucking delegate. And even the fucking airlines are calling.''

''Let them come and vote for Hanover,'' Addis said.

The others looked at him.

''The delegates. On the first ballot. Most are committed, right? Then, I suppose, we'll have an open convention.''

''I have someone researching the rules,'' Finn said.

''And after the first ballot, who will they vote for?'' Carey asked.

''I guess that's the question,'' Addis said.

Finn stood up and began pacing. He never bumped into the furniture.

''Could state chairs get together first?'' Finn asked. ''Make a decision?''

''And enforce it?'' Carey asked. ''Good luck. You know we're talking chaos, if we do not settle this damn soon.''

''May not be ours to settle,'' Addis said.

Finn ran his fingers across the mounted samurai sword McGreer kept in a corner of the office. The intercom on the desk sounded, and McGreer picked up the phone. He frowned, hung up, and switched on the television.

Margaret Hanover was on CNN. She was in a hallway in the old Executive Office Building, outside the makeshift White House pressroom. A crowd of reporters surrounded her. Behind her stood M. T. O'Connor, twirling her hair, and Lem Jordan.

''Fuck,'' McGreer said softly, as he raised the volume.

''I am touched by the outpouring of support that has come from across the nation and from around the world,'' Margaret was saying. ''It has meant so much to me and to Jack—and everyone who works here.''

''Mrs. Hanover, do you believe that security was too lax at the White House?'' asked a reporter from the *Wall Street Journal*.

''No, no. These people have such a heavy burden here. They never got credit for those attempts they stopped. Even once when Jack and I were . . . I don't think I should go into that. But I know they did their best. Every security system has lapses. I hope we can learn from this."

She was somber. She looked at the reporters, not the cameras.

"If Mumfries decides to run, will you support him?" The questioner was off-screen. Addis recognized the voice—a producer for ABC News and a friend of O'Connor.

"Shit," Carey said.

"As you know, President"—she said the word slowly—"Mumfries has not announced his intentions yet. So it would be unfair of me to speculate. I will say this: I am grateful for the support he gave my husband, and I hope that in the months ahead, if not the years after that, he will join me in fighting for the policies that Bob initiated."

" 'Join me'?" Finn said.

"Have you thought about running?" Again, it was the ABC producer.

Margaret let out a slight laugh. "Now there's an idea," she said. "But seriously, today I am just thinking about Jack—what will be best for him. Our family has always been devoted to public service. They may have killed Bob, but not what he stood for. . . ."

She was starting to cry. A reporter offered her a handkerchief, and she dabbed at her cheeks.

"I probably should be going now," she said. "I just wanted to see some friendly faces. Thank you."

She walked out of the room.

McGreer turned off the television.

"Did you fucking know about this?" McGreer asked Addis.

"No, not at all."

"Does she have . . . plans, Nick?" Finn asked.

"Nothing I've been told."

"Well, there's continuity, and then there's continuity," Carey said.

And if she runs you're still in the thick of it.

Addis guessed that was what Carey was thinking. Carey and Margaret rarely agreed on policy matters but they had worked well together. They both had been loyal to the same overriding principle: what would be best for Bob Hanover.

"That certainly was off-message," Finn remarked. "How'd she look?"

"As purposeful as ever," Carey replied. He was smirking.

"Well, I think we should find out what we fucking can," McGreer said in a way that indicated the meeting was done.

About what? Addis thought.

On the way out, Finn placed his hand on Addis's shoulder.

"Thanks for joining us, Nick," he said. "Let us know if you learn any-thing . . . pertinent."

M. T. O'Connor was not in her office. Her assistant told Addis she might be with Margaret in the East Wing. Addis headed that way. At the corridor that connected the two wings, he passed Kelly and Wenner. The CIA director stopped to say hello. Addis recalled their first meeting, in the early days of the administration, when Wenner had invited Addis to the CIA for lunch. In his personal dining room, he asked Addis to explain the Honduras business. Off the record. For curiosity's sake.

Addis laid it out for Wenner. When Mumfries had chaired the Senate intelligence committee during the previous administration, he and his senior staff tacitly approved—with a nod and a wink, nothing on paper—a CIA operation that funneled funds to a band of drugged-up, thuggish generals in Honduras. The generals were using this money to supply arms to a rightist rebel insurgency next door. Per their understanding with Langley, they were keeping a percentage of the money for shipping and handling. Official policy was that Washington had no favorites in the civil war in the neighboring country; a majority of Congress was opposed to intervention. But the President and Mumfries—hardliners from opposing parties—agreed that public policy should not prevent them from proceeding with behind-the-scenes action. But after the CIA program had been initiated, a leak occurred, and the details reached the front pages. The source of the leak was never publicly identified. The best guesses traced the tip-off to Senator Palmer, who previously had blocked the administration's attempts to openly assist the right-wing rebels. And since Palmer took no significant action without the input of his chief of staff, Nick Addis was blamed by the national security crowd and Mumfries's staff—and that included Hamilton Kelly—for the scandal-causing leak. Hearings had to be held. Newspaper editorialists huffed about spies running amok. Mumfries claimed a miscommunication had transpired between his staff and certain CIA officers, and he survived the scandal with little political damage.

After Addis had finished recounting the episode over lunch, Wenner had not asked him who had leaked. Addis had appreciated that.

"How are you, Nick?" Wenner now inquired.

Shit, I should really get an answer to that question.

"Like everyone else, sir."

"Hard days, hard days," Wenner said.

"Yes, they are sir."

"Yes, indeed," Kelly interrupted. "And, Nick, you and I need to talk soon. . . . About future considerations."

"Sure."

Kelly and Wenner started to move off.

"And that appearance a few minutes ago." Kelly had stopped and was facing Addis. "Interesting. Don't you think?"

Kelly was trying to be melodramatic. Wenner, lost in thought, wasn't paying attention. Addis shrugged.

"We'll talk," Kelly said and guided Wenner toward the Oval Office.

"Can't wait," Addis said, to no one in particular. He looked at the Rose Garden and walked on.

Neither O'Connor nor Margaret were in the widow's office. He ambled down the hall, and he saw Jack in the library. Addis entered the box-filled room, wondering if Lem Jordan was near.

"Hi, Jack."

Jack, with his back to the door, was startled. He wheeled himself around.

"Hey, Nick," he muttered. His eyes brightened to see Addis.

The car accident, nine years ago, had left him paralyzed from the waist down. It also had turned him from a gregarious child into a withdrawn, sullen boy. He occasionally entered what the doctors called conscious blackouts. He would be awake but coma-like, impenetrable, nearly autistic. The specialists had not been able to find the cause of these retreats. Psychologists and psychiatrists came up with various theories. It was the shock, the anger, the guilt for not being the perfect son. No treatments had taken hold.

Jack wiped his stringy blond hair from his face. Was he getting thinner? He was wearing an Orioles T-shirt. Addis squatted next to him.

"Whatcha doing?" Addis asked.

"Helping Mom pack."

"And what are you packing?"

"Old stuff."

Addis sat on a sealed box. He looked at the open cartons. They were filled with books, knickknacks, old newspapers.

"How you doing?" Addis asked.

"I keep the list," Jack said. He held up a clipboard. "Then Mom puts it in the box."

Addis pulled a scrapbook out of the box at Jack's feet.

"These are my mom's boxes," Jack said, pointing to the ones closest to him. "Those"—he pointed across the room—"are my dad's."

Addis flipped through the scrapbook. Margaret's report cards from grade school. Always straight As. A picture of her next to a handmade poster that read, "Vote Mason." Had she run for class office in middle school? A large group photo taken at what appeared to be a wedding reception. Margaret stood out—sixteen years old or so, but the same wince-like smile. And the tall young man standing to the side of the group? Was that Mumfries? On the next page was stapled a copy of *Voices*, the literary magazine at her boarding school. The masthead listed her as an associate editor.

"You know," Addis said, nodding toward the emblem on Jack's T-shirt, "maybe we should go to another ball game."

"Sure. But the seats won't be the same." At opening day, months earlier, Addis had sat with the President and Jack at the edge of the playing field.

"I bet we can get some good ones."

"I bet you can," Jack said.

"I'll just say they're for you."

Jack wiggled his mouth; it was nearly a smile.

Addis turned a bristled page. A *Harvard Crimson* was tucked into the book. The subscription label was addressed to a library at Yale. Addis carefully unfolded the issue. Nothing on the front page seemed significant. He gingerly opened the paper.

"What's that?" Jack asked.

"A newspaper from where your father went to college."

"This is one of my mom's boxes."

"Yes, but she must have kept it for him."

There it was. Toward the back, a four-paragraph story with the headline, "Hanover to Star as Romeo." The article—there was no picture—previewed a production that was to open later in the week. Addis knew the tale. Margaret had met Bob after a performance of the play. She must have saved this *Crimson* as a special souvenir.

"Let me see," Jack said.

Addis held the page in front of him, and Jack looked at the short article.

But, Addis noticed, it was dated prior to the night Margaret met Bob, for the play had not yet opened. Could she have . . . ? he began to wonder. Had she gone to the play because she already knew Hanover would be in it? Had she engineered a chance meeting? Perhaps after that first encounter she had rummaged through the library at school and retrieved this back issue of the *Crimson*. But not the issue that contained a review of the play? There must have been more elaborate coverage of the production. Why go back and collect just this brief mention? Had another issue of the *Crimson* fallen out of the scrapbook long ago? Or had Margaret, while at Yale, been reading the newspaper of another school, searching for references to a man she did not yet know? That would have been methodical. Damn methodical.

Addis pulled the paper from Jack. He felt he had discovered a secret. He slipped the paper back between the pages and returned the scrapbook to the carton.

"Really shouldn't be going through her stuff," Addis said.

"My mom didn't say I couldn't."

"I know. But sometimes it's better to respect people's privacy."

Jack was rocking himself in his wheelchair.

"You miss him?" he asked Addis.

"Yes, I do, and so do millions."

"But not like . . ."

"Not like you and your mom."

Addis stood, as if he were about to leave.

"What do you got to do now?" Jack was asking him to stay.

"Lots of things, lots," Addis said. "But they can wait a little."

Yeah, come up with a list of historians.

And there were preliminary calls to be made regarding the Louisiana Land Deal.

I'd rather deal with the historians.

Jordan came into the room.

"Wh-wh-what you up to, N-nick?" he asked.

"Just talking to Jack," Addis said. "Told him we should go to a ball game soon."

"S-s-sure," Jordan replied.

"Now that you're here, I think I'll get back to it all. Is that okay, Jack?"

"Guess so."

"See you later, then. Bye."

Jack wheeled himself toward the window. He didn't say good-bye.

14

Dupont Circle

June 25

Dunne sat in the front seat of his Buick. He nodded at the police officer dressed in civvies in the Toyota across the street. Both men had unobstructed views of the Moroccan embassy. In his hand, Dunne held the daily report of the Interagency Assassination Task Force.

Earlier in the day, after dropping by what soon would be his new office in the main Treasury building—Personnel/Training/Management Development—he had been whistled into the Secretary Louis Alter's office. Alter asked him about the headlines. Dunne replied that he had never seen any memo from Kelly regarding Mumfries's suggestion that White House security procedures be reviewed.

"Is Kelly making this up?" Alter said.

"Maybe," Dunne answered.

"Why?"

"I don't know." Dunne had his suspicions, but he did not want to share them with the Secretary. "Except that as far as I can see they're going to dump as much of the load on me as they can."

Alter thanked Dunne for his time, and the meeting was over. In the hallway, Dunne ran into a friend from the Secret Service. They chatted about wives and children for a short time. Nothing about anything official. As they parted, the friend patted Dunne on the back and handed him a manila envelope.

"Supposed to be restricted," he said. "But seems like everyone gets it. Just in case you didn't."

Without opening the envelope, Dunne said good-bye.

Now, in the car, he read the report. Ballistics had not produced any leads. Analysts at the CIA and the Bureau were combing through records of terrorist attacks around the world, looking for the presence of similar weapons. Nothing in the report referred to whether any U.S. agencies used such weapons.

Dental records had turned up nothing. The effort to trace the tattoo's origin had yielded no information. The component agencies of the IATF were checking 347 people named Max Bridge. None appeared promising at the moment, and a group of psychiatric profilers could not agree on whether the suspect's use of this name was significant. Maybe, they concluded. And they had not yet reached any conclusions on the meaning of *HAPPY*.

Dunne shook his head and continued reading.

Modest progress had been made in processing the flood of tips that had poured into the Bureau. Tens of thousands of Americans thought they knew the assassin. The unsolicited leads were being categorized and evaluated. Several men who had worked on a fishing trawler in Alaska reported that an old shipmate named Chet resembled the suspect. Three Marines thought that the assassin looked like a fellow who had attended the first weeks of basic training before dropping out. A search of the available Marine records turned up nothing. Some kids in New Hampshire swore that the suspect had once been a substitute teacher. The list was long. A part-time catcher for a minor-league baseball team in North Carolina. A right-wing survivalist in Idaho who used to be the night manager at a freight yard. My own son, claimed several parents. My ex-husband, claimed several wives. The Bureau was checking each lead as fast as possible.

The IATF had reached a preliminary finding on one point. Regarding the involvement of Brady Sandlin and Allison Meade, the obvious explanation was the most probable. The assassin had used Meade to entice Sandlin to the hotel room. It appeared unlikely that either was an active participant in the plot to kill the President.

"No shit," Dunne said to himself.

He again nodded toward his partner of the moment. The fellow, on unofficial loan from the Metropolitan Police, was alert. A car came out of the embassy driveway. The officer shook his head. Dunne kept on reading.

The briefing report noted that later in the day Mumfries would meet with the presidential commission he had created to oversee and review the work of the IATF. The list of commission members included Senator Palmer, Secretary Alter, and CIA Director Wenner.

Another car was leaving the embassy, an aqua-green BMW convertible with diplomatic tags. The police officer placed a finger on his nose.

Dunne started his car and moved the Buick behind the BMW. The convertible raced through the pothole-filled streets of a neighborhood filled with embassies and grand houses. Dunne cursed the city administration with each alignment-ruining bump. At Massachusetts Avenue, the BMW turned right. It drove past the mosque and made a left after the Naval Observatory.

Dunne followed closely in the noontime traffic. The BMW stopped on Wisconsin Avenue at a stretch of restaurants, bars, and shops. Its driver parked in a no-standing zone. Diplomatic immunity, Dunne thought.

Dunne double-parked a few cars behind the BMW and watched the Moroccan cross the street and enter a bar with no windows. A parking space opened up down the street. Dunne guided his car next to the meter. As he got out, he dug into his pockets. No change. He'd have to take the ticket. And there would be a ticket, for the one thing the city did well was enforce parking laws.

Dunne entered the bar. Only a few patrons were present—a couple at the bar, a few at tables in front of a low stage. Still, the air was heavy with smoke. The lights were low. A woman wearing only garters was at the edge of the stage and leaning forward. Dunne did not look closely. Generic disco music was playing. He spotted the Moroccan at a table near the stage. Dunne sat at the bar.

"No one's at the door, mister, but we still got a five-dollar cover," the bartender said. He was a skinny fellow, in his thirties, with long thin black hair that fell below his shoulder blades.

Dunne put a five on the counter.

"And a two-drink minimum," the bartender said.

"A club soda," Dunne said.

"Got to charge you as much as a mixed drink."

"Fine."

The Moroccan ordered a drink from the waitress, a black woman with a 1970s-style Afro who was wearing stiletto heels and a one-piece body suit matching the color of her skin. He rubbed her backside as she left.

Dunne watched the Moroccan, not what was happening on stage. He recalled one of his first assignments as a cop in Atlanta. A stripper had failed to report to work for two days, and one of the other girls dropped by her place and persuaded the super to let her in the apartment. They found the stripper dead and naked in the kitchen. Every knife and sharp kitchen utensil she owned had been stuck into a different part of her. Dunne was the first officer on the scene. By the time he had arrived, the blood had seeped through the floorboards and begun to stain the ceiling of the apartment below. The case was easily solved. A detective went to the bar, asked a few questions, discovered the victim had a fan who came to see her every day. The detective, with Dunne and another officer, went to the suspect's home and found him dead and bloody in the bathtub.

"Debbie, she's a GW student, pre-med," the bartender said to Dunne, eyeing the woman on the stage. "We got a few who are doing poli-sci.

Imagine if they go into politics. Wish I could take photos, in case one of them becomes famous. Wouldn't that be a fuckin' kick? But boss-lady won't let me."

Dunne asked for another club soda.

"Sure, dude," the bartender said.

Dunne hated being called that. He said nothing.

The Moroccan stayed for about an hour. Several of the dancers came over to his table after they finished their routines. He handed each a few bills. A regular. When the Moroccan called for his bill, Dunne paid his own. Then Dunne followed him out, putting on sunglasses before leaving the bar.

Dunne looked up and down the street; there was little pedestrian traffic. He walked up alongside the Moroccan.

"Mr. Al-Fusah?"

The Moroccan turned toward him. He had a thin moustache and blood-shot eyes.

"I'd like to speak with you a moment," Dunne continued.

The Moroccan tried to step away from Dunne. But Dunne gripped the man's arm. He pulled him closer.

"I am sorry, I am very busy now," Al-Fusah said. He twisted to break free of Dunne. But Dunne held on firmly.

"I insist," Dunne said. With his free hand, he pulled back his jacket to reveal a gun in a shoulder holster. "Just take a little walk with me."

"I am a diplomat," Al-Fusah protested. "You cannot do this to me."

"Please," Dunne said, "don't make a scene—especially here, in front of . . ."

He tightened his grip, and Al-Fusah reluctantly began walking with him up Wisconsin Avenue.

"What of me do you want?" Al-Fusah asked.

Dunne put a finger to his lips.

They passed a few stores, and Dunne guided Al-Fusah down a set of steps and toward an empty baseball field. Al-Fusah came to a halt.

"I told you people before. To leave me alone."

Dunne stood still.

"What people?"

"You people. You CIA."

"When was this?"

"When I was in Paris and you Americans bothered me there. I said leave me alone."

Dunne chuckled. "We Americans are not all the same. This has nothing to do with that. Let's sit down there"—he gestured toward the third-base dugout—"and have a little talk."

He shoved Al-Fusah, and the Moroccan stumbled down the stairs. No one was on the field, and the dugout was shielded from the view of anyone on the street. Dunne pushed Al-Fusah on to the bench and continued to stand.

"A friend of yours got into trouble with an American girl the other night. He said something to the police officers that interests me."

Al-Fusah jumped to his feet. "That was not me. I know nothing about that."

Dunne slammed his fist into the man's stomach. He had pulled the punch—it was more to shock than hurt Al-Fusah. Still, the Moroccan's head heaved over his knees, and when he returned to an upright position, his face was red and his breathing quick.

"I am a diplomat," Al-Fusah said between breaths. "You cannot . . . demand you return . . ."

"Listen, I'm not going to explain everything to you. But take my word: I'm a desperate man. Worrying about getting into trouble with the State Department is the last thing on my mind today. Answer a few questions and you can be on your way—and nobody, including the fundamentalist opposition back home, will have to know about your friendly relations with certain Americans. Understand?"

The Moroccan was silent.

"It would be very easy," Dunne said, "to leak a police report on that episode—which also would note you are a regular at the Riviera Bar, which features the loveliest of naked ladies—to the international news service in town that is a front for an intelligence service unfriendly to your government."

Playing the role of the heavy, Dunne told himself. He never liked it—mainly because he had known too many who relished it. But it usually worked. And now more than ever he cared only about results. He waited and looked at the baseline dust on the concrete floor.

"So what do you want me to say?"

"Your friend, the one who was sent home. He told the police that he knew the girl in the papers. Was he talking about the one in the hotel?"

"Yes."

"The one found with the reporter."

"Yes."

"Allison Meade was her name."

"I do not know."

"How did he know her?" Dunne asked.

"From the service."

"What service?"

The Moroccan was staring at his feet as he talked. Dunne grabbed him by his short black hair and yanked up his head.

"I'm going to take a wild guess here," Dunne said. "Escort?"

Al-Fusah nodded.

"And you knew her, too."

"Maybe . . . He says to me the photo in the newspaper looked like her. I see it and I do not know for sure. But he says to him it looked like her."

"The name of the service, please."

"I do not know. He was the one who called always."

Dunne hit the Moroccan in the stomach again. He had to admit to himself it felt good to strike someone, something—after the past few days.

Al-Fusah recovered his breath and said, "Really I do not know. Maybe some name like a joke. I remember he laughed about it. Said maybe they'd send"—he hesitated—"Mrs. Hanover."

Dunne wondered if the pause meant that Al-Fusah had recognized Dunne.

"You remember there was a joke, but not the name?"

"He laughed about it. But he called, not me. And it was only once or twice."

"When?"

He thought for a moment.

"Maybe two months ago. Before the new ambassador came. And once before that."

"Okay," Dunne said. "Those times did you meet anyone else from this service?"

"She came with the same girl."

"Each time? To that apartment?"

"Yes."

Dunne waited for more information.

"She was white girl, also. Long blond hair."

"Age?"

"Like the other girl."

"And their names?"

"I do not know."

Dunne placed his hand on Al-Fusah's shoulder and started to squeeze.

"I do not know," the Moroccan repeated. "Maybe one say it was . . . like diamonds. . . . I think, Tiffany. I do not know."

"Did either one say anything you remember now?"

Al-Fusah shook his head.

"And the girl from two nights ago—did she come from the same service?"

"I do not know."

Dunne went through the checklist in his mind. He concluded he had obtained all he could from this low-level diplomat.

"Fine," he said. "We're done. But you're not going to disappear now, too, like your friend? I'd like to know I can reach you again, if I need to."

The Moroccan said nothing.

"Because if I can't, I can always drop off that police report with you-know-who and see what happens."

Al-Fusah nodded.

"See you around, and thanks," Dunne said. He began to leave the dugout. "I mean that. Thanks."

"It was clean," Al-Fusah said, a trace of protest in his voice. "Very clean. We did not do what you think. They were not those kind of girls."

"Whatever you say, Mr. Al-Fusah," Dunne replied.

Dunne returned to his car and pulled a ticket out from under the wiper blade.

15

Capitol Hill
June 25

Damn ugly, she thought.

Lancette walked by the concrete planters placed behind the Supreme Court; it was as if they were designed by the city planners in charge of East Berlin during the communist years. Wasn't there a less unsightly way to protect government buildings from foreign terrorists and made-in-the-USA antigovernment extremists? In recent years, these planters had sprouted throughout Washington like weeds. Streets had been closed, traffic rerouted, metal detectors installed in federal offices. Had anyone, she wondered, bothered to study the health effects of repeated exposure to those machines? Maybe we're all being zapped to death by security precautions. A guard patrolling the perimeter of the court smiled at her. The Cold War done, and we need to hide behind half-ton plant holders. Go figure.

The genealogy room at the Library of Congress was empty when she entered and took a seat. It was near closing time. A note from a stranger and here she was at a secret rendezvous. Her very first. She wasn't sure why she had decided to come. A change in routine? Curiosity? The possibility she'd get a story to tell out of this? Her family used to press her for details of what they imagined to be her clandestine exploits as a modern-day Mata Hari. But the only danger she had faced in the Agency came from office politics. The CIA, a paper-pushing bureaucracy? Who wanted to hear about that? But it was the Agency she knew. And no one had ever made a movie about that reality.

Lancette skimmed through a newspaper. On the front page was a photograph of mourners visiting Hanover's grave. A story on the investigation reported that the inquiry was going nowhere. An editorial called on President Mumfries to announce soon whether he intended to run for reelection. A young man with a ponytail and a backpack walked in.

"Guy gave me a twenty to give you this," he said, and handed her an envelope.

"Where is he?"

"Said not to say anything. Just tell you to read the note."

She let a look of concern form on her face.

"Okay, okay, outside in the back, in a brown car." He spun around and left the room.

That's what the note said. It asked Lancette to meet him in the parking lot. It was not signed. In a penny, in a pound, she thought.

She exited the library. A car flashed its headlights. The guy from the gift shop was behind the wheel. The window next to him was open. The engine was on.

"Glad you came," Charlie Walters said. "Sorry for the melodrama . . . the notes and all this."

He was nervous. She stayed back from the car.

"But there are reasons," he continued.

"Good ones, I'm sure," Lancette replied.

Walters slid over to the passenger side.

"Please, get in for a moment. We can talk."

"Long day behind the desk. I prefer to stand."

Walters fumbled something he was holding and cursed under his breath. Lancette took a step forward to see better inside the car. He raised an arm. A gun was in his hand. Six inches from the tip of her nose.

"Please, get in," he said. His hand was shaking. She thought about running, but she worried a sudden movement might prompt him to shoot. She opened the door and slid behind the wheel.

"What the hell do you think you're doing?" she said.

"Turn left when we leave the lot."

"So what is this? A kidnaping? A rape? A new way to impress a girl on a first date? You should know that I left notes at home and at my office saying I was meeting you, just in case something happened."

"You did not." He waved the gun at her. "Drive."

"Did too. Good tradecraft, isn't it?"

"Then let's hope they're not paying attention to you yet."

"Who?" she asked.

He poked her with the pistol, and she pulled the car out of the lot.

Lancette was surprising herself. She was not frightened. Walters ordered her to turn right and then right again.

"That's a one-way street," she said. "The other way."

"Do it."

She looked at him.

"That way you can tell if anyone is following," he said.

"They teach you this?"

"No, saw it on television."

She turned into the one-way residential street and toward the head-lights of an oncoming car. A horn sounded. She veered to the right and the other car passed. Walters checked to see if anyone was behind them. A truck came toward the car. She swerved again. At the end of the block, she hit the brakes.

"Keep going."

"Isn't this enough?" she asked.

"Go." He shook the gun.

At the next intersection, he instructed her to make a left and to return to normal traffic.

"All clear," he said.

"I'm delighted," she replied.

Walters directed her away from the Capitol, down Pennsylvania Avenue, and toward the dilapidated neighborhoods of Anacostia. Near the river, he told her to make a U-turn, pull over, and get out. He took the keys from her. They were standing in front of Wink's, a windowless bar. The neon Budweiser sign over the door was not working. A hand-painted sign read, "Pool 50¢." The gun was not in sight.

"A drink?" he asked.

"You're crazy," she said. "I should run."

"You can. But if you care about . . . You should have a drink."

This is not about fucking me or hurting me, she thought. It's something else. She tried for a tough-sounding response.

"Okay . . . but you're paying."

Not quite, but close, she thought, as he opened the door to the bar for her.

Inside the bar was dark, the air smoke-drenched. She followed him to a booth in the back. Everyone stared. He sat with his back to the wall.

"I'm guessing they don't get too many white patrons in here," she said.

"That's the point," he said. "We don't have too many black people to worry about."

A waitress took their order. Two beers.

"Okay," Lancette said. "You had your fun. You got me here. Anyone white walks in the door and we'll know it. So what do you want?"

With his index finger, Walters drew small circles in the sticky film covering the tabletop.

"Really, it's what you want—or wanted."

"And what's that?"

"An ICEMAN report."

The front door opened; a shaft of streetlight sliced through the smoke. Walters raised a hand to block the beam. Lancette turned to see three black men in overalls entering.

"Doubt they could get anyone here that fast," he said.

"They? You mean us?"

"Hard to think of it that way sometimes. Too many of us who are not us, you know. It's a big place."

"Okay, okay. The ICEMAN report. What are you talking about?"

"Listen to this," he said.

Walters was a psychiatrist and worked in DA/MA/P. He had been with the Agency seven years. He joined it after a short stint as deputy head of penal research with the Michigan Department of Corrections. He spent his first two years at the CIA in the euphemistically named Occupational Health/ Behavior Rehabilitation office, the office that looked after the many agency employees who had become too familiar with alcohol and controlled substances. It was known throughout the Agency as Dry Out. Then Walters graduated from Dry Out to MA/P.

The morning after the President was shot, Walters received the ICEMAN request. It came in the standard form, containing a written physical description of the assassin and various photographs that Lancette had selected. Walters read the report and realized he possessed a clue to the most awful crime decades.

He had not recognized the man in the photographs. But the tattoo that was etched into the killer's chest—the letter *M* pierced by a dagger— seemed familiar to him. He could not recall where he had seen it. Perhaps on an inmate in Michigan? He probably had stared at hundreds of tattoos there. Or on one of the hundreds of CIA people he had counseled, treated, interviewed, or screened? He was not sure.

The request for information was urgent, so he quickly wrote up a memo. It was short:

> *The undersigned believes he once encountered a person bearing a tattoo similar to the one found on the subject's chest. (An arrow through an* M.) *The undersigned cannot recall where he saw the tattoo previously. But he believes there are two possibilities: (a) when he was working with inmates in Michigan correctional facilities; (b) when he was treating employees of CIA. The undersigned is trying to recall more precisely.*

He carried two copies of the memo to the office of Dr. Stan Blum, the head of DA/MA/P. Blum was not there. Walters had the secretary, a new gal, initial both copies. He left one with the secretary, returned to his own office, and waited for interrogators to burst in.

No one came. That is, no one from the Office of Security, no one from the FBI, no one from Secret Service. Just Blum. Thank you for the report, he told Walters. It's been taken care of. And if you think of whoever that was with the tattoo, do let me know. In the meantime, place your copy in the MA/P central files, so we can locate it if you're not around. And, remember, you are not to discuss this matter with anyone. Not with anyone.

Blum left the office, and Walters knew—just knew—that his report no longer existed. He was scared.

That night—three days ago—Walters went home to his apartment in the Kennedy-Warren, the large residential complex on Connecticut Avenue. He rummaged through a box in his bedroom closet and found the journal he kept during the months he had worked for the state of Michigan. These were the notes for a book he once considered writing. For the first time in years, he read through all the entries, even the ones about the assault and attempted rape that had left him with an injured kidney and caused him to resign.

A Sam Cooke song started playing on the jukebox. Walters leaned closer to Lancette. "I am not a brave man," he said. He drank his beer and resumed the story.

There was nothing in the diary about that tattoo. So he went to his storage room in the dank and cavernous basement. He kept two composition books in a crate. In these he had been recording—against regulations—his experiences at the Agency. Notes for another book, this one a novel.

The notebooks were a collection of key words and phrases, not a full-fledged account. The pages contained cryptic references meant to stir his memory later. "Couple/Art dealers/EE" referred to a husband-wife team of officers who posed as art dealers in Eastern Europe. Both were utter drunks. "Multiple fem/Sri": a female case officer with multiple personality disorder who had to be extracted from Sri Lanka. She had been overseeing a penetration of a Chinese operation to procure restricted computer technology. At a meeting with an asset, the personality of an eleven-year-old girl had emerged. The asset bolted; the mission fell apart. "Nam/twelve-year-old": twenty-five years after serving in Vietnam, a former DO man who now worked in the credit union began having horrific nightmares about an adolescent agent he had recruited during the war. She had been killed in a free-fire zone.

Lancette waited patiently as Walters explained himself.

In the basement storage area, Walters had reviewed his notes. Toward the middle of the first book, he found the entry: "Outsider/Hotel/Exp. drug/The Gauntlet."

It had been several years ago, after he had left Dry Out. His supervisor, Dr. Killigren, had introduced him to a man with one of those nondescript names: Mr. White, Mr. Brown, something like that. Go with him, the boss had said, and take our newest concoction. Killigren handed him a vial of pills and explained that the Agency had been experimenting with a new drug that in certain cases diminished the cravings of hardcore alcoholics. The medication had been cooked up, practically accidentally, at one of the labs of the Directorate of Science and Technology. The side-effects included impotence, dizziness, and profound nausea. The drug was being kept a secret from Dry Out. They'd go wild, Killigren had said, if they thought such an easy fix had been found. But his office had used it a few times, in discreet tests. Of course, it's a secret from the FDA, Killigren said.

Mr. White—if that was his name—escorted Walters to a suite in the Rosslyn Marriott. The room was filthy. The air held a stench. A lamp was smashed. Jagged glass littered the carpet. Furniture was overturned, the bed linen soiled by bodily fluids. And a man was slumped in a chair watching a soap opera.

Walters's guide explained to him that the semi-conscious fellow was a "friend" who had been through a rough patch. You could say we owe him, Mr. White remarked. Perhaps the pills.

This man needs more than a pill, Walters said. This is all we can do for him right now, Mr. White said. The man in the chair said nothing. He did not seem to notice that others had joined him in the room.

Walters shut off the television set and sat in front of his subject. Can you tell me what happened? he asked the man in the chair. No, Mr. White said. No questions. Tell him about the pills.

This is ridiculous, Walters thought. The fellow was barely awake. He studied him. A week-old beard, thick wrists, unkempt, thinning brown hair, a scar on his ear. One eye was shut tight, and he held something in his hand. As if to explain, the man opened his fist. In his palm was a glass eye. He placed it back within his eye socket.

He wore combat boots, an unbuttoned leather vest over a bare chest, and a baseball cap bearing an emblem that read "The Gauntlet." What's that? Walters defiantly asked, pointing to the words on the hat. The man in the chair blinked repeatedly; he coughed.

Place where I work—sometimes, he mumbled.

Enough, said Mr. White. Explain the pills.

Walters reached into his pocket and removed the vial. These pills, he said, will cut down on your desire to drink. Not erase it completely but make it less. They block the interface between the alcohol and the chemical receptors in your brain.

The man's eyes began to close. Walter's escort shook the fellow in the chair; the eyes opened.

Walters went on: One in the morning, one at night. If you experience dizziness, a decline in sexual appetite, stomach troubles, you should contact me immediately. Here's my number.

Walters wrote it down on a piece of hotel stationary. He looked at Mr. White and realized he would never hear back from this person. He held out the container of pills. The man leaned forward to take the vial, and the flaps of his vest separated to reveal a tattoo on his chest. It looked like an *M* pierced by an arrow.

Okay, let's go, Mr. White said. He patted the man in the chair and turned on the television. You take care, he said. See ya later.

In the hallway, Walters protested. The man in the room clearly required more than a poorly tested drug. Sometimes a little is the absolute best we can do, Mr. White said, and, to tell the fucked-up truth, this guy is damn lucky. Doesn't look it, but damn lucky.

Walters never saw Mr. White again. He never saw the man in the chair again. He never heard from him. A few days after the visit, he asked Killigren if he could conduct a follow-up session. Some meetings never really occurred, Killigren told him. Walters tried to argue, invoking medical ethics. It's hard to be a doctor in the dark, Killigren said. But if that's where your patient is . . .

Lancette realized she had scraped the label off her beer bottle. She gathered the pieces and placed them in the plastic ash tray on the table.

"In retrospect, seems hard to believe that I didn't right away remember the tattoo," Walters said. He sipped his beer. "But there have been even odder days."

An Aretha Franklin song blared from the jukebox.

"Ever find out what the Gauntlet was?" she asked.

"No. But then I never went looking. I told you, I'm not a brave man." He emptied his glass.

"And it was a dagger through an *M*?"

"Something like that. Can't swear it, but. . . ."

"And the photographs—none looked like the man you met in the hotel room?"

"Not that I could see. But did that Max Bridge guy have a glass eye?"

Not as far as Lancette knew. But you could never be sure that all information was being shared.

The door to the bar opened, and light fell upon Walters's face. Lancette saw concern in his eyes. She looked over her shoulder. A black man and a white man had entered. They sat at the bar.

"When was this?" Lancette asked.

"Little over four years ago."

"And that was it? Period? Done?"

"Like I said."

"And no one has asked you about your ICEMAN report?"

"No one."

The white man left his seat and passed Lancette and Walters on his way to the men's room.

"And how did you find me?" she asked.

"Too easily, I have to say. A friend in Security—helped him after his son committed suicide. I asked him about ICEMAN reports. He told me about you. Then I asked Mrs. Novek about you. She really does know everyone. Told her that I was, well, interested in meeting you. You know what she's like. A wonderful coincidence, she told me. You had an appointment with Wenner that day. She called me when you were finishing the meeting, and I found you in the gift shop."

"Sounds like quite the coincidence."

"Coincidence sometimes do happen."

"I have to tell myself that every day."

"And another coincidence. Today I was ordered to Burundi. Seems one of our colleagues was found in the embassy communications room naked and delusional. I asked for more details. They told me that the chief of station would brief me on my arrival—tomorrow. Feels like I'm in a bad movie, you know. A cliché. The guy with the clue who . . ."

The white man passed them as he returned to join his friend. Another pair of men—black and white—entered the bar and sat with the first two.

"Coincidence or not?" Walters asked.

Lancette glanced at the men.

"Time to go," he said.

"What do you want me to do?" she asked.

"Whatever you think you should. I just had to tell someone. I'm not doing anything more."

"And if I want to contact you?"

He quickly wrote his number on a napkin and passed it to her.

"They say I'll be back in a few days. But keep an eye out for that headline: State Department Officials Die in Bujumbura Car Crash."

He tried to laugh but instead a clicking sound came out of his throat.

"We should leave separately," he said. "There's an alley in the back. I checked it out earlier. We'll get up. I'll head to the men's room. You go out the front, like you're going to wait for me outside the door. If they're here for us, they'll wait for me to come out of the bathroom before they move."

"And then how do I get home?"

"They have cabs up here."

The two stood, and Walters dropped money on the table.

"Do you have a copy of your memo?" she asked.

But Walters already was heading toward the back.

"I'll wait out front," she called after him.

The men at the bar looked at her without moving their heads. She opened the door and left. Across the street, a woman was huddled in the entranceway to a boarded-up building. Next to her was a pile of cardboard boxes. Two little feet stuck out of the boxes. The feet of a child? Lancette wondered.

Lancette flagged a taxi.

"Toward Arlington, please," she said.

"Sure," the cabbie said. He was a young fellow. Armenian, she guessed. She looked for his license. It wasn't displayed.

"What you doing up here?" he asked, as the cab cruised toward the illuminated dome of the Capitol.

"Seeing a friend."

"A friend?"

Questions, she thought.

"The address?"

"Just head straight for a little." She stared out the window. The cab descended Capitol Hill.

"You know what," she said. "Forgot something in my office. You can let me off here."

The cabbie came to a stop by the Rayburn House Office Building. He asked if she wanted him to wait. She said no, handed him six dollars, and stepped out of the cab. She walked toward the entrance to the building. When the taxi pulled away, she changed direction and headed to the Metro.

In the station, she sat on a stone bench. She was alone on the platform. Must have just missed a train, she thought.

16

Adams Morgan
June 26

Addis rested his head against the tile and felt the water of the shower cascade over him. He had slept in this morning—the first time in years—but he had not slept well. He wanted a week—a month, a year, maybe more—away. Too much bullshit, he thought; not even a grace period for mourning.

He tried to recall an exercise he once had read about in a book on yoga in the bathroom of a girlfriend. Damn, he couldn't remember which girlfriend, which bathroom, which city, which year. That made him feel even more worn. Enough, he told himself. The exercise. It was trite. Stand straight but not stiff beneath the showerhead, arms at your side. Try to imagine that you are the water, you are merging with the water. Listen to the stream. Feel yourself flowing. Breathe deep through your nose. Use your diaphragm. Close your eyes.

Addis breathed. He exhaled. Nothing. He couldn't concentrate. Instead, he again thought about seeing M. T. O'Connor and Dan Carey leave the White House together the previous night. They were deep in conversation and did not notice Addis behind them. He had been able to catch only one full sentence. "That can be taken care of," Carey said. They both got into her car.

Addis felt the water and remembered a story O'Connor once told him about the consultant. At the start of the administration, O'Connor's father had died suddenly when an aneuryism burst. While she was working frantically to place scheduling matters in order before flying to Georgia for the funeral, Carey dropped by her office. I heard the news, he said, sorry. She thanked him for the condolences. Then he added: "At least it didn't happen during an election year."

No other anecdote so encapsulated what Addis thought was the small soul of Dan Carey. For years, Addis and O'Connor had shared a private complaint: Carey and the other technicians—the pay-to-play pollsters, the media advisers, the focus-group engineers, the communications specialists—were crowding out the politicos like Addis and O'Connor, who were drawn to the game because they wanted not only to win but to alter policy outcomes as well. Politics—in the White House, on Capitol Hill, across the nation—was becoming ever more dominated by sharpies obsessed with the means. Hundreds of young men and women were enrolled in graduate programs that taught them how to be campaign managers and consultants. There was no requirement they care about anything other than the mechanisms of politics. Addis occasionally was asked to speak at these programs. In the first half of the administration, he had accepted several such invitations, hoping he could discern in the students a reason for optimism. He rarely found it. These days he routinely sent regrets when invited.

Now O'Connor and Carey were talking, sharing a ride somewhere.

Addis shut off the water. So much for do-it-yourself meditation, he thought. He dried off, dressed, and left his house through the back door.

"Mr. Addis, a moment please."

A thin man in a crumpled white suit was standing next to Addis's Honda. He was fifty or so, had a craggy, pale face, with dark rings beneath narrow eyes. His accent was British.

My alleyway is turning into Grand Central Station.

"Mr. Evan Hynes-Pierce," he said and held out a hand. *"Pittsburgh Courier-Press."*

Addis ignored the outstretched hand. He had not met Hynes-Pierce but he knew of him. Hynes-Pierce was the reporter probing the Hanovers' land deal in Rapides Parish. And he was the fellow who, three weeks before the last presidential election, had aired an interview on a television tabloid show with a woman who years earlier had filed a sexual harassment complaint against Margaret Hanover. The woman's story was accurate to a degree: She had submitted such a complaint when Margaret Hanover was an administrator at a community college in New Orleans. But the accusation had been dismissed quickly by a review board. After the broadcast aired, it had taken less than a day for reporters to locate relatives and friends of the complainant. They explained that the woman had a long history of mental illness and that she had accused numerous men and women of sexual harassment. After the election, Hynes-Pierce was hired by the *Courier-Press*, where his speciality—skewering the Hanovers and their associates—was much appreciated by the right-wing, millionaire recluse who owned the paper.

"Excuse me, but this is my home," Addis said.

"Yes it is. Rather ill-mannered of me to intrude on such a fine morning." He lifted his head to the sky, and the sunlight illuminated the crevices in his face. His teeth were shaded yellow. "But I have a delicate issue to discuss."

"Call me at work? I promise I'll get back to you. Things are a little crazy these days. Surely, you can understand that."

Addis stepped toward his car. Hynes-Pierce leaned against the door on the driver's side.

"Why were you making calls to New Orleans and Rapides yesterday?" Hynes-Pierce asked. "Getting ducks in their row, perhaps?"

Addis had been on the phone the previous day to Louisiana. He had spoken to Flip Whalen, who had been Hanover's chief of staff during the gubernatorial years. Whalen had stayed in Louisiana after the election to tend to his wife, who was battling a variety of cancers. A paper-thin wisp of a man, Whalen was the keeper of the Hanover history. If anything came up that was pre-White House, he was the first call.

The Hanovers had a few deals over the years, Whalen had told Addis. Maybe something in Rapides, but nothing that ever demanded Whalen's attention. Other money matters had required troubleshooting. Margaret had been on the board of a nursing home firm that was charged with Medicaid fraud, but she resigned promptly. And then there was a financial adviser they had used who was charged with promoting fraudulent securities solicitations. That had sparked a run of newspaper stories, but the episode blew over. Talk to Harris Griffith, Whalen advised, he was their accountant for many years. But be gentle with Griffith, Whalen cautioned, he had gotten caught up in some funny savings-and-loan business and had lost his job at a fancy downtown firm.

When Addis had rung Griffith, his call was answered by a machine. He left a message and next called Mickey Burton, the party's chair in Rapides Parish. At twenty-seven, Burton was the youngest parish chair in the state. Burton told Addis that a Brit fellow had been nosing around asking about a deal involving the Hanovers and some land near the county airport.

So here, leaning against Addis's car, was the jerk who was forcing Addis to spend his time digging into the distant finances of a dead man. And Hynes-Pierce knew about the phone calls Addis had made.

"You don't believe in letting someone rest in peace," Addis said.

"Actually, I do. Most certainly. The worms don't care whether their lunch had unfinished business. I am sympathetic to that point of view. Quite reasonable. But, you see, not everyone else involved believes in resting in peace. Look at the grieving widow. Hardly a rester there, right?"

"Fuck you," Addis said.

"Yes, but as the story continues . . . Well, the story continues, doesn't it?"

"Maybe this time you can prove Margaret's a lesbian."

90

"Never did say that."

"But you didn't mind other people thinking it—after you rushed to air a story full of holes."

"It is an imperfect craft. I'll grant you that. But I do believe in making available as quickly as possible all information that is available. You do realize, the full story rarely comes out all at once. Would you mind telling me whom you were calling in Rapides Parish and why you were placing such calls—while you were toiling as a government employee and being paid by the American taxpayers?"

"I do mind. But, for your own information, I was talking to old friends. A lot of people these days want to talk. Hard to believe, isn't it?"

"Fine, fine. Trying days. Sad days. I do appreciate. And no one much cares for those of us who pick over dirty bones. But a broader question, if I may? What would you, Mr. Addis, do if you discovered that one of the great men whom you have so ably served, out of, no doubt, your own allegiance to worthwhile causes and principles, had acted, unethically, untowardly, or illegally? Would the public be consigned to the dark?"

"You know, great illuminators like yourself might do better if you weren't such assholes. Now, excuse me."

Hynes-Pierce moved away from the car, and Addis unlocked the door.

"So in the fashion of all the professional spinners and concocters in this town, you prefer not to answer legitimate queries?"

"Nice try."

"Well, a lad can try." He flashed a jagged smile. "Not even on background?"

"You must be—"

"Then perhaps next time."

Hynes-Pierce held out a business card. Addis did not take it; he got into the car.

"I'm hoping there won't be a next time," Addis said. He shut the door and started the engine.

"There always is," said Hynes-Pierce, beneath the sound of the car.

As Addis walked down 37th Street, past the row houses, to Georgetown University, he wondered how Hynes-Pierce had learned of the calls to Louisiana. There were only two choices: this end and that end. Louisiana or the White House. Maybe Mickey Burton had asked around and word had traveled back to Hynes-Pierce. That would be damn quick, Addis thought. The other option was more disconcerting.

As he entered the campus, he passed a Secret Service agent standing at the corner. Addis said hello. The agent's nod was barely discernible. Not a good time for these guys, Addis thought.

He considered the other option: a leak from within the White House. That ordinarily would not be a surprise. But he had told no one about the calls, and Hynes-Pierce was not the normal recipient of White House tips. Most were dished out rather strategically to the major national reporters, who were delighted to be accomplices in the turf fights of the President's courtiers. Addis worried about his Louisiana project.

Black bunting hung at the front of Gaston Hall. Addis entered through the front, amid a stream of students. He shook hands with the few who insisted. He displayed his White House pass and went through a magneto-meter. A uniformed officer then patted him down. Everyone had to be searched under the new security precautions.

Only days ago, Hanover had been scheduled to deliver a noontime speech here. He was going to unveil a billion-dollar plan to outfit pub-lic grade schools with computers. Smart Schools for Smart Kids— O'Connor had proposed the name. Originally, the money was to come from reductions in corporate welfare. But when word of the cuts had leaked, party and campaign fund-raisers requested that the President protect the subsidies enjoyed by companies that were being generous to the reelection effort. At the White House, Mike Finn, Brew Mc-Greer, Dan Carey, and Addis huddled. We can deal with the details later, Carey had asserted. Announce the general plan. Do not propose specific cuts. Vagueness carried a benefit. The industries threatened would be sure to donate, as long as they believed they still had a chance to preserve their cherished tax preferences. Addis argued for specific cuts so the computer initiative would be regarded seriously. Af-ter the aides wrangled, McGreer drafted a memo for the President, suggesting that Hanover order a list of *potential* cuts for his future *con-sideration*. Hanover took the advice.

All that was now moot. Mumfries had placed the program on hold. Instead, he planned to use the occasion for a speech on how the country needed to move past the tragedy. Kelly had decided it would be manda-tory for the entire White House senior staff to attend. Mumfries also in-vited Margaret Hanover.

Addis was directed to the bleachers on the stage. One of Kelly's aides was running about with a seating chart; there were assigned spots for each staff member.

One big happy family.

Television crews filled the back of the room. M. T. O'Connor took her place next to Addis.

"Nice little show," she said.

"Yeah."

"Always wanted to be a prop for Sam Mumfries."

Kelly trundled across the stage, conferring with assistants and Secret Service agents. He pointed McGreer to his seat in the front row of the bleachers. Finn, Byrd, Ann Herson, Hanover's white-haired secretary, and others were there.

"Don't see Dan here," Addis said.

"He's on the party payroll, so the invitation didn't apply. Lucky guy."

That explanation came a little too quick.

"I'm sure," Addis said. "Getting along with him?"

"This is a nightmare. Mumfries shit-cans computers-in-schools and does a stupid rah-rah instead."

"No surprise there."

"Believe me, I have no expectations. But I can still get pissed. You, my friend, don't seem to give two shits. Everything's not done and finished. Not yet. Why don't you care? Yeah, he's gone. But we're not."

"That's not it," Addis said.

"What is it?"

I really don't want to get into it. Really. Believe me, I have a reason. A damn good one. But not now.

"I'm just worn."

"We don't have time for that. Kelly's put one of his factotums into my office. Already, he's overruling me."

"You won't have to do much more scheduling, I guess."

"Not for this S.O.B.," O'Connor said.

The student body president was at the podium, explaining the program schedule to the students and warning that they could not leave the hall once the President arrived.

"What have you been doing?" O'Connor asked.

"Not all that much," Addis said.

"Margaret told me about your project."

"Well, I haven't really done a lot on that front, either."

"Anything there?"

"What does she say?"

"She shrugs, says Bob would know, and wonders why the attacks never stop."

"They never will," Addis said. "Especially if she decides to—"

"Tell me if there's anything, okay?"

Kelly stood in front of the bleachers. He signaled to Addis.

"Thanks for the list," Kelly said. "The President is meeting with the history boys for dinner tonight. Feel free to stop by—before dinner."

Addis nodded; Kelly darted off.

"That's what I've been doing," Addis said to O'Connor. "Helping Kelly feel like he's so damn smart."

"One minute," a voice on the P.A. system said.

The audience went silent. The technicians and assistants cleared the stage. Behind the podium were several empty chairs.

Addis looked at the side of the stage. Margaret Hanover stood with Sally Mumfries and the two Mumfries girls. Jake Grayton was next to Mumfries. Lem Jordan was a few feet behind them. Jordan's eyes never stayed still. He scanned the crowd, his hands clenched. When Jordan concentrated, Addis had noticed long ago, he tightened his fists.

The student body president returned to the podium.

"Mrs. Sally Mumfries, and Carla and Ruth Mumfries," he said.

The three women walked on to the stage and sat in the seats behind the podium. There was a rustle in the audience. No one knew whether or not to applaud.

"Mrs. Margaret Mason Hanover," the student president declared.

She moved toward the center of the stage, holding herself in a regal pose, chin tilted up. She wore a dark-gray dress. Her hair was in its bun. Again, there was an awkward silence. Everyone in the audience seemed to be asking, do you applaud a presidential widow?

"Clap," O'Connor said softly.

Toward the rear of the hall, a woman stood and began clapping. A few students followed tentatively, applauding but remaining in their seats. More joined in. Several rose to their feet. The applause gained momentum. It grew louder. More students stood. The clapping picked up pace. Addis saw young men and women crying. Then everyone in the hall was standing and applauding. The volume increased.

Margaret had taken a seat next to Sally Mumfries. She nodded to the crowd. The ovation continued. She clasped her hands at chest level. The audience would not stop.

"Speech," one student cried.

O'Connor was smiling; a tear ran down her cheek. We must be nearing a minute, Addis thought.

Sally Mumfries handed Margaret a handkerchief and said something to her. Margaret stood up, and the applause went on. She walked to the podium. The student president stepped aside. Margaret's face was red. She wiped her tears with the handkerchief.

"Please, please," she said into the microphone. "Please."

The students remained on their feet. The clapping did not cease.

"Please, please," she repeated.

Slowly, the applause faded. The crowd began to sit.

"Please," she said once more.

The audience became quiet.

"Thank you. I had not expected to say anything today. But that welcome was—"

She sobbed once. Addis looked at Mumfries. He was standing stoic, off-stage. Kelly was red-faced; he was fidgeting, and looked at his watch. Yes, Ham, Addis said to himself, this is live on the networks and the cable news channels.

"All I can say is thank you. I know our son Jack would appreciate it, if he were here. I can't wait to tell him about it."

She paused and again wiped a tear. O'Connor was squeezing Addis's arm.

"As you know, my husband was supposed to give a speech here today to announce a program that would bring computers to needy children in schools across the country. Though he is no longer with us, I hope that his ideas and ideals will live on. That's the least we owe him."

Applause. A few students returned to their feet. Kelly was whispering to Mumfries. Margaret Hanover waited for the crowd to sit.

"And I want to ask each of you—even those who may not have supported his administration—to promise that, in his memory, you will give a little of yourself. This country doesn't need grieving. It only needs its citizens—especially its young people—to share themselves with the public good. Bob always enjoyed talking to young people."

Her voice cracked.

" 'They're more idealistic than we give them credit for,' he said to me. I know he was right, and I hope all of you will show that he was, and join me in fulfilling that promise."

Join me? There it was again. How close could she get? Addis wondered.

"So today another President is here to talk about other things. He and Sally have been so supportive of Jack and me. I cannot thank them enough. Our new President has been called to lead our nation in a difficult time. Please keep him in your prayers in the days ahead. Thank you."

Days, she said. Not weeks, months, or years.

One more standing ovation. It ended when Margaret sat down. The student body president returned to the microphone.

"The President of the United States," he said. "Samuel Mumfries."

Mumfries strode toward the podium. The students rose to their feet again. But it was clear: the applause was less enthusiastic. The staff in the bleachers looked at each other. Kelly slapped his hand against his leg. The audience quickly settled down. Fifteen seconds, Addis estimated to himself.

"Amazing," O'Connor said.

Mumfries took a drink from the glass of water on the podium.

"I just want to thank you all for that heartwarming welcome you gave to Mrs. Hanover," he said. "She bears a burden that few of us will ever know. I thank *her* for the support she has given me this past week. And I do hope she will continue to provide us with her valuable counsel. This nation owes her a debt that never can be repaid."

Nice job, Addis thought.

Mumfries's speech was predictable. "The sign of a great nation," he said, "is how it bears adversity." There were quotes from the Bible—both Old and New Testament. He referred to a passage from *Profiles in Courage*. He commended to a new generation the most famous line ever uttered by Franklin Delano Roosevelt: "We have nothing to fear . . ." Nothing about the assassination investigation. Nothing about policy. Nothing about Mumfries's political intentions. Nothing that galvanized the hall. At the end of the speech, Mumfries received a respectful standing ovation, more obligatory than charged. Addis could envision the network reports this evening. The story would not be Hanover's attempt to comfort and motivate a nation but a packed auditorium embracing the grieving widow. Emotion trumps content—especially when content's so thin.

Mumfries was shaking hands with college officials and top faculty members. Grayton was by his side. The White House staff filed out of the bleachers. Addis passed Kelly.

"Good idea, Ham," he said. "The President gave a fine speech."

Kelly grunted in reply.

As Mumfries departed the building, reporters shouted questions at him about his political plans. He pretended not to hear and entered a limousine with his wife and children. Margaret got into another car. O'Connor pushed past Addis at the auditorium's rear exit.

"I'm going to ride back with her," she said. "You want to come?"

"No, I have my car here."

"We should talk. Maybe you should talk to Dan, too."

"About what?"

"What comes next."

"I'm not sure I want to know. And I'm not sure it's a good idea. Getting applause as the wife of a slain president is not the same thing as getting votes."

"Nick, you think this just happened? Come on. Nothing just happens. You should know that. I know you think Dan's a sleazebag, but he's smart. And he cares probably more than you think he does. That girl who first started clapping, she was—well, never mind that. You really should talk to Dan."

O'Connor ran to the motorcade and jumped into the limousine with Margaret. He pictured O'Connor at a shooting range firing a .357 at a silhouette target. That was two years ago on a rare Saturday afternoon off. She had taken him to a gun club in Virginia to explain her fondness for recreational shooting. This short woman with thin arms discharging a weapon—Addis laughed when he remembered how she had yelled out "Boom!" each time she squeezed the trigger.

That was real clever, Addis thought, as he walked back to his car. Seed the audience. One person could set it off. Damn clever.

"Mr. Addis?"

A woman in a Georgetown University sweatshirt, jeans, and a baseball cap was walking at his side.

"Yes," he said and kept moving.

"Uh, can I, like, talk to you a minute?"

One more person who wants to tell me how sorry they are?

"I have to get back to the White House," he lied.

"It's important—kinda."

He stopped. They were standing by an ivy-covered fence that surrounded an athletic track.

"I knew Allison Meade," she said.

His face was blank.

"You know, the girl in the hotel, with that reporter."

"Sorry. I don't know anything more than what's been in the paper."

"I do."

Addis didn't know what to say.

"She was a friend, and, uh, we worked together," she said. The woman was nervous. She took off her cap and twirled it around a finger. Her brown hair was in a pony-tail.

"Where?"

"This is going to sound real weird. . . . For this service—it's called an escort service. But it isn't like what you think. I mean, we don't *do* it. It's like a scam. Or a partial scam. You call up and ask for a girl, and they tell you this is not a sex service. No prostitution. And the guy always says, sure. He thinks, they just got to say that. And they tell you—the girl— where to go. And you get there. And the first thing you say, is, you know, this is not a sex service. You can look. You can talk to me. I can talk to you. I'll get undressed. And you can do whatever you want without touching me. Or we can go out somewhere. Or I can tell you what to do. You know, some guys—that's what they really want. But this is not a sex service. And they're kinda mad, because they didn't believe it. But you already got their credit card number. So usually they complain but then they find a way to . . . have fun. Like I said, weird, isn't it? Some even call back. If they like us."

A gust of wind blew a newspaper page across the sidewalk. An elderly woman pushing a stroller approached them. Addis said nothing until she passed by.

"No prostitution, then?"

"Not at all. I swear. But I've seen some strange shit."

"And Allison?"

"We sometimes worked together. Like sometimes you get a call for a twofer. Mainly out-of-towners. Lots of foreigners, diplomats. One night the two of us drove around in a limo with these Arab guys. We were naked, except for the fur coats they had us wear. We didn't get to keep the coats. It was good money, and without having to . . ."

"Was she out on a job that night?"

"Don't know. Maybe, I guess. She worked more than I did. She didn't always tell me what she was up to. But she never mentioned that reporter guy before. It could've been a job. But there's just no way she could've known, that she could've been involved. . . ."

She was crying. Her lips were trembling.

"She called that day. But I was out and didn't get the message until late. I tried to call her, but she was already . . ."

Her body heaved with the sobs.

"Okay, okay," Addis said and put a hand on her shoulder. "Let's go sit down somewhere."

She told him that she lived a few blocks away.

"Let's go there," he said.

He searched his pockets for a tissue. He found none. As they walked, she calmed down. He asked whether she had told anyone else. She had not. She was afraid.

"And the 'rents would go ape-shit," she explained.

"So then why are you—?"

"—I had to tell someone. Hoped that I could find someone, not the police or anyone like them, who could do something and, I guess, keep me . . ."

"Out of it?"

"Yeah."

"But why me?"

She nodded. "This is going to sound major sicko. But I always wanted to meet you. You seem so . . ."

Is this a con? A sorority prank? Are her girlfriends waiting to see if she can bring Nick Addis back to her house?

". . . nice, and I thought . . . God, this sounds so dumb."

"No, no," Addis reassured. He figured he had to ride it out.

"I tried to talk to you the other night, but I got scared."

The woman in the alley?

"But your hair?"

"Oh, a wig. Got a bunch, for when clients ask for something specific. It's not like they expect it really to be real."

The two walked along without talking. Addis studied her face. The chin was pointy. There were dark patches beneath her eyes. She appeared to be in genuine distress. They crossed a cobblestoned street. He realized he had not asked her name.

"Just halfway up," she said. "A group house. But no one else will be around." Addis braced himself for whatever surprise might be in store.

When they approached the house, Clarence Dunne was sitting on the stoop. He looked at Addis and then at the woman.

"Gillian Silva?" he asked.

17

U.S. Treasury Department
June 26

Earlier that morning, Dunne had been sitting in an uncomfortable plastic chair in a hallway. Two armed guards stood nearby. He was waiting for a dubious honor—to be the first witness called before the Commission on the Assassination of President Robert Hanover. The commission was holding its opening session in an auditorium at the Treasury Department. With the inquiry short of hard facts, the commissioners had decided to begin with "contextual matters." Today that meant security at the White House.

A uniformed guard escorted Dunne to the witness chair. All commission members were present, including Treasury Secretary Alter, CIA Director Wenner, former U.N. Ambassador Melissa Shea, Senator Palmer, and House Majority Leader Wynn Gravitt. Alter nodded slightly toward Dunne, as Dunne took a seat. The commissioners sat behind two cheap, metal, fold-up conference tables. Dunne was sworn in.

The questioning was conducted by the staff director, a former Capitol Hill investigator who had moved on to a K Street firm. He asked Dunne about his qualifications for the post of White House security chief. He had Dunne describe how previous assassination attempts had been thwarted. They covered the budget for White House security and the quality of the security staff at the White House.

"Were you familiar," the lawyer asked, "with the memorandum written by Mr. Kelly during the presidential transition that conveyed Mr. Mumfries's concerns about lax security at the White House?"

"No, I was not," Dunne said.

"The memo was cc'ed to you."

"I don't recall seeing it."

"Is it possible that you have forgotten seeing it?"

"Possible, but not likely."

"And why not likely?"

"I tend to take the suggestions of vice presidents seriously."

Several commissioners grinned.

"So how do you explain this discrepancy?" Representative Gravitt interrupted. "Can it be that the White House is so disorganized that memos about security get lost?"

Typical, Dunne thought. Gravitt, the former owner of a pest-control business in Orange County, was a rising star in his party. The *Washington Post* had reported that morning that he had pressured the House Speaker to recommend his appointment to the commission.

"This memo was supposedly written before the current administration inhabited the White House," Dunne replied.

"But you were already security chief at the White House, right?" Gravitt, an athletic-built, thick-lipped fellow with lacquered sandy hair, looked pleased.

"Yes."

"And once the administration came in," Gravitt continued, "this memo was never acted upon?"

"Not that I know of."

"And did Vice President Mumfries ever follow up on the matter."

"Not that I saw."

"So he let it drop?"

"And last I checked," Alter interrupted, "the Vice President's job is not to oversee who comes and goes from the White House. Isn't that true, Mr. Dunne?"

Before Dunne could answer, the staff director spoke: "Thank you, Secretary Alter, Congressman. I'd like to ask Mr. Dunne if, regardless of the memo, there ever was a full review of the screening process for individuals, including media representatives, who had access to the White House?"

"Not a comprehensive one."

"And should there have been?"

"The answer is obvious."

Dunne was questioned for an hour-and-a-half. Gravitt interrupted several times. Wenner said nothing. At the end of the interview, the staff director asked if Dunne had anything else to say about the assassination.

Dunne paused for a moment. Mr. Al-Fusah and his friends? No, a scapegoat-to-be should hold on to something. That was his way into the investigation. Mention it now and Grayton would grab that lead.

"No, sir."

Dunne left the building, crossed 15th Street, and entered the Hotel Washington. He called home, let the phone ring three times, and hung up. He

101

waited twenty seconds, then dialed again. He knew his wife, Alma, hated such nonsense. She would not admit it, but he realized this scared her.

On the fifth ring, she picked up. He did not say anything.

"608 H Street Southwest. Suite 219."

He returned the receiver to its cradle. He had taught her a simple code. Subtract from each digit of the street address the amount corresponding to the number's place in the series. 608 meant 721. And change the first part of the quadrant. It was not a foolproof system. Nothing was foolproof. It was a matter of rendering life more difficult for whoever might be paying attention.

Chinatown, he thought.

He knew from his wife's response what had happened that morning. An old friend—a private detective—had dropped by his house and handed Alma an envelope. She opened it, memorized the address written on a slip of paper, and then burned the paper. If none of that had happened, she would have picked up the phone on the tenth ring. And he would have said, "Hello, dear."

The day before, after Dunne left the Moroccan official, he returned to his White House office and opened the Yellow Pages. He remembered what Al-Fusah had told him: "Maybe some name like a joke. . . . Said maybe they'd send Mrs. Hanover."

Dunne read through the pages for escort services: Potomac Escorts, Ecstasy Escorts, Exclusive Escorts. A few bore more imaginative names: High Positions Escorts, Executive Power Escorts. He turned the page: First Ladies.

That fit the punchline. There was a phone number but no address. He called; the number was disconnected. He phoned a friend at a large private investigation firm. Can you get me an address for a phone number? Dunne asked. Can't the Secret Service get its own information? the friend replied. It's for me, Dunne explained. Not until tomorrow morning, the friend said. Fine, Dunne said. They went over the arrangements for dropping off the information.

After hanging up the phone in the lobby, Dunne left the hotel and walked down F Street. Three Secret agents he knew were heading toward him. An awkward moment began. He could tell what they were thinking: Should we stop to talk? That's understandable, Dunne thought. He was an awkward man. Perhaps the most awkward in the service's history.

"Off to grab a bagel," Dunne said. That is, no need to start a conversation. The three men said hello and walked on.

Dunne entered the mall attached to the National Press Building. He rode the escalator to the lower level. He headed toward the bathroom and went through a firedoor to a flight of stairs. He climbed two levels and followed the hallway that led to the Marriott. He moved through the hotel lobby and jumped into a cab. He order the cabbie to take him to the Cannon House Office Building.

As the taxi navigated traffic, Dunne wondered why he was engaging in such precautions. He had no reason to suspect he was being watched. Perhaps it was a guilty reaction to having not told the commission about Al-Fusah. He had lied under oath. Fuck, that was easy, Dunne mumbled to himself. But enough self-analysis. Playing it cautious, running a countersurveillance exercise was always good practice.

At Cannon, he entered the building at the side and found the stairs to the basement. He walked through the long tunnel to the U.S. Capitol, then followed the maze-like path through the sub-basement of the Capitol and came to the underground corridor that led to the Senate office buildings. Several aides and a few senators rushing to the floor for a vote recognized him. He was accustomed to that. He used to joke that he had appeared in more photographs with President Hanover than Margaret had. Newspapers and television news shows had flashed his image repeatedly since the assassination.

For the first time since leaving the Treasury Department, he looked behind. Down the length of the tunnel, he saw no one hurrying to keep up with him.

Dunne arrived at the Dirksen Building—imagine, he thought, a defender of segregation being commemorated by an office building that now sits two blocks away from the Thurgood Marshall Judiciary Building—and took the stairs to the street level. He exited the building and hailed a cab.

"Convention Center," he said.

Dunne got out at the Convention Center and entered the building. A computer exposition filled the hall. He paused over literature at a display table and looked out through the windows. He spotted no one. But then if they—whoever they might be—were doing their jobs well, he would not see them. He pocketed a few brochures and departed the center. He was two blocks away from the address for First Ladies.

The suite on the second floor was locked. Dunne knocked, and nobody answered. Dunne smelled the food being cooked in the Chinese restaurant below.

"Ain't nobody home."

Dunne turned around. A tall, young black man wearing wraparound sunglasses, baggy nylon pants, a Redskins T-shirt with the sleeves cut off, and hiking boots was speaking to him. His hair was closely cropped, his chin dimpled. He folded his brawny arms—a weight lifter's arms—in front of his chest.

"Where did they go?" Dunne asked.

"Why you asking?"

"My name is Clarence Dunne."

"And?"

"I'm here on government work."

"Big shit. My name's Twayne Marcus Starrell. And I hate the government."

"You work around here?"

"Maybe I do."

"They close up shop recently?"

"I heard this guy on television last night. And this was it: He says information is a fuckin' resource. More valuable than gold, he says. He says, anyone give anything away for nothing is a god-damn fool's chump. Do I look like a fool's chump?"

"No, you don't, Mr. Starrell."

"Fuckin' right. You a cop? I ain't playin' squeals."

"No, I work for the Department of Treasury."

"You a money man?" Starrell laughed. "Got some fresh Mack Bennies for me?"

"Wish I did. It's not that sort of a job. But I'll pay you for your time." Dunne checked his wallet.

"Fifty dollars, if you help me out."

"You a cheap nigger-in-a-white-man's-suit."

"It's all I have now."

"Well, a Mister Money Man with no money. Don't believe in ATMing? You knocking on that door? I know I got some good shit for you worth more than change. If you can be dropping more."

Dunne put away the wallet. He took out his Secret Service badge and flipped it at Starrell.

"Take a long view, son. Some day you may need help from someone like me."

"Fuck, you said you ain't no cop."

"Not a cop. Secret Service."

"A spy man? No shit. But not all of us black men get into trouble that we need your help getting out of. Ain't that way with me. I'm a working man. So take your badge and down-ass out of this building. My uncle owns it, and when he ain't here what I say is word."

Damn, Dunne thought, I misplayed this one. He's too big and too full of himself to intimidate. And he has more to prove in this encounter than I do.

Starrell stepped aside to clear a path between Dunne and the stairwell.

"Listen, Mr. Starrell, I didn't mean any disrespect. You caught me on a bad day. You help me now, and I'll reimburse you for your efforts. If you want more money, you'll have to trust me for it. If you want"—he looked at the T-shirt—"Redskins tickets—"

"Pardon the fuck out of me, they ain't playing now."

"Well, when they are, I'll get you good seats."

"Like I can't cop my own?"

Fuck you, thought Dunne.

"Your uncle trusts you to look after the building while he's gone?"

"Got trouble with that?"

"Not after today, he won't." Dunne moved toward Starrell, keeping the young man's hands in his field of vision.

"What you mean?" Starrell asked. He formed two fists.

"Because I am going to leave this building. Then I am going to dial a number at the city office building. Then this afternoon, a building inspector's going to be in your basement. And when he's done, your uncle will be facing a few thousand dollars in fines and the god-damn headache of rewiring the building. After that inspector man leaves, I'm going to come back and tell your uncle why he was here in the first place—because his stupid, big-mouth nephew was too dumb to answer some polite questions. And if you don't think I have the"—Dunne paused—"the juice to pull that off, then you don't know shit about nothing."

Dunne could not see anything behind Starrell's sunglasses. He wondered if the young man was carrying a knife or gun.

Starrell swished the saliva in his mouth. He put one hand in a pocket.

"Gimme the fifty," he said. "And you're going to owe me another hundred, got it?"

"If it's worth a hundred, you got it."

"Trust me, Mr. Black Secret Agent Man, it is."

"Sure," Dunne said. He handed Starrell the money. Together, they went down the stairs.

In the basement, Starrell removed a tarp that was covering a pile of stuffed, gray plastic garbage bags.

"They shut down extra quick. Took anything worth anything. Phones. Computers. Left the chairs, the desks. Left my unc hangin' for two months' rent. Dumped a bunch of shit in garbage bags. I brought it down here."

"Why did you do that, Mr. Starrell?" Dunne asked.

"I knew what they was running. And saw they were booking. And I guessed there'd be some interesting shit being tanked. Stuff you could do something with."

"Like what?"

"You know . . . whatever."

"Like blackmail someone?"

105

"Never know what you might find, right? Like I seen this story on TV. These people found all sorts of things in people's garbage."

Dunne untied a bag and reached in. He withdrew his hand. It was covered with coffee grinds. Starrell smirked at him: "Most of it's paper. But there's mess here and there."

Dunne grabbed a piece of paper and wiped off his hand. He slid a crate near the bags and sat on it.

"This is going to take a while," Dunne said. "If you have other things to do, go ahead."

"No way, man. I'm staying here. Just in case."

"Just in case I . . . strike gold?"

"Yeah, that's it. Gold, man. Garbage into gold." Starrell laughed.

"Then you can help," Dunne said. He threw one of the bags at Starrell. "Separate the papers from the other garbage."

"And we're going to do a dogg-dogg even-split, man?"

"Yeah, on any gold we find."

It took Dunne nearly two hours to review the garbage of the First Ladies Escort Service. In that time, he learned that Starrell's eighteen-year-old girlfriend was pregnant. That she planned to keep the child and had refused his marriage proposal. That she told him she didn't want to be tied down to a man with no future. That he worried there was someone else. Or maybe the baby wasn't his. But, he told Dunne, he wanted to act like a man. Dunne also learned that the owner of the escort business was a white man named Raymond who looked like a squirrel. It was a small operation. The rent was paid in cash. Starrell recalled once talking with the Latina receptionist and joking about the nature of the business. She became upset and told him, "Our girls are good girls." Starrell didn't know what that meant. The pages for the current month were torn out. He thought she was lying, like women got to do, to make the world a prettier place. Raymond had left no forwarding number or address. His uncle didn't even know Raymond's last name.

Most of the trash was useless. No listing of escorts; no listing of clients. But in the last bag, Dunne found a calendar book with scheduled appointments. He found an entry two months prior to the assassination, with an address on New Hampshire Avenue. There were two initials—A. and G.— and a phone number by each one.

"You have a phone?" Dunne asked.

"You got gold?" Starrell asked.

"Maybe."

Starrell led Dunne to his unc's office. Dunne dialed the number next to the G. It was disconnected.

"Whatcha scoping?" Starrell asked.

"Trying to find the person who goes with the number."

"No prob."

Starrell took the phone and punched in a number.

"Willie-boy, yo, it's me," he said into the phone. "Got some digits, you look it for up for me? . . . Yeah, I know the one. She's damn real. . . . Yeah, I know about Tamika, but I don't know if that means I got to give this one to you. . . . Just look up the damn number, okay? . . . Yeah, yeah, I'll do intros—maybe. Just look it up."

Starrell recited the number, then placed his hand over the receiver.

"Willie's into computer shit," he explained to Dunne. "And he can get on this thing and find any digits you want. Or, if you got a number, the address. It helps when you want to trip on some bitch."

"Gotcha," Dunne said. He picked up the Nation of Islam newspaper on the desk.

"That shit's my unc's," Starrell said to Dunne. "Believes in all that back-to-Africa bullshit. Like I want to go back to where they got killer-jack viruses."

Starrell listened into the phone. He repeated to Dunne the name and address that Willie had found for the number on the calendar.

"Yeah, Willie, yeah," Starrell said into the phone. "I'll tell her 'bout you. . . . Okay, okay." He hung up the phone.

"Thanks," Dunne said.

"And what about that other stuff downstairs?"

"Don't think it's worth much."

"Nothing?"

"Besides, that's nasty business."

"Man, all business is nasty business," Starrell said.

"Yeah, but some business is nastier," Dunne said. "I should go."

"You owe me a hundred."

"I'll be back with it."

"Like I'll see that."

"You will. And I thought we said, one-fifty."

Starrell smiled. "Okay, Mr. Money Man, okay."

"Thank you, Mr. Starrell," Dunne said. "And good luck with Tamika."

18

Upper Georgetown
June 26

Gillian Silva led Dunne and Addis into the kitchen of her group house. Against one wall was a bookcase full of lunch boxes depicting television shows of the 1960s. A housemate, she explained, was a collector. None of the other residents were home. She asked the two men if they wanted coffee. Both declined.

"Oh, yeah, Coke," she said to Addis. "I should've asked. Want one?"

Every profile of him included the obligatory reference to his fondness for—or near-addiction to—Coke. A documentary on the election showed a wall of his campaign office entirely covered with empty Coke cans, each affixed by electrical tape. During the transition, an advertising firm had offered him a large sum for doing a commercial for Coke. He turned it down.

"No thank you," he said now.

Silva started the coffee-maker and then excused herself and went to the bathroom. Dunne in a low voice explained to Addis how he had located her.

"That was a lucky guess about First Ladies," Addis said.

"I think I deserved it," Dunne replied. "I can't depend on enticing key witnesses with my boyish looks. . . . She tell you anything yet?"

"She's friends with Allison Meade. Worked with her in this funny escort business, maybe more of a scam—she claims there's no sex—but doesn't know what her friend was up to at the Mayflower."

Dunne recalled to himself what Al-Fusah had said: "It was clean." What an odd world, Dunne thought.

Silva joined them at the kitchen table. She had taken her hair out of the ponytail.

"May I ask you a few questions, Miss Silva?" Dunne inquired. He placed his hands on the table, palms down.

She looked toward Addis.

"It's okay," Addis said.

"I've seen your face before," she said to Dunne. "I got this great visual memory. Can tell you exactly what everyone I saw yesterday was wearing. Even the day before. And I've seen you—on TV, or something like that."

"I'm the . . . I was head of the Secret Service detail at the White House until—"

"Until the assassination?" she asked and then feared she had made an impolitic remark. "Oh, sorry."

"No, that's alright," Dunne said.

"But I was telling Nick—okay, if I call you that?"

"Please," Addis said.

"I was telling him, I don't want my name in all this. I think it would kill my grandmother. And she just had this operation. And my 'rents would go ballistic. They'd be so . . ." She took a sip of the coffee.

"Miss Silva, I don't make promises I can't keep. At least for now I can try to keep you out of this. But I may not be able to guarantee that forever. But—and I don't want to pressure you—if you don't help now, then you may become the subject of some official action, perhaps a subpoena, and then your name will be linked to the assassination investigation."

"That's not very nice," Silva said. She turned to Addis for support. He shrugged.

Slamming diplomats, intimidating a young woman—we desperate men are not polite, Dunne thought.

"Okay," she said. "But please, okay?"

"I will try, Miss Silva."

Dunne asked about Allison Meade. Silva said that Allison had introduced her to First Ladies, that she and Allison had kept their work a secret from their friends and families, that Allison worked more than she did.

"She's prettier than me. Or, I guess, was. Her eyes—they were different colors, blue and gray. You wanted to keep looking at her, to figure that out. She was good when people got pissed off. You know, when they thought they were getting something they weren't. She'd talk to them, sexy-like. Let them smell her. And they would . . . you know. As long as they didn't get her messy. Sometimes she'd play S&M games with them. But the rule was: You can't touch. You can't be busted for prostitution, then, Raymond told us. He was the guy who ran this thing. He said he'd can us if we did tricks. But Allison was real cute. So some guys called back for her, even if they couldn't do everything. And that was fine with me. There were few guys I ever wanted to see again. Most were greasy—guess I shouldn't say that, but they were—foreigners, junior diplomat types, the World Bank and all that. It wasn't an ego thing for me if they didn't ask for me again. Really, it wasn't."

Addis tried to imagine Allison Meade. He had seen a wire photo; it did not compare with Silva's description of her friend. He wondered what he and Dunne would do with this information. Could they *not* immediately relay it to the proper authorities? He had never practiced law. But shit, he thought, there had to be some statute about interfering with a federal investigation.

"When was the last time you saw her?" Dunne asked

"In psych class, the day before . . ."

"And she said nothing about any upcoming jobs?"

"No. Sometimes she'd tell me. Sometimes she just smiled at me like she had this story to tell but she wouldn't tell it."

"And she never mentioned to you anyone who sounded like the suspect in the assassination? You've seen the pictures?"

"Yeah, sure. And, no, she never said anything about anyone like that. How come you guys with all your computers and everything can't find out who this guy is?"

"We will," Dunne said.

"He does all the talking?" she asked Addis, nodding at Dunne. She was pulling at the ends of her hair.

"Right now, he's doing most," Addis said. She was angling for a certain kind of notice from Addis. He leaned across the table, brushed her hand with his, and asked if he could use the phone. She smiled and said yes.

Good touch, Dunne thought.

Addis went into the living room. A stack of fashion magazines was on a coffee table. A lava lamp and a bong were on the mantle above the fireplace. A framed poster commemorating a Monet exhibit was on the wall. On the couch was a pile of Jane Austen novels. Studying Sartre and de Beauvoir by day, servicing international bureaucrats at night—Addis wondered how much of a secret world truly existed. Spouses lying to each other. Employees padding books. Children deceiving parents and vice versa. Community leaders doing the unspeakable. Who was renting all those behind-the-counter videos in those nice shopping malls? Calling those 900 numbers?

After years of working in government, Addis had changed his view on how the world works. He had grown up a devotee of Watergate. He could cite whole passages of the tapes. As an adolescent, he had pored over the Warren Commission report and could list the dozens of suspicious holes and contradictions in the official account. He had believed then that the official reality open to public inspection merely veiled a hidden world, where the true power resided and the truly significant decisions were reached. But government service had prompted him to reconsider. Bureaucracies were too incompetent to create, manage, and maintain extensive conspiracies. Interagency competition would doom any plot that

110

relied on cooperation among various portions of the government. Spend a week in government, and anyone would see that it was impossible for the Pentagon, the FBI, the Secret Service, the CIA to agree on anything, let alone how to cover up a presidential assassination for decades. Most government malfeasance was actually nonfeasance—bumbling conducted by cover-your-ass bureaucrats, not intricate schemes authored by masterminds.

There were secrets. Secret meetings, secret plans, secret wars, secret deals. Addis had seen a few, yet nothing monumental, and few that would profoundly affect history's overall shape. A favor for a contributor. A private understanding between the President and a foreign head of state that was not shared with Congress. But these secrets did not comprise an entire other world. Addis had concluded that, in general, life is pretty much what it appears to be. Oswald probably had done it. But recent events—events that had transpired before the Hanover assassination—had caused him to reevaluate, to wonder if the world revolved upon *small* secrets. Nothing grand, no global plots, but a long line of modest, economy-size secrets—like Silva's secrets—that, taken together, formed a covert patchwork that blended seamlessly into the pattern of everyday life as we see it.

Addis called the White House and checked his messages. There were no calls he wanted to return. From the living room, he could hear Dunne gently interrogating Silva.

"So tell me about Raymond," Dunne asked. "What's his last name?"

Silva did not know. The name of the receptionist in the office? She only had been told the first name: Maria.

"Listen," she said. "This was not like Citibank. We didn't have staff meetings. I saw him once in a while, but usually it was all over the phone. And I'd pick up the money. Mostly from Maria."

She described Raymond: short, thin, muddy-brown hair, pronounced nose, thin moustache, angular face, maybe forty-five. Looked like a squirrel.

"What else?" Dunne queried.

"Once he told me he was in the Marines. I couldn't see it. Don't they have a height requirement or something?"

"And . . . " Dunne said. He could tell she was keeping something back.

"I hate getting into this stuff," she said.

"What stuff, Miss Silva?"

"It's so stereotypical."

"What is?"

She was silent.

"What is?" Dunne repeated.

"You're missing the good stuff," she called to Addis in the living room.

111

Addis returned to the kitchen and leaned against the counter.

"Ms. Silva?" Dunne said.

She tossed her head.

"Okay, he's gay," she said. "Runs an escort service—well, not exactly an escort service, but close enough—and he's gay and hangs out in the bars. I don't know. It's like too much a type. You know what I mean?"

"I appreciate your sentiments," Dunne replied, "but I'm just asking for details that might be useful in case we want to find him."

"Yeah, it's not like I'm so PC, but . . ."

"How do you know about Raymond's social life?"

"He mentioned it to me when he first interviewed me. I think to convince me that he doesn't hit on his girls. It wasn't a big deal. He paid well and never tried any funny stuff. That's all I cared about."

Silva was talking to Dunne, but her eyes were on Addis.

"Do you know which bars?" Dunne asked.

"No."

"Would you know where to find him if you had to?"

"I guess not," she said. "Just at the office. When I heard about Allison, I called him, and there was no answer. I didn't know what to do . . ."

A tear moved down her face and met her lip.

"And never any word from Raymond."

She shook her head.

"After that you immediately changed your phone number?"

"Yes."

Dunne thanked Silva for her cooperation. He gave her his home phone number and asked her to call if she thought of anything else.

"And do you have a number?" she said to Addis.

"You can call the White House switchboard and ask for me."

She looked disappointed.

"But you're going to keep my name out of this, right?" She was still talking to Addis.

He did not see how that could be done in the long run. He waited for Dunne to speak.

"As long as possible, Miss Silva," Dunne said.

On the way out, Silva pointed to a framed photograph of herself hanging on the wall. She was wearing a black leather bustier and a bikini bottom. Much of her body was exposed. She looked good, Addis thought.

"My cousin's a fashion photographer in New York," she explained. "Shoots lingerie catalogs."

"It's nice," Addis said.

Silva smiled at him. "Good luck," she whispered.

Dunne and Addis stood in front of the group house.

"So now what, Clarence?" Addis asked. "You're not about to tell the task force about this interview, are you?"

"I may . . . eventually. Is that okay?"

"I don't know. Been a while since I checked the criminal code about screwing with a federal investigation."

The two walked toward campus. A car passed by. A man was driving; another was in the passenger seat. Through the tinted windows, Dunne could not make them out.

Surveillance? If so, Dunne knew how he would do it. Three teams mobile, one stationary and tracking, rotations every fifteen minutes—

"So you want to keep this to yourself for now?" Addis asked.

"Yep."

"Why?"

"Don't have a good answer for you."

"Trying to save the day all on your own?"

"Probably."

"And what else?"

"Can't really tell you. Something's off with the way they're handling this investigation. Don't know what. But it is."

"Fuck it, Clarence, you want me to withhold information from the task force and a presidential commission because something *feels* wrong?"

Addis put on his sunglasses. Shit, he thought, is this how a cover-up starts? Will conspiracy buffs—or, worse, congressional aides and federal investigators—one day be examining accounts of this conversation now occurring on a lovely Georgetown street on a sunny afternoon? Earlier in the day Addis had heard on the radio that the most popular Internet sites this week were those devoted to conspiracy theories on the Hanover assassination. One theory referred to a budget memo—leaked last month—that raised the possibility of cutting spending for the Pentagon and the intelligence community. Addis knew that idea was DOA and that the memo, written by a low-level analyst in the budget office, posed no threat to the generals and the spies. Yet that did not stop hundreds—or thousands?—of his fellow citizens from drawing a certain conclusion.

"It's all I have right now," Dunne said.

"Okay—for a while."

"How long is 'a while,' Nick?"

"I can't say. But I'll let you know when it starts to run out, if you let me know what you're doing."

"Sure."

113

"You're lucky I'm in a don't-give-a-good-god-damn mood these days."

Dunne looked at him for more of an explanation.

"My secret," Addis said.

19

White House
June 26

The President would like to see you.

The note was on Addis's desk. He logged on his computer to check Mumfries's schedule. NO DATA AVAILABLE, the screen read. New security precautions, he assumed.

Next he called the Office of White House Administration and asked how White House telephone records were kept. Could he look at the records of his long-distance calls in order to find an old number? It was all in the computer, he was informed. Yes, he could review his own records. Could anyone else? Not anyone; only a few senior staff had access.

On the way to the Oval Office, Addis passed Mike Finn and Dan Carey outside McGreer's office. "The Georgetown event—something, wasn't it?" Carey asked Addis. He was beaming. Addis noticed how well Carey's suit fit. Why didn't his wig?

"The President was fine. He—"

"Not him," Carey interrupted. "Margaret. That was something. I wasn't in the room. But on TV. . . ."

Which for you is all that matters.

". . . it was something, really something."

And all because of Dan Carey, right?

"She handled herself very well," Addis said.

"Sounds like something Kelly would say," Carey replied and laughed.

Finn was tapping his cane gently against his shoe. McGreer was in the doorway, frowning. Addis could tell the lineup remained the same. McGreer was holding on to Mumfries. Carey was pushing Margaret. And Finn was waiting—and probably talking to both camps. But with no declared candidates, there were no declared allegiances.

"Talk to you later, Nick," McGreer said and shut the door.

Mumfries was at his desk, when Addis entered the Oval Office. His right hand was squeezing a golf ball. The books that Hanover had kept on the table behind the desk—a biography of Theodore Roosevelt, a history of New Orleans, and a first edition of *Let Us Now Praise Famous Men*—were gone.

"Sit down, Nick," Mumfries said.

Addis took a seat in the wooden chair facing the desk.

"Can Millie get you anything? A Coke?"

Addis shook his head. He was surprised. In the hundreds of meetings he had had with Hanover here, the President had never offered him a drink in the Oval Office. It felt odd.

"Nick"—Mumfries leaned forward—"all the pundits and party hacks, and the god-damn weed pickers at the *Post* have been on my hump for me to say if I'm running. Of course, I intend to. But hell, I thought it was decent to wait a piece. The body's not even—sorry, you know what I mean."

"I do, sir, and I appreciate that."

Mumfries rolled the golf ball across the desk and caught it with his left hand.

"I've been considering options, and I want your advice."

"Yes, sir," Addis said.

"You boys did a pretty good job making sure there was no competition in the primaries. And I know Pratt won't be a problem in the general. . . ."

Addis wondered if Kelly already had run a poll matching Mumfries against Wesley Pratt. The onetime country-and-western crooner had suspended his campaign and called for a fortnight of prayer.

"But the convention is going to be full of Hanover delegates. Who's going to be controlling them?"

Mumfries was pumping the golf ball with his left hand.

"I don't know, sir."

"The Reelect? State chairs? Should we start working on the delegations now, one-by-one, the old-fashioned way?"

"That would be one strategy."

"Or wait until the convention next week? Out of respect to Bob."

"You could do that."

"But there's a risk. Someone else might get into it before then."

Mumfries mentioned no names. He placed his hands together, with the golf ball between them. He was waiting, looking for information from Addis.

"I think you've laid it out pretty well, sir," Addis said.

"Nick, I'm going to have to make an announcement soon. All those son-of-a-bitch gnats won't stop buzzing until I do. And I'd like to announce that the senior staff will stay on. You know, I'll have to do a little shuffling. Get something else for Brew. Fiddle with the Cabinet. Maybe find an official slot for Margaret. An ambassadorship, maybe one of those U.N. outfits that does all that children's stuff. That's if she wants it. Maybe she just wants to go home with Jack."

Mumfries paused; he was asking for advice, without asking. Offering a job, and hoping for something in return.

"That sounds very generous, sir. And I think it will be well received by most of the staff. I'll stay until the election, but I'm leaving after that."

"Already made up your mind?"

"Have other things I want to do," Addis lied.

"In politics?" Mumfries asked.

"Hopefully not," Addis replied, knowing that was the truth.

"You're still young. My daddy once told me a man should have three careers. . . . But you're aboard until the election?"

He was—and that surprised Addis. Why am I staying on? he wondered. Because it was the default position? He could think of only one reason not to leave: to see what was going to happen. After years of access, he was not yet ready to be an outside observer. How god-damned clinical, he thought.

It also was hard to look into the face of a President and not say what the President wanted to hear. Addis was still bemused by this fact. But it explained much of what had gone wrong in the Oval Office throughout history.

"These days," Addis said, "I feel like I'm drifting. But if I can be of service in the months ahead, I'll try. I hope you understand."

"I do."

Because that means there's one less person on Margaret's side?

Mumfries stood up and left the golf ball on the desk. Addis was not sure if Mumfries did understand. But then he didn't care what the President thought.

Kelly was waiting outside the office. His ears were red. Addis noticed a blue ink stain on Kelly's white shirt just above the waistline.

"A nice chat?" Kelly asked.

"Yes. And I told him I would stay until the election. Then I'm gone."

Addis guessed that Kelly had opposed Mumfries's intention to issue a blanket invitation to Hanover's senior staff. But Mumfries, for all his ego, bore a streak of insecurity. Most of them did, Addis supposed. Those pols who every few years had to plead for the public's support—they all wanted to be hoisted on to the shoulders of people they did not know.

117

"So you already got something worked out for after the election?"

You can't believe I'm not signing up with Margaret. You want to know why, but you don't have the balls to ask.

"Not really," Addis said, "but his offer was on the clumsy side."

"It was straight up. He's hoping you'll stick with him."

You didn't say "us."

Kelly ran his fingers through his two patches of fine blond hair.

"Hell," Kelly said, "you know he thinks he's responsible for you being here in the first place."

What the hell are you talking about?

Kelly read Addis's face.

"You don't know?" he asked.

"Know what?"

"Shit," Kelly said. He laughed and then checked his tie pin. "I probably shouldn't tell you." He stepped into the hallway, and Addis followed, hating himself for chasing the bait.

"What are you talking about?" Addis asked.

"Nick, this is like the prime directive on *Star Trek*: Don't fuck with the past. Forget it."

"Just tell me."

"Alright. It's not a big deal. I assumed you knew. But you know how you got your job with Hanover?"

"Yeah, I do."

"Well, maybe not all of it. When Hanover was thinking about running early on, he called Mumfries. He knew Sam was thinking about running, too. And they're almost family. That is, the Mumfries and the Masons. Think he almost went out with Margaret, after he came back from Laos or somewhere—you should get him to tell you the stories about when he was with the Special Forces—before he moved to Texas and got into politics. Too much, isn't it?"

Kelly was enjoying this. He hooked both thumbs behind his suspenders.

"Anyway, Hanover called him up. I know because I was in the room. He wants to ask Sam not to run against him, but he can't really do that. But he's trying to scare Sam out, let him know he's going to do the deed. So he asks Sam for help. Like, 'Hey, Sam, I'm starting to pull together a lil' ol' campaign staff. Got any bright ideas for me?' "

A security patrol passed by. Two bomb-sniffing German shepherds were part of the unit.

"So Sam covers the phone," Kelly continued, "and tells me what Hanover wants. 'Think I'll recommend you,' he says to me, and we both laughed. Then he says to me, 'Hey, what about our favorite S.O.B. who screwed us on Honduras?' And he says into the phone, 'Well, Bob, there's

118

this sharp young man up here who works for Palmer.' And that's it. He hangs up the phone and says—and he's talking about you—'He'll never be on our team. Better if he's out there with Hanover whizzing against the tent than being around here and making it rain.' And this was when nobody, Sam included, thought the President could be beat."

Kelly stopped talking to see how this was registering. Addis did not say anything.

"So you see, Sam got you your job and look what happened." He extended an arm. "All this. . . . Now, I'm not saying you wouldn't have hooked up with Hanover one way or another. Maybe his next call was to Palmer. And maybe Palmer—since he wasn't running—was going to send you off to him wrapped up with a pretty bow. Maybe this. Maybe that. But who knows? Who the fuck knows?"

"Thanks," Addis said.

"It's funny, don't you think? I just assumed that Hanover told you about that."

He never got around to it.

"Maybe he didn't want to give Sam credit for such a good decision," Kelly said, an edge in his voice.

"Thanks," Addis said. "That's one for the history books."

"Sure is," Kelly said. "See you later with those historians, right?"

He bounded toward the Oval Office. Addis had to think a moment about what to do next. His days used to be overloaded with meetings. In the absence of pressing official duties, he went to the East Wing to find Margaret Hanover.

Margaret's office was almost completely disassembled. The desk was gone. The books were packed in boxes. The filing cabinets were covered with packing quilts. She sat on a crate. M. T. O'Connor was perched on another, reading from a folder.

"The invitations keep coming in," O'Connor was saying, when Addis rapped on the open door.

"Not yet," Margaret told O'Connor. She looked tired. She held a Bible, and caught Addis looking at it. "He took his inaugural oath on this Bible," she said.

"How's Jack?" he asked.

"He's pretty quiet. But he's always quiet."

"I told him we should go to a ball game."

"That would be good. I don't think Security will let that happen for a little while, but then . . . He's with Lem, now. They're watching a movie downstairs."

She put the Bible in a box.

"What can I do for you, Nick?"

He didn't want to say in front of O'Connor.

"Didn't have much to do," he said. "Thought I'd come by to see if you needed any help."

"Cleaning out my office?" she asked. "We can talk with M. T. Pull up a crate. Nothing but the finest accommodations."

O'Connor patted a box next to her. "Health and Human Services budgets," she said.

Addis hiked up his pants and sat on the box.

Was it only two months ago, he thought, that we were on Air Force One, flying back from Ireland? President Hanover was napping, and Margaret and M. T. were contending with the raving sister of the senior senator from New Hampshire. She could not find her panty hose and was shouting at the First Lady, demanding that Margaret determine who had stolen her panty hose.

"I've looked at the records, made a few calls," he said to Margaret.

She picked up an ornamental mortar and pestle—the bowl bore a snowy forest scene—and placed them in a box.

"From the First Lady of Estonia," she said. "If it's under a hundred dollars in value, I can keep it."

"What do you remember about the land deal?" he asked. "As far as I can tell, you bought the parcel from a limited partnership for about $30,000. Held it for two years and then sold it to another limited partnership and made about $120,000. How did you and"—Addis stumbled as he referred to Hanover—"he come to—"

"You can call him Bob," she interrupted.

"—come to invest in this property?"

"It was Bob's deal. A friend of his brought it to our attention. It was near a river. Said it could be a good investment. Then, it turned out, they were going to expand the nearby airport and Southern Chicken was going to build a big processing plant there. We sold the land to some people who I think were putting this deal together. I don't remember the details."

"This all happened when he was governor?" Addis asked.

"Yes, and there was an ethics officer who reviewed all of our finances. So I presumed this was checked out."

"Good. We should find him. What's the ethics officer's name?"

"Flip will know."

Addis took a breath.

"And any connection with your father? This scummy reporter's been asking about him."

"Nick, you know I had no contact with Chasie after the AG campaign. . . . I wonder what he'd be thinking now, if he were still here."

Margaret's eyes were becoming moist. O'Connor placed a hand on Margaret's arm. She moved out from under it.

"Damnit, I've cried enough," Margaret said. She tucked a strand of hair into her bun.

"So nothing sticks out to you?" Addis asked. "There's nothing there?"

"There's always something, because there's always someone who's busy making anything into something. We should know what people are saying about it. That can be more important than what really happened. Right?"

"I suppose," he said.

"So you're going down there?"

He nodded.

"Without having to say why?"

"I have an idea. And it will be good to get out of here for a few days."

Shit, I shouldn't have said that.

O'Connor shot him a look that screamed, "You insensitive bastard." But Margaret did not pay attention to his remark. He got up. "I'll let you finish here," he said.

"Thank you, Nick," she said.

"Don't worry about it," he replied.

She began rummaging through another box. "Old calendars," she explained.

O'Connor accompanied Addis back to the West Wing.

"Is she doing alright?" he asked.

"She's strong. A fighter."

"You know, I don't think it's a good idea."

Shit, I can't bring myself to say it: Margaret running for President.

"Not good for who?" O'Connor asked. "Not good for Mumfries, Kelly, and their cronies?"

"I don't care about them."

"Not good for her? How condescending is that?"

"She can do what she wants, but it won't go well for her. She'll look too ambitious."

"And a woman can't do that?"

"Not easily, unfortunately. But there are other reasons: She's never held office; she's a magnet for too much shit."

"And I suppose it's not good for Nick Addis, who has checked out of the game and is now above it all?"

"I don't matter."

"Spoken like a true self-pitying martyr." She finished the sentence with a chuckle, trying to take the sharpness off her words.

121

"And what about Jack?" he asked.

"Maybe we ought to pack him and Margaret off to a wax museum in New Orleans," she replied. "That will be great for him."

"Okay, okay, you've convinced me. Go for it. Have a blast. Smite all foes."

O'Connor hugged him.

"That's it?" she said with a smirk. "I have your blessings? Thank you, padre." He laughed at her and said good-bye.

Addis went back to his office. He returned a few calls. His parents were not in their offices. He spoke to a few friends scattered throughout the administration. They each wanted to know what was going to happen. He reported that he did not know. He did the same with a couple of journalists he respected. He answered a call from Senator Palmer. The senator was on the floor.

Then he called Holly Rudd.

She was with a client, the receptionist said, but she would be right with him. He listened to Muzak.

"Hi," she said.

"Sorry I've been hard to get."

"Are you okay—"

"You busy?"

"Not really. Had a president from one of the unions in here, and I had to explain why he couldn't postpone a union election he's not going to win. . . . So, how are you?"

"Pushing through the muck."

"I'm sorry—"

"Yeah, I know. Everybody is."

"Yeah," she muttered.

"Well, here we are . . . talking."

She didn't reply. Addis could tell she was considering what to say next.

"If there's anything I can do."

He felt a slight shake in his knees. Why was this so god-damn hard? How much time does it take?

"I was kind of hoping you'd say that."

There was silence on the other end.

"I need a favor," he continued.

"Okay." Her voice was tentative. He wanted to hang up. This is dumb, he told himself. But it was the best idea he could concoct. Or was he fooling himself?

"I do need it."

"Okay, what?"

"I'd rather tell you in person. Besides, in a minute, I've got to have

122

cocktails with a bunch of historians and discuss the nature of national tragedies."

They arranged to meet later. Then Addis called his travel agent and asked her to book two tickets to New Orleans.

"To be billed to the party?" she asked.

"No," he said, "it's personal."

20

Rosslyn

June 26

Julia Lancette did not recognize the phone number. The 456 exchange—which flashed on her caller-identification readout—indicated the call was coming from the White House. She answered with a curt "hello."

"Ms. Lancette, please," a male voice said.

"Who's calling?" she asked.

"Jake Grayton."

"Hold on." She punched the hold button. She had seen him at Wenner's office yesterday. Why would he be calling? She reconnected the call and tried to speak in a slightly different voice.

"This is Julia Lancette."

"Hi, this is Jake Grayton," he said. "I hope this doesn't sound too strange, but Mrs. Novek said I should give you a call. We almost met—but didn't—in the director's office. And she thought we might share some interests. So I was wondering—to get to the point—if you'd like to have dinner."

Damn straightforward, she thought.

"You're not too busy these days, Mr. Grayton?" she asked.

"Yes, but we all have to eat and I didn't promise a long dinner. And call me Jake."

"I don't know, Jake."

"We can invite Mrs. Novek to join us."

Lancette laughed and then silently chided herself for doing so.

"See?" he said. "We'll have fun."

"This is not really the time to be having fun, is it?"

"Then we won't. I give you my word."

First, a whacked-out CIA shrink, she thought, now a date with one of the big honchos in the community. Perhaps she should borrow a touch of Dr. Charlie Walters's paranoia. Her mother's voice sounded in her head: "You can never know if a chance is a good one or a bad one, so take it." As Lancette had gotten older—and remained unmarried—her mother had become more daring in the advice she offered.

"Sure," she said. "When?"

"Tonight? Tomorrow?"

She was free that evening. She was free most nights when she wasn't being forced to Anacostia by a gun-toting colleague.

"Tomorrow looks good," she said.

He suggested an expensive, well-known Cajun restaurant.

After she finished with Grayton, Lancette tried to do some work. An American banker had been gunned down, mob-style, in Moscow. Might he have been an agent? An asset? The Agency, she knew, had increased its contacts with business executives working overseas, especially in Russia. She considered which offices should be sent an ICEMAN request on this case.

It was hard to keep her mind on the task at hand. She was puzzling over her conversation with Walters. What, if anything, should she do in response? Should she inform Wenner? Tell him that she had been kidnaped by a CIA psychiatrist who claimed his ICEMAN report had been spiked? A report that contained vague information. Walters's superiors would probably brand him as overly excitable—which Lancette could confirm—and argue that he was not reliable. Surely, they had some excuse, real or manufactured, to fall back on, should their handling of the report be questioned. Perhaps it would be best to determine first if Walters should be taken seriously.

She left her office and crossed the street to a Vietnamese restaurant. So many had sprouted in northern Virginia in the years after the war. The most loyal customers were former Company men and ex-military officers who gathered in these establishments to sop booze and repeat their stories of glory days in inglorious times. Four white-haired men—she recognized their made-in-the-military bearing—were shouting at each other at the 5THbar. She found the pay phone and dialed Walters's number. This was not complete security, she knew. But better than none. A woman answered, and Lancette asked for Dr. Walters.

"He's not in," the woman said. "He's on travel."

"Oh, the Africa trip, right?" Lancette said. "I forgot."

"He's on travel," she repeated. "Would you care to leave a message?"

"No." She put the receiver down. Well, she thought, he had told her the truth about being packed off. Still, that did not provide much guidance.

She picked up a Washington phonebook.

"Fuckin'-A!" one of the men at the bar yelled. "I fucked her—not you! Remember you met her fucking sister at one of those pussy parties at the Duc Hotel after a cocktail thing at Mau's."

The owner of the restaurant rushed over to quiet the customer. Once a captain in the special police in Saigon, the owner now served gin to Americans who used to advise him on how to wage war. Some people win even when they lose, Lancette told herself.

She found a listing for a business called the Gauntlet. That was the name on the cap worn by the man in Walters's story—the man who bore a tattoo similar to the one found on the assassin of President Bob Hanover. There was an address on 5th Street Northwest. It was near downtown Washington, in a desolate neighborhood. She knew there was a police station three blocks away. During her initial orientation at the CIA, she had been told that operations people were required to memorize the locations of all police offices and hospitals in the metropolitan area. As an analyst-to-be, it was not necessary for her to do so. Nevertheless, she had committed the list to memory.

Outside the restaurant, she hailed a cab. She gave the driver an address that would be a block away from her destination. As the taxi headed across the Key Bridge, she watched the local college crew teams rowing on a muddy Potomac. You can never know if a chance is a good one or a bad one, she said to herself.

There was no sign on the front of the building, a four-story brownstone with peeling paint and shuttered windows. Next door was a boarded-up shop. In its brick facade, a few faded painted words remained: Goldstein's Pawn. On the other side was a collapsing building. Its windows were gone, replaced by bricks and cement. Glassine envelopes were scattered on the sidewalk. Further down the block was a square of land filled with rubble and surrounded by a cyclone fence.

Three young black men were hanging across the street. She knew they were watching her. She walked to the rear of the building. There were several tall oak trees behind it. The trees obscured the view of the balconies attached to the second and third floors. She heard voices coming from the closed-up brownstone and returned to the street.

Next to the front door was a mailbox. A small piece of paper bearing the handwritten word Gauntlet was taped to the receptacle. She pressed the doorbell.

A large white man—about six-and-a-half-feet tall and weighing three hundred pounds—answered the door. He was in his mid-forties and had a curly red beard that came to a point halfway down his chest.

"Don't open until six," he said and started to shut the door.

"Wait," she said.

The door closed with force. She rang again.

The same man opened the door.

"Not open," he said.

"I'm not here for that," she said, wondering what "that" might be.

"Then what you want?"

"Can I come in?" she asked.

"Depends."

"On what?"

"On what you want? You a lawyer?"

"No. I'm looking for someone."

"You're a dick?"

"No, just trying to help a friend."

"Bullshit," he said. "Bull-fucking-shit. But come fucking in anyway. Sun's not good for me. Doc says I'm susceptible to melanomas."

She stepped into the building. In the hallway, a pair of steer horns hung from the ceiling. On the wall to each side was a mounted wagon wheel. The place was dark. But she could see that the entire first floor was one open room. Tables and chairs were set up. Cowboy posters were on the wall. Ornate saddles were mounted on stands. A jukebox was glowing. There was a bar at the end of the room. Three men were sitting at it. A young man wearing a white apron was mopping a dance floor.

"I've had three fucking melanoma operations," the bearded man said. "Doc says that I need to live like a god-damn vampire."

He guided her to the bar and told her to sit. He took a place behind the bar.

"Big Daddy Lopez," he said, introducing himself.

The men at the bar looked at Lancette with little interest. They each had a buzz cut. "So he told him," one was saying, "that he couldn't take it anymore. That either he put his name on the lease or that was it—"

"But I ain't no spic," Lopez said to Lancette. "My name's Lopez. But as far back as we can trace, ain't no spic blood, just a spic name, okay?"

"Okay," Lancette said.

"Who you looking for? Not me, right?"

"No, not you. Looking for a fellow who, I think, used to work here a few years ago. He—"

"Why you looking for him?" He took a draw from a long-necked bottle of beer.

"Someone asked me to help find him—"

"Thought you said you're no dick."

"No dick? Hey, stop talking about Gregory!" one of the men shouted at Lopez. The others laughed. The young man mopping the floor glowered at them.

"Mind your own fuckin' girlie business," Lopez said to them. His attention returned to Lancette.

"Who asked you to help?"

"It was"—she thought for a moment—"his family."

"And what's his name?"

"They're trying not to use his name. He—"

"Sounds like a scam, sweetie. How do they expect to find him?"

"Well, they believe he's using a different name now—and they don't know what that name is. But he's hard to miss. He has a scar on his ear and a glass eye."

She said nothing about the tattoo. The tattoo found on the assassin had been described in the media. If she mentioned it, Lopez would know why she was interested in the man.

She paid close attention to Lopez's face. It did not change as she described the man.

"And why are they looking for the hombre-with-no-name?"

"I don't know all the details. Something to do with a will. He might have some money coming his way."

"Yeah, right. Money coming his way, so maybe I'd want to help out then, right?" Lopez laughed.

The front door opened and a man came in carrying a valet bag.

"Big, I forgot," he said. "Did you say chaps or jeans tonight?"

"Chaps, you ditz," Lopez yelled.

"Don't get yourself in a huff," the man said. "I brought both."

"Think you can help?" Lancette asked.

"What else does he look like?"

"Glass eye, a scar on his ear, I said."

"And?"

Lancette looked puzzled.

"In a place like this, that's not enough," he explained, grinning.

He's jerking me around, she thought.

"Wouldn't you know if he worked here?" she asked.

"I've been running this place about two years now. Bought it from a couple of faggots who moved to Indiana for some god-damn reason. But I'll ask around. Maybe. Hold on." He opened the beer chest and then slammed it shut.

"Fuckit, Gregory," Lopez said to the man with the mop. "Told you to make sure we had the Corona. I don't see one here."

"They haven't delivered it yet," Gregory replied.

"And don't you think I should know that." Lopez lumbered out from behind the bar to tend to the beer problem. While he was gone, Lancette listened to the men at the bar.

"Fucking Sarge keeps busting my balls," one said.

128

"Thinks he knows?" asked another.

"Don't think so. Even so don't think it would matter. He's just a ball-buster. Gotta report back for an overnight." He placed an empty beer bottle on the bar. "Later, boys."

He looks like a Marine, Lancette thought.

"Later, Big Daddy," the fellow called to Lopez.

"See ya, Slick," Lopez yelled back, as he returned to the bar. "Semper Fi them in the you-know-what!"

He smacked a fist into his palm.

"So say I find something," Lopez said to Lancette, "how do I reach you?"

"I'll come back," she replied.

"Wrong!" he said. "Most of our patrons come here and don't want to be found. So I don't want people knowing Big Daddy runs a finder service. You come by once, that's a fluke. You come by again, and they ask, what's up? So I'll call you. Let me have one of your cards. This is fuckin' Washington, if you're legit, you got a card, right?"

"Sure," Lancette said. She pulled out a business card and handed it to him.

"Janet Lang, Inter-Business Media," he read. "What's that?"

"A news service. I'm a desk editor."

"Okay, pretty lady, Big Daddy will call you if he comes up with the right prize."

One of the men at the bar had gone over to the jukebox. He dropped in a quarter and punched the buttons. As Lancette left the bar, she heard a woman singing:

He takes me to
The places you
And I used to go.

She knew the song: Patsy Cline's "Why Can't He Be You?"

129

21

White House
June 26

Addis was in his office preparing to leave for the night. He had finished with the historians. In the White House Map Room, he had collected condolences, accepted best wishes conveyed to his parents, and nodded his head respectfully whenever one of the sages had cornered him to pass on political advice. Addis had buttonholed McGreer and asked if he could take off a few days. For what? the chief of staff asked. A trip to New Orleans, Addis replied. Not on that old business? McGreer asked, suspicion in his voice. No, Addis said, it was personal. McGreer raised an eyebrow. Have fun, he advised. Next, Addis took Kelly aside. Kelly displayed no interest in why Addis was heading out of town. Just make sure my office has a number for you, he said and separated himself from Addis to reclaim his position next to Mumfries.

As he left the West Wing, Addis was grabbed by the arm. Startled, he stopped walking.

"Keep going," Dunne said.

Addis tripped over his feet and recovered his balance.

"Let's go to your car," Dunne said.

They walked past a military Jeep with a gun mounted on its back. Addis led Dunne to his Honda. Both men got into the car.

"What's the matter?" Addis asked.

"She's dead," Dunne said.

"Who?"

"Gillian Silva. Just on local news. Got hit by a car while riding her bike."

"Shit, Clarence," Addis muttered.

"I know."

Both were silent for a moment.

"What did you do after we . . ." Addis began to ask.

"Nothing. That is, nothing about this. Had to attend an orientation session for the training center. Filled out papers."

"So what is this? An accident?"

"Car didn't stop. No one saw the license plate. And an accident? How damn unlucky can two girls be?"

"I didn't tell anyone."

"No one? No one at all? You got to let me know if you did, Nick."

"No one, Clarence."

"And you met her just before I saw you, right? She walked up to you? Like you said?"

"Like I told you, yes."

"Maybe it was me," Dunne said, more in the direction of the windshield than Addis. "Through me." He was gripping his legs tightly.

"Maybe someone found her like you did," Addis said.

"I don't know . . . I was followed. Somehow or another."

"So what does this mean?"

"There's bad shit out there."

"Clarence, maybe it's time to share what we know—"

"No," he interrupted. "If this is an accident, there's not much to be done besides what I'm going to do. If it's not an accident, then we can't let anyone know."

"This is getting kind of big to keep to ourselves."

"You don't have to. But you have to make me one promise."

"What?"

"If you're going to tell someone, you'll let me know first."

"Sure, Clarence, sure."

Dunne reached into his coat.

"Take this," he said.

He held out a gun.

"N-no, that's alright, really," Addis sputtered. "Besides, you probably need it more than I do."

"Nick, be real. Don't you think I have others? If someone killed her, they probably know we were there, that we know what she knows— or used to know."

"I don't want it," Addis said of the gun.

"Take it—until we know more."

Addis kept his hands at his side. Dunne opened the glove compartment.

"Don't," Addis said.

Dunne placed the gun inside the glovebox.

"I'm going out of town," Addis said. "I don't need it. And, Jesus, I'm not going through a metal detector carrying that thing."

"Just have it nearby."

"Fuck, Clarence. I don't know how to use it. M. T.'s the shooter. I'm better with a cell phone. You think someone's really going to take a shot at a senior White House—"

Addis stopped, realizing how stupid he sounded. You idiot, he told himself, someone killed the President. Dunne had the courtesy not to reply.

"Where are you off to?" he asked.

"New Orleans. It's personal. Two or three days, I guess."

"Lucky man."

"Yeah. You going to be okay?"

"Me? Sure."

"Clarence, I don't like being part of a conspiracy."

"You're not," Dunne said. "You're part of the anti-conspiracy."

"Isn't it pretty to think so," Addis replied.

Dunne considered putting a question to Addis: You're a politico, the type always pushing an agenda to help your career or that of whomever you're serving. So why are you going along with me, a politically radio-active has-been? Why not run to Mumfries—or Margaret Hanover or Jake Grayton—and tell them about this lead to the crime of the century? Dunne decided not to ask.

Addis wondered if the circular patch of gray hair on Dunne's head had enlarged in the past week.

"I'll see you when you get back," Dunne said.

He left the car. Addis opened the glove compartment and emptied the gun of the bullets. He then folded a piece of paper around the ammunition and returned the gun and the bullets to the glovebox. He locked it and started the car engine.

Addis drove by the reinforced barricade at the rear of the parking area. Armed units were still patrolling the perimeter of the White House grounds. As Addis sat at a traffic light on Connecticut Avenue and gazed at a mobile soup kitchen, he noted to himself that in an hour he was going to see Holly Rudd for the first time in four years. Since she had moved to Washington, the two had not spoken. In this small, claustrophobic city, their paths had not intersected. But, then, he had not enjoyed much of a regular life. The White House had been all consuming. There had been the occasional dinner party in Georgetown, and a short affair with a fa-mous fashion model. But he spent little time outside the White House bubble. And it had taken the assassination to prompt her to contact him.

The light changed, and a horn blared behind him. He shifted into first gear. Through the side window, he saw a homeless man take a sandwich and hurl it into the rush of cars heading out of the city.

22

Flight 847
June 27

She smells too damn good.

As the 767 fought against the jet stream, Holly Rudd slept, her head resting on Addis's shoulder. Whenever she was a passenger in a moving vehicle she lost consciousness. Train, bus, car, airplane—give her a humming, mechanical drone and swaying motion, and she could not resist. Yet in bed at night, she had tossed, she had pushed, she had kicked. In the old days, after they made love, Addis would roll to the far side of the bed to avoid the writhing to come.

On the crowded airplane, as she dozed peacefully, he went over their dinner the night before. She had arrived at Havana Village, had kissed him quickly on the cheek—a glancing kiss—and had sat down at the table. She looked good. Her brown, almost black wavy hair, shoulder-length, was longer than he had ever seen it. Her eyelashes so fine, her dark eyes like dots on a round, smooth face. From what he could tell, she was still muscular and trim.

"How are—"

"Fine," he said.

"It's so—"

"I know."

He asked about her job and her family. She supplied the basics about the firm and her parents and sister.

Four years, how do you cover four years?

The waiter, one of the owner's sons, brought them beer and took their orders.

"What can I do for you, Nick?" she asked. "You said you needed something."

The prelims are over, he thought. He sipped his beer and hesitated in replying.

133

"You said you need a favor."

Was that reluctance in her voice, or was the whole damn thing too strange? Shit, here goes.

Addis told her that he had to travel to New Orleans on confidential business. He did not want to have to explain his travel to any curious parties—in the press or elsewhere.

"A trip with an old friend—"

"An old girlfriend," she interrupted.

"Would not provoke too many questions."

"Not those sort of questions," she said. "But others."

"Sounds silly, I know," he said. "But I'm in a jam. It's asking a lot, but can you give me a few days?"

"It's connected to the . . . ?" she asked.

"Not really," he replied.

"Does it have something to do with the race? Is it true what the papers are saying, that Margaret's going to—"

"I can't get into it. Not now. If you have to know, then let's forget about it."

"Okay, okay," she said. "I did offer. I just don't want you to think that . . ."

"To think what?" he asked. But he knew what she meant.

Do you think I'm trying to use this tragedy? Damnit, am I looking to find something, someone, to fix myself to?

"Maybe I should tell you—"

"You're seeing someone." He had heard: a lobbyist for an environmental group. She nodded.

"It's serious," she said.

You had to throw that in, didn't you?

"Would it be a problem," he asked, "for you—and him—if you . . ."

"He's in Rio for a conference this week," Rudd said.

"If we travel together, you know what people will say, what will happen?"

"I remember: the news photographers, the gossip columns. Is this really the only way—"

"All I can come up with."

"You're really pushing it, Nick."

"I know. One last push for old times?"

"One last push?" She smiled for a moment. "But I can only be gone two days."

"Thanks, I just need a friend to help."

He wondered if this were true.

How do you know when you're pulling off a really good job of self-deception?

134

He had booked a suite with two rooms, he told her. She would only have to accompany him to a few meals, perhaps a show.

"Maybe Jeff will see something in the Rio paper," she said.

"We can tell everyone, 'just friends.' Can he read Portuguese?"

"No. But he can read a picture."

"I can call him, if you like."

She laughed in reply.

"No, I'll deal with it. It will be fine. He's too damn secure, anyway."

Why is she agreeing? Does she want there to be a problem with Jeff? Shit, stop thinking this way. It's just a pity-fuck.

"Besides," she added. "Maybe we'll have—"

"Here you go," said the waiter, who had arrived with their food. He looked at Addis with sad eyes. "I just want to say that I feel—"

The waiter was embarrassed; he did not know how to finish the sentence.

"I know," Addis said with sympathy. "I know."

"Yes, yes." The waiter placed the plates in front of them and backed away.

"Must be hard to be consoling everyone else," Rudd said.

"Comes with the territory."

But what were you going to say?

The conversation drifted back to small talk. She picked at the food and mentioned that she had been in Alaska. On a vacation with Jeff? She didn't say. She passed on dessert and coffee. Outside the restaurant, they went over the travel arrangements and she flagged a cab. She touched his hand as she said good-bye. But it was a tentative gesture, hard to read. She entered the cab.

"Thank you," he said through the window. "I know this is weird, but—"

A bus rumbled past, smothering her reply, and the taxi left the curb. Had she said, "Life is weird"?

Rolando, the owner, was smoking a cigar outside the restaurant.

"A good meal, my friend?" he asked Addis.

"Delicious," Addis said.

"And your friend, did she—"

"How's business tonight?"

"Good, good. But the dumbwaiter is not working as it should. So Johnny and Esteban had to use the stairs. I think their knees are not so good." Rolando laughed and held out a cigar to Addis.

"Not tonight," Addis said.

A pocket of turbulence knocked the aircraft, and Addis stopped replaying the previous evening. Rudd stirred but did not awaken. Her hair fell

135

across his jacket. He wanted to touch the hair. But he knew that he shouldn't, that if he did she would choose that moment to end her sleep.

There was something he wanted to tell her. Not about the land deal, the supposed point of this trip. That would bore her, it would seem trivial, another political sideshow supplanting substance. He remembered her rants. Why couldn't politics just focus on what policies are best for the nation? How could he put up with all the bullshit? Why was the nation constantly being distracted by negative ads, personal attacks, and irrelevant questions about the private lives of candidates? For the same reason, he had replied more than once, that television networks broadcast crap, that lawyers encourage clients to sue when they don't have a chance, that the Pentagon demands weapons for which there are no true targets, that the Chinese want Disney stores, that investment bankers care more about the on-paper value of a firm than what it produces.

It was unreal to expect the political system to be more noble an institution than any other. Those who wanted to do good within the system—those who wanted to better the odds for people not represented by well-tailored corporate lobbyists and deep-pocketed political action committees—had to tote plenty of garbage. If you couldn't stand the stench and opted out, then you were making room for those who had no sense of smell. He had tried to convince her of this—perhaps tried too hard.

Let old bones rest in peace, he thought. And turn to powder.

No, what he wanted to tell her at this moment would be important to her. She would be held enrapt. She would feel vindicated and enraged. She might be disappointed by him even more.

About a month ago—ages before the assassination—Flip Whalen, the Hanovers' unofficial ambassador to back-home, had called from New Orleans. McGreer was traveling with President Hanover in Asia, so Whalen asked for Addis, who was recovering from a sinus infection and unable to fly.

"Want to give you all a heads-up," Whalen told him.

An itinerant laborer had been arrested in Opelousas. He had come home drunk and hacked his wife to death with a machete. He then sliced their nine-month-old daughter nearly in half and tossed the child's body out the window of their second-floor apartment. When the police arrived at his apartment he was sitting in front of a stove with the gas running. All the windows were now closed. In one hand was an unlit match. He was poised to strike it. The police officers held their fire, fearing a mis-aimed shot might spark an explosion. They tried to talk to him but he was mumbling gibberish. Then he moved to light the match.

It did not ignite. The matchbook cover was wet with blood and sweat. The man was apprehended.

As he had listened, Addis wondered why Whalen considered this a White House concern.

At the police station, Whalen continued, the fellow confessed—not only to the murder of the woman and the child, but also to three other murders in the past ten years. A drunk in a bar. A fellow day laborer who had chiseled him out of thirty-five dollars. An owner of a convenience store outside New Roads, shot dead during a botched robbery attempt.

"Flip, so what?" Addis asked.

"That's the same fellow Donny Lee Mondreau killed."

"Shit."

"Yeah. Shit, double-shit, and triple-shit."

Mondreau had been executed for this murder. The case against Mondreau was mostly circumstantial. A trucker had testified that he saw Mondreau running from the store at the time of the killing. Mondreau, whose mental abilities were diminished, had told the police different stories pertaining to his whereabouts. A jury found him guilty; an appeals court validated the sentence rendered. Hanover had flown to Baton Rouge to sign the execution order. And a far-off consequence was a fight between Addis and Rudd in a New Orleans hotel room.

"So what do we know for sure?" Addis had asked Whalen. He reached for a pad and a pen. Then he caught himself and pushed both away.

"Not much. He's a doper. A lot of mumbo jumbo so far. But they've got to check it out."

"Any indication he knew that someone had been arrested for the New Roads killing?"

"Don't know," Whalen replied.

"Does his story match the details of the killing?"

"Don't know yet, either."

"Can we get some answers?"

"Yeah, I'm on it. The sheriff is a cousin of the parish chairman. He's a good man."

Good in what way?

"And who else knows?"

"Just the cops, as far as I know—and the sheriff's cousin."

"Keep me posted, Flip. I want to know."

I really fucking want to know.

Whalen did not call back for two days. In that time, Addis wondered how Hanover would respond if it turned out an innocent man had been executed on his watch. Would Wesley Pratt try to exploit this during the campaign? The polls showed Pratt was sunk. He was an amiable fellow, but he could not help referring to Jesus whenever he appeared in public. This habit had won him the support of a devoted following, enough to triumph in the primaries. But, according to the polls, it had alienated most

137

people likely to vote in the November election. One mistaken conviction could not change the calculus of this election, and Addis could envision a contrite Hanover pledging to push for criminal justice reforms—not the abolition of the death penalty—to ensure such a tragedy was never repeated. He would be sincere, all sincerity. Most of the public would forgive the President. Still, a man would be dead.

When Whalen finally rang back, Addis cut short a conversation with a network anchor to accept the call.

"No more problem," Whalen reported.

"Why not?" Addis asked.

"The great humanitarian in question decided that he himself did not deserve to live."

"And?"

"Last night he took his sheets and . . . was found this morning. Long gone. That's it."

"That's it?"

"Sheriff says his other stories didn't match with known cases. So that's it. Case closed."

"Flip, did they check the New Roads—"

"Nick, the sheriff says the case is closed. It was a false alarm. You want to go second-guessing local law enforcement?"

"But what if they . . . ?" He did not want to say what he suspected.

"C'mon, Nick. There's no reason to believe it's anything other than what they say it is. And I don't see any reason to discuss it further. Do you?"

"Guess not."

"You don't go chasing after bears when they're showing you tail, do you?"

After he finished with Whalen, Addis sat at his desk and stared at his hands. He let the phone ring. About forty-five minutes later, an aide rushed in, holding a memo written by a Cabinet member that decried the administration's budget figures. At least three reporters already had a copy. Addis left his desk and headed toward the Situation Room to send a high-priority message about the memo to McGreer on Air Force One. The phone calls from Whalen? Didn't one cancel out the other? But he knew: He was spinning himself.

That was four weeks ago. That was before. . . .

The pilot announced that the aircraft had begun the descent into New Orleans. Rudd awoke and lifted her head from Addis's shoulder. She showed no sign of self-consciousness.

"Almost there?" she asked.

"Close," Addis said.

She picked up a newspaper and read. On the front page of the metro section, Addis saw a photograph of a smiling Gillian Silva. He recalled the photo she had showed him yesterday. Plump breasts. Sleek legs. Pouty lips. Now cold flesh.

Rudd saw that he was looking at the story about Silva.

"Imagine being her parents," she said.

"I couldn't," Addis said.

23

Downtown Washington
June 27

Twayne Starrell's uncle asked Clarence Dunne if he belonged to a church. He frowned when Dunne mentioned an Episcopalian house in suburban Maryland. He handed Dunne a flyer for a new church.

"For true Africans," he said.

Dunne was waiting for Starrell in the uncle's small office. The uncle had sent Starrell out for rat traps. The city had cut back its rodent office, the winter was mild, and they're damn well everywhere, the uncle explained to Dunne. He then apologized for cursing. The uncle returned to the paperwork piled on his desk. Dunne pondered the request he had received that morning from Jake Grayton: *Please prepare an evaluation of each member of the security detail at the White House.* Grayton wanted the report completed tomorrow. That should keep me busy, Dunne said to himself.

Starrell was surprised when he returned and found Dunne in the office. Dunne wanted to shake his head. Starrell was wearing a thick gold chain, a University of Maryland sweatshirt with the sleeves cut off, and the same bad-ass sunglasses from the previous day. Dunne recognized Starrell's sneakers from a newspaper story. They cost nearly two hundred dollars and young black men were fighting each other—even slaughtering each other—over these shoes.

"Mr. Money Man, the black Clint Eastwood returns to the scene of the crime," Starrell said. "Wasn't sure that would happen."

He handed his uncle the bag of traps.

"We're going huntin'," Starrell said to Dunne. "Looking for those ghetto ponies. Ride 'em, cowboy. Buffalo cowboys, right, Unc?"

"Buffalo soldiers," the uncle said.

"Yeah, but after they were done fighting for the Man, they got good jobs, right, Unc? Fancy cowboy jobs, right?"

The uncle ignored the remark.

"Would you mind if I borrowed Mr. Starrell for a few hours, maybe the day?" Dunne asked the uncle.

"Who says I want to be borrowed?" Starrell said. He pressed his hands together and flexed his muscles.

"Here," Dunne said. He gave Starrell an envelope containing one hundred and fifty dollars.

"Borrowed was a euphemism," Dunne said. "You'll be paid."

"To be a Secret Agent man?" Starrell said and laughed. "A government man? Unc, he tell you where he's from?"

Dunne turned to the uncle.

"Does he have your permission?" Dunne asked.

"Fuck, I don't need his permission."

Dunne stared into the reflective plastic of Starrell's sunglasses. "You work for him. He's your uncle. You need his permission."

"You work for the government?" the uncle asked.

Dunne nodded.

"The white man's government?"

"Everybody's government," he said.

The uncle chuckled in disdain: "Well, I don't give no nevermind. Take him and give me peace for one day. But tomorrow he better fix the toilet on the fourth floor. We just got one working now. Boy won't tell you. But he's good at plumbing, wiring, and building. Only reason why I put up with all that."

Dunne took *that* to mean the dress, the attitude, the disrespect.

"He must be good, then," Dunne said with a smile.

He left the office. Starrell waited several seconds before following. Outside the building, Starrell rousted a homeless man sitting by the entrance.

"Told your skanky HIV-ass to beat it," Starrell said. He poked the man with his foot. The fellow crawled a few feet, then got up, and moved off. Dunne gently placed a hand on Starrell's shoulder. Starrell jerked back and waited for Dunne to remonstrate him.

"Any place to get a good burger around here?" Dunne asked.

"Just Mickey D's. My unc says there used to be all these lunch counters around. Lunch counters, lunch counters. He goes on like it's a fuckin' fairy tale. Run by black men. Where black men ate black and talked black. But the chinks squeezed 'em out. Now it's all chink around here."

"Let's try this one," Dunne said.

The two entered a Chinese restaurant and sat in the back.

"Please take off your glasses," Dunne said.

"What's it to you?" Starrell shot back.

"I like to see someone's face when I do business with them."

Starrell took off the sunglasses and hung them from the collar of his sweatshirt. He had what Dunne called seeing eyes.

A waiter came by, and Dunne said several words to him in Chinese. The waiter nodded and left two menus.

"Whatcha say?" Starrell asked.

"It was just a Chinese greeting."

"You know Chink?"

"Mandarin, a few words."

"So what's the business?" Starrell asked.

"I want you to help me find the guy who rented that office in your building. Raymond."

"And how am I supposed to do that?"

"I've been told where he likes to hang out."

"Where's that?"

"Bars."

"Only a million of those."

"A certain kind."

"What kind?"

"I'll pay you well."

"You deaf. I said, what kind?"

"Twice as much as those sneakers."

"What is it?"

"Gay bars."

"NFW, man. You think I'm cruisin' in and out of the bender joints, looking for a fuckin' 'mo? That stuff makes me sick."

Dunne pointed to the sneakers: "Three times as much."

"Shit, I can do that by truckin' a paper bag 'cross the street."

"But you don't. Do you?"

Starrell took his sunglasses and tapped them against the Formica tabletop.

"Why not?" Dunne asked.

" 'Cause."

"Because why?"

"Just 'cause."

"Bullshit. You scared?"

"You want a fuckin' reason. I'll give you a fuckin' reason. Willie's little brother, Marco. You want more?"

Starrell was shouting, and the waiters were staring.

"I'll give you more. Steven Reeves. Macky Dobb's sister. Ty Forrest. Hitch Blackwell. Tamika's brother Wendell. My cousin Barry. Ask my unc about him."

"All dead?"

"You're a fuckin' genius," Starrell muttered.

Dunne called over the waiter and ordered for both of them.

"I hate this slop," Starrell said.

"It won't be too hard. You go to the bars, you look around, you ask for Raymond. You know what he looks like. And if anyone asks why, you tell them he left stuff behind when he moved his office and you have it."

"Why don't you go lookin' for the fag?"

"If I go looking for him, people will wonder why. I'm a little more visible than you. My picture's been in the papers a lot this week."

" 'Cause of the blow-away at the White House?"

"Yeah, the blow-away."

"And what if any of my buds catches my ass going into an ass-fuckers hole?"

"Tell them Raymond owes your uncle money and you're looking for his sorry ass."

"And how I'm supposed to know where to be going?"

"I have a list."

Starrell raised an eyebrow.

"Consulted with a friend," Dunne said.

"If one of those pussies fuckin' looks at me—"

Dunne leaned in close to Starrell.

"You do nothing," Dunne said, his voice steely. "You walk away, and you keep looking for Raymond. This is a job. If you can't do it straight up, then screw it."

"How much?"

"The sneaks times three. That's for today. After that, we'll negotiate the additional pay."

"Rockford got five C's a day. And that was a long-ass time ago. Before fuckin' cable."

"Prove to me you're worth it."

"I'm fuckin' worth it."

"Just like you got to prove it to Tamika."

Starrell frowned; he crossed his arms.

"Don't you ever . . ."

Can't finish that sentence, can you? Dunne thought.

"Don't," Starrell said.

The food came. Dunne started in on the chow fung noodles. Starrell pushed aside his plate.

"Told you," he said.

Dunne poured tea into the two cups on the table.

"Okay," Starrell said, "but you got to tell me one thing."

"What's that?" Dunne asked.

"Why you're looking for that squirrel-face."

"Can't." Dunne spooned out hot chilies over the noodles.

"Then you don't got nobody to chase your cocksucker."

"Okay. And you go back to the toilet. Without six hundred dollars. And don't forget to tell Tamika what you turned down. So be it."

"So be your Tommin' ass."

Starrell slid back his chair, as if he were preparing to stand.

"It's about Big Man being dropped at the White House?"

"Can't say, Mr. Starrell. You want them to wrap this up for you? Maybe for your uncle?"

"You know what he says. He calls it white-on-white violence. That's fuckin' funny. Why should I fuckin' care he got popped?"

"You don't have to care. No one has to care."

Starrell remained in an about-to-stand position.

"Go on," Dunne said. "Don't give a damn. Go clear the shit out of the pipes. This is honest work"—Dunne wondered to himself as he said this— "and if your head is too hard or your heart is too scared to do it and pocket a week's pay in a day, then get going. This only works if I can trust you."

Starrell leaned forward.

"And if I trust you," he said.

"That's right. Two hundred up front, the rest at the end of the run. Deal?"

"But, you know, I'm just doin' this for my unc. Don't want nobody running out on him. And it's three at the start."

"Two-fifty," Dunne said. He put out his hand. Starrell traced his fingers against Dunne's.

"This shit taste any better if you put that on it?" Starrell pointed at the hot chili.

"Yes, but go light. And we've got to do something about your clothes."

"Fuck that," Starrell said. He scooped up a large spoonful of the chilies and dumped it on his noodles. He took a bite and winced. Starrell said nothing. He looked Dunne in the eye, chewed, and swallowed.

24

Addis and Rudd were halfway through New Orleans International when a black women rushed toward them. She was carrying a sign that read "Stop the Killing." Behind her were a dozen other black women; several were holding on to small children. She had recognized Addis.

"You have to tell the President, that new President Mumfries, what's going on down here," she shouted in Addis's face.

"Please do something," urged another. "Our babies are dying. Our people are being killed." Others surrounded Addis.

Rudd stepped to the side. She picked up a leaflet the women were distributing. The literature cited New Orleans as the city with the most murders per capita. It noted that the local police force was underfunded, corrupt, and inefficient—the worst in the nation. It asked all tourists visiting New Orleans to express their concern about public safety in the city.

An airport security guard pushed the women away from Addis. But Addis dismissed the guard, and he calmed the group. He asked them to explain what they were doing. He listened intently. He promised he would bring their leaflet back to the White House.

"Bless you in Jesus' name," said a woman wearing a red hat. She engulfed Addis in a hug.

He wished them well. Then he and Rudd proceeded to the rental car counter. "Think you can help them?" Rudd asked.

"No," he answered.

They checked into a bed-and-breakfast in the lower French Quarter. It was several blocks from the small hotel where they had stayed four years before. Their suite looked like an antique shop, cluttered with pieces and knickknacks from various periods. Dark red drapes hung over the windows. The wallpaper had a fish pattern. In the main room was a four-poster bed with a feather mattress. The door to the adjoining room was open, and Addis tossed his bag on the bed there—a clear reminder, he thought. He asked Rudd if she wanted to have lunch at Antoine's. Sure, she said. He told her that he first had to make a few phone calls.

"That's alright," she said. "I'll walk to the river. I can never get over that the river is above the city."

How strange is this?

"Have fun," he said.

After Rudd left, Addis went to the pay phone in the alcove off the lobby. He called Whalen and arranged to visit him that afternoon. He then tried Harris Griffith, the accountant, and got the answering machine again. He called directory assistance and obtained an address for Griffith. Next Addis dialed Mickey Burton, the parish chair in Alexandria, and made plans to see him the next day. He returned to the room. When Rudd came back, they went to lunch.

The maitre d' at Antoine's hugged Addis at the door. He cried and offered his condolences.

"He was loved," the host said. "You see that now."

"Yes, he was," Addis replied.

The maitre d' did not ask if he had a reservation. He seated them in a booth and wiped his face with a handkerchief. He patted his moustache.

"And how long are you in town?" he asked.

"A few days. A short break."

"And you are staying where?"

Always working. Everybody is always working. Tell him; he tells the Times-Picayune, *and there's a photographer stationed there. A trip to New Orleans by a senior Hanover aide counts as news here.*

"Nearby," Addis answered. He knew to expect a reporter outside the restaurant by the end of the meal. That could not be avoided, and that was the point. Best to hide in plain sight, he thought. Better to be photographed, he figured, than to be caught avoiding being photographed. Having Rudd at his side helped.

"Can I have the chef prepare something special for you and your friend?"

"Please."

The meal arrived—a crayfish stew. And when they were done, the waiter refused to provide a bill. Instead the maitre d' came over and said the meal was a gift from him.

"But I'm not allowed to accept gifts," Addis explained.

"Then it is a gift for your lovely friend." He nodded toward Rudd.

"Thank you," she said.

A reporter was waiting for Addis outside the door. He was a young man, his face pock-marked. Next to him was a photographer.

"Nat Ridenhauer," he said. "The *Picayune*. Don't want to be a shit. But would you mind if I ask why you're visiting New Orleans?" He held out a tape recorder.

"Not a problem," Addis said. "I just wanted to get out of Washington for a few days with a friend."

"And her name?"

Rudd had moved away.

"If you think it's necessary. It's Holly Rudd." He spelled the last name.

"And what line of work is she in?"

"That's not important," he said. "She's an old friend, that's all. But I'm sure you can find her on Nexis if you're determined."

"And no business here?"

"No."

"You're not going to stop in on the governor, then, to talk about—"

"It's nothing personal, but no—"

"About what President Mumfries is doing next—"

"Really, I'm here on personal time. A few days. So I'm not going to get into any—"

"Well, then can you share your feelings about what you think Mrs. Hanover should do?"

"Not today, Nat. Is that enough? . . . I think that's about it."

"I guess it will have to be," the reporter said. "Thanks a lot."

Rudd joined Addis, as he walked away. She tried not to pay attention to the photographer shooting them.

"Thanks again," he said. "I owe you."

"No you don't," she said. "But it does bring back memories."

Good? Bad?

"Do photos of you still make the wires?" she asked.

"Not as much as they used to."

"That must make life easier."

"Guess I haven't noticed," he said.

She chuckled, and Addis asked why she had laughed.

"I'm not sure," she said.

Addis dropped Rudd off at the Tulane law library. She had brought work with her and preferred to sit in the library rather than in their suite. He told her he'd be back in a couple of hours.

Flip Whalen lived near the school. Set back from the road, behind a cast-iron fence with a rose pattern, the house was pure Greek Revival, built, Addis recalled, in 1856 by a molasses mogul. Fluted Corinthian columns flanked a veranda in front. Jefferson Davis had spent three weeks here after the Civil War. The first time Addis had visited, Whalen escorted him through the grounds. He showed off the trees: crepe myrtle, sweet olive, pear, Japanese plum.

Addis walked the path that led from the driveway. He remembered the late-night sessions that Whalen hosted here during the campaign. In leather chairs in the library, Hanover, Addis, Finn, McGreer, Whalen, Margaret, and the others strategized and fine-tuned the campaign. Whalen's father had been the chief counsel to one of the oil companies that used to run the state, and he left his only child with a fortune. Whalen had devoted a portion of that inheritance to Hanover's first political campaign, when Hanover ran for attorney general and attacked the system that had done so well for the Whalens.

The front door was open. Addis shouted hello. No one came. He went to the back and found Whalen and his wife Amelia in the sunroom. The stereo was playing Bach. Whalen was helping Amelia get comfortable on a flower-patterned couch. Addis had not seen her since the inauguration. Her hair was gone, her skin pale yellow. Cancer had been traveling through her body: first, breast, then lymph nodes, and, most recently, throat. Addis waited by the door until Whalen finished arranging the pillows for Amelia.

"Flip," he said. "I let myself in. Hope you don't mind."

"Nah, buddy," Whalen replied. "*Mi casa es* . . . you know. Come here."

The two men embraced. There was little between Whalen's chest and back. Addis wondered if Whalen was getting slimmer. One good squeeze, and he would break like a breadstick.

Addis bent down and kissed Amelia on the cheek. It was hard for her to speak. She forced out a scratchy "hello" and then grabbed his hand. He felt her fingers trembling.

"Good to see you," Whalen said. "Here, sit. Can I get you anything?" Addis shook his head. "You know we were sorry we couldn't be in Washington for the. . . . But"—he looked at his wife—"we couldn't because . . . She had a few bad days."

"Everyone knows," Addis said. "They do."

"Yeah." Whalen stared out of the room and toward a flock of grackle on the back lawn. He was wearing a jacket and a tie. Even at home, Whalen always dressed up.

"How's she doing?" Whalen asked.

"Pretty well, I think."

"Ready for the run?"

Does he mean me or her?

"I don't know. I'm staying clear. What does she tell you?"

"And how's Jackie-boy?"

"He's holding up. Spending a lot of time with Lem."

Whalen shot out a laugh. "That Lem. Always by their side." He pulled a cigar out of his coat pocket and unwrapped it.

"Don't smoke 'em," he said. "Just chew 'em. . . . What can I do for you, Nick?"

"It's about that reporter. The one asking about that land deal in Rapides."

"Yeah, he came by. I'd gone to the store. Patty, the cleaning woman, let him in. I came back and found him trying to talk to Amelia about all that. I escorted him out. Roughly, too."

His wife managed to smile at him.

"Told you most of what I know on the phone. But there was another little problem we had. Margaret was asked to be on the board of this company building day-care centers. Turns out one of the backers was a lawyer in Metarie who represents mob guys. The *Picayune* got ahold of it. We got her out. She gave the money back. Twenty-five grand a year. Real money for them."

"You mentioned an ethics officer who vetted the finances of state officials."

"Yeah. I checked after we talked. I should have remembered. But I was blind-trusted and never had to deal with it. His name was Cummings. George Cummings."

"And where's he now?"

"Maybe chatting up a storm with Bob. Died a few months ago. Prostate."

"And the records of his review?" Addis asked. "Would they be somewhere?"

"Supposed to be," Whalen replied. "All supposed to be preserved like holy texts until Kingdom Come. But you go try to find something in the state archives. They couldn't even locate the central files of our first term when I was thinking of doing that book on the early years. Then there was a fire. They can't even tell us what was lost."

"Tell me about the accountant."

"Griffith, Harris Griffith. Didn't look like an accountant. Tall, thickly built fellow, with this full beard. Looked like a lumberjack. Don't know how they chose him. But he got into trouble with the feds. He was the accountant for one of these S&Ls. The bank crashed, had to be bailed out, upwards to thirty mil. You know the drill: bad real estate loans, lending to directors, et cetera. The officers and directors got caught with empty pockets. So the feds went after the lawyers and the accountants who had signed off on reports saying everything's jim-dandy. A while back, I got a call from Griffith. Asked if I could talk to Bob about him. I said, 'Nope.

Can't do it.' He said he understood. The feds kept after him. The firm kinda fell apart."

Amelia was making a stuttering sound. She was pointing at her mouth. Whalen went to the kitchen and returned with a glass of water and a straw. He placed the straw in her mouth and held the glass for her. With his free hand, he stroked her head.

"Do you think that Mason could have been involved?" Addis asked.

"With that land deal? Doubt it. After that first campaign, the blood was so bad. Those stories were true. Didn't have to make it up for that TV movie. Boy, did Chasie hate me. He and my daddy did business together. I was a traitor to the regime. My daddy once told me that he had seen Chasie at the Jefferson Club in Baton Rouge. This must've been when Bob was still AG, but right after Jackie was born. 'Don't it break you up you can't see him?' my daddy asked. 'Yeah, sure,' Chasie said. 'But he's still my flesh and blood. And they can't ever take that away.' You know, I don't know if Chasie ever got to see the boy. That is, in person."

Whalen removed the straw from his wife's mouth and placed the glass on a table.

"What's the deal with Margaret and Mumfries?" Addis asked. "I still can't figure that out."

"Don't see how it's related to this. But Mumfries's family owned a bunch of businesses here. Some freight companies. Natural gas. Construction. Bunch of local papers. Had to be some crossover with Chasie. Sam, though, never went into all that. Cut out on his own. Got far, far away. All the way to . . . the state next door. They never liked each other. But, you know, funny thing is that if it weren't for her, he wouldn't be President today."

Addis's expression asked why.

"Was on her advice," Whalen said, "that Bob took on Sam."

"I never saw her push for Mumfries. In all those meetings, she only asked questions about whoever was being discussed."

"I was there, too. But I was also here, in this room. Night before he made up his mind. She asked if I wouldn't mind leaving them be for a minute or so. I did and went to the kitchen. But I could still hear them. She said he had to pick Sam. For the obvious reasons. He balanced out the ticket in politics, and he could give them Texas. 'Thought you hated him,' he said. 'Doesn't matter,' she said. 'Only one thing matters.' I got to feeling guilty—listening in like that—and went out to the veranda."

He paused. "First time I think I ever told anyone that. Right, Amelia?"

She nodded.

"Except for Amelia."

She smiled again.

"And the thing of it is, we would've won without Texas. But who knew that then?"

"You think Margaret has reason to worry about this deal?" Addis asked.

Whalen rearranged the books on the coffee table in front of Amelia.

"Not that I know, but she's a thorough woman. Always has been."

Amelia rolled her eyes. Her husband did not notice. For my benefit? Addis wondered. Or an involuntary sign of discomfort?

"Guess I should be going," Addis said.

He said good-bye to Amelia. There was a tear at the edge of her eye. Whalen removed a handkerchief from his pocket and dabbed at it. He then took Addis by the arm and escorted him from the sunroom.

"Gets pretty emotional. You can imagine." Before Addis could reply, Whalen was on to another subject: "Was playing golf with Bob a few months back. He told me that he thought Sam was being a bit too friendly with this woman in the White House. Katie somebody. But then Bob always thought that about everyone."

Addis knew whom he meant. She worked in the domestic policy shop. He had heard the rumors. He didn't want to be drawn into this conversation.

"Do you think Margaret should?" Addis asked.

"Don't think Bob would have any problem with it. Probably get a kick out of it."

At the door, Whalen gave Addis a hearty handshake.

"Flip, one more thing," Addis said.

"What's that?" Whalen asked.

Addis discerned a trace of irritation in Whalen's voice.

He knows what I'm going to ask about. He must. Or is he just tired? Didn't he already say there was nothing to it? The guy was on drugs. His other stories didn't check out. Case closed, right? A stiff swinging in the county lockup. A suicide. Case closed. Live with it.

"Nothing, Flip. It was great to see you and Amelia."

"She's a fighter, Nick, I got to tell you. She's a fighter."

"I can tell."

Addis stood before a rundown building a few blocks from the criminal courthouse, an area of unused warehouses and cheap office space. There were three bail bondsmen storefronts on the street. In the lobby, he found a directory written on a piece of cardboard and taped to the inside of what once was a glass case. He started up the stairs, grabbing the wooden railing. A slab of dry paint came off in his hand.

151

On the third floor, Addis rapped on a grime-encrusted glass door. No one answered, but the door opened. He stepped in gingerly.

"Harris, you mother-fucking—"

A woman ran out of the other room in the suite. She was tall, her hair platinum blond. She wore high heels and a short black skirt. She was waving a gun and came to a stop when she saw him.

"You're not Harris."

"Thank God," he said.

She put the gun in the shiny black purse slung over her shoulder.

"He gave it to me," she said of the gun, and shrugged.

No one else was in the suite. The room held two filing cabinets. One desk had a cheap calculator on it. A stack of papers sat on another desk. Cardboard storage boxes was piled against the wall. On the opposite wall, a calendar was turned to the wrong page: a bucolic snowy scene of a country church.

"You know where he is?" she asked.

"No. I just came by to see him."

"That shit. I went to the safe deposit box. Two pair of earrings, a neck-lace, a broach, and a bracelet—all missing. He gave them to me when he was riding high. Told me I had the only key to the box."

Her nails were bright red, her lips the same. Orange patches glowed on her cheeks. She wore flashy rings on six of her fingers. She was in her late forties, he thought. But the skin around her eyes was drum-tight.

"So I came to get them back. What do you want with the snake?"

"To talk to him about some old business. I guess you don't know where he is?"

"No, and his lawyer won't say where he's at. I want this divorce over and done with. His asshole creditors are driving me nuts."

Addis asked for the lawyer's name. She pulled a business card out of the purse.

"Can hardly say it. Fucking Polack."

Addis wrote the name and number on a scrap of paper.

"I think I'm going to wait a while," she said. "See if the scumbag shows."

She took a seat and put her feet on a desk. She patted the bulge in her purse. Addis started asking questions. She told him that Griffith's firm had fallen apart after the banking investigators began their inquiry. At the same time, his investments—primarily risky future options—collapsed. He filed bankruptcy. She kicked him out. She let him back. He tried to keep a practice going. He hooked up with this export/import guy whom she suspected was smuggling dope. And Griffith was using. She booted him again. She let him back again. She came home one day, and he and the export-import dealer were in the house with two bimbos. There were

152

coke lines on the coffee table. She threw him out, and that was it. Their attorneys were in charge now. The bank case was going to trial. Her jewelry was gone.

"If you find him before I do, let me know, hon, okay?" she asked.

He promised.

"Tracy Griffith," she said.

She recited her phone number and waited for him to write it down.

"Thanks a bunch," she said. "And close the door for me on the way out. I'd like this to be a surprise. He probably forgot I have the keys."

He moved to the door.

"And, hon, sorry about Mr. Hanover. I didn't vote for him 'cause of the capital gains stuff. I needed the break. But I'm sorry all the same."

Addis found Rudd in the Tulane law library. She asked for fifteen more minutes. He called McGreer's office. There was nothing for which he was needed. He checked his messages—no calls from Dunne. Then he called the lawyer with the Polish name.

"Yeah," a man answered.

Addis stumbled over the pronunciation.

"Just say, 'Joe Mik,' " the gruff voice advised.

Addis introduced himself and said he was looking for Harris Griffith.

"Listen," Joe Mikolajczyk said, "I'm not sure I should even tell you I know where he is. What do you need from him?"

"Some old paperwork needs to be resolved. I thought he could help."

"I gotta tell you: he's not in a very helpful mood these days. And as one of the people he owes big I do try to encourage him to spend his time in pursuits that enhance his financial position."

"I understand. Please ask him to call me here or in Washington."

"And I gotta tell you, don't think you can come around and expect us to jump. I don't play the game everyone else down here plays. Got that? I don't jump. Not for dead guys. Not for live guys."

"I do, Mr. Mikolajczyk." He spoke the name deliberately.

"That's good. You almost got it right." Mikolajczyk hung up.

On the way back to the library, Addis passed a student lounge. The news was on the television. Wynn Gravitt, the House Majority Leader, was on the screen criticizing the lack of progress in the assassination investigation. Addis paused to watch and ignored the students' stares.

"As a member of the commission, I am simply appalled that we don't know more than we do," Gravitt was proclaiming. "This is not the time for partisan shots. But I have sent a letter to President Mumfries setting out my concerns."

Wesley Pratt might be too polite to exploit an assassination, Addis thought, but not Gravitt.

As Addis and Rudd drove back to the bed-and-breakfast, she asked if they could swing by First Street and Liberty.

"Sure," he said. "Why?"

"There's this book that's a favorite of a friend of mine. Part of it takes place on that corner. Just wanted to see it. Tell him I did."

"Okay."

She's not going to volunteer more. I'm not going to ask.

When they reached the corner Rudd turned her head to absorb each quadrant of the intersection: a brown brick church, an empty lot covered with litter, a child-care center with wrought-iron security bars on the doors and windows, a white cottage with blue trim. A young black man was pacing by the lot. He looked like he was waiting for someone.

"Not too special, is it?" Addis said.

"No, not at all."

He glanced at her. She was looking out the window and smiling.

"Maybe K-Paul's tonight?" he asked.

"More photographs?"

"Maybe."

"If that's what you *need*," she said.

"Thank you," he said and glanced at her. She was looking at the corner as they drove away.

Jeff's favorite book, right? She's comparing us.

"I'd ask you how it went today," she said, "but I don't think I'd get much out of you."

"Not yet."

"Someday?"

"Maybe. When I can."

"That's what I thought."

At the bed-and-breakfast, there was one message for him. It was from Evan Hynes-Pierce, and the number was local.

154

25

Dupont Circle

June 27

Starrell burst through the doors of the fast-food restaurant and bound up the stairs to the second floor. Dunne was in a booth at the back.

"I hate those cake-boys!" Starrell said and slammed his body into the booth. He pounded his hands against the tabletop.

They got to make noise, Dunne thought. That's how they can tell they're here.

"This white dude comes up to me and says, 'Know what I like more than anything else? Chocolate blow pops.' This shit's too much, man."

"And what did you do?" Dunne asked.

"Shit, should've messed him. . . . But I walked away from the fucker." Starrell grabbed French fries from Dunne's tray.

"Did the drill. Looked around. Didn't see him. Asked this freak behind the bar—man, he had all this metal shit sticking out of his body—if he knew this Raymond fuck. He says, 'Oh, you looking for a daddy.' I keep my cool and tell him the story. He don't know Raymond either. He says, 'Maybe I can help you tonight.' I don't think so, cocksucker."

Dunne sipped his coffee.

"Don't be looking at me like that," Starrell said. "I didn't say that. I just say thanks and I book. That makes three of these joints. And I ain't liking it any better. Thought I saw a homey going into the record place next door. But if he see me, he wouldn't know it, right? Not in these Joe College rags."

Starrell was wearing dark slacks, dark shoes, and a white shirt with a collar. Old church clothes, he had explained when Dunne picked him up at the Bennington Gardens projects. What he wore to funerals. The gold chain, the dark sunglasses were gone.

"There's two more bars around the corner," Dunne said.

"Man, I bet he ran his squirrelly ass out of town. I should get me a burger."

"I'll treat you to some real food when you're done. If there's nothing at the first, you can go straight to the other one. Then meet me across the street. I'll be upstairs at the Greek place."

"Shit, you be stuffing your face, and this hungry nigger's starving."

"See you in forty-five minutes. Remember, don't rush in and out. Stay for a few minutes in each one. Okay?"

Starrell nodded.

Dunne crumbled up the food wrapping on his tray and got up.

"And wait a minute after I leave before you do."

"That's heavy spy shit, man."

Dunne checked his watch. Forty-five minutes exactly. No way, he thought, I'm going to have those personnel evaluations done for Grayton tomorrow. The door opened, and Starrell came in.

"First joint same as the others."

"And the other?"

"Don't see him there. So I be talking to the guy at the door. Big-ass nigger. Don't look like no bitch to me. Used to work for one of those Congress guys. Tells me the name. I don't know it. Who cares about those fucks? But I don't tell him that. He asks me, 'What you want?' Like he knows I ain't there to party. I tell him about Raymond. He don't says he knows him. He don't says he don't. So I ask him where else to go, like where would Raymond be hangin' near Chinktown. But I don't call it that. So he tells me about this other place. He writes it down—the address."

"Why did you start talking to this fellow in the first place?" Dunne asked.

"Don't know. Just did. Getting sick of this empty trip."

"And you want to follow this lead?"

"Ain't too far from my unc's building. He could walk it."

"Good thinking, Mr. Starrell."

Dunne gave him a ten-dollar bill and told him to take a cab and then find him afterward at the Italian restaurant at the corner of Sixth and New York, the one with the bright neon sign.

"Where you been?" Starrell asked. "Don't you know no rag-head cabbie gonna pick up a nigger?"

"In those clothes, you'll be fine."

"Yeah, that's right. Like this is it: I got the magic fuckin' white-man cammies. Bet your ass, I could get me a job at the White House in this."

"I'm glad you think so. This time you leave first and I'll wait."

"And I want my money tonight. Don't FedEx me. No next-day delivery shit, this time."

"Yes sir, Mr. Starrell," Dunne said. "Now go to work."

The room was dark, and Starrell squinted. Shit, he thought, there's cowboy shit everywhere. Cowboy posters on the walls. Cowboy hats hanging, too. Those white skulls with the horns you always see in the movies. The jukebox was loud. Some sad-voiced woman was wailing:

Loneliness surrounds me
Without your arms around me.

The place was crowded. Waiters were wearing open leather vests with nothing on beneath them and those type of pants you see on riders in the rodeo. Starrell's uncle once had made him watch a television show about black men in the West. Starrell hated watching all that stuff about slavery. But he remembered this black rodeo champion who was shot and killed in a bar after winning a big rodeo. Some white fuck didn't like how he was celebrating his victory.

This is buggin', Starrell told himself. Cowboy bitches.

His eyes adjusted to the light. He started roaming and looking for Raymond. He tried not to mind the stares he drew. In the back room, there was a mechanical bull. He'd seen that in a movie, too. By the stairs, he saw a life-size poster of a scraggly white boy wearing a rumpled hat, a bandana, and dusty old boots. In his left hand the boy held a beat-up rifle as if the gun were a cane. If Starrell weren't in a gay bar, he might have laughed at the picture. This white boy had a smooth face, half-closed eyes, and a crooked nose. Looks like a retard dressed up for Halloween, he thought. He read the panel next to the photograph: "William Bonney, 1878, a.k.a. Billy the Kid." Shit, he knew who that was. And Starrell had grown up with a guy who had joined a crew at Bennington. By the time the guy was fourteen, he had popped six suckers. Everyone started calling him Billy the Kid. Then he was popped walking his momma to the clinic.

Starrell took the stairs to the second and third floors, each had a bar and a balcony. There were only a few people on the third floor. No Raymond. He went back down to the second. The bar was mostly empty. But the balcony was packed with leather boys, cowboy boys, and bare-chested muscle-boys milling about. As they passed one another, bodies brushed. No one said "Excuse me." At the doorway to the balcony, a group of tall, brawny men in T-shirts and buzz-cuts were drinking Buds.

Shit, Starrell thought, no fuckin' way to check this out without . . .

He considered taking a pass on the balcony. But what if that fuckin'

157

Raymond was out there? he asked himself. So fuckin' what? Mister Man won't know. I ain't being paid enough to be meat. But . . .

"Fuck this shit," he said under his breath.

He clenched his fist and stepped out to the balcony.

"Hey, private," one of the Bud-drinking men said to him. "Hello."

He placed a hand on Starrell's shoulder.

Starrell's reflexes kicked in. He knocked the hand away and faced the man head-on.

"Fuck you," he said.

"The balcony is for friendlies, little big man. You ought to know the rules. Or leave."

The man's friends formed a half-circle around Starrell.

"I think you owe my friend here an apology," one said.

"Just don't be touching me," Starrell snapped.

"Doesn't sound like an apology to me," another said.

Shit, cool it down, Starrell told himself.

"I'm just lookin' for somebody," he muttered.

"Still not an apology," one of the men said.

"And you know," said the man who had touched Starrell, "we're all just looking for somebody. That's why we're here."

He turned to his friends: "This young man does not understand the rules. I think it would be a public service if we—"

Two of the men grabbed Starrell by the arms. He tried to squirm out of their holds. But the grips were tight. He kicked at them. But his feet found no target. He felt himself being lifted off the ground. He was carried inside to the bar area.

"Let go, motherfuckers!" he shouted.

He heard the men laughing.

Then a huge hand passed by his face and connected with one of the hands holding his right arm.

"Shit," someone said in pain.

"Break it up, you fags," a new voice was saying. "Stop it. Now!"

The grips loosened and Starrell's feet returned to the floor. A large man with a long red beard was pushing the men away from Starrell.

"Shit, it's not even past eight o'clock. What the hell's going on?"

"Sorry, Big Daddy, this punk was not being friendly on the balcony," one explained, "so we decided to remove him from the field of action."

"Do I pay you boys to MP my place?" Lopez asked.

No one said anything.

"Fucking-A right, I don't."

He waved his hands at them: "Go back to your party. And let me worry about what goes on here."

158

The gang shuffled toward the balcony. Starrell thought about bolting. But this scene was too weird and this man too big.

"You—come with me!"

Lopez grabbed Starrell and pulled him down the stairs, to an office in the back of the ground floor. He pushed Starrell into a wooden chair. An arm to the chair fell off.

"Got to get that fixed," Lopez said. "Pound it back in for me, okay?"

He sat behind his desk and introduced himself: "But I ain't no spic. Not that there's something wrong with spics. Just want people to know."

"Sure, alright," Starrell said.

Motherfucker could be a pro wrestler, Starrell thought. With that long red beard, he could call himself the Viking Volcano.

"Boy, now what are you doing here?" Lopez asked. "And don't you get stressed-out; that 'boy' ain't no black thing. I call everybody 'boy'. Okay?"

"Can I call you 'boy'?" Starrell stared hard at Lopez.

Lopez laughed and slapped the desk.

"Call me whatever you fucking want. But tell me what you're doing here. My queer radar don't pick up a signal. So what do you want?"

"Looking for this Raymond dude. Looks squirrelly. You know him?"

"Fuck, this ain't no lost and found. Yesterday, and now this. What is it? Find-a-fag week?"

Starrell didn't follow him. But he watched as Lopez picked up a business card from his desk.

"Why you looking for him?" Lopez asked.

"Got some stuff of his. Some papers."

"And what are you going to do when you find him?"

"Ask if he wants them back."

"So you're a do-gooder, then?"

The door opened, and a blond-haired man came into the room.

"What is it?" Lopez barked.

"Another of the narc boys is here. Says he wants to talk to you."

"Tell him, I'll be right there."

The door closed, and Lopez stood. He dropped the card on the desk.

"Fucking cops," he said to Starrell. "They keep coming in here and telling me they think this place is a major transit point. That's camel shit. They want to look around. But if I drop a *C* on them, it's gonna be cool. The cost of doing business in the capital of the fucking Free World. You"—he pointed at Starrell—"don't move your butt. I'll be back."

Alone, Starrell examined the empty office. There was a poster for an old movie on one wall. He knew one of the names on the poster: Marilyn Monroe. But he didn't know the other two names. Both were men. There was a photo of Lopez with his arms around two white guys. They were wearing T-shirts and military khakis and standing in front of a helicopter. Hanging on the door was a black bull whip. His arms hurt where the men had held him.

Lopez returned to the office.

"You can stop a lot of useless talk with a hundred," he said.

He leaned against the desk.

"You're lucky, boy, that I landed when I did. You were messing with America's finest."

Starrell didn't catch the reference.

"Marines, you motherfucker."

"Those guys upstairs?"

"Affirmative."

"Shit, man, you're telling me they're fag Marines?"

Lopez put his hands together as if he were praying.

"Thank the fucking Lord, my son."

"No way."

"Fucking way, boy. What could be better for a fag-bar owner? Those lads can drink a god-damn sea all night and still run their six in the A.M."

"And . . . you?"

"I own the place. That's all anyone has to know about me."

"But is you . . . was you a Marine?"

Starrell nodded toward the photograph of Lopez by a helicopter.

"Kinda. But my story's not priority-one here, ace. You are. Why are you looking for Brother Raymond?"

Fuck, Starrell thought, he knows him.

"I told you."

"Tell me again."

Starrell went through the story.

"And why'd you come here?"

"A girl who worked there was complaining to me he never was there to TCB. She told me about here. Said she knew he be coming here. So I came to scope."

"Listen," Lopez said. "I don't suffer bullshit. And I don't like punks snooping around here. I make my money off a clientele that appreciates privacy. You see a scene out front like they got on P Street?"

Starrell shook his head.

"Damn straight. Can't even tell what's going on inside. And we've been here for years. On a need-to-know basis."

Lopez pulled on his beard and put his face in front of Starrell's.

"So don't *be* scoping round here no more. Got it?"

Starrell could taste Lopez's stale breath.

"Yeah," he said. "But I got to find Raymond. You know him?"

160

"If what you've got is important, I'm sure Raymond will find you. People got a way of knowing when they're being looked for."

"But if you see him, you tell him, okay? He probably don't know what he left behind is important."

"We all leave stuff behind. And speaking of that . . ."

Lopez grabbed Starrell's arm, right where it hurt. He yanked him toward the door.

"Excuse my manners," Lopez said. "But if I stop watching these fags for five minutes, the shit hits the rotor."

They left the office and Lopez pushed Starrell across the dance floor. The bar was filling up. Starrell bumped into a short, skinny man wearing cowboy boots, latex shorts, and a tank top. As Lopez propelled him along, Starrell searched the crowd for Raymond. Be a pro, he told himself. Do the job.

At the door, Lopez released his hold on Starrell and slapped Starrell's rear. "Now scoot," he said. Two patrons entering the bar laughed at the sight. But Starrell didn't care. He had found a place where Raymond could be found. And he could see the neon sign of the Italian restaurant where Dunne was waiting.

26

Foggy Bottom
June 27

The bar at Kinkead's was emptying out. Julia Lancette ran a finger along the rim of the wine glass. Above the bar, the television was turned to CNN. Only in Washington, she thought. Grayton was late. He had called her office twice to inform her he was running behind. That had given her more time to sit in her office chair, stare at her desk, and consider what she should do regarding her conversation with Charlie Walters. She had not heard anything from the red-bearded man at the Gauntlet bar, nothing about the man with a glass eye and the tattoo. She did not know what to do next.

President Mumfries was on the television. The sound was too low for Lancette to hear, but she knew what he was saying. Earlier in the day, at a luncheon held by a business lobbying group, he had declared he would run for President. As he made the announcement, Lancette's mother called, and they watched the speech together. "You know why he's making his announcement there," her mother had said. "Because there are no reporters to ask him what he thinks about Margaret Hanover running."

She pursed her lips. The lipstick felt odd. It had been a long time since she had worn any. Her hair was pulled back and held in place by a hair clip. She was wearing a knee-length, black dress, modestly cut, but it did accentuate her long neck and shoulders. Two men at the other end of the bar were staring at her. Both wore gray suits. One directed a half-smile at her. She tried to keep her face blank. The smiling man called the bartender over, spoke softly to him, and nodded his head toward her. Oh shit, she thought.

Grayton sat down on the stool next to her.

"I hate to begin with an apology, so instead: 'It's nice to meet you, Julia.' "

He held out his hand and she took it.

"No apologies needed."

"Hungry?"

She nodded.

"Good. To the table, then."

The hostess guided them to a booth. Grayton asked the hostess to inform Michael that he was here tonight and that he had brought plastic pouches to collect evidence. She laughed and walked away.

"The sous-chef used to be in the Bureau," Grayton explained to Lancette. "Left us, studied cooking, and—bang!—a whole new life. Last time President Hanover came here—shit, shouldn't have said 'last time,' but it was—he got food poisoning. Bad oyster. Nothing the place could have done about that. Hanover was great. Sent Bertis, the chef, a note inviting him to the White House for dinner. 'No hard feelings,' he wrote. 'But watch out. I'll be cooking.' Bertis and Michael were so relieved no one found out about the incident. Think of the publicity. But you didn't see anything about that, did you?"

"No, I didn't."

"And you must read a lot of papers and watch a lot of news."

Was he referring to her job?

"Yes, I do," she said.

"And nothing on this. See, some secrets can be kept. . . . Want to try the oysters?" He laughed.

"No thanks. . . . And if no one found out about the bad oyster, how do you know about it?"

"Well, no one rarely means *no one.*"

Without consulting the wine list, Grayton ordered a bottle. He suggested several choices for dinner that were not on the menu. They ordered.

"On to the obligatory portion of the evening?" he asked.

"Sure," she said.

He went first: Dartmouth, Eighty-second Airborne, NSC staff aide, several jobs in the community, headed the Bureau's antiterrorism office, then deputy directory. He mentioned the divorce.

"One fun fact: One summer, when I was kid, I stayed at my grandparents' on the eastern shore. Had this job driving cars across the Chesapeake Bay Bridge. Believe it or not, some folks cannot handle driving that four miles. Too long, too high. Panic attack. So the state paid us to drive them across in their cars. Then we'd wait for another anxiety case going back the other way. Back and forth, back and forth. A lot of miles. Not much distance. . . . And you?"

"Nothing all that exciting."

Washington University in St. Louis, the Woodrow Wilson School, and then straight to the DI. She assumed he knew the circumstances of her departure from the Directorate of Intelligence.

"And now, this," she said.

"Could you please be more vague?" he asked and laughed.

"Don't think so. But, I'm sure you know . . ."

"Yes, I do. I did my research. And as deputy director of the Bureau I would not ask you to disclose classified information. But it must be fascinating—maybe disconcerting?—to sift dirt from dirt."

"Never had it put that way. Just trying to help the DCI stay ahead of the bad P.R., which—"

"Never seems to end."

"Never seems to end," she repeated.

"And how do you feel about that?"

The appetizers arrived. A straw was sticking out of the crab and corn chowder Grayton had ordered. There was writing on the paper wrapper covering the tip: "Beware of warnings in soup." Grayton showed it to Lancette and drew a plastic pouch from his pocket.

"See? I was serious."

He placed the paper in the bag and sealed it. He wrote "Exhibit A" on the pouch. Smiling, Grayton asked the waiter to deliver it to Michael in the kitchen.

Fun and games, Lancette thought.

"The last week must have been hard on you," she said.

"Yes, a tough one. Unfortunately, those in our profession do not have the luxury of grieving during such times."

It's not *our* profession, she said to herself.

"I wish that everything could shut down for a while, so we could—"

"Feel?" He started the soup.

"Yes, I suppose so."

Grayton pointed the spoon at her.

"There's still a lot to do," he said.

"Did he do this on his own?"

"Probably. Usually the case."

"But usually we know the name," she said.

"That is right."

The waiter returned to their table.

"I have a message from the kitchen," he said. " 'There's no crime, if there's no evidence. Flush.' " He held out two empty hands and then left.

Lancette ignored the joke.

"Did you work much with President Hanover?" she asked.

"Sure. Not much one-on-one. But meetings on terrorist threats. Budgets. International crime. Gun stuff. I know Mumfries better."

"Why?"

"Coordinated a lot with him when he was running the intel committee. He was always supportive of us in the community, understood our work."

Our work—she felt jumpy. Just have dinner, she told herself. His call, this rendezvous—it could all be coincidence. They had passed in Wenner's office. Viv Novek was a notorious gossip. He was handsome, mildly amusing. She liked the line of his jaw. She counted the months she had been alone. Months? It was time to use the word *year.*

"Tell me about your family," he said. He refilled her wine glass.

Her father was a retired Army doctor and had moved his family from one military base to another around the world. During World War II, he was a junior clerk with a meteorological unit in England. Then one day everyone in his office was given a business suit and a pair of wingtip shoes and put on a plane, the destination a secret. They landed in Portugal, a supposedly neutral country, and set up shop in a closed insane asylum—from where they observed weather patterns in secret, wearing their business attire, not uniforms, and relayed the information to Allied command.

"We're both children of the military," Grayton said.

His father had been a welder who worked on nuclear submarines in a Connecticut shipyard.

The entrées arrived. As they ate, they talked about recent developments in the Balkans. He told her several funny stories about Wenner's meetings with visiting chiefs of foreign intelligence services. She mentioned she was considering getting a dog. She felt the wine and declined his offer of an after-dinner brandy. She said she should be going. He signaled for the check.

"You never did say how it makes you feel," he said.

"How what makes me feel?" she asked.

"Digging up the secrets of the community for which you work."

She dragged a fork across a plate and reorganized the chocolate torte crumbs.

"I don't really look at it as 'digging up' secrets," she said. "It's more like tending to weeds. And no one—"

She dropped the fork, and it fell to the floor.

"But maybe you should ask me again," she continued, "when I haven't had three glasses of wine."

At the door, he offered to drive her home. She said she could manage the short ride. She was parked across the street. He walked her to her car. The 1965 Dodge Dart was still damaged from the crash near headquarters, but it was running.

"What happened here?" he asked, inspecting the back of the car.

"An in-the-family accident, that's all."

"Sure you don't want a nightcap?"

One more drink, she thought, and I'd end up waking someplace I've never seen.

"No, thank you."

She got in, lowered the window, and turned the key. The starter made a clicking noise and went dead. She tried again. The engine caught, and she pumped the gas. The car rumbled. Grayton gave her a thumbs-up.

"I hope we can, again," he said.

"Okay," she said. "Thanks for the dinner. Good luck finding answers."

"We're both searchers, aren't we?" he asked. His smile was slightly skewed, but warm.

"Yeah," she said. "Two of a kind." She drove off.

It was past one o'clock. A tail light was out; her car was rattling more than usual. She knew she could not pass a DWI test. She drove slowly.

Could she like this jerk? Was he fishing for something? Was he or one of his buddies in the community—god, she hated that euphemistic term—concerned about her conversation with Walters? Hell, the last thing this bunch was—this collection of spies, saboteurs, covert warriors, satellite watchers, and clandestine managers—was a community. She had to tell someone about Walters. Should she inform Wenner of her trip to the bar? It probably violated several regulations. Was it improper use of official cover for nonofficial purpose? Or was it unauthorized assumption of duties?

Tending to weeds—she had never before explained her work that way. Not the same as growing something, she thought. Perhaps certain people were fated to clear space for others. Yet is that what she really wanted to do with her life, why she had gone to expensive schools, why she had put up with all the bullshit of "the community"? It's time to think, she told herself. Once all this—whatever "this" may be—was over.

She passed the Lincoln Memorial, crossed the bridge, and noticed a car close behind her. She tried to determine if there were any lights on its roof. She could not tell. She checked her speedometer; she was under the limit. She tapped her brakes. The car behind hers—it was a four-by-four—remained close. On the other side of the Potomac, she followed the signs for the George Washington Parkway. The four-by-four took the same exit. On the parkway, Lancette stuck to the right lane, hoping the other car would speed by. It switched lanes and began passing her. She turned on the AM radio.

The four-by-four slammed into the Dart. The impact threw her away from the wheel. The tires beneath her hit the gravel of the shoulder. She lunged for the wheel. Her car was heading for a steep embankment that

166

led to a slip of water. She pulled hard to the left. The Dart regained hold of the road.

Lancette looked to the left. The four-by-four was pacing her. The windows were tinted. She could not see the driver. The four-by-four plowed into her again and pushed the Dart to the edge of the road. She punched the accelerator, held the wheel tightly, and stayed on the road.

The four-by-four pulled back and then crashed once more into the Dart. Lancette's car skipped across the road toward the embankment. She heard the sound of the two cars grinding against each other. She heard herself yelling: "You fuck! You fuck! You fuck!" She felt her car losing the road, flying across the shoulder, toward the water.

She turned her face toward the four-by-four. She could see nothing behind the window.

Then the four-by-four jerked forward, as if pushed from behind. It shot ahead of her. She saw the black stretch of water. She yanked the wheel to the left.

A tree, damnit! She pounded the brakes and ducked. Metal slammed against wood. Her head hit the wheel. The windshield shattered. Lights streaked by. Glass fell on her. Pain raced through her chest, shoulder, and neck. She waited for another crash, another explosion, and before it arrived, she dropped into nothingness.

"Miss Lang. Miss Lang."

She tried to focus. Someone's hands were on her. A pounding echoed in her head. She was afraid to move. She felt pieces of the windshield in her hair.

"Miss Lang. Can you . . . ?"

She opened her eyes. A black man was next to her.

"Sit up if you can. But if it hurts, lie still."

She placed her right arm against the seat—no bolt of pain—and then pushed. Slowly, she propped herself upright. Glass tumbled off her.

"There you go. It's not too bad. I called for an ambulance."

She touched her forehead. It was wet, warm.

"You're banged up there, but it's not cut deep. Take this."

He placed a handkerchief in her hand and guided it to the wound.

"Don't press too hard."

There were no lights on the parkway. She could barely see the man. Then he leaned against the opened door and the interior light came on. Late-fifties, she guessed. A gray circle in his hair. His face was covered with sweat. He looked familiar. She wiggled her toes and carefully changed the position of her legs. They seemed fine. She tried to slide toward the door.

"Take it easy," he said.

"I think I'm okay," she said. "Let me try."

He moved out of her way, and she swung her legs out of the car. Her left shoulder and arm hurt.

"What happened?" she asked.

"I was behind you and saw this car smack right into you. Looked like he was trying to force you off the road. I came up on his rear and drove straight into him—pretty fast—to push him away. You went flying off the road. Hit this tree."

"And where'd he go?"

"He tore out of here. I couldn't chase after him. My headlights were gone, and a piece of metal was caught in one of the wheels. I pulled over."

He pointed down the parkway. She couldn't make out his car.

"An ambulance will be here soon," he said.

"Did you see who—"

"Got the license. . . . You don't know?"

She shook her head. She was trying to clear away the fog. The pain became sharper. She wanted to stand up and grabbed for the side of the door. He placed his hand on her shoulder.

"I think we should wait for the medics," he said.

Several cars drove by. The interior light went off. She did not want to look at the front of the car.

"Who are you?" she asked.

"My name is Clarence," he said.

"I've seen you. . . ."

"Dunne," he added.

A thought struck, and she felt frightened.

"You called me Miss Lang."

Shit, Dunne thought, a rookie mistake.

"Just trying to see if you'd wake up."

How the fuck does he know my cover? she asked herself. She moved back into the car.

"You should keep still," he said.

"How'd you know that was my name?"

"Went through your bag looking for I.D. But, don't worry, I didn't take anything."

She saw her bag on the front seat. There was glass on it.

Using both feet she kicked him in the stomach and pushed him back. She shut the door. Glass from the windshield fell into the car.

"Stay away!" she yelled. "Stay back!"

Dunne stepped toward the front of the car. He held his hands up. He spoke through the windshield frame.

"You're right. I lied. I didn't go through your bag. I was following you."

168

Lancette wished she had a gun.

"Why?" she shouted.

"Because we were both looking for someone in the same place."

"What place? Where?"

She looked around her car. Maybe she could find a loose screwdriver, a socket wrench.

"The Gauntlet," Dunne said.

She wondered if he had called an ambulance. How long had she been out? How long does it take for an ambulance to arrive?

"And?"

"And I thought we might see if our searches overlapped."

"And how'd you know I'd been there?"

"An associate of mine saw the business card you left behind there."

"So you followed me?"

"Went by your office tonight, saw you leaving. Took a shot. Got lucky."

"Instead of just approaching me?"

"My mistake. I apologize. I wanted to see what I could learn about you before I did approach you. But it's a good thing I did—"

"Yeah, real good. How do I know you weren't driving that car?"

"Guess you don't," Dunne said. "But it's unlikely I tried to kill you and then called 911, isn't it?"

Lancette could see flashing lights down the highway.

"Listen," Dunne said. "I was chief of security at the White House. And these days I'm not on Jake Grayton's A-list. I saw you with him tonight. So maybe it's stupid for me to be talking to you."

She didn't say anything. She heard a siren getting louder.

"I think we should have a chat and see if we have any mutual interests."

First Walters, she thought, then Grayton, then someone tries to kill me, now this guy wants to talk.

"Maybe," she said.

Dunne stepped toward the door of the car.

"But stay the fuck back for now!" she yelled at him.

He stood still.

Lancette closed her eyes and listened to the wailing of the ambulance.

27

Interstate Highway 10, Louisiana
June 28

Holly Rudd sat next to him in the car, doing *The New York Times Magazine* crossword puzzle. Addis kept the speedometer needle on 80. He knew that if he were pulled over in this state he would receive condolences, not a ticket. He tried to focus on what he needed to ask Mickey Burton, the party chair in Alexandria. He wondered how Hynes-Pierce had located him in New Orleans. He kept a watch for cars that might be following him. But he was distracted by Rudd.

So far, she had been a good sport. She had not bolted the previous night when a television camera crew filmed them leaving the restaurant. On the walk home she had pulled him by the arm when they passed a young man wearing a nun's habit and playing heavy-metal songs on an acoustic guitar. He shared a smile with her at the sight of the street performer, and he noticed that her hand lingered on his arm longer than necessary.

"Have you been happy, Nick?" she had asked. "I mean, well, up until . . . Sorry, that was stupid."

"Hard to tell," he had replied. "And you?"

"Think so. But . . ."

She didn't finish the sentence. They walked the rest of the way in silence. Not awkward silence. It had been the silence of memories. He had wondered what she was thinking, but he had not asked. He never liked it when someone posed that question to him, and he long ago resolved not to ask it himself. What's important is what's said, he thought. If anything.

Once back in the suite, he had said goodnight. The door between the rooms would not shut tight. He pushed on it and jiggled the knob so the door would stay closed. When he was in bed, the door popped open. A crack of light entered the darkened room. He could hear Rudd rustling the pages of the legal brief she was reading in bed. Soon she turned off the light. Thirty minutes later, he left the bed and peered through the space at the doorway. He could see her, in the glow of a streetlamp, a figure beneath the covers. He was curious if she still thrashed about at night. He watched her for several minutes. Not once · did she toss.

The car sped along, and they passed a barn with a faded advertisement for chewing tobacco on its side. Had he asked her here mainly to concoct an alibi? Or was he looking to reconnect with her? To return to a time before a certain discussion in a New Orleans hotel room, a time before a particular execution? If he could win her back, would that blot out what happened between then and now? How damn pathetic can one be? he asked himself.

Ten miles south of Baton Rouge, Addis clicked on the turn indicator.

"Gas?" Rudd asked.

"No, I want to show you something."

"What?"

"Won't take long," he said.

He exited the interstate and followed the signs to Duplessis. Before they hit town, he turned off the state highway and on to a dirt road.

"Where are we—"

"Just hold on," he interrupted.

The car bounced past a falling-down shed. The road led over a hollow and cut through the woods. Rudd noticed a wooden sign nailed to a post. The words were hand-painted in white: "For Gloria," above an arrow that pointed in the direction they were traveling.

Addis stopped the car in front of a ramshackle house. Smoke was coming out of the chimney. A horse was tethered by the front of the house. The front porch was crammed with junk: bashed-in television sets, beat-up furniture, rusty farm equipment. A chicken coop was on one side of the house, a barn on the other. Addis honked the horn and got out of the car. She followed and nearly stepped on a rooster running by.

A thin, elderly black man in overalls came out of the house.

"Mr. Addis!" he yelled.

"Mr. Pearson!" Addis shouted back.

The man stepped off the porch and grabbed Addis by the shoulders.

"I heard on the radio," he said, "you were down in the city, but . . . My, oh my, what are you doing here?"

"Taking a few days off."

"Guess you got it coming. I've been crying my eyes out. Just crying like a baby. Even this morning when I got up and heard this other fellow on the radio talking about it. I know it's an unholy world, but what makes someone want to go and do something like that?"

171

"Let me introduce you to a friend. Mr. Anthony Pearson, this is Holly Rudd."

Pearson took her hand.

"A pleasure, miss," he said.

"Do you have time for a quick tour?" Addis asked.

"You know the answer, Mr. Addis. C'mon."

Pearson led the pair to the barn.

"Mind them horse droppings," he said to Rudd. "The nag's got intestinal problems."

Above the entrance to the barn was another handmade sign that read, "For Gloria." Rudd looked at Addis and silently mouthed, "What is this?" He ignored the question, took her by the arm, and walked into the dark barn. Pearson hit a switch and a series of spotlights turned on.

The barn was full of shining sculptures of angels. Wherever she looked, Rudd saw another piece. Cherubic angels. Wise-old-men angels. Voluptuous women angels. She saw a soldier with wings, a little boy with wings, a farmer with wings. She guessed there were several hundred angels crammed into the barn. They all glittered. She looked closely at the nearest one—a woman with wings holding a baby—and saw the surface was aluminum foil.

"And see over there?" Addis asked.

"My god," Rudd whispered.

There was a life-size sculpted replica of Da Vinci's *Last Supper* against one side of the barn.

"Been doing this since my wife died in 1978," Pearson said. "Started the day after she died. Didn't know what else to do."

"Gloria?" Rudd asked.

"Yes," Pearson answered. "Finest woman ever."

He led Rudd through the barn. There was not much open space, and they had to squeeze between pieces. He explained that he used wire, papier-mâché, modeling clay, and foil, that he had made four hundred and thirty-seven pieces. All were angels, except for Jesus and his disciples. He pointed out the first angel he had made, the pieces that looked like his relatives, the sculptures that were based on famous people. The facial details were crude, but Rudd could identify two presidents, Frank Sinatra, and Henry Aaron. Some wore pieces of real clothing. Several had broken wings or missing details.

"Don't know whether I should be fixing the old ones or keep making new ones," Pearson explained. "It ain't like there are any rules for this."

"It's gotten pretty jammed in here, Mr. Pearson," Addis said. "What are you going to do?"

Pearson bent over and picked up a brown fedora that had fallen off an angel holding a briefcase. He put the hat back on the head.

172

"Been thinking about the ceiling. Maybe an etching in foil of what they got up there in the Sistine Chapel. My baby girl sent me a good book with all that laid out. But I ain't figured out how to do it. Can't get no scaffolding in here and"—he let out a raspy laugh—"my back ain't so good. But I was thinking, maybe I could cheat a little. Do it in the house— foil on plywood—and then hang it up in here. Think that would work?"

"I think it would be magnificent," Addis said.

"And you, Miss Rudd?"

She was, Addis could tell, stunned by Pearson's angels.

"Yes, sure," she replied.

Pearson tended to one set of wings that was hanging loose from a fireman. Rudd moved next to Addis.

"This is amazing," she muttered. "All for Gloria?"

"True love," Addis said. "Can you imagine?"

"Amazing," she repeated.

Pearson invited them into the house for lemonade, but Addis declined, explaining he had a meeting in Alexandria. Pearson escorted them out of the barn.

"Are any of these . . . is there one of Gloria?" Rudd asked him.

"I wouldn't dare," Pearson said quietly.

Rudd started to apologize for asking, but he held up a hand.

"Nah, nah. Everybody asks. Guess it's the natural thing to do."

At the car, Pearson told them to wait a moment. He ran into the house and returned with a camera.

"May I?" he asked Rudd.

"Okay," she said.

"You can be an inspiration."

He took the shot without asking her to smile.

"Now you tell Mrs. Hanover," he said to Addis, "that I've been praying for her and for the boy, okay?"

"I will," Addis said.

"And she should do whatever's in the heart. I been listening to the radio, so I know what's happening there."

"I'll tell her, Mr. Pearson."

Pearson started crying. He wiped his face with his sleeve.

"See, Mr. Addis, I told you," he said. "I'll go do this inside. You got to get going."

Pearson walked away.

Rudd didn't say anything to Addis until they were back on the state highway. She asked how he had first discovered Pearson and his angels.

"During the campaign," he said. "After . . . after the primaries. Heard about him from the guys on the gubernatorial staff. I asked Margaret if the story was for real. She said she and Bob had been out here a few times, when campaigning. So when I had the chance I came to see it for myself."

"Who'd you come with?"

You always know what to ask.

He had come with the deputy press secretary. They had slept together that night, when they returned to New Orleans. She had been the first woman he had made love to after splitting up with Rudd.

"A few people from the press office," he lied.

"And why did you bring me there?"

"I thought you'd like to see it."

"That's all?"

"That's all."

Rudd was silent for a few minutes.

"Damnit, Nick. You're always two places at once. Always operating on more than one level. I'm not even sure if you can see it."

He knew what she meant.

"God, did I hate you," she said.

"For what?"

"For being you and for not being you . . . For making me decide."

"Making you decide what?"

He steered the car on to the interstate and kept his eyes straight ahead.

"Between you and my . . . Oh, what the hell does it matter?"

She sounded like she was crying. He didn't want to look.

"You know," he said, "sometimes I think that maybe, maybe you were right about . . ."

He was edging toward it. Tell her or not? He knew they were both thinking about that conversation and the execution of a man neither of them ever met.

"I know, I know, I know," she said. "That's what makes it so goddamn awful and sad. Don't you see that? Don't you?"

"What do you mean?" he asked.

But he knew.

"Oh, forget it. We should've hashed this all out years ago. It doesn't matter now. It really doesn't. Really. I called you up after the assassination because I felt bad. Not only for that, but because I, I—"

"Never returned my calls?"

"Yeah—and never gave you the chance."

"For what?"

"To be mad at me. To tell me you were."

And this is your expiation? Be by my side, so poor Nick can let it all out? And you can move on. Be with what's-his-face.

"So now you're giving me the chance?"

"No, that's not it. I thought that . . ."

174

"Thought what?"

"Just that it would be good to see you and . . ."

Now that you're serious with someone else.

"And see if . . ."

"See what?" he asked.

"Oh, I don't know. I don't."

Addis stared at the stripes on the road. She can't say it, he thought. She can't tell me she's doing a compare-and-contrast before making a decision.

"And why, why really did you ask me to come down here with you?" Rudd said.

"For your help."

"That's it."

"Holly . . ."

She waited for more. But he did not know how to continue.

"Then it looks like," she said, "we both got what we wanted."

Rudd picked up the crossword puzzle and pulled a pen out of her pocketbook.

"How much longer do we have?" she asked.

He looked at her. Her face was red, her eyes wet.

"About two-and-a-half hours," he said.

"Okay," she said. "If you want me to drive some, let me know."

She stared at the puzzle and then wrote over several letters.

Mickey Burton was waiting for them at the bar in the Chesterfield Hotel. He was in his late twenties, short, big-eared, and wide-mouthed. He shook hands with Addis and his eyes drifted toward Rudd's chest. He took them on a brief tour of the hotel, which had been owned by his family for four generations. He noted that his grandfather had kept a suite on reserve for Huey Long's "private meetings." Then Rudd excused herself to stroll through town.

Burton brought Addis to the restaurant. He pointed at three elderly men sitting in a booth. "I invited some of the old boys down, but first we can talk," he said.

The two sat at the empty bar.

"Got a call this morning from Joe Rego," Burton said. "From Mumfries's Texas organization. He asked if I'm ready to endorse Mumfries. Shit, I say to myself, they're faster than a hound. He said they're calling all the chairs. 'In Louisiana?' I asked. 'Everywhere . . . So, Mickey, what's it gonna be?' I say, 'Joe, you probably got me, but I got to get used to the fact first, alright?' He gave me the usual line: 'We're going to remember the early ones.' I know that. 'Put me down as a leaner,' I said, 'But I'm

175

not getting married today.' Especially when I know you're coming to see me."

"That's not what I'm here about."

Burton lit up a cigarette and moved the ashtray away from Addis.

"Yeah, but Margaret may . . . And I've always liked her. When my mother was dying, she—"

"Mickey, that's really not why I came," Addis interrupted.

As if your endorsement is so damn important.

"Sure, sure. But can't blame me for thinking that. . . ."

"No, I can't. Could I get a Coke, please?"

Burton whistled at the bartender.

"It's that land deal I called you about."

"And that don't have anything to do with why Joe Rego's bothering with me? Only doing it for the history books?"

"I'm finishing up a job."

The bartender placed a Coke in front of Addis.

"Okay," Burton said. "I asked around. Found out a little. Mostly what you know. Hanovers bought this parcel in a stretch called Blue Ridge. On the edge of the state forest. Don't know why it's called that. There's no ridge. But it's a nice spot, near the Calcasieu River. Pretty remote, but not too far from Route One-sixty-five. Then sometime later they sold it to these boys putting together an industrial park deal, to go with expanding a local airstrip into a real airport. They were going to get companies to set up manufacturing right next to it. Fly parts in, assemble the goods, fly 'em out. They were trying to line up Southern Chicken for a processing plant, too."

"And then what happened?"

"Deal fell through. One of the banks financing it went belly-up. The state pulled out."

"The state?"

"Yeah. Money for the airport was coming from the state industrial development fund. But only when the private money got squared."

"The fund set up when Bob was governor?"

"Yeah, but the private money never came together, so Baton Rouge never had to do anything. One way to look at it, though, is that the Hanovers were the only ones who made any money off this land."

"Who owned it before the Hanovers?"

"Not sure. Some partnership. A local before that."

"Who owns it now?"

"Think it's the same guys who bought it from the Hanovers. But it's been pretty quiet ever since."

Addis tilted his head toward the old men still sitting in the booth. "Let's go say hello."

176

The men were arguing over whether the local high school football team could win its third state championship in a row this coming fall. "We're crazy about the Cougars," Burton explained to Addis. He waited for a pause in the conversation and then introduced him.

"That's Mr. Andrew Manning, used to be mayor. That's Mr. Shepherd Vaullet, used to head up the First National. And that's Billy Irwin, Senior used to be state senator, then handed the seat to Billy, Junior"

"A lot of used-to-be's at this table," Manning said.

The others laughed.

"Sorry about the governor," Manning said to Addis.

His table-mates muttered their condolences.

Burton and Addis sat down. Addis started to explain why he was in town.

"Know all about it," Manning said. "That British fellow came through here. He found me at the barber shop. He went out to Shep's house. Asking his questions in that snotty, smart-ass way. 'Just looking for the truth,' he said. 'No one should be afraid of telling the truth.' Fuck him."

"That's what I told him," Shepherd said.

"And I chased him out of the barber shop," Manning said. "And told Mickey about it. Because I'm a loyal party man. Always been. Even when someone in the party bad-mouths the party and then becomes attorney general and then governor, I'm loyal. That's what loyalty is, sticking to a friend or a party, even when you think they're doing something wrong."

Hell, old wounds sure stay tender. Stop busting my balls.

"I appreciate that, Mayor," Addis said.

"Glad someone does," Manning said. "And when someone helps you get something—like, say, a nice big house in Washington—you stick to him, when it's his turn. Right?"

Joe Rego called you, too?

"I see your point," Addis said.

"Do you?"

"So how can we help?" Irwin interrupted.

"Just wondering what you remember about Blue Ridge and the airport deal?" Addis said.

"Wasn't a local deal," Vaullet said. "They came out of Baton Rouge. We had some meetings. They were buying up land near the old strip. Said they had friends in Baton Rouge who were helping. Had a bank behind them. One of them owned dog tracks down state. Another was in the construction business. They seemed serious. Then the money wasn't there. That was it."

"Were any of them connected to Chasie Mason?" Addis asked.

"Now, why are you asking about that?" Manning said.

"I'm just asking." Addis said. "Covering all the bases."

177

"It was a damn shame what happened in that family. Picture it from Chasie's side. Couldn't see his own grandson," Manning said.

"You got to understand something, Mr. Addis," Vaullet said. "Chasie knew everyone. Knew all of us. I counted him as a friend, and everyone else at this table probably did." The other two nodded. "Asking if a businessman in Louisiana was connected to Chasie Mason is like asking if one wave in the ocean was connected to another. But the boys on the airport deal never mentioned his name, far as I can recall."

"Never did," Manning said. "Can't blame this on a dead man."

Did anyone know, Addis asked, about this partnership that sold the land to the Hanovers? No one did.

"Listen, Mr. Addis," Manning said. "Us codgers at this table saw our share of deals made on the windy side of the street. It's no different here than in Baton Rouge or where you come from. But I don't remember anything about this business that would lose me any peace of mind."

"Why do you think the Hanovers bought the land?" Addis asked.

"Hell, why should we know?" Manning said. "Seems to me you know someone who knows. You should be swimming upstream."

"She says it was Bob's idea."

Vaullet let out a guffaw. "How old was the boy, when this happened?"

"A year or so when they bought it."

"Then she knew," Gaullet remarked.

"How do you know that, Shep?" Burton asked.

"Mickey, I was a banker for forty-seven years. I saw lots of couples come in through those doors. Hundreds. Thousands, maybe. Sometimes the wife would be all quiet, just like the little woman. But if she'd just been a new mother, she'd ask questions, a tubful of questions. She knew exactly how much money they had and what they didn't have."

"Maybe you should ask Mumfries for the lowdown," Manning snorted.

"Oh, shut up with that, Andy," Irwin said.

"Why Mumfries?" Addis asked.

"His idea of a bad joke, right Andy?" Irwin said.

"Right. I'm a batty old man. That's all."

Addis didn't understand. He turned to Burton. The young party chair was biting his lip.

Addis thanked the men for their time.

"And tell Margaret," Irwin said, "that we're all sorry."

"Yeah, tell her," Manning added, "we wish her well . . . and that we hope she and the boy come home soon."

Addis and Burton were sitting at a table on the front porch of the hotel, eating the chicken sandwiches they had ordered and waiting for Rudd to return.

"What was all that," Addis asked, "about me asking Mumfries?"

"I dunno. Geezer gibberish."

You don't bite your lip at gibberish.

"No, I don't think so, Mickey."

"It's nothing."

"Then we'll talk about nothing for a while."

"A stupid story."

"About?"

"Just local bull."

"All politics is local. Mickey. Tell me."

Burton's face looked like it was in a vice.

"Okay. I'm only guessing. But there's this story my father told me about. He's dead, but he was in with all those guys. He heard it from them. You know the accident, the one with Jack, when Bob was governor?"

"Of course."

"Well, this rumor went around back then that the local paper up in Natchitoches Parish had a story it was going to run that said a state trooper smelled alcohol on Hanover's breath when they pulled him out of the truck. But the paper was one of those weeklies owned by the Mumfries family. The story never came out. Some people thought, you know, since the Mumfries were close to the Masons, even if Chasie and Margaret weren't speaking, that . . . well, you know. Then when he picked Mumfries, the old-timers said, 'Hey, we know why.' You never heard any of this?"

Addis said no.

"Well, it was only talk."

"Only talk," Addis repeated. He sucked in an ice cube from his glass and swirled it in his mouth.

One dead man can change a lot of history.

A waiter brought Burton another beer and Addis a Coke.

"You know my dad told me not to get involved in all this," Burton said.

"In what?"

"Politics. Wanted me to tend to the hotel and look after a pipe-fitting business he co-owned. Pissed I went off to law school. Know what he told me once?"

"What?" Addis asked.

"Told me, 'The only thing wrong with politics is politicians. You gotta sign up with somebody. And that means you're signing up with everything that person ever done.' "

"Pretty insightful. And you didn't take his advice?"
Burton took a swig of beer.
"Hell, you want to run pipe fitters all day?"
"I wouldn't know what that's like," Addis said.
"Guess you wouldn't."
"Wonder where your lady friend is," Burton said.
"Me, too."

28

Arlington Hospital, Arlington, Virginia

June 28

Slight concussion, two stitches in the forehead, bruised ribs, a wrenched shoulder—Julia Lancette reported her condition to Clarence Dunne, who was sitting next to her bed in the hospital room. The nurse had told her she could leave as soon as the doctor came by. Dunne noticed that the chart hanging on the bed bore a different name than the one he had called her the previous night.

"I'd like to say thank you," Lancette said. "Any news about our friend?"

"The license plate was stolen. No word on the car."

"And I still haven't figured out what you were doing there."

"Maybe if we talk, it will help you sort things out."

"You sound like my mom."

"I have three boys. . . . Perhaps you'll permit me to go first?"

"Shoot."

"What should I call you?"

"Julia Lancette. The name on the chart. You read it on the way in."

"But your business card. . . ."

"If you search a newspaper index you'll find out I used to be an analyst with the CIA. Got into a pissing match about an estimate and almost got canned. It was my fifteen minutes."

"I remember. But you were reinstated?"

"Right. But once you irritate these guys, reinstatement is meaningless. It's like they let you back into the store and then tell you nothing is for sale."

"And now you're with Inter-Business Media. Never heard of it."

"A news service. A small outfit."

Dunne raised an eyebrow.

"A front?" he asked.

"Small outfit," she said. "When I first joined there was a mistake and I received business cards with the wrong name, but, coincidentally, the same initials. We couldn't figure out why. I kept the cards. Use them as a joke once in a while. I was in that bar, and this fellow demanded I give him a card. I gave him a phony one."

Dunne did not believe her. But he admired her ability to think fast.

"I see. . . . And who were you looking for at the Gauntlet?"

"Who were you looking for, Mr. Dunne?"

Dunne decided to speak freely with her—more or less freely. Often you have to yield information to gain information. But mostly Dunne felt unencumbered by caution. His career was over. He had one shot here.

"Trying to find a man named Raymond who ran something like an escort service. That wouldn't be who you were—"

" 'Something like'? Why were you looking for him?"

"A tip that he might have information on the assassination."

Lancette propped herself up in the bed.

"You're working on the official investigation?" she asked.

"Not exactly. I wanted to vet this lead before turning it over."

"And it vetted?"

"Not yet."

She recalled the recent newspaper stories about Dunne. He had been accused of not sufficiently reviewing security procedures. He had been replaced as head of the White House detail. He had lost a president. Now he was on his own.

"I'm sorry," she said.

"And you?" he asked.

"A tip, too."

She told him. Not everything, but much of it. A source had informed her that a man—the source did not know his name—who used to work at the Gauntlet might have information regarding the murder. The man had a scar on his ear and a glass eye. She went to the bar looking for him. Nothing came of it. She said nothing about the tattoo. That, she thought, might be too much.

"And your source?" Dunne asked.

"And yours?"

"Mine is no longer available."

"Neither is mine now."

"Trust is a funny thing, Ms. Lancette."

There was a rap on the door. Jake Grayton entered, carrying yellow tulips.

"Hello," he said. He paused to look at Dunne. "Small world."

Grayton placed the flowers on a table.

"Doing alright?" he asked her.

"Not too bad."

"Sorry I didn't insist on driving you home. Hope it wasn't the wine."

"Had nothing to do with the wine," she said.

Grayton pulled a chair to the side of the bed opposite Dunne.

"Guess you have a pretty good excuse," he said to Dunne, "for not finishing the personnel evaluations."

"Still working on them, Jake."

"Good. What a surprise to see that you two were involved in the same accident last night. Never met before?"

"No," Lancette answered.

"You're lucky Clarence was there to help?"

"Yes," she said. "Very."

"Clarence, what were you doing on the parkway? I thought you lived in Bethesda?"

"My wife left her glasses at our boy's house. I was running over to pick them up."

"So late at night," Grayton remarked. "That was fortunate. And the other driver?"

"Didn't stop," Dunne said. "No word on him yet."

"Asshole," Grayton said. "Julia, I'm sorry I let you drive home alone—"

"That wasn't the problem."

"You need a ride now?" Grayton asked.

She thought of her bashed-up Dart sitting at a repair shop.

"Clarence already offered," Lancette said.

Dunne hadn't, but he nodded.

"Okay, I hope you don't mind if I check in on you later?" Grayton said.

"Not at all," she replied. "Thanks for the flowers."

"I have to be going. . . . I'll call the parkway police. Let them know I'm interested in finding out who did this."

"Good," Lancette said.

As Grayton opened the door, he turned toward Dunne: "Clarence, end-of-day tomorrow on those evaluations?"

"Yes, Jake."

"Small world," Grayton said.

"You said that on the way in," Dunne noted.

"And the size hasn't changed since then."

Grayton left the room.

———

183

Dunne drove Lancette home in his wife's Volvo sedan. He followed Lancette's directions through the large complex of identical brick townhouses and pulled up in front of her house. In her lap were the tulips.

"So what do we do now?" she asked.

"Tell each other what we lied about?" he said.

"Only if we get Grayton into the conversation."

Dunne almost laughed.

"Someone's out there," he said.

"Think I'll stay at my parents' tonight."

"Same last name?"

She nodded.

"Try a friend, then," he suggested.

"Good advice."

"Yeah. I know how to protect."

Both were silent for a moment. Two mothers with their toddlers walked past the car.

"I'm mad," she said. "I hate being made afraid."

Dunne hoped she would explain more. Give her room, he told himself. She used her index finger to flick aside a tear.

"Hate it," she said.

Nothing else was coming, Dunne thought.

"We should talk some more," he said.

"Maybe," she said. "I need to . . ."

She didn't finish the sentence. Dunne wrote his phone numbers on a card and handed it to her.

"Where are you going to be?" he asked.

"I'm not sure."

"Don't stay here," he said sternly.

"I won't. I'll call you. I will."

"If you're on to something and anything happens," Dunne said, "I won't know where to pick up."

Lancette got out of the car.

"I could say the same about you," she said.

She went inside and examined herself in the bathroom mirror. It hurt to comb her hair. She could feel a headache growing. The pain suppressants were wearing off. She placed a few strands of hair over the wound on her forehead. She went to the kitchen, found the phonebook, and dialed a car service.

"I'd like to schedule a pickup for later today," she said.

29

"When do we go home?"

Those were the first words Rudd said when she and Addis returned to the bed-and-breakfast.

"Tomorrow," he said.

"In the morning?"

"I may have to see someone. Let me find out."

"Can we stay in tonight? Order some food?"

She kicked off her shoes and grabbed a file of legal papers.

"Sure," he said.

Addis picked up the phone messages that had been slipped under the door to the suite.

"I'll be right back," he said.

"You can use the phone up here, if you like. I promise I won't listen."

"Thanks," he said and started for the door.

"It's up to you," she muttered.

From the pay phone in the alcove off the lobby, he returned McGreer's call. The chief of staff wanted to know when Addis would be back. "Getting crazy here," McGreer said.

Ham Kelly was lining up commitments for Mumfries across the nation. The *Post* was running an editorial tomorrow calling on Margaret to respond to the whispers she might challenge Mumfries for the nomination. A rumor was flying about that Pratt was going to select as his running mate Howard Rivers, the only African American congressman in Pratt's party and a former basketball star. Senators were inquiring if the White House still wanted to go ahead with the China treaty hearings, which had been scheduled for the week after the convention.

Shit, the body's not even . . . and the corporate lobbies can't wait.

Addis knew what the pro-treaty senators—and the corporate lobbyists urging them to call the White House—were thinking. Before Hanover had decided to push for the China treaty, Margaret had been lobbied, privately, by unions, environmental groups, and human rights outfits, all urging her to oppose the accord. She was sympathetic to their concerns, but she refused to say anything in public against the treaty while her husband was considering it. Once Hanover resolved to move forward with the treaty, she repeated the same arguments for the treaty that he offered. If the White House was about to split into two camps—Mumfries versus Margaret—might the treaty foes get another chance at enlisting Margaret? The K-Street crowd was concerned.

McGreer had more to report. House Majority Leader Wynn Gravitt had proposed that the House form a committee to oversee the assassination commission. Kelly had ordered the party to stop payments to Dan Carey and had brought in another pollster. An item in a trade newsletter reported that Mike Finn had been asked by the life insurance lobby to leave the White House and become president of its trade association, at $300,000 a year. And Margaret had scheduled a network interview for later in the week without informing the White House communications office.

"But you come home when you're fucking ready," McGreer said.

Addis promised to be back the following afternoon. He attempted to return a call from M. T. O'Connor, but she was not in her office. He ripped in half a message from Evan Hynes-Pierce. The last message was from Harris Griffith's attorney. Before dialing, he practiced saying the lawyer's name.

"Mikolajczyk," he answered. "Talk to me."

"It's Addis."

"Good, good. It's your lucky day. I spoke to Harris. Three weeks I hear squat from him. I have to put up with his gun-crazy wife. Today, he calls."

"Is he in town?"

"Slow down, junior. He is and he says he'd be royally honored to meet you."

"When?"

"Slow the fuck down, I said. First he wants to know if you're in a position to help him in his current difficulties."

"Mr. Mikolajczyk, I can't even begin to have a conversation like that."

"In that case, my client has authorized me to respond in the following manner."

Mikolajczyk hung up the phone. Addis redialed the number.

"Don't waste my time," Mikolajczyk said.

"Don't ask me to break the law."

Addis tried to keep the anger out of his voice.

"Don't ask my client to put out without getting a piece back."

"I just would like to talk to him briefly about a financial matter he handled for the Hanovers. Shouldn't take very long."

"Yeah, I think I know what you want to talk about."

Addis did not respond.

"So, say you get together," Mikolajczyk continued. "You talk. You ask a few questions. He answers a few questions—if he can. Then would you listen to what *he* had to say? About a *financial matter* that he cares about, that's ruining him, that may compel his residency in a fucking federal institution?"

Addis wondered if Mikolajczyk was taping their conversation.

"I'm a good listener. But so there is no misunderstanding, listening means just that—listening. I listen to lots of people."

"Can the crap. Is this loyalty? Did they ask him to do their numbers when they went big time? Hell no. So take your fucking ethics and protect your ass all the way back to Washington. We got others interested."

Others? What others?

"Maybe the three of us could talk? Tomorrow morning? Maybe on a conference call?" Addis suggested.

"Yale Law, right? And you don't understand the principle of legal representation? An LSUer can teach you something, eh?"

Addis felt the dampness under his arms. He could not figure out a line to pitch him.

"Don't say anything else," Mikolajczyk barked into the phone. " 'Cause I'm done listening. I told Harris you were going to be a putz. We'll call you, if we got anything else to say. See ya around, junior."

The line went dead. Addis slammed the phone down.

"Shit," he muttered to himself.

What a trip, he thought. His conversation with Rudd. The old geezers in the restaurant bearing grudges of yesteryear. Burton's yellowing gossip about the car accident. This asshole on the phone. Damn few answers, he thought. He hadn't even pressed Flip Whalen on the Donny Lee Mondreau business; whether there was a reason to wonder if a suicide in a jail cell wasn't actually a suicide. He wanted to return to Washington. Not to the White House, but to his unkempt home, his cat, his . . . There was not much else. But that didn't matter.

"No luck today?" asked a man behind him.

Addis saw Evan Hynes-Pierce standing in the doorway. He wore a white linen suit with a vest and a Panama hat. His collar was open. There was no tie.

What god-damn great timing.

"Mr. Graham Greene, I presume," Addis said.

"I am chasing after the power and the glory."

"And the dirt."

187

"Curious isn't it? How well they mix."

"I hope you don't mind if I don't feel like bantering."

Addis headed toward the stairwell.

"Had a tough time in Alexandria?"

Addis stopped; he clenched a fist and took a breath.

"Stalking me?" he asked. "The Secret Service might be interested in that."

"Yes, file a complaint straightaway. But do we really want to draw attention to our trip—yours and mine—to the city first peopled by French discards?"

Hynes-Pierce placed a crooked finger before his lips.

"This is more than a cozy getaway with a lovely ex-lover. Don't take offense, but you do not look relaxed."

"How did you know I was in Alexandria?"

"People like to talk. Have you ever noticed that? Even when they don't want to. I've been in this business for twenty-three years—went to the *Sun* instead of university, I did—and I'm still stunned by what people will tell you."

"And what do you expect me to tell you?"

"In this instance, I have no illusions. Fancy a walk?"

"What do you want?"

"Actually, I'm here to reach out, to share information. Come along."

He nodded toward the door and adjusted his hat.

"For a minute or two," Addis said.

The two walked along Bourbon Street. The sun was setting and tourists were filling the Quarter. Frat boys and German backpackers were purchasing Hurricanes at streetside counters. They passed a bar with a pianist playing a jazz version of "Amazing Grace."

"Tourist jazz," Hynes-Pierce said. "A disgrace to the departed."

Addis shrugged.

"Earlier today, I had a moment," the reporter continued, "and I visited Storyville—or what used to be Storyville, the prostitute paradise for the fine seamen of your Navy—until a no doubt god-fearing Navy official in 1917 ordered the brothels closed. Fine, the buggers had to find elsewhere to make landfall. But these places of evil were also refuges for musicians: King Oliver, Jelly Roll Morton, and Louis Armstrong. They all began their careers by entertaining the clientele of whores. Now today, if you visit Storyville, what do you find?"

"Please," Addis said. "Do tell."

"Public housing that would make a squatter in Brighton feel quite fortunate. Broken windows. Refuse in the hallways. Plastic vials littering the street. Oh, there was this lovely statue of a Mexican leader with the inspiring inscription: 'Peace is based on the respect of the rights of others.' "

"That's fascinating," Addis said.

"What did you make of President Hanover's decision not to add any money to the federal housing budget?"

Hynes-Pierce's mouth formed a droopy smile. One side of his face, Addis noticed, hung lower than the other.

"What did you want to tell me?" Addis asked.

"Do you think Mrs. Hanover would be of more help to those people?"

"And you care? When you dig up sleaze for a right-wing ideologue who wants to end all social programs?"

"You misunderstand. I do not hide my loyalties. I believe in letting God, not government, sort it all out. And if there is no God, then we all must make do on our own. I admit this is a much easier philosophy to live by than yours, which motivates self-professed samaritans to preach social improvement and force others to live by their prescriptions—and, at the same time, win political elections."

A photographer wearing a red clown nose and large, floppy shoes approached and asked if they wanted him to take their picture.

"A nice souvenir," Hynes-Pierce said.

Addis waved off the photographer.

"Hard as it may be for you to believe," Addis said to the reporter, "I'm not interested in discussing political philosophy with you. Can we cut to the chase?"

"Indeed. We must save time. So valuable it is. Let us proceed. Step this way."

Hynes-Pierce led Addis toward an alley. A street performer was dancing ballroom style with a blow-up doll. The doll's feet were attached to his shoes. Together they danced to a tango, spinning and swirling, the doll's dress fanning out. A small crowd watched.

The reporter passed the dancing pair and stepped into the alley. Addis followed. Hynes-Pierce removed his hat—a true drama queen, Addis thought—and cleared his throat.

"My research indicates that if the Hanovers did not receive what you call a sweetheart deal, then it was certainly a kissing-cousin arrangement. Two principals in the Elva partnership, which sold the land to the Hanovers at a very attractive price, were involved in business dealings with one Mr. Robert Charles Mason. Then, at least one of the financial associates of the firm that purchased the land from the Hanovers at a considerably higher sum was also a commercial confederate of our friend, Mr. Mason. Shared an interest in a dog track, I am told. So, did father help daughter? Did daughter and son-in-law go along with a no-risk series of

189

land transfers that netted them more than one hundred thousand dollars—back in the days when that sum meant something? How does this square with that lovely television movie in which a strong woman stands with her courageous husband, the political reformer, against the corrupt father? Sacrificing succor, adhering to honesty and integrity—and to love—she is forced tragically to bid farewell to her padre and his millions. Uplifting and sad, it was."

Shit, Addis wondered, what does he have?

"Hell, you know that anyone who ever gave change for a dollar bill in Louisiana had some connection to Mason."

"Well, I have faith that further excavation will unearth additional congruences," Hynes-Pierce said. "And, then, we can let the citizenry decide between coincidence and conspiracy. Truth will out."

"Why are you telling me this?"

"Thought I could help you."

"Help me?"

"Or a friend. This information will reach the public. But the timing of that, and, thus, its impact, will be determined by those far above my lofty quarters. Or pay grade, as you Americans say. My employer would prefer, at the moment, to see a narrow reaction—that is, for it not to be *publicly* relevant to the great events of the day."

Addis began to understand. The owner of Hynes-Pierce's paper did not want Margaret in the race. But was the publisher hoping she would stay out if she knew such an article awaited her entrance?

"Shouldn't he be drooling for a catfight between Mumfries and Margaret?" Addis said. "It's the one thing that might give Pratt a chance."

"Seems he's comfortable with the status quo. A Mumfries presidency would be . . . predictable. And he is not certain that Pratt, under any circumstances, could beat the wife of a slain leader."

And how many more millions will his conglomerate and its high-tech firms make if the China treaty goes through? Sure, the owner of Hynes-Pierce's rag might be a right-winger. But there's conservative, then there's conservative. Pratt keeps saying you shouldn't do business with folks who lock up Christians. And that's not good for business.

"It's China, the damn treaty, isn't it?"

"Not my privilege to know."

"But why go through this little dance? Go ahead and publish it. Wouldn't that get him what he wants: Margaret out of the race?"

"I suppose the question is, will an ancient piece of history be deemed terribly significant by an electorate sympathetic to a grieving widow?"

Addis calculated quickly: The publisher could run the story and hope it sparked enough bad publicity to persuade Margaret not to run. But if it failed to do so, she would have weathered a storm, and he'd be without ammunition for further use. No, the smarter play was to threaten publication first—attempt to intimidate her out of the race—and, if that did not work, then publish the piece at an opportune moment.

Hynes-Pierce placed a cigarette in his mouth and took a matchbook out of his pocket.

"You enjoy being a rich man's messenger boy?" Addis asked. "Guess it's a night off for the seeker of truth."

"The story will run. I'm still dotting *i*'s, crossing *t*'s, for I want this piece to be incontrovertible. But I know from whence comes my living, and I can live with that. I am doing my master a favor. I see the situation very clearly. I think that's a good way to live. It's beneficial for the soul."

"No comment—that's what I should have said at the start."

"As you wish. But now, you do *your* duty and report the details of our chat to your master. Or mistress."

Addis left the alley.

"I notice there was no denial," Hynes-Pierce shouted after him.

Addis wheeled around.

"How can I deny what I don't know?" he asked.

"That is the question, isn't it?" Hynes-Pierce said.

He lit a match. Before it hit the ground, Addis was gone.

Rudd was on the phone when Addis returned to the suite. Legal documents were scattered across the bed. She was laughing. She placed a hand over the receiver. "M. T.," she said.

Addis went into the other room and flopped on the bed.

"So then," Rudd was saying into the phone, "the vice president of the union asks, 'Can I give this to him in cash?' "

She laughed again.

"How would you like to be the one to tell him that two Justice Department officials are in the other room? Okay . . . he just came in. . . . Yeah, it was good talking to you, too. . . . Hope it all works out. . . . Here he is."

Rudd waited for Addis to pick up the other phone, she then hung up and told him she was going to take a bath. She closed the bathroom door behind her.

"Margaret asked me to call," O'Connor said.

"I talked to Brew earlier. Sounds like a busy day."

"She wanted to know how it's going."

"Of course," he said.

He lowered his voice. He told O'Connor about his discussions with

191

Whalen and the men in Alexandria. He mentioned the trouble he was having reaching Griffith and the phone calls with Joe Mik. He recounted his conversation with Hynes-Pierce.

"He's a pig," O'Connor said.

"Yes, and a diligent one. . . . You will tell Margaret about this offer?"

"Where is he getting his information?"

"Must be Griffith. His lawyer made it sound like Griffith is talking."

"Jesus."

"He's probably trying to sell the story. Maybe to Hynes-Pierce."

"And is it true?" she asked. "The sellers and then the buyers were associated with Chasie?"

"It could be."

"That's a lot of help, Nick. You know what this could mean?"

"M. T., I'm not an idiot."

"And this Griffith jerk has proof? This is what happened?"

"I wasn't there when they bought the land. . . . You're going to tell her, right?"

"He's just a sotty hack blowing smoke. That's what this is. You know the other stories he's done."

"Even a trash collector finds something valuable once in a while. And it's her decision. Tell her what he said. Otherwise, I will."

"She doesn't have enough to worry about?" O'Connor asked.

"Now she has one more thing."

"I'll take care of it," O'Connor said. "You know, she's all moved out of the residence. We're like a camp behind enemy lines here. Dan won't even come on the White House grounds."

"A true loss." He pictured Carey and O'Connor scheming together—and cringed.

"But we're moving everything to Blair House. And it's not always wrong to listen to what Dan has to say."

"Sure."

"So you're going to sit it out, the campaign?"

Addis didn't feel like answering.

"Doing nothing is doing something," O'Connor said. "There are other drivers on the road."

"Guess I'm out of gas. You can pitch me later."

Addis realized he was gripping the phone tightly. His palm was sweaty. He looked out the window. A young boy was pushing a big bass drum on a dolly down the street by himself.

"Okay, I should go," she said. "But you and Holly?"

"It's nothing, M. T. Really. Just keeping me company. I'll tell you about it when I'm back."

"Sure thing, Romeo."

192

"Really. She's seeing this guy."

"Then she's probably doing a reality check with you."

Glad I could be of help.

"Good night, comrade," he said.

"Later," O'Connor replied.

Addis returned the receiver to its cradle. He realized that he still did not know how Hynes-Pierce had learned of his trip to New Orleans. He stared out the window and listened to the water pouring into the tub.

30

The Gauntlet

June 28

Stares. Lancette felt covered with them as she moved through the packed bar. She pushed at bodies to clear a path. Her hand slid across sweaty flesh. She was jostled. Her head ached; her body was sore. She avoided meeting the eyes trained on her. As she headed toward the office, she went over her list of suspects. One was Lopez—or a friend of his. But then it might be someone in the Agency. Walters had been scared. Perhaps she should have been. Grayton maybe? How melodramatic: a romantic dinner, then an assault on the highway. She certainly couldn't tell Wenner that someone from within—a member of the community—*may* have chased her off the road, without telling him why. Best to start with Lopez. She didn't have to answer his questions.

Without knocking, she opened the door to his office. He was in his chair, on the phone, his back to the door.

"Now try again," he said, without bothering to turn. "And this time make believe you have god-damn manners and knock."

Lancette walked up to the desk.

"Who did you tell about me?" she asked.

Big Daddy Lopez wheeled his chair around.

"I'm on a personal call at the moment, missy. You wait outside and I'll be right with you."

"No. Hang up the god-damn phone."

A bemused smile formed on Lopez's face.

"A nice tough-guy act. I ain't going anywhere. You give me a minute, then I'll give you yours."

He turned his back to her and resumed the phone conversation. He waved a hand at her. She stepped out of the office and leaned against the wall. A shirtless waiter came over and asked if she wanted a drink. She stopped him with a sharp "no."

194

"Be nice," he replied. "Us girls have to stick together."

Lopez opened the door and offered her a chair.

"Still looking for a monkey with a glass eye?"

"Did you tell anyone I was looking for them?" she said.

"Fuck you. You come into my place of business, ask me for a favor, to help you find someone. But you won't give me his precious name. I say I'll see what I can do but ask you to stay out of here. And then two days later, you barge in here. . . . Tell me, what sort of relationship do we have, Miss"—he picked up the business card she had left—"Lang?"

"Somebody ran me off the road last night. Nearly . . ."

Lopez looked at the bandage on her forehead. A moment passed before he responded.

"So what? A drunk on the road. A bad driver. An old boyfriend. Ain't got nothing to do with me."

Lancette placed her hands on the desk. She took a breath and it hurt. She wanted to wince. Instead, she smiled at him.

"I am sorry to be so rude. It's irritating to be chased off the road and nearly killed. I was just wondering if you had told anyone I had come in here looking for that former employee."

"You wanted me to find the guy, didn't you? Yeah, I mentioned it. . . . But I think you should leave now."

"I will, if you tell me who you told."

"Sorry. That don't fly—especially when you won't tell me what you're really doing here."

"Okay, Mr. Lopez, enough bullshit," she said. "I work for a government agency. And I was informed that this fellow might possess information related to a serious federal crime—"

"The details of which, of course, you are not at liberty to discuss."

God damnit, she thought to herself, why am I doing this? Should I tell him it's about the assassination of President Hanover?

"Got a badge?" he asked.

"Are you harboring a person possessing information pertaining to a federal crime?"

She was trying to sound as official as she could.

"Not that I am aware of. And that's all that counts. You can't obstruct what you are not aware of."

"And you don't want to assist?"

"And you don't want to flash a badge?"

"I don't work for law enforcement."

"No shit," he said. "But it don't make no difference. I don't care what initials come after your name. I don't cooperate with anyone I don't know *and* trust. If I ever come across any serious shit that I think my friendly federal government needs to know about, I have people to call. And believe-the-fuck-me I know plenty of well-wired honchos. See some in here. . . . Now, I'm giving you a good piece of advice: Leave now."

He knew something, she could tell. But he wasn't going to say. She stood up.

"I don't appreciate being fucked with," she said. "So if you know anyone who cares, please pass that along."

"You, go, girl," he said with a snort.

Lancette left the door open on her way out.

Outside the bar, she took a deep breath. She ran her fingers through her hair, wishing she could wipe off the smoke. She walked toward Massachusetts Avenue, where she could find a cab.

A man grabbed her arm from behind. She felt a sharp point dig into her side.

"A knife," the man said. "A real sharp knife. And you better be quiet."

He steered her into an alley that led to the back of the bar. They stepped among shards of broken glass.

"There's about fifty dollars in my handbag," she said. "It's—"

"Shut up," he said and pushed the point into her side. The metal tip slipped through the fabric of her blouse and was against her skin. Halfway down the alley, beyond the reach of the nearest streetlamp, he threw her against a wall. She could hear music from the bar and people's voices from the rooftop. She wondered if she should scream.

"Why you looking for me?" he asked.

She squinted and tried to discern the face in the darkness. His hair was scraggly and shoulder-length, receding. His face was gaunt. It was hard to tell but maybe there was something wrong with one eye. He stepped toward her, placed a hand around the base of the neck, pinned her to the wall, and positioned the tip of a Bowie knife beneath her chin. He smelled sweaty; his breath was boozy.

"Why are you looking for me?" he repeated.

The odd eye shined differently.

"Someone who met you a long time ago was trying to find you," she said.

"Who's that?"

He tightened his hold on her throat. She considered kneeing him in the groin. But if his hand jerked upward, she would be cut.

"A doctor. Dr. Charlie Walters. But you may not remember his name. He saw you in a hotel a few years ago. Gave you some pills to help you."

"Help me with what?"

"Help you with . . . the drinking."

The tattoo. On the chest. Her assailant was wearing a beat-up leather vest over a T-shirt.

196

"Fuck them all," he said right into her face. "They fucked us."

"Who?" she asked.

"All of them."

He shoved her against the wall. Her foot kicked to the side and knocked over a carton of discarded electrical cords.

"Who do you work for?" he asked.

"Walters is a friend. He asked me to look for you. Wondered how you were. Said he couldn't do it himself because of some bureaucratic bullshit."

"You fucking bastards want to kill me. So I don't say anything."

He lifted the handle of the knife so that the blade pressed harder against the skin beneath her chin.

"No, I don't. I just wanted to talk."

"This ain't how I'm going down in fucking history. No fucking way."

He wasn't listening to her. He was becoming more agitated. He's going to do it, she thought. He's—

"Drop the knife, motherfucker."

Twayne Starrell stood ten yards behind the man with the knife. He was pointing a .9 mm pistol at him.

The man with the knife turned his head slightly to see Starrell.

"Step the fuck back!" Starrell shouted. "Now, motherfucker!"

The man lowered the knife and backed away from Lancette.

"Drop the god-damn knife!" Starrell yelled.

The man let it fall and slowly turned to face Starrell.

"You!" Starrell shouted, jerking his head toward Lancette. "You stand over here."

He pointed to a spot next to him. Lancette walked to his side. Starrell tried to keep both the man and the woman in his view. He ordered the man to kick the knife toward him. The man followed Starrell's instruction without saying a word. Starrell carefully bent his knees, kept his eyes on both of them, and picked up the knife. He threw it over a fence and into a vacant lot.

"Make him take off his vest and shirt," Lancette said.

"What are you talking about?" Starrell snapped.

"Make him take them off," she repeated.

"I ain't playing no games here!" he yelled at her. "Shut up, bitch!"

"Tell him to pull up his shirt!" she shouted.

She realized she was shaking.

"Shut the fuck up!"

Starrell waved the gun at her then brought it back to the man. He noticed that the man's hands were slightly curled, as if he were ready to spring.

197

"Okay, fucker, we're all going to trip out real smooth," he said to the man. "You'll be right in front of me and my friend here"—he shook the gun—"and the lady will be right at my side."

He grabbed Lancette by the arm and yanked her close to him. Shit, he thought, what the fuck to do? Homeboy with a gun leading a white man out of an alley and holding on to a white woman. That's hard shit to pull off.

"Okay, knife-man, you walk slow. Or picture this: Mr. Niner saying hello and good-bye to your pumpkin head."

The man took a step toward the street, and Starrell positioned himself and Lancette a few feet behind him.

A bottle thrown off the rooftop landed in the alley and exploded. All three were startled. One piece struck Starrell in the side of the face. On reflex, he brought his free hand toward the wound.

The man in front of him dropped to the ground and grabbed a screwdriver that was lying among the electrical cords. He threw it at Starrell. The handle hit Starrell in the neck. He staggered forward and dropped to his knees. A glass shard sliced his knee. He looked around. The man was running down the alleyway.

Starrell jumped up and started to chase. The gun was still in his hand. He rushed past Lancette and then realized he had a choice: her or him.

"Fucker!" he yelled.

He grabbed her.

"C'mon, let's go," he said. "Got somebody for you to talk to."

He put the gun in his pocket and pulled her out of the alley.

"You Janet Lang?" he asked.

"Let me guess," she said. "You want me to talk to a Mr. Dunne?"

Starrell stopped walking.

"What's the fuckin' game here?"

"He and I have already met," she said. "Were you watching for me?"

"Nope, I was scoping for this squirrelly dude. But I saw you come out, and thought maybe you was the girl here before looking for someone. That freakin' red-head monster said something about you. Then that asshole snatches you. Is he the fucker you was looking for?"

"It would be an odd coincidence if he wasn't."

She glanced at the bloodstain on his pants leg.

"Fuckin' new jeans," he said. "Man, what was all that shit about his shirt?"

"Thought he might have a gun under it. . . . I hope Mr. Dunne is going to pay for a new pair of pants."

"He better be."

"Mind if I ask your name?"

"Yeah, I do," he said.

198

Starrell's uncle was working late in his office. His eyes widened when Starrell and Lancette entered.

"What do you have there?" the uncle asked, looking at the bulge in Starrell's pocket.

Starrell took out the gun.

"God-damnit, boy," the uncle sputtered. "I told you not to bring any street stuff into my building. I told you—"

Starrell held the butt of the gun toward him.

"It's empty," he said.

Lancette looked at him.

"Had to scare some motherfucker. Got it from Willie. Thing don't even work. Jammed up or something. He found it wrapped up in newspaper in the bathroom at church." He turned to Lancette: "No shit."

"You watch your mouth," the uncle said.

"Now I got to use the phone."

"And I have something to show you."

The uncle handed Starrell a page from the day's newspaper and pointed to a photograph of a man and a news story.

"Guess we're not getting any back rent," the uncle said.

Lancette read the story over Starrell's shoulder. A Raymond DeNoefri had been found dead in his apartment in Foggy Bottom. He had been garroted. The police had no suspects yet. DeNoefri, the article reported, once had been arrested for writing bad checks. The photograph showed him standing on an apartment balcony next to a barbecue grill.

"So have you found who we were looking for?" she asked.

Starrell found the piece of paper on which Dunne earlier in the day had written his cellular phone number. That was when Dunne had hired Starrell to stake out the bar and watch for Raymond. Don't say your name or mine or anything specific when you call this number, Dunne had instructed. Starrell told Dunne that anybody who spent time with the brothers in Bennington Gardens knew the badges could cop cell-phone conversations.

Starrell dialed the number.

"Got some four-one-one for you," he said.

199

31

New Orleans
June 29

The tendrils of sunlight passing through the wooden shutters woke up Addis. It was early and he lay in bed. He wondered what else there was to do? He could dig through corporate records to ascertain the various business connections of the individuals involved in the land deal. Verify if Hynes-Pierce had the story right. But sorting through financial records was not his specialty, and a news story about a senior White House aide appearing at a state office and requesting documents on local businesses would not be useful. That left Harris Griffith, the accountant.

Addis had gotten nowhere with Griffith's lawyer. A trip to Mikola-jczyk's carried a high risk. Again, Addis had to consider the possible headline: "White House Official Visits Lawyer for S&L Accountant under Investigation." It's funny, he thought, most people assume that if you work in the White House you possess tremendous power. One could direct large amounts of campaign cash to political allies, help contributors contend with pesky federal bureaucrats, find jobs for friends, affect military actions, and, of course, shape legislation. But there were limits. An inquiry from Addis on almost any subject had the potential of blowing up into a controversy over undue, unlawful, or unethical White House interference. When Addis once called a friend at a Miami newspaper and asked her opinion of Wesley Pratt, another newspaper disclosed he was running a "secret White House intelligence-gathering effort." Political power, he thought, is more easily exercised by those who do not appear on news-magazine covers.

Addis did not have much to show for the trip. His top accomplishment was transmitting a blackmail threat from Hynes-Pierce. And the informal tangent to his informal mission—the confession and subsequent suicide of the itinerant laborer in Opelousas—should he have pursued that with more vigor? Drop by the sheriff's office in a Podunk parish and say, "Hello boys, mind telling me if that suicide of a no-good child-killer was really a suicide? Or did you . . ." As if that would work.

Excuses or realities. Isn't that too often the question?

He heard Rudd get out of the bed in the next room and open the window shades.

At the airport, Addis called Mikolajczyk. "Talk to me," said the lawyer's recorded voice. Addis hung up.

Through the flight to National Airport, Rudd worked on a crossword puzzle. Addis flipped through magazines. It was raining in Washington when they arrived. At the curb, he asked if she wanted to share a cab.

"Think I'll take my own," she said, "and go straight to the office."

"Do you have a moment for me to thank you," he said.

She shifted on her feet.

"I think so," she said.

"I know this was a lot to ask. I appreciate it."

"And thanks for showing me those angels. That was . . ."

"Something."

"Yeah, something. . . . And maybe we should talk some more some-time."

Thanks, but I think I'll look for solid ground elsewhere.

"Okay," he said.

"I hope the trip helped you figure out whatever you have to figure out. I'm sure I'll read something in the newspaper soon, and it will all make sense."

"When I can, I'll let you know what it was—"

"No," she interrupted, "that's okay. I don't need to know."

The taxi dispatcher waved at her. Rudd had a melancholy expression. Don't confuse it with regret, Addis told himself. Don't.

She said good-bye and entered the cab. He got into the next one.

"The White House, please," he said.

"Yes, I think so," the driver said. He was wearing a skullcap. A small flag—Eritrean, Addis thought—hung from the rearview mirror. He steered the taxi into the congested traffic.

"Must be a very sad place," he said.

"Yes, it is."

"But we get along. People get along."

"Usually. I suppose they have to."

The cab crept along.

"Terrible traffic," the driver said. "Terrible."

Through the windshield, in between movements of the wipers, Addis could see the cab ahead. Rudd was sitting in the backseat.

Military Jeeps were still patrolling the White House grounds. The hastily constructed barricades that controlled pedestrian traffic on the grounds had not come down. Addis passed through the southern gate and wondered if the new security measures would become a permanent fixture, further isolating the White House from rest of the world.

Another flood of messages, including one from Dunne. Addis asked an intern to check the newspapers of the past two days for stories on the Georgetown University student who was hit by a car and killed while bicycling. The niece of a friend of a friend, Addis explained.

He left the building and crossed Pennsylvania Avenue. Since the funeral, Lafayette Square had been cordoned off. It was empty, except for security details and pigeons. No secretaries sitting on the park benches eating take-out salads. The ragged protesters who lived in cardboard huts in direct view of the front gate—their signs had decried nuclear bombs, the neglect of the poor, the corporatization of the health care system—had been cleared away. Addis recalled the time Hanover had walked across the street and chatted with them. They asked him to cut military spending in half, to help all the poor children, to invest billions in solar power, to promote a week during which all businesses would be shut down and no one would consume anything other than the essentials. "Not such bad ideas," Hanover had said to Addis. "I don't know whether to wonder why they do this or why more people don't."

Addis passed through security at Blair House: metal detector, verification of his hard pass, and a mandatory pat-down. Jack was in the library, watching music videos. Addis said hello.

"Hey, Nick," Jack said, turning from the television.

"What's on?"

"Nothing much. But this one's kinda cool. They all turn into cartoons, see? Lem likes it."

"I haven't seen this one," Addis said.

"Most are pretty dumb. . . . We going to a game soon?"

"I haven't forgotten. Maybe in a few days, when things calm down. Me, you, and Lem, okay?"

"Lem's not here," Jack said.

"Where is he?"

"He went home. His mom's sick."

"Well, he'll be back soon."

"Okay," Jack said. "You promise?"

"Sure do. I'll see you later."

"Alright." He started flipping channels.

Addis went up to the second-floor office. Dan Carey was leaving the

202

room as Addis entered. The consultant turned and asked Margaret if he should stay. She said no, and invited Addis into the office. She was at the desk. O'Connor was sitting cross-legged in a chair next to her. They both had been poring over the papers spread out on her desk. Margaret swept them into a pile.

Carey's numbers, Addis thought.

Margaret came out from behind the desk and greeted Addis with a dry kiss on the cheek. She sat on the couch and pointed to the spot next to her. He took his place.

"First," she said. "Thank you."

Before he could respond, she went on: "Second, I'm going to run. I'm going to make an official statement day after tomorrow. A speech at the Children's Aid Fund. Bob was supposed to be there. They've asked for me. Not Sam. And I'll be doing that show tomorrow night. I know I'm going to be pressed on my intentions. So I'll give a short yes, and say watch the speech."

When you'll have live coverage on all the networks.

"I'd rather wait, but Sam is locking up commitments, and I've been getting calls. I haven't told anyone yet but M. T. and Dan—and now you."

"And Jack?"

"I'll tell him."

"Did M. T. tell you about—"

"Yes, she did. All about it."

Addis wanted to be certain that O'Connor had fully relayed his conversation with Hynes-Pierce.

"So, then, you don't care about Hynes-Pierce and his boss's offer?"

"Oh, I care. Very much. But I'm not going to allow them to blackmail me."

"You're prepared to deal with the story about you and . . . Bob benefiting from a rigged land deal? I'm not saying that's what happened. But that's how it will be portrayed—and that your father was a part of it. So they're going to accuse you of being a liar, a hypocrite, or a fraud. Probably all three."

"They don't really have any hard proof, do they?"

"I'm not sure."

"No one who will come forward and say anything—"

"I'm not sure. There's one person, Harris—"

"I'm not worried," she interrupted.

What does she know?

Margaret grasped Addis's hand.

"I'm going to do this, Nick. I've thought about it. Sam is a pig. He'll open the troughs for the other pigs. The good Bob did will be washed away. Sam's budget will be the same as Wynn Gravitt's. They'll dump the education loan expansions, the low-income tax credits. This stuff does matter to people, doesn't it? Don't we owe it to them to try? Sam won't take up the second-term agenda, the pension protections, the Medi-kids program, public school revitalization. Bob's promise will never be realized. I can't let that happen. I just can't. No matter what . . . I won't."

Margaret, Addis thought, would never acknowledge that Hanover's first three years in office had been disappointing. To her, the best would always have been to come. But the mythical second term had been stolen from her husband—and from her. Unless she claimed it for herself.

"And," Margaret continued, "he's so . . ." She searched for the word. Then her eyes narrowed: "Distasteful . . . So distasteful."

"You're right about Mumfries," Addis said. "But he's not the issue."

She raised an eyebrow. The gesture reminded him of a magazine cover that had depicted Margaret as a schoolmarm.

"You are," he continued. "Forget about the question, 'Is America ready for a woman president?' Is the public willing to see you as a bona fide candidate and not a grieving widow who's gone around the bend? A wife who can't let go. A woman mourning by running for president. Do you want to suffer through all the comparisons to Evita Perón?"

She placed both hands on her lap.

"Don't tell me about suffering," she said.

"I'm sorry. But many people will see you as a power-grabber. Not a lawyer, teacher, globe-trotting ambassador of goodwill, but something of—I'm sorry to say—a political gold-digger."

"Dan's polling and focus groups," O'Connor interrupted, "don't say that."

"Of course not," Addis replied. "People are not going to confront their feelings about such an unprecedented move until they have to. They may even have the decency not to share those thoughts with a focus group moderator. And Dan has an interest—"

He decided not to complete the sentence.

"And your interest?" Margaret asked. "What is it?"

He looked at the portrait of Truman above the fireplace.

"Don't think I have one," he said.

Margaret grinned at him.

"That's an unusual position to have," she said.

"I'm always willing to help you. The trip to New Orleans—"

"But . . . " she interrupted.

"I just don't know about this."

"That's fine, Nick. You don't have to say anything right now."

"I told Mumfries I would stick around until the election. Then I'm gone."

"But that doesn't mean you're going to be supporting—"

204

"Not at all."

"Well, I hope I can still ask you to—"

"Of course, you can."

She let out a long breath.

"I have a question for you," he said.

She nodded.

"As far as you know, was your father involved in any of the land transactions?"

Addis could feel O'Connor's gaze. He avoided her eyes.

"Not as far as I knew then. It really was Bob's deal. Some people came to him. He asked me. I told him it was up to him."

"Okay," he said.

"Nick, think about it some more. I'm sure Sam would understand— he wouldn't be happy, but he would understand—if you had a change of heart and joined us. And thanks for being honest with me."

"Remember," he added, "you have the full sympathy of the public right now. Until you declare that you—someone who has never held elected office—want to challenge a sitting President. Then it's uncharted territory."

"There is such a thing as too much honesty," Margaret said with half a laugh.

Addis and O'Connor scattered a flock of pigeons as they headed though the square toward the White House.

"Why does she hate Mumfries so much?" Addis asked.

"You know," O'Connor answered. "He's only in it for himself and his bloodsucking pals."

"Yeah, I know. But there's something else. The family stuff? The Mumfries and the Masons. What is it?"

O'Connor came to a stop in the middle of Pennsylvania Avenue.

"She once told me that they had been at some family function when she was pretty young. He was there, just back from military service. Seems like their families were pushing them together."

"And?"

"It was weird. I asked what had happened. She said, 'Well, he was drinking and—' She stopped right there. She wouldn't say. But it wasn't a happy memory."

"A grope?" Addis asked. "Something more?"

"I don't know."

"And you didn't ask?"

"Some things you don't ask," she said defensively.

Shit. Talk about history. Say it's all true. He did something sleazy when he's

205

a military buck and she's a young southern girl. Years later, his family buries the story that Hanover had been drinking the night he drove off the road and crippled Jack. Was that a favor to Chasie? Or an IOU, to be redeemed later? Then, again years later, she lobbies for his place on the ticket, so her husband can win it all. Now. . . .

"Jesus, M. T. Is this all because she's pissed at—"

"No, it's not. It's about stopping Mumfries from screwing up everything."

"Things are pretty screwed up already, don't you think?"

"Nick, how long have you been in Washington? As fucked up as things are, they can always be fucked up a lot more."

"There must be a bottom somewhere," he said, as they passed through the guard booth.

"You'd think so, wouldn't you?" she replied.

Hamilton Kelly rushed up to Addis and O'Connor in the lobby of the West Wing.

"Shit, Byrd just got a call from a reporter at a tabloid," Kelly said. "Asked if the press office had any photos of Sam and Katie Cleary together. You know what this is about, don't you?"

They were both aware of the rumors. Flip Whalen had asked Addis about the gossip.

" 'Why are you interested?' Byrd asked the snot. 'Well,' he said, 'wouldn't it be natural for there to be photographs of the Vice President and the assistant domestic policy adviser together? I find out who's behind this and it will be fucking *ca-runk* for them. *Ca-runk!'* "

Kelly saw the question on their faces.

"On our farm in the Florida panhandle, we had gators in the lakes and ponds. We used to catch armadillos and toss them to the gators. And they chomped on them. Made a sound like you never heard. Loud, and it'd scare you out of your balls. *Ca-runk!* Fucking *ca-runk.*"

Kelly stared at O'Connor and repeated the word: "*Ca-runk.*" Then he left them.

"This is ridiculous," Addis said to O'Connor. "Who's doing this?"

"Don't look at me," she said.

Carey? It had to be.

"But you know who."

"Actually, I don't," she said.

"Then maybe that's the problem," he said and left her.

Addis returned to his office. On his desk was a news story on the hit-and-run death of Gillian Silva. No leads, the police said.

32

Capitol Hill

June 29

Addis stood before a closed diner and thought Dunne had given him the wrong address. The windows were boarded up. He saw a gang-banger sitting in a car and thought about several friends who complained they could not find buyers for their homes in this Capitol Hill neighborhood. A townhouse across the street had bricks cemented in the doorway. Three white vans were parked in front of the house. Renovators or narcs, he wondered.

On the front door of the restaurant was a note: "Due to arson, Benny P's will be closed indefinitely." He knew the place. He had eaten here when he worked in the Senate. It was not a regular haunt for aides and lobbyists. It was a spot to escape the power-suits. Grilled cheese sandwich, greasy fries, and a Coke. Addis tried the door; it opened.

The smell of soot was in the air. The floor tiling crackled beneath his feet. Smoke stains covered the walls. A large piece of the ventilation system hung from the pressed-tin ceiling. Dunne was in the only remaining booth in the diner. With him was a woman with thick, naturally pink lips and straw-yellow hair. A small bandage was on her forehead.

Addis gingerly stepped between pieces of debris and sat next to Dunne and across from the woman. Late-twenties, he thought, a lot in her eyes.

"Friend owns this place," Dunne said. "Been in the family for twenty-seven years. Some punks broke in. Smashed it up. Then started playing with the stove. Burnt the place down. Insurance money may not cover it."

"Too bad," Addis said. "I used to come here."

Dunne introduced him to Julia Lancette.

"We think that's her name," Dunne joked.

He did not explain further. Addis tried not to let Lancette draw a disproportionate amount of his attention.

207

"There's another death," Dunne said. "Raymond, the owner of First Ladies."

Before replying, Addis glanced at Lancette.

"She knows," Dunne said. "We're engaged in an unprecedented act of interagency cooperation. The Secret Service, the White House and"—he paused for dramatic effect—"the CIA. Ms. Lancette works for our *friends* across the river. A scout for skeletons and old ghosts, if I have it right."

"That's close," she said.

Addis watched her mouth move.

"She was engaged in extracurricular work of her own," Dunne said, "and her project overlapped with ours. She's been looking for a man with a tattoo, similar to the one found on the fellow still known as Max Bridge. And she doesn't think everyone in her world appreciates her efforts."

Addis had a dozen questions. He wanted to know more about her. But he told himself to stay focused.

"Raymond—what happened?" he asked.

"Killed in his own apartment. Police say it looks professional. Their theory—not for public dissemination: the never officially acknowledged DC mob. That he didn't pony up for them. They've been making a move on the escort business."

"And you?"

"All I know is that whoever I go looking for ends up on the done-and-gone-forever list. I'd be at a dead end if it weren't for—"

A tall black man in dungarees entered the diner through a door behind the counter.

"Benny Junior and I were on the Atlanta force years ago," Dunne said.

"Sorry to interrupt," Benny said. "Good to see you again, Mr. Addis. Been a long piece. Sorry there's no Coke for you."

Addis stood up to shake Benny's hand.

What do you say to someone who's lost twenty-odd years of work?

"Me, too," he said.

"Like I said, I don't want to interrupt. But I had the television on. Heard something I thought you might want to know."

"What is it?" Dunne asked.

"Had a report on this program saying that they got evidence the guy who shot up President Hanover was mixed in with white supremacists."

"Who has evidence?" Dunne asked.

"Don't know. The reporter didn't say what the evidence was. And they're still not sure of his real name. But they know he done it because he hated black people? Figure that one out."

"Thanks, Benny," Dunne said.

Benny read the signal.

"Okay, Clarence. Just thought you should know. I'm next door, if you need me. Nice to see you again, Mr. Addis."

He stepped through the mess and left the diner.

Dunne picked up a piece of newspaper that was on the floor and took out a pen. On the paper he wrote the name *Max Bridge*.

"Our *happy* assassin," Dunne said.

He then diagramed the chain: Bridge to Allison Meade to Raymond DeNoefri to the Gauntlet to the man Lancette was looking for, the man with the tattoo.

Gillian Silva doesn't even make the chart, Addis thought.

"It's not a straight line," Lancette said.

She took the pen and drew an arrow from the tattoo man to Bridge.

"A circle," she said. "If the tattoos match."

Dunne pulled out another pen and underlined "Gauntlet."

"Gay bar," he explained to Addis. "Seems to specialize in don't ask/ don't tell for unconventional Marines. And its owner is trying to keep a secret. Maybe about this one." He tapped his pen against tattoo man.

"He lied to me," Lancette said. "Told me he had the bar only two years," Lancette said. "He's been the owner for six."

She paused, and Addis waited for the explanation.

"I checked the liquor license," she added. "And I think our friend"— she pointed to tattoo man—"worked there during that time."

"And you don't know who this guy with the tattoo is?"

"No," Dunne said. "But the bar owner seems to. Or is it all a coincidence?"

"Clarence, have you shared any of this with the task force?" he asked. Dunne was silent.

"And you're a freelancer, too?" he said to Lancette. "Haven't told Wenner?"

Before she could reply, Dunne answered.

"For some reason," he said, "Jake Grayton recently has taken a very personal interest in Ms. Lancette."

"Well, there might be several reasons for that," Addis said.

Her expression changed for a moment, but he could not tell if she had smiled at him.

"But at this particular moment in the history of the known universe," Addis said, "we don't know much, do we?"

"We know five people are dead," Dunne said.

"Six," Addis said. "You probably forgot Hanover."

He immediately regretted saying that. He was feeling irritated, frustrated. There's too much to process, he told himself.

"What do you want me to do?" Addis asked.

"Two nights ago," Dunne said, "a car tried to run her off the George Washington Parkway."

Addis touched his forehead. She nodded.

"Nick, we're not seeing it all," Dunne said. "But it's deep. They got the paperwork piling up on my desk, like they want to keep me inside the office. We have nervous nellies across the river. We're adding to the District's body count. And someone wants Ms. Lancette face-down. I'm going to poke around. Will you look after her tonight?"

"He insists," Lancette said to Addis. "I stayed at a friend's last night, but she left town on business today."

"Glad to," Addis said, hoping he didn't sound too eager.

Addis stood up so Dunne could get out of the booth.

"So where are you going?" he asked Dunne.

"To our favorite bar."

Lancette started to speak: "On your—"

"You've had enough excitement for the week," Dunne interrupted. "You and Nick stay at his place tonight. I'll check in later."

He started to walk to the door and then turned around.

"And how was New Orleans?" he asked Addis.

"That's another story," Addis answered.

Dunne said good-bye, and Addis sat down across from Lancette.

"A few questions?" he asked.

"I have nowhere to go," she said.

She told him about her job, about her past at the Agency. He remembered her run-in with the Agency brass.

"And I remember yours," she said, "back when Mumfries was chairing the committee. Honduran business. Guess we have something in common."

"Yeah, we're both on the same shit-list at Langley."

"Well, I happen to know there is no list. It's really a small metal box containing index cards."

He smiled at the joke.

"You're going to stay on at the White House?" she asked.

"For the time being."

"But they gave you time off to go to New Orleans. . . . I saw your picture in the paper . . . with your girlfriend."

"She's not my girlfriend," he said.

"Right, an ex. Just friends?"

"I don't know. Just echoes."

Lancette said nothing in response.

"You like Cuban food?" he asked.

"Yes. Reminds me of the Agency's most foolish days."

"Good."

They left the diner and got into his car. He took East Capitol toward the Capitol and saw that one of the white vans had pulled behind him. The sun was low on the horizon.

"See how orange the Supreme Court looks?" she said. "I have a friend who's a cinematographer in Hollywood. They call this time of day 'magic hour.' Must be when they take all those postcard shots. I love the way Washington looks in this light. Almost makes you—"

"Believe," he interrupted. "Almost."

The van stayed behind Addis's Honda as he headed toward Union Station and followed him west on Massachusetts. When he turned on 6th Street Northwest, the van kept going straight.

33

The Gauntlet

June 29

Dunne stood in the alley behind the bar. He pictured Starrell facing down Lancette's assailant. Inside he had been told that Lopez was in the basement with the plumber and would not see him.

He picked up a broken brick and threw it toward a window. The glass shattered. He waited a few seconds and hurled a stone through another closed window. The back door opened. A man wearing spandex shorts shouted at him.

"What the fuck are you doing?!"

"Please tell Mr. Lopez I'm waiting for him," Dunne said.

Dunne found another rock and tossed it hard toward a basement window. It skipped against the ground and crashed into the glass.

"You're fucking crazy," the man shouted at him. "He's gonna kill you."

"Tell him I'm waiting."

Thirty seconds later, Lopez burst through the back door.

Shit, he's big, Dunne thought. Starrell hadn't exaggerated.

Lopez took two strides toward Dunne before he saw the gun Dunne was holding. He came to a stop.

"You're a dead man," he said.

"Turn around," Dunne said.

"Deader than dead," Lopez said.

Lopez faced the brick wall. Dunne pushed Lopez against it. Dunne noticed several men standing by the back door.

"Stay back," Dunne yelled at them.

They did not move. He lowered his voice so only Lopez could hear him.

"I imagine they have standing orders not to call the police unless you tell them to."

"Something like that," Lopez said.

He shoved the gun barrel into the back of Lopez's neck.

"Tell them to go back inside," Dunne said.

"Leave this fuck to me," Lopez shouted at them. "But he pulls any shit, you call the cops and the whole wide world and tell them that Clarence Dunne, the asshole in charge when Hanover was wasted, went nuts behind a gay bar."

The men went inside and closed the door.

"Nice to meet you, too," Dunne said.

He backed away from Lopez and told him to turn around. Dunne kept the gun trained on him.

"To what do I owe this fucking pleasure?" Lopez asked.

"Just tell me where to find the man who used to work here, the one with the glass eye, the scar on the ear."

"First the mystery girl and now you."

"No bullshit," Dunne said. "You told her you weren't the owner when he worked here. That's not what the liquor board says."

"Very good, Dick Tracy. And if I don't cooperate you're going to blow me away? I don't think so. That would make this a very bad month for you, seeing how about a dozen witnesses would send your black ass away."

"You're smart for a former government man," Dunne said.

He lowered the gun. Lopez waited for Dunne to say more.

"It's amazing what you can find out when you ask a few friends in the bureaucracy to check a name. . . . Born in Wilmington, Delaware. Marines. Then U.S. Army. Special Forces. Detailed to South Korea. Then the Philippines, counterinsurgency. Then to Afghanistan. A TDY for the Agency, I'm guessing. Trained the *mujhadeen*. Distinguished write-ups. But there was one problem. The Hekhtabar clan you were advising developed a creative method for financing its war against the Soviets. They learned that a supply line can work in both directions—in and out. And a DEA agent was paying attention. He tracked a supply from Mexico to Paris to Peshawar and to the Badakhshan hills controlled by Hekhtabar. He even turned a courier, who told him about an American—a very big American—who was helping out back home. The agent forwarded the case to Justice and waited. Nothing happened. Most DEA agents learn not to push inconvenient cases. But this guy was a real ballbuster. He kicked and screamed. He didn't get his way, and it was suggested that his career might flourish elsewhere. He took the advice—but not before making sure there was a paper trail. It was classified, but at least it was there. And his last accomplishment: finding out the name of that American he never got to question—Ernest Ivan Lopez. I bet your Afghan friends got a kick out of the Ivan. But they probably didn't know your real name anyway."

213

Lopez's jaw was clenched.

"I wasn't involved in no heroin shipments," he said.

"But you knew," Dunne said. His tone was between that of a question and a statement.

"I wasn't involved, I said. You go to the end of the earth and help some rag-heads who are up against the second biggest military power in God's entire fucking universe. I was sent to help them kick Moscow butt, not to examine every package on every stinking mule train."

"Fair enough. But don't you think Mr. Hekhtabar might have thought your presence meant they had a degree of protection?"

"No one ever told them that. I sure as hell didn't."

"Not all societies are as plain-speaking as ours. . . . Anyway, Mr. Lopez, I didn't drop by tonight to rehash old ground. I came to ask for your help."

"You have a pretty damn funny way of asking for it. And if I don't help, what are you going to do? Sic the DEA on me?"

"No. But what do you think might happen if that DEA report somehow ended up with a reporter and a story came out? Imagine it: local bar owner once advised CIA-backed drug traffickers. I suspect the District liquor board might be interested. And so would all those community activists who claim the CIA has been working with drug dealers and flooding inner-city neighborhoods with shit and pain. You can read this stuff all the time in the local black papers—which you may not get around to. You see, Mr. Lopez, these people are desperate to explain the devastation that's struck their communities. You and I know they overstate the argument. But what would happen if they had a real-life symbol of their dark speculations? One living and working in their own neighborhood."

Dunne did not actually possess a copy of the DEA report. A friend at DEA had read him portions over the phone. But judging from the look on Lopez's face, he concluded the report was accurate. *Paper wars*—that's what we fight in Washington, Dunne thought. Bloodless battles of leaks.

The tension in Lopez's body lessened. He dropped his shoulders.

"Fucking extortionist," he said. "I don't deal with scum."

"Not asking for a deal. Just asking for help."

"I don't help people who think they can blackmail me."

His pride was talking now, Dunne thought. Not his head.

"I'll say please, then," Dunne said. "Please tell me where to find him. That's all. Then he can tell me whatever he wants to. You know him? You worked together?"

"Semper fi, man."

"You knew Raymond DeNoefri?"

"Yeah."

"Heard what happened to him?"

"Yeah. . . . That fucking black kid who came in here—he's part of this, too?"

"He was helping me. Raymond ever talk to your friend, the one with the glass eye?"

Lopez did not reply. Dunne asked again.

"They say Raymond pissed off the wrong people," Lopez said. "Told them he didn't want any partners. You don't do that."

"Maybe. Maybe it was something else. Was he a friend of yours?"

"Shit, man, you stand behind a bar in a straight joint and every god-damn sad-sack you pour a glass for thinks you're his A-number-one best bud of all time. What do you think happens in a gay bar?"

"And I'm guessing that friend of yours might know something about Raymond, too?"

"You do a lot of guessing, man."

"These days I have to. Have you asked him about Raymond? What does he think?"

Lopez tugged on his beard.

"I don't speak for nobody but me."

Acknowledgment, Dunne thought, that Lopez knew the man with the glass eye.

"So let me ask him myself," Dunne said.

Lopez was silent.

"Raymond was ex-Marine, right? Hanover was a decorated vet. How about some semper fi for them?"

Lopez crossed his arms.

"Come on," Dunne said. "Take me to see him. Kick my black ass, if you don't like how it goes down. Unless you already know everything, you got to be curious, too."

"I stopped being curious. It's bad for business."

"You know the girl that was killed with the reporter in the Mayflower? She worked for Raymond."

Dunne paused to let Lopez absorb that fact.

"You see the picture here?" Dunne asked. "I know you do. The asshole who killed the President murdered a young woman who happened to work for your pal Raymond, who then was murdered in the comfort of his own home. And your friend with the glass eye, somehow he's messed up in all this."

Lopez kicked a tin can to the side of the alley.

"Please, Mr. Lopez. Semper fi for everyone."

Dunne placed the gun back in its shoulder holster.

"Alright," Lopez said.

He opened the back door and shouted that he would be gone for an hour or so. He then headed out of the alley; Dunne followed.

"Got a few apartments around the corner," Lopez said. "Crash pads for customers. A place to go if they're too drunk or they need privacy."

"And he used to work for you?"

"Yeah, a few years back. Odds and ends. Working the door. Security. But it didn't work out. He hates fags."

"In the service together?"

"Fort Bragg and Korea . . ."

"And?"

"Afghanistan. He passed through . . . It's a fucking cliché. But I owe him for some major shit."

"And now."

"Burn-out city. You'll see. Can't do much of anything. Got some pension or something. Been through some heavy stuff. I was just trying to watch his back."

"And his name?"

Lopez ignored the question. The two walked up 5th Street and made a right on M Street.

"So why all the Marines and other military jocks at your place?" Dunne asked.

"Guys who started it were jarheads. Word got out: a safe place to go for fags in uniform when they were out of uniform. If you're a new puppy at the Eighth Street barracks, you hear about the Gauntlet in the first week."

"And he hates homosexuals, but you and he—"

"Hell, this is just a business opportunity for me. That's all."

They came to a small apartment building. Lopez took out his keys, but he saw that the lock was broken. With a push, the door opened.

"It's not Georgetown," Lopez said. "Proximity. Not style."

The light in the front hallway was dim. The bulb shined through a discolored glass covering. The paint on the walls was peeling off in sheets. They took the stairs to the fourth floor. Lopez stopped before a door that had a three-foot-high paper cross taped to it.

"His idea," Lopez said.

He knocked on the door. There was no answer. They could hear the sound of talking coming from within the apartment. He knocked again.

"It's me," Lopez said.

No one responded. Lopez unlocked the door and opened it slowly. He placed a hand on Dunne's shoulder, indicating he wanted him to stay in the hallway. He then stepped into the apartment.

"So you're saying that if we reinstituted school prayer, teenage pregnancy rates would drop—"

Sounds like a radio, Dunne thought.

A piece of the wooden doorjamb exploded; Dunne ducked.

"You little fuck!" he heard Lopez yell.

Dunne peered into the room. Lopez was striding toward a man sitting in an easy chair facing the door. Lopez raised his right arm and grabbed a pistol from the man in the chair. There was a silencer on the gun.

"You dumb bastard!" Lopez screamed at him. "You fucking dumb bastard!"

Dunne walked into the studio apartment. It smelled of stale beer and cigarettes. The bed was unmade. Empty bottles were scattered. A loud-playing radio was on the floor next to the bed and tuned to a talk show. Lopez clicked it off.

Dunne took an inventory of the man in the chair. Pushing forty. Receding hair. Scar on the right ear. The left eye was the odd one. A pug nose. His mouth tilted to the left. Patchy stubble covered his face. Stocky. He wore military-style boots, jeans, and a black T-shirt with the name of what Dunne assumed was a heavy metal band.

"Man, what's wrong with you?"

"Sorry, Big. Thought you were somebody else." He spoke in a slow drawl.

"It's fucking hard to mistake me for anyone else, don't you think?"

"Yeah, I suppose."

The man's arms hung limply over the sides. Boozed up, Dunne thought. Lopez sat on the bed. He signaled for Dunne to pull over a wooden chair.

"This man here wants to talk to you," Lopez said. "He used to be at the White House. You don't have to tell him anything you don't want to. Okay?"

"Sure," the man mumbled.

Dunne noticed that Lopez had not used the man's name.

"My name is Clarence Dunne," he said.

"I seen you on the television," the man said.

"Could well be."

"They said you fucked up or something."

"Yeah."

"I fucked up, too."

"How's that?" Dunne asked.

The man picked up a bottle of rum lying on the floor. He held the bottle in front of his face. There was a puddle at the bottom. He put the bottle to his lips and sucked out the contents.

"I was born," he said.

"Did you know Raymond DeNoefri?" Dunne asked.

"I don't want to talk about none of that."

217

"What do you want to talk about?"

"How you fucking sign up for duty, trust the fuckers, and then they fuck you up the ass. You know what I mean?"

"I think so. Which fuckers do you have in mind?"

"All of them."

He looked at the floor, searching for a bottle that wasn't empty.

"Let me," Dunne said.

He spotted an unopened bottle of rum on the kitchen counter. Next to it was a plastic cup. Dunne rinsed out the cup in the yellow-stained sink. He opened the rum and poured out half a glass.

"Don't you think he's had enough?" Lopez asked.

Dunne had hoped that Lopez would protest.

"Fuck you, Big," the man said.

"I want him to be comfortable," Dunne said.

He gave the cup to the man.

"So tell me about the fuckers," Dunne said. He took a pen and a small notebook out of his jacket pocket. The man didn't pay attention to that.

"You know. You do your job. You do it straight-up. Then they say, hey boy, you're a good old boy, we got something real damn special for you. Ain't no one going to know about it. Can't tell your folks. But if they knew they'd be real proud of their boy. Real fucking proud. Just like when you sacked the quarterback from Talladega and won the championship. You know?"

He gulped the rum.

"Or when they first saw you when you came home from Basic in your uniform. Like you were fucking superman. A god-damn Marine."

He looked hard at Dunne and scratched the ear with the scar.

"Best friend in Basic was a colored boy, he was."

"What was this special something they had for you?" Dunne asked.

"Ain't even got a name. Like it don't exist. If you work for something that don't exist, what's that mean? You don't exist, right?"

"Right," Dunne said.

"Fucking right. They brought us in, from all over. Destroyed all our records. Said, you boys don't exist. But you do. Gave us special-ass training. Then said, you do the stuff no one else can do. You know, the stuff we can't do ah-fish-al-lee. You know?"

"Yes, I do. When was this?"

"Back when I had two eyes . . . Told us to not use our real names anymore or say where we was from. Hell, we was no longer Americans. Turned me into a fucking Canadian . . . Shit, there's no more beer. Maybe we all should go to Big's place. It's full of Marine-fags, you know?"

Dunne nodded and kept scribbling in the notebook.

"We weren't fags. Man, we did the ugliest shit they had."

"Where?"

"All over the fucking planet. We popped this guy in Hong Kong. He was selling high-tech shit to the Chinks. I don't know what it was. In Germany, we torched this office and five-fingered a bunch of files. Most of it was in the Middle East, man. All those A-rabs, man. Took out some crazies. Then the shit went down. Where I bought all this. Became One-Eyed Jack, Jack."

He finished the rum in the cup. Dunne poured more. Lopez was sitting quietly on the bed.

"Tell me about it," Dunne said.

"Fucking Tangiers. The deal was, take out the boys running this one group. You know, the fucking Holy Warriors. But, you know, don't be so clean about it. Make it look like a pissing match between the towel-heads. Right? So it's fucking obvious, man: a car bomb. But it all got all fucked. The night before, they packed it in and moved. So our intel was no good. Then the damn thing went off before we even got it there. Don't know fucking why. Wasn't my thing. I didn't do demo. But it did. Took out a whole damn block. Killed something like twenty-seven people. Bunch of those beggar-kids they got everywhere. Couple of Americans. Like what the fuck were they doing there? And we lost half of our fucking team. I was a trailer. Got caught in the blast. A fucking mess. Three of us left, including T. L."

"T. L.?" Dunne asked.

"Team leader," Lopez answered.

"He was a-o-fucking-kay. Mattie got his face beat up."

"Mattie?"

The man went on: "Broke his nose and a cheekbone or something. Fucking changed his face. Me—mostly just the fucking eye, and screwed up my leg. Shattered some shit. T. L. dragged both of us out. I don't re-member that too good. Got us a doctor somewhere. Don't remember all of that either. Then we had to get out of the fucking country. Left behind all this shit. Sat-phones. C-4. We fucking drove across it. Hell yes, I re-member that. Every fucking bump. Thought I was going to die."

"And they brought you back to the States?" Dunne asked.

"Not right then. First to Germany. Saw some doctors there. They gave me this eye. It ain't glass, you know. Some high-tech plastic. Then back to the States. Put us up in different hotel rooms. Kept us apart. Lots of questions. Then they said, man, that's it. See ya, don't wanna be ya. A five-hundred-a-week pension. Straight into a bank account. Don't even know from where. No taxes. And no medals. Can't be no ah-fish-all rec-ord, they said. Jesus Christ, even when I asked for help they gave me the middle of the doughnut, you know. Come around, hold my hand, take off. Then they said I had to stop calling the number we had. That's all I had. No names, just one number. They disconnected the damn thing."

"Who knew about your outfit?"

"No one. They said the President knows. They said the numero uno at the CIA knows, the one who's dead now, but no one else there's supposed to know. You ain't really CIA they said. They wanted to make sure we know that. And they said some fools in Congress know. Guess that's where they got the funny money."

He knocked back the rum.

"And the other two?" Dunne asked.

"Went separate ways. Until . . . Well, I ain't never seen one of them, T. L., and . . ."

He was drifting. He started looking at his hands. He turned sharply toward Lopez.

"You ain't taking my gun," he said.

"I'm not giving it to no drunk," Lopez replied.

"Okay," Dunne said, trying to gain control. "Okay. You never saw T. L. But the other one?"

"I don't want to talk about it," the man said.

Dunne ignored his reply.

"You saw him again, right?" he said.

There was no response.

"Do you have a tattoo on your chest?"

Still, no response.

"An *M* with an arrow going through it?" Dunne asked.

The man's eyes widened.

"Oh shit," Lopez said softly.

"Where'd you get it?" Dunne asked.

"No need-to-know."

"Can I see it?"

"Fuck you. You a fag?"

Lopez stood up.

"I'd like to see it, too," he said.

"Told you that would happen if you stuck around those fags for so long," the man said. He tried to laugh.

Lopez picked up the hunting knife that was on the night table next to the bed. He grabbed the man by the shirt and pulled on the collar.

"Fuck you, Big," the man said. But he did not resist.

Lopez stabbed the knife into the edge of the shirt and sliced the material. He ripped the shirt apart. The tattoo was on the left side of his chest.

Exactly the same place, Dunne thought.

"Where did you get that?" he asked.

220

"Cairo," he said. "It's not really an *M*, just looks like one. The guy told us it was an old symbol that protected warriors from getting shot."

"You and . . . " Dunne said.

"You fucking know. . . . Me and . . . Mattie and . . ."

"The team?" Dunne asked.

"Yeah, the whole team," the man muttered. "Except for the black one. Said something about not wanting to make his momma cry . . ."

The man coughed and wiped his mouth on his sleeve.

"And it was Mattie who shot President Hanover?" Dunne asked.

The man grabbed the bottle from Dunne and took a long gulp. He positioned the hanging pieces of the T-shirt over the tattoo. Dunne repeated the question.

"I didn't know nothing about that," the man said. "Not a god-damned thing. He didn't tell me nothing. Just came to town. Found me 'cause when I was all blasted up and they were trying to get me a doctor, I thought I wasn't gonna make it, so I gave him my dad's phone number. Wasn't supposed to do that. Violation of the rules, you know. The fucking rules. But I wasn't checking out like that without someone telling my dad what went down. I don't care what they said. You got a right to know what happens to your son, right? So they split us up and all this time goes by—and a few weeks back, he calls my dad and gets my number up here. I got this room over in Arlington. Off Wilson. Too close to the damn highway. Thought I had me a job, too, with this company that goes overseas and tells American companies how to protect their dumb-fuck executives. But it didn't come through. Man, I can't tell them what I did for two years, you know."

"Doesn't make it easy," Dunne said.

"Fucking-A."

"So Mattie shows up . . ."

"Yeah. He comes to town. Calls me up. Asks to stay at my place. Sure, I say. What the fuck do I know? Tells me he was in Africa. Doing ops for this South African company. I'm thinking weapons shit. But he don't say. He says he just got back. He ain't acting alright. But he doesn't say nothing about it. Not that he's nuts. But I think he's leaning too far into the well. Talking to himself. I see him do this twitchy thing. And it really pisses him off when it happens. Had a thick bushy beard. Guess he shaved it off right before he—"

He tapped the side of the chair with his right hand.

"Says his dad just died. And he goes on about how he hates all the fuckers that did this to us. And all the fuckers who did something to his dad. And, man, he sees the President on the television, and he starts cussing. Like he was the one that fucked us, man. But he don't say nothing about doing anything about it. Swear to God, man."

221

The man crossed his arms and held himself. He hunched forward. Dunne thought he was close to crying. He wondered if tears would come out of the socket containing the eye made of high-tech plastic.

"And then what?" he asked.

"He stayed at the place. Went out a few times. Said he had things to do."

"And he asked for help?"

"I fucking told you," he shouted. "I didn't know anything about that."

He swung his arms and knocked the bottle of rum. It flew off his lap and landed on the wood floor. The rum flowed into the floorboards.

"Shit," he said. "I shouldn't have done that."

"So what did he ask you to do?" Dunne asked.

"Said he needed a woman. Said he would pay. Not for him. But for some business associate."

"You fixed him up with Raymond, who you knew from the bar?"

"But I didn't know what it was all about. I fucking swear it."

"And then?"

"Then he said he was going away for a few days. But no big deal. Like he was going to be back soon. Left some stuff. In my place. Then he . . . I bugged out of my place after that."

He stared into space and rubbed one hand across the stubble on his face. Dunne wrote in the notebook.

"He was a fucking good man. He fucking was."

"I'm sure he was," Dunne said. "And his last name?"

"We weren't supposed to tell each other that. Went by those names they gave us. Like me: Albert Peters. There's a fucking name for you."

"It wasn't Max Bridge? Do you know why he would use that name?"

"No fucking clue—except that we used to sometimes call ourselves the fucking Maxes, like we're going to take it to the max. It was a joke. That's why we liked that tattoo. I mean, it looked like an *M* for Max."

"Do you know where he was from?"

"A GOB like me."

Dunne raised his eyebrows.

"Good ol' boy. You know, another goober. From the South. Don't know where. Used to talk about fishing and hunting with his dad. Told me he shot a copperhead when he was ten or something."

"And how did he come to join your team?"

"I figured he'd been sent over from one of the services like I was. But one time—maybe when we were in Berlin—he said he went through Basic in the Marines but it didn't work out. And never said nothing else about that."

His eyes were beginning to droop. He was slurring words. What else to ask? Dunne wondered.

"Okay, who ran the team in Washington?"

"Who the fuck knows."

"Well, you must have talked to someone, right?"

"Yeah. Had one fucking meeting. Told to report to this office in fucking Crystal City. Got there. A bunch of suits—all had soft hands, you can tell— and they ask me these questions. Then gave me money—cash—and told me to check into a hotel down the street and wait. Two days later, a suit came and took me to this house. The others were there. That's how it began. Never saw one god-damn piece of paper."

"And the men in the office, no names?"

He scowled at Dunne.

"Who the hell are you?" he said. "No fucking names at all. But, you know, I saw this fellow on the television the other day, looked like one of them."

"Who was that?"

"I don't know. He was going into Congress or the White House or something. To talk about all this you-know-what. I don't know. Like he's in charge. The sound was off."

God-damn it, Dunne thought. Could it be?

"Shit, Big, I forgot to tell you, I think I fucked up the television. It don't get nothing now."

"We'll deal with that later," Lopez said.

"And that fellow you saw?" Dunne said.

"Fuck, who knows? My memory's shot. Can't even remember all the pussy I got. Told Big that I left my best days and nights in Tangiers. All got blown right out of my head."

Dunne slid his chair closer to the man.

"Did you kill Raymond?" he asked.

The man lunged and grabbed Dunne by the collar. Lopez jumped off the bed, and wrapped his hands around the man's wrists.

"It's okay, okay," Dunne shouted at Lopez.

Lopez froze, his hands still holding the man.

"I didn't fucking kill nobody," the man said.

"Not Raymond? Not because he knew you knew this guy?"

"No-fucking-body," he growled.

"Not the girl on the bicycle?"

"What are you fucking talking about?"

The man let go of Dunne's collar. Lopez freed the man's wrists and backed away.

"What about the woman who was looking for you?" Dunne asked. "The one you grabbed?"

"Didn't want to be looked for. It's pretty fucking obvious why."

"And did you run her off the road?"

223

"Man, I didn't want nobody looking for me. Don't bug me on that. She's okay, right? And it was Big who got me all worked up about that. He told me that if she kept coming around, I'd have to book."

Lopez looked at Dunne and shrugged.

"And she ain't the only one come looking," the man said.

Dunne moved his chair back.

"What do you mean?"

"After I bivouacked here, I called my landlady, ol' Nhu Nguyen. Madam Nhu. Vietnamese. Told her I'm not coming back. She said an old friend came 'round to see me. Didn't give a name. That was two days after, you know. I don't need any more people looking for me. Don't want any other people. Don't want them. No, thank you."

His breathing was becoming heavier. He's zoning out, Dunne thought.

"What's your name?" Dunne asked.

"Jimmy," he said.

"Jimmy who?"

"Jimmy . . . Jimmy Shit-for-brains."

He closed his eyes.

Dunne reached out to stir him.

"Let him be," Lopez said.

"I think we should get him out of here," Dunne said.

"No way," Lopez said. "I'm not letting him go anywhere. I'll keep watch over him." He picked up the gun. "No one knows he's here. Only you and me. Besides, your record isn't too hot."

"Thanks," Dunne said.

Lopez pulled a sheet off the bed and draped it over Jimmy.

"He and I don't put much trust in ah-fish-als," Lopez said, mimicking Jimmy's drawl. "I don't think you'll get him before the commission. Besides, I wouldn't be too sure they'd want him there."

"Then maybe we'll get him a lawyer. He can do a video affadavit. We'll keep him protected."

"Or he can sell his story, right? Why give it away? This is a million dollars for him."

And for you, too? Dunne thought.

"You knew of this special unit?" Dunne asked.

"Only from what he told me."

"Ever see proof it existed?"

"Proof? Fuck it. Just look at him."

"When was it operational?"

"Five years back or so."

Shit, Dunne thought, when Mumfries ran the Senate intelligence committee.

"Okay, so let me bring a lawyer to see him. Get the story on tape. You

224

and he can decide what to do with it—as long as it gets out somehow. And you'll stay with him here until the morning. Deal?"

Lopez picked up the phone and dialed a number.

"Get me Sandy," he said into the receiver.

Jimmy was slumped over in the chair, in a deep sleep, wheezing through his mouth.

"Sandy," Lopez barked. "I'm not coming back tonight. Got some business. So you're in fucking charge of the fairies—and the cash at the end of the night. Put it all in the safe. I'll call in a few hours to check on everything. If any of the assholes from the precinct come by, tell them I'm fucking my brains out with a beauty queen and I'll be there tomorrow. Got it? Good."

He hung up and looked at Dunne.

"Deal."

Dunne took the phone number for the apartment and left. Outside the building, three prostitutes passed him.

"Hey sugar," one said to him. "Want a date?"

"You can pop the cherry tonight," another said.

"No thanks," Dunne replied.

In his car, he took out his cell phone and called the office of the Secretary of the Treasury. He then called another number.

"What's up?" a voice said.

Dunne recognized the voice. "Don't say anything. I'm coming by in an hour. I'll meet you in the front."

34

Adams Morgan
June 29

Rolando brought over two plates of grilled shrimp and two glasses of wine. Addis and Lancette were seated at the back of the first-floor dining room. This was where he had sat with Rudd three nights earlier.

"Okay," Addis said after the owner left, "let's have it."

"Have what?"

"Your story."

"My story? Like this is a date?"

"Sure, why not?"

"It's not that interesting."

"Then give me your cover story."

"That's even duller."

"Okay, then how about those Wizards? Can you believe what a messed-up season they had. Nothing in the paint. No leadership—"

"Okay, you win," she said. "My story."

She went through it like she had done with Grayton, but with more details. She told him how she had found her way to the CIA. It started with her thesis at the Woodrow Wilson school: an examination of Tito's campaign to undermine and absorb political dissent in Yugoslovia. Impressed by the paper, a professor had recommended her to a friend in Washington, a fellow at an institute dedicated to foreign policy. She had visited the friend, and they had chatted about prospects for democracy in the Balkans. He asked if she might be interested in working further in that area. She said yes. He picked up the phone and called an acquaintance in the CIA. I get five hundred dollars a head, he had told her. She was not sure whether he was joking.

"The rest is you-know-what," she said.

"Current events," he said. "But that whole flap?"

"Not now."

"Something like, you wouldn't go along with some report on . . ."

"Assessing the political strengths and weaknesses of various Serbian players."

"They wanted you to fix it, give a boost to somebody?"

She stared at a couple at another table. They were laughing. The man was making faces as he told a story.

"Okay," she said. "The thing was, they were shooting for the right policy. It was all about who should get a nod of support from us. But the folks who deserved it were the worst organized. And it doesn't help to send a paper to the NSC saying the people we ought to be helping are a bunch of fuck-ups. So they wanted that shaved."

"And you didn't want to be a shaver?"

"It's not what I was paid to do," she said.

"Not even when it could have helped."

"Not even. I was naive. I didn't think it was up to me to rig the record."

She looked at her hands.

"That's about it," she added.

"Commendable."

"Or foolish and arrogant."

Enough pushing on this front, Addis thought.

"Okay, is it my turn?" he asked.

"You don't have to bother," she said. "I've read the profiles. Seen the interviews. And I have a confession."

Jesus, I love the way your mouth moves.

"Yes?" he asked.

"A close friend of mine is intensely preoccupied with you. She'd be disappointed—actually, she'd feel betrayed—if I didn't try to introduce her to you. She's really nice. A lawyer at the DOE. So maybe when all this is . . ."

She trailed off.

Bad sign, he told himself.

"Sure," he said. "Sure."

He sipped the wine.

"Care to tell me how you got into this thing?" she asked.

"A product of celebrity. See what happens when—"

"They put your face on the cover of magazines."

"Yeah," he said.

He thought of Gillian Silva. He poked a shrimp across his plate.

"A woman who wanted to meet me. Had what she believed was important information. She got it to me and . . ."

"And what?"

227

"She was hit by a car and killed. I can't say it's connected. But . . ."

Lancette moved her hand on the table toward his, but it stopped inches short.

"Mr. Dunne asked me not to tell the director about any of this."

"Clarence is obsessed these days. That's understandable. He wants to be in control. I'm not fighting him on that."

"It's hard to sit on this. I'm supposed to bring Wenner everything. That's the whole point. No surprises—"

"No skeletons, no bumps in the middle of night," Addis said.

"Something like that," she said. "He called twice today. He saved my ass, saved my career. He's going to be royally p.o.'ed."

"Well, go ahead. I'm not going to fight you, either."

Addis lifted his wine in mock toast to her and drank.

"You're not exactly what I expected," she said.

"Or your friend, I bet."

"Probably."

"Well, Julia"—it was the first time he used her name—"it's been an unusual time for me—"

"I can imagine," she interrupted. "It must be very—"

"It's not just that. Even before this . . . I was getting tired of gaming out one situation after another. I'm not so certain life is so malleable. Sure, major events—momentous events—can turn on small decisions. You know, the pebble in the pond and all the ripples. But you can spend so much time trying to figure out what pebble to throw where to get precisely the right ripple. And then, anyway, a flash flood comes racing in and washes over the ripples you've so carefully orchestrated."

"How many hours a day do you put in at the White House?"

"Usually—and it hasn't been 'usual' lately—fourteen or so."

"And you've been doing this for almost four years?"

Almost five, if you count the campaign, he thought. He nodded.

"Then let me suggest a radical diagnosis: burnout."

"That's part of it. But there's more. When I'm honest with myself, I know that."

"You're not always honest with yourself?" she asked.

"That's a hard one, don't you think? How can you tell if you're honest with yourself? Say you're really good at spinning the truth, then how can you?"

"You just can. In the CIA they say they want us to be objective analysts. Just the facts, ma'am. But the whole weight of the culture, of the bureaucracy, is to produce material that pleases whoever is above you. The President or just the guy who can give you a promotion. Still, you know damn well when you're pushing a piece of evidence too far or ignoring information that contradicts what you believe—or want to believe. I've seen a lot of smart and good people who act as if they really do believe their own tilted reports. But I have to think that at one level they know what they're doing, that . . ."

She thought for a second.

"That they're aware they're juggling the truth. It's not that they're liars. But from their perspective they're—let's be kind—animating the truth with other concerns. For noble reasons, of course. Nobody likes to think of themselves as—"

"A shit," he said.

Lancette laughed and lifted her glass.

"Exactly. The human capacity for self-justification is endless."

He clinked his glass against hers, and Addis waved to Rolando and ordered another round.

On the way out, they passed a group of twenty-somethings heading toward the dance room on the second floor.

"Do you like to dance?" Lancette asked.

" 'He dances like an epileptic string bean.' That's what a writer for *Vanity Fair* wrote about me during the campaign. I made the mistake of letting him come out with us one of the few nights we took time off. Since he proceeded to get drunk at world-record speed, I always thought his observation was—"

"Enhanced?"

"Precisely. Not exactly the truth, but . . ."

"Not exactly not *not* the truth?"

"Right," he said. "Right, not *not* the truth. I like that."

They walked out into the night. The air held a cool moistness. In the breeze he could smell the trees of nearby Rock Creek Park. He was enjoying the buzz—from the wine and from her. Let's just ignore the remark about her girlfriend, he told himself.

They crossed Columbia Road and passed a crowd of African diplomats heading toward a world beat club.

"Actually," he said, "I do have a story you haven't already read about."

"Really? I hope it's not classified. I don't think I want to know any more state secrets."

"Don't think this one belongs to the state."

"Then, feel free," she said and smiled.

Shit, why the fuck not?

"Remember Donny Lee Mondreau?" he asked.

Her eyebrows moved together.

"It's a familiar . . ."

229

Addis gave her a moment. Her face eased. She did not make the connection.

"A retarded man. Convicted of killing a convenience store owner in Louisiana and got the death sentence—"

"And President Hanover flew back," she interrupted.

"Yes. But he wasn't President then. It was during the campaign."

"I remember."

They reached Addis's house. He stepped inside first and felt something beneath his foot. Cat shit, he knew. He hit the light switch.

"Watch out where you walk," he said.

On a table was a note. He read it and gave it to Lancette.

"It's from Samantha," he said. "She's twelve, lives next door. She takes care of the cat when I'm gone."

"I fed Eric," the note said. "But he's in a bad mood. Maybe you shouldn't go away so much. Or maybe you should get another cat. Samantha."

Addis guided Lancette to the living room couch. He then headed to the kitchen to retrieve paper towels and stain remover. The cat was not in sight.

"Do you think," Lancette shouted at him, "she meant that you should replace your cat or that you should get an additional one so he'd have company?"

"Good question," he said on the way to the front hallway.

"She's a pistol," Addis said, as he cleaned the mess. "The other day she asked me if I believed in God. I said, 'Mostly.' She didn't like that. I could tell. She then asked if I wanted to marry a woman who believed in God. I said I'd like to marry a woman who had some faith. Then she said, 'Would you marry a woman who didn't believe in God but who went to church anyway?' "

"What did you say?"

"I said there are a lot of reasons for going to church. Some people go because they know what they're going to find. Some people go to look. And she said, 'But wouldn't she be a phony?' I said, not if she knew the difference between the two."

"So when you're not running the world, you assist young girls in their spiritual development," Lancette said.

Addis passed through the living room on his way back to the kitchen.

"Everyone needs a hobby."

Damn, he thought, she's good. I've missed this.

She inspected the stack of memorabilia piled on a rocking chair. There was a hat from the *U.S.S. Constitution*. A photograph of Addis at a ceremony at the Rock and Roll Hall of Fame, his arms around two famous musicians. A folder of letters from schoolchildren. A framed citation, signed by Hanover, thanking Addis for his participation in the passage of an education bill. A postcard with a photograph of the Empire State Building. Lancette flipped it over. "From one sin city to another," the handwritten message read, "Love, J." She recalled the news reports of Addis's affair with a famous model who went by a single name that began with the letter *J*.

Addis returned to the room. She dropped the card on the pile.

"Do you want coffee, tea, or anything?" he asked. "Hot chocolate?"

She picked up from the floor a cardboard container for a six-pack. But instead of beer, there were miniature bottles of champagne in the slots. Each had the presidential seal on it.

"Product endorsements?" she asked.

"If you go to the Kennedy Center and sit in the President's box, they have a refrigerator there. With a combination lock on it—"

"And you have the combination."

"Yes. Six-six-six, believe it or not. Don't tell the Christian right."

"Do you think they change it with each administration?"

"If they do, I'll probably never know. Should I open one?"

"No, no," she said. "You'll want to keep these."

She wiped the dust off the bottles and put them back on the floor.

"And would it be real or fake?" she asked.

He looked puzzled.

"The hot chocolate. Are you going to actually heat up milk and add true chocolate syrup? Or is it, rip open a package of powder and pour in boiling District water?"

"Let me try to find some clean sheets," he said.

"What about the story you promised? Mondreau?"

"Oh, yeah."

He looked around the room. Every chair was covered with books and papers but the one at the desk. He pulled it over and sat in front of her.

He told her about the phone call from Flip Whalen, the suspect's confession, the reported suicide. He told her about his role in advising Hanover on Mondreau's execution. He did not mention the breach that his advice had caused between him and Rudd. As he spoke, he stared out the bay windows and watched people heading toward the nightlife of Adams Morgan. When he finished, he looked at her. Her elbows were on her knees, her chin resting against her palms.

"Is that why you were in New Orleans?" she asked.

"Not really. I thought about asking around a little, but . . ."

"You didn't want to know?"

"I don't *think* that's it," he said. "I just don't know how you show up at a sheriff's office and say 'Hey, did you boys kill a nigger as a favor to the President?' "

"You tell anyone about the call?"

231

"No, no one."

You can do the math. That means you're the first. This is much more intimate than sex.

"I'm honored," she said.

She smiled to show she was not kidding.

"And you still don't know what to do about it?" she asked. "If anything?"

He nodded.

She gently shook her head: "That's a tough one. Are you going to let it drop?"

"So far I have."

"I don't know what I'd do."

They were silent for a moment. This is a woman who stood up to the CIA—and from the inside, he thought. She'd really let the episode fade? Let official history go undisturbed?

"Thanks for not judging," he said.

Lancette touched her bottom lip with her index finger. She leaned back into the couch and gazed out the window at a crowd of club-hoppers. Two men were loudly singing an old disco song. A black van drove past the house. Addis thought he had seen it a few minutes earlier. A poor soul circling for parking? Or . . .

"I'll get around to it," she said. "Some judgments take longer than others."

He wondered if they ever would kiss. The singing outside turned into a howl.

"You know," she said, "I was reading an interview with this Dutch architect. He was saying, 'the street is dead,' but—"

"Not here," Addis interrupted.

"That's what I was thinking."

The phone rang. Addis picked up the cordless phone on the desk. The battery was dead.

"I'll let it ring," he said.

The answering machine picked up.

"Nick, it's M. T., are you there? Are you screening? Jesus Christ, pick up the phone. It's important."

He ran into the kitchen.

"Fuckit, Nick, pick up," O'Connor said.

He grabbed the phone and said hello.

"Damnit, Nick," Lancette heard O'Connor complaining. "I got to—"

The phone machine shut off.

Lancette stood and looked at the message machine. The number 15 was illuminated. From one of the piles, she picked up a baseball. She could

232

not read the autograph. Stop snooping, she told herself. She thought about the phone call from Flip Whalen.

Addis came out of the kitchen. He had gone pale. She dropped the ball. It landed on the rug and rolled several feet.

"They shot Clarence," he said.

She froze in place.

"Who?"

"No one knows."

"Where?"

"Near Bennington Gardens. A housing project in the Southeast. They call it, 'Simple City.' "

"Shit. And?"

"They don't know. He's at G.W. Unconscious, but still alive."

Addis pushed aside the papers on his desk and found the remote for the television. He clicked it on.

"Another Washington tragedy," a news anchor was saying.

A live shot showed the outside of George Washington University Hospital. There was nothing to see. The anchor cut to a reporter at the hospital. He had no facts other than what O'Connor had relayed to Addis.

"The police," the reporter said, "have no idea about the motive."

Shit, Gillian Silva, Raymond DeNoefri, now Dunne. . . .

The show returned to the local anchor: "Sadly, these days motives are not always needed. And on a personal note, let me say. . . ."

He went on to report that he knew Dunne socially, that Dunne had been of help to him when the anchor developed a substance abuse problem, that he was certain some people will question what Dunne had been doing in such a notorious and dangerous neighborhood on his own, late in the evening, and that . . .

Addis turned off the set before the anchor finished his point. He saw a black van drive past his house again.

"Let's get out of here," he said.

"Where?"

"Ever been inside the White House?" he asked.

233

35

The White House
June 29

The meeting was under way when Addis entered McGreer's suite.

"Do we have to do anything," Ken Byrd asked, "other than issue a statement expressing shock and saying the President and Sally are praying for him?"

Kelly cracked his knuckles. "What's important," he said, "is that we look like we're in control."

"Put a special FBI team on it?" McGreer asked.

"That makes sense," Mike Finn said.

They all looked toward Jake Grayton.

"I just got off the phone with the police chief," Grayton said calmly. "He's throwing everything he's got into this. I think we should let them handle it initially. I hate this, too. But a shooting in Simple City isn't that extraordinary. And, to be candid, the cops know how to work that turf better than the Bureau. We will, of course, offer them all the support."

An uncharacteristically immodest moment for Grayton, Addis thought. He cleared his throat.

"I'd like to remind people," Addis said, "that not only was Clarence until recently an official at the White House, he also was a key witness before a presidential commission investigating a presidential assassination. If you don't do anything, people will wonder."

"Wonder what?" Grayton asked. "Wonder what he was doing there on his own? Wonder why the attempted murder of an *ex*-White House official receives more attention than the murder yesterday of a fifteen-year-old on a bus, on her way to tutoring some kids?"

"Alfre Marvin," Byrd said.

Grayton looked angry at being interrupted.

"That's her name," Byrd said nervously.

"Since the assassination, Clarence has been acting erratic. Not showing

234

up to meetings or training classes. Not filing reports. Who knows what's going on in his head? Do you, Mr. Addis? Any ideas what he's been up to?"

Addis did not say anything. McGreer broke the silence.

"What the fuck's going on here? We're all on the same fucking team. It's fucking obvious. Ken, put out the god-damn press statement and note that President Mumfries has called Mrs. Dunne and told her that all the fucking available resources will be be made fucking available immediately to catch the fuckers. Alma's probably at the hospital. Send Sally over there to be with her. If not tonight, then first thing tomorrow. Jake should make sure there's a liaison between the fucking D.C. cops and the Bureau. Everyone fucking agree with this?"

They all turned toward Kelly. Using a handkerchief, Kelly wiped sweat off the back of his neck.

He's going to be great on television, Addis said to himself.

"Yeah, sounds good," Kelly said.

"Good," McGreer said. "Let's fucking go."

McGreer stood up, and Kelly followed.

"What a way to head into the convention," Kelly mumbled.

On the way to his office, where Lancette was waiting, Addis was stopped twice by Secret Service agents who asked what he knew about the attack on Dunne. Just what everybody else does, he said.

I don't like lying, so stop asking me. Please.

"Nick."

O'Connor was in the hallway with Lem Jordan.

"Do we know anything yet?" she asked.

"No," he said.

Addis waited a moment for Jordan to say something. But he just stood there looking tired.

"What are you doing?" Addis asked O'Connor.

"Came over from Blair House to pick up some stuff." She was carrying several files. "They wouldn't let us in on what's happening with Clarence."

"Not surprising," Addis said.

"Hear anything from your friend, Hynes-Pierce?"

"Not today. I'm sure he's creeping about. Margaret hasn't changed her mind?"

"Anyone been saying anything about the story on Mumfries and Katie?"

"Not to me," Addis replied.

"I was told the press office hasn't heard back from the *Express*."

"So maybe there's a truce," Addis said with a smile. "Hear anything along those lines, M. T.?"

She shook her head. Jordan wasn't talking. His hands were in his pocket.

"You okay, Lem?" Addis asked.

"Yeah, s-s-sure."

"He just got back from New Orleans," O'Connor said.

"How's your mom?" Addis asked.

"S-she's al-r-r-right," Jordan replied. "Kind of a f-f-fal-fal—"

"False alarm," O'Connor said.

"Good," Addis said.

"We have to go," O'Connor said.

"Before Kelly sees you?"

She ignored his comment.

"L-l-let's go," Jordan said.

"Okay, Lem." She took a step toward Addis. "Call me if you hear anything about Clarence. Please."

"Sure, M. T. Full disclosure."

Addis watched as O'Connor and Jordan headed out. An odd couple, he thought. She walked as if she were a marionette that barely touched the ground. He plowed forward like a highway steamroller. Had they dropped by now because this was an opportune moment to retrieve information—party contact lists, scheduling records?—that Kelly might not want Margaret to have?

"Shit, I hate thinking this way," Addis said to himself. Then he realized he had said it aloud.

Lancette was sitting at his desk when Addis returned. She held up a memo.

"A reminder that you can be called in for a random drug test at any time."

"In the home of the free."

She put the memo down.

"What did you tell them?" she asked.

"Nothing."

"And did they tell you anything?"

"Nothing we don't already know. Your friend Grayton was there. Not too eager to dump the Bureau on top of the D.C. cops."

"And what would that mean?"

"I don't know. That he's hoping the police will do their usual job."

"And what do we do?" Lancette asked.

"I don't know."

She picked up the framed cartoon in which Hanover's predecessor was

236

denigrating the names of famous Americans with foreign-sounding names, the cartoon signed by Hanover.

"You were pretty close to him, weren't you?" Lancette asked.

"I thought so."

"Thought so?"

"I don't know what else there is to do tonight. Maybe we should get some sleep. See how Clarence is doing in the morning. Maybe we can talk to him then. If not, make some decisions of our own."

"You want to go back to your house? I'm not ashamed to say I'm a little bit spooked."

He thought of the black van. How often had it driven past?

"No. Clarence would bite our heads off for doing that. The White House always has rooms reserved at the Mayflower."

"You and me?"

"Afraid of getting your name in the papers?"

"No. Doesn't everyone in the White House know about these rooms?"

"Yes."

"And isn't that where they found . . . ?"

Allison Meade and Brady Sandlin, he thought.

"You mind a professional's opinion?" she asked. "It's not very secure."

"Okay," he said. "Another idea."

They left his office and took the stairs to the ground floor. In the hallway outside the press office, they saw Grayton.

"Shit," Lancette muttered.

He trotted up to them.

"Julia, you get around," Grayton said.

"We're old friends," she said, nodding toward Addis. "We were having dinner when we heard about Clar . . . Mr. Dunne."

"That's odd," Grayton said. "Clarence happens to be on the parkway when you're run off the road. Then you happen to be with Nick when Clarence is shot."

"Almost unbelievable," Addis said.

"I had an instructor at the Academy," Grayton replied. "He said a coincidence is what happens when there's not enough room in the world for all of us to move around."

Addis and Lancette didn't say anything in response.

"Anyway," Grayton went on, "I'm sure Nick's been keeping you informed of what we know about Clarence."

"He has," Lancette said. "Now he's going to see me home."

"Good," Grayton said. "You and Clarence have not had much luck lately. I hope it doesn't spread." He looked at Addis. "Good night." Grayton walked away.

Addis and Lancette headed through the old pressroom. Much of it had been removed: the podium was gone, the blue curtain and the White House seal that had hung on it, the chairs in the row in which the assassin had sat. Seats were still upturned. Lighting wiring and adhesive tape were strewn about. It was the first time Addis had been in the room since the murder. In the days after the assassination, there had been talk of sealing the room and maintaining it as a memorial. But Margaret Hanover had objected. Addis remembered what she had told one reporter: "I do not want to see the people's White House, the very symbol of our democracy, turned into a tomb."

"Nick," Lancette started to say. But then she realized she had nothing else to tell him.

He stood in the middle of the room.

"That's where Mary sat," he said, pointing to an overturned seat in the front row. "She always got the first question. Been here the longest. Always let the press secretary know what she was going to ask about. Thought it looked bad for the President to appear surprised on television around the world."

He pointed to a seat in the second row. A crumpled fast food-bag was next to it.

"That was Jeffrey's spot. Pompous prick. Did that story on the President bringing in a masseuse. Demanded to know where the masseuse was from. And when he didn't get an answer within an hour—shit, we didn't know and the President was traveling—he said the White House was stonewalling. After the piece was on, he told me, 'Sorry, I'm renegotiating my contract and I need lots of airtime.' Shithead. When he was flying with us on the plane during the campaign he was sleeping with an assistant press secretary in the White House."

Addis stared at a wall, as if he could see through it to the press office.

"She worked right there. . . . Conflict of interest? Didn't stop him. Did we complain? What do you do? Make a stink and then they're all out to get you."

Another seat: "Paige. Fox News. Invited me to dinner at her house. Tried to. . . . Well, you know. I said no. The next week she did this piece saying Dan Carey was pushing me aside, that the President had . . . had lost confidence in me. Wasn't true. Though I'm sure she accurately reported what Carey was telling her."

"Okay, Nick, okay." Lancette placed a hand on his arm. "Let's get out of here."

They walked across the room. A reporter's notebook was lying on the floor. A stack of old press releases was on a table by the door. They left the building.

"No matter what Margaret says," he said, "it will always feel like a tomb."

At the entrance to Blair House a guard stopped them. No more visitors tonight, the guard had been told.

"I assume Ms. O'Connor is still inside," Addis said. "Please tell her I'm here."

The guard picked up the phone. O'Connor was there in less than a minute and escorted them into the building.

"Mind if we use one of the guest rooms?" Addis asked.

O'Connor glanced at Lancette and raised an eyebrow.

"This is Julia Lancette," Addis said. "She's an analyst with the secret-keepers across the river. And it's not like that. Clarence asked me to look after her tonight. And now . . ."

O'Connor pulled Addis away from Lancette and spoke in whispers.

"What's friggin' going on?" she asked.

"I don't even know. A few nights ago, Julia was driving home and this nut tried to run her off the road. Clarence happened to be—"

"There," O'Connor interrupted.

"Yeah, and he rammed this other driver, and, I guess, saved her. Right?"

"Yes," Lancette said, sidling up next to Addis.

"And then she got these threatening calls," Addis lied. "Like they're from the same guy. And Clarence thought she should be careful. So when—"

"This sounds like bullshit, Nick," O'Connor said. She squared off in front of Lancette: "And why is someone after you?"

"No idea," she replied. "I got my name in the paper a while ago. Said I was with the Agency. Got a few calls from crazies. Asked if I was beaming signals into their fillings. That sort of thing. But nothing like this—"

O'Connor pulled Addis aside. "I don't believe this. Nick, we've always told each other everything."

"I don't know everything. But, then, do I know everything you know these days?"

"That's different," O'Connor said. He noticed the lines at the side of her eyes were deeper than usual.

"I don't know if it's different or not. But I need your help. We have to stay somewhere."

"Margaret's already in bed. Why don't you camp out in the study on the second floor? You can use the couch. The floor. There are some big pillows. A quilt. Is that good enough?"

"Sure, thanks, M. T."

Addis showed Lancette to the wood-paneled study. They each took a turn in the attached bathroom. He offered her the couch.

239

"I'll use some of the pillows," he said, "and sleep on the floor."

"Well . . ."

Is she going to suggest something else?

"That's nice of you."

He started to gather the pillows. She found a quilt in a closet and unfolded it.

"But can you set them up right here?" she asked, pointing to the floor next to the couch.

Did she merely want to feel secure? he asked himself.

"My pleasure," he said.

Addis arranged his sleeping spot, and she lay down on the couch. He turned off the lamp, and positioned himself on the cushions. An orangish light from outside filled the room. She fixed the quilt so that it covered her and draped over Addis.

"Good night, Nick. Thanks for dinner and . . ."

He could smell her and felt a trembling within.

"It's okay."

Try to sleep. Try.

"I don't think I'm going to sleep much tonight," she said.

"Me neither," he said. "Good night."

Fifteen minutes later, she was asleep. He could tell from her breathing. He stared across the room at a portrait hanging on the wall. Dwight David Eisenhower was watching them.

She rolled over, and her hand gently dropped upon Addis's shoulder. It was still there when he drifted off.

36

Bennington Gardens

June 29

Starrell banged his fist against the apartment door.

"Open up, fuckin' Jesus Christ, open up the fuckin' door," he shouted. He pounded again. His heart was racing. His chest hurt. Sweat was stinging his eyes.

"Come on, Willie! Open the god-damn door!"

The locks clicked; then the door opened as far as the chain would allow. Starrell saw his friend's face in the crack.

"C'mon, man, quick, open up."

"You fuckin' nuts, Twayne. What the fuck you doing?"

Starrell grabbed at the chain.

"Willie, open the god-damn, motherfuckin' door, now. Let me in."

The door closed. He heard Willie Jameson undo the chain. The door swung open. Starrell bolted in, and Jameson quickly shut the door. Starrell plopped on to a couch covered with a white sheet. Jameson was wearing a T-shirt, white athletic socks pulled up to his calves, and black boxer shorts that revealed his long, skinny legs.

"What's the fuck's going on?" Jameson asked.

"Just seen somebody capped. Look at this shit."

There was a dark splotch on the left side of Starrell's T-shirt.

"Man, blood and skank right on me. . . . If anyone comes to the door, don't let no one in."

"Don't be bringing no gangsta shit into my house, Twayne. My momma's sick like I ain't ever seen. Coughing up this yellow shit."

Starrell was breathing hard.

"Okay, okay, you stay your ass there," Jameson said. "I'll get you some water."

When Jameson came back, Starrell chugged the water and handed the glass back to Jameson. He then took a long breath.

241

"This is what it is," Starrell said. "Got a call from this dude who used to be a big-dick nigger at the White House. I'm doing some favors for him. He's paying big, you know."

Jameson started to ask a question, but Starrell kept talking.

"So he calls me and says he got more for me to be doing. Says he's coming over. We sit in his car. He tells me some heavy shit, man. Fuckin' like a flick. I ain't getting into it now. But heavy. Then he says I'm gonna be watching this ratty-ass apartment building for him and see if this weird dude cuts out. And then, man, the fuckin' glass explodes and he gets shot in the neck. Blood spits out, like a motherfuckin' hydrant. Shit, I start yelling. Then there's another one and another one. I'm fuckin' kissing the car seat. I look up at him. His eyes are open but they look dead. He says, 'Take the notebook and get the fuck out.' I see it sticking out of his pocket. He says it again: 'Take it and get the fuck out. Go.' With all this blood comin' out of his mouth, like he's drinkin' it. So I grab it and fly. And someone takes a fuckin' shot at me. It hits the street, man, and these pieces go flying. One got me almost right on my fuckin' bone-man."

Starrell put his hands on his head and drew in another deep breath.

"I start to run. I don't know where the fuck I'm going. I think there's some fucker behind me, but I ain't stopping to check it out. I go past the school and remember that what's-his-name, that Jamaican-man, the teacher there—"

"Lannie."

"Yeah, Lannie. He leaves this window open so the crew can get in and play roundball. So I check the window. It's open. I crawl in and it's dark. And I feel all this moist shit on my shirt. Fuckin' buggin'. I run through the school. Ain't nobody playin'. I go down to the basement. See this room with all this equipment stuff. Close and lock the door. I fuckin' waited for I don't know."

"Probably an hour."

"Yeah, a fuckin' hour. My heart was fuckin' bombin'. Got this little window there, so I read the notebook. It was the stuff he told me. Then I got out. By the alley where the crew did that guy's sister. Didn't see nobody. So I ran here. . . . Man, he must be dead."

"He ain't," Jameson said. "Saw it on the news. He's all shot up, but they got him in a hospital. He's crit, ain't awake. And I know who the fuck he is. So whatcha doing for him?"

"Nigger, I don't even know. Helping him find somebody. In some strange motherfuckin' places. But then he told me some wicked shit tonight."

"What shit?"

Starrell took out the notebook, which he had tucked inside the waistband of his nylon sweatpants. Jameson grabbed for it. Starrell pulled it back. He saw Jameson's computer was on the table near the kitchen. The screen was lit.

"Man," Starrell said, "you still trying to cop a white computer-bitch for some hand lovin'?"

"Fuck you, Twayne. Tell me the shit he told you. What's in the book?"

Starrell ignored the request. "Your brother Anjean's still running with the crew?"

Jameson nodded.

"Think he'll help me, if I need it tonight?"

"What's in it for him?"

"Fuck if I know. Payback for when I told him the Dwee was after his mean-fucker ass."

"That was a long time ago. . . . Besides, momma don't let him in the house no more. Not since Marco, man. . . . Look what I found in the closet."

Jameson handed Starrell a small sketch book. Inside were pen and pencil drawings: guys hanging out on a street corner, basketball players on the court, small children playing with discarded vials, a couple of funeral scenes, teenagers ignoring a teacher in a classroom, boarded-up storefronts. The front page said, "Life in Simple City as sene by Marco Jameson."

"He was fuckin' good," Starrell said, as he flipped through the book. "I didn't know Marco could do this shit."

"Neither did me and momma."

Neither said anything for a moment.

"I don't know what I got for Anjean," Starrell said. "But you call him and ask if he can get his ass over here now. Tell him maybe he'll get on TV again—and not as no kiddie-killer now."

"Yeah. . . . okay. But I got to go downstairs to use the phone. I don't want momma to catch me talking to Anjean."

"Okay, this black man ain't going nowhere."

Starrell looked again at the computer.

"And you find people on that thing, right?"

"Sometimes. Depends on what you already know about them."

"Their name and kinda where they live?"

"You got a chance."

"Then after you call Anjean I got someone for you to look for."

The computer chimed, signaling a message for Jameson.

"Yo, Willie man," Starrell said, "one of your machine-bitches is calling."

Jameson went over to the computer. He typed a few words, then hit a series of commands. The screen went dark.

"Hey, I wouldn't cop a look at your lover-boy notes," Starrell said.

Jameson shook his head at Starrell: "You better tell me more when I get back."

He opened the door and checked the corridor.

"B-R-B," he said.

"Huh?" Starrell said.

The door shut. Starrell heard Jameson's mother cough in the next room. He opened Dunne's notebook. Man, he thought, this nigger's handwriting was damn straight, like printing in a book.

37

Addis felt hot. His shirt was moist. He had been sweating in his sleep. He shifted his position on the pillows. Lancette stirred on the couch.

"Julia," he said.

She muttered a few words.

"Good morning."

She rolled over and mumbled again. She was far away.

His beeper sounded. Startled, she bolted upright. He reached for the pager and read the message.

" 'Call DCI Wenner,' " he said.

"That's what it says?" Lancette asked. She was now fully awake.

"Yeah. And the number."

He saw his reflection in the television screen. His hair was sticking out. He tried to turn away from her casually and pat it into place.

"What does he want?" she asked.

"I guess we should find out."

Addis picked up the phone and dialed the number.

"It's Addis," he said.

Lancette imagined the other half of the conversation.

"Blair House," he said.

She looked at the grandfather clock in the corner. Seven-thirty.

"She's with me."

Addis handed her the receiver.

"Sir," she said into the phone.

She listened, said "Yes, sir," and then hung up.

"Said he was sending someone for me."

There was a rap on the door. "Come in," Addis said, and O'Connor entered.

"There's news," O'Connor said.

Addis stared at her.

"About the assassination," she added. "They called Margaret and said there's going to be an announcement."

"And they didn't tell her what it is?" Addis said.

"No, the bastards."

O'Connor examined Lancette. She's searching for signs, Addis thought. Whether we did or did not. Lancette tucked in her blouse. She pulled at her hair.

"She said you should come watch with us," O'Connor said.

"She knows we're here?" Addis asked.

"Yep," O'Connor said.

Lancette was trying to smooth the wrinkles out of her clothes.

"You look fine," O'Connor said.

O'Connor led them to the second-floor office. Margaret Mason Hanover was behind the desk, in her bathrobe. Dan Carey was sitting in a chair next to her, wearing a well-pressed Italian suit. Flip Whalen was on the couch. Addis was surprised to see him in Washington. But this was a big day for Margaret; tonight she would openly declare her intention to challenge Mumfries. On the television was the press briefing room at FBI headquarters; the sound was off.

"Good morning, Nick," Margaret said.

He introduced Lancette. Margaret nodded toward the television. "They called me ten minutes ago and said to turn on the television. That's all they said. I don't hear from Brew, Ken, or Mike or anyone else."

"Margaret," Carey said. "It's going to get worse. They chose the wrong side. I have new—"

"Yes, yes," she interrupted. "New numbers. Show them to Nick. I don't need to see new numbers today."

She waved Addis and Lancette toward chairs. "I trust the accommodations were satisfactory."

Addis rubbed his tongue across the inside of his mouth. It was dry.

"Fine, thank you," he said.

"Would you mind telling me why you needed a place to hide out?"

"It's something of a long story," he said.

Margaret waited for him to continue. Whalen was smirking at him. Addis went into the same story he had told O'Connor the night before. When he mentioned Dunne's name, Margaret cut him off.

"M. T., call the hospital to check on him. See when would be the best time for me to come by. It's so sad. Poor Alma."

Her eyes returned to Addis. He finished the explanation.

"So when Ms. Lancette heard Clarence had been shot in Bennington Gardens," Margaret said, "she thought that maybe it had something to do with the fellow in the car and she was frightened?"

246

"Yes," Addis said.

"And Nick offered to provide you a safe spot for the night?" she asked Lancette.

"Yes," Lancette said.

"But not in his house?"

This is where it falls apart, Addis thought.

"After we heard about Clarence," Lancette said, "I wanted to be somewhere that was—"

"More secure than your average D.C. residence?" Margaret asked. Lancette nodded.

Not bad, Addis thought. Still thin, though.

"So, Nick brought me here."

"And you work at the—"

Margaret held up her hand. The live shot from the FBI showed Jake Grayton at the podium. He was reading from a piece of paper. O'Connor increased the volume on the television. Addis noticed Lem Jordan standing by the door to the office.

". . . to tell you of a breakthrough we've had in the assassination investigation," Grayton was saying. "Very early this morning—shortly after two—federal agents, following a confidential tip, raided an apartment in downtown Washington, D.C., in the hope of apprehending an individual, tentatively identified as James Edwin Dawkins, who is believed to have been an accomplice of the assassin of President Hanover. The agents announced themselves at the door and as they entered, they were fired upon. The agents returned the fire. In the ensuing exchange, the suspect received a lethal wound. Another individual, identified as Ernest Ivan Lopez, the owner of a local bar and in whose name the apartment was leased, was also wounded fatally. None of the agents involved in the raid were injured. A subsequent search of the premises found written material espousing the cause of white supremacy and material on how to conduct acts of terrorism. Included in this material was a guide to manufacturing the sort of weapon used in the assassination of President Hanover. A preliminary examination of the body of Dawkins found a tattoo similar to the one on the body of the assassin. An investigation into the background of Mr. Dawkins is being conducted. Our initial information indicates he served in the U.S. Marine Corps several years ago. It is unclear what he has done since his service. Material located in the apartment suggests that he knew the assassin, whom we are now identifying as Matthew Levon Morrison, and that both men shared an interest in white supremacism and harbored a deep hatred of the U.S. government. The relationship of Lopez to Dawkins or Morrison is unclear. We are continuing the investigation. We will not be taking questions at this point."

So there's the conspiracy, Addis thought. All arranged. He glanced at

247

Lancette. She was twirling her hair. She caught him looking at her. Very slowly, she shook her head and mouthed the word "no."

"Now, let me go over procedure a little," Grayton said. He put down the written statement. "After the raid last night, we contacted the White House. I spoke to Hamilton Kelly, a senior aide to President Mumfries. I am told that Mr. Kelly woke the President and informed him of the event. Starting at six o'clock this morning, we began notifying members of the commission. We still have a lot of work to do. The site of the raid has been sealed. To give our forensic experts a little peace in which to work, we are not releasing the location of the apartment. But I am certain that members of the press will be there within minutes. We are continuing to investigate the individuals involved. We will try to determine if any other accomplices remain at large. All the information we have to date indicates there is no outstanding threat to any government official. We hope to have more details for public release later in the day. And if we do, we may be able to have a more extensive press conference and give you the chance to ask questions. But there is a lot for us to do right now."

Grayton cleared his throat.

"On a different matter, let me briefly say regarding the shooting of Clarence Dunne last night, the prayers of everyone here go out to him and his family. We understand there has not been much change in his condition. We are hoping for the best. And to the members of the press, thank you for your patience and understanding."

Grayton stepped away from the podium. Reporters shouted questions at him.

"Who fired the first shot in the apartment?"

"Where are the bodies right now?"

"What's the significance of the tattoo?"

"Did either one have the word *HAPPY* carved into their skin?"

"What was Mrs. Hanover's reaction when you told her? Will this affect the announcement she is expected to make tonight?"

"Will President Mumfries be making any statement?"

"Which federal agents conducted the raid? Mr. Grayton, was it the SWAT team you established last year?"

Grayton did not stop to respond. He left the room. An anchor recapped the statement. O'Connor hit the mute button on the television.

"That's it?" Margaret asked.

"Seems to be," Whalen said.

"Should I call Brew and request more information?" O'Connor asked.

Margaret Hanover shook her head.

"Believe me, I want to know what caused this," she said, "and why these, these"—she could not find the words—"these fuckers killed my husband. I have to know. But I'm not asking them for any favors today.

248

We'll hear from them. Think of how it will look if they don't keep me informed."

Her eyes were moist. She stood up and tightened the belt of her robe. "Time to get dressed. Dan, do we have to put out a statement?"

Carey had been scribbling on a yellow legal pad.

"Nothing elaborate," he said. "You're following developments and you expect you will be kept posted. You are glad none of the agents involved in the raid were injured. That's all. And that your schedule today remains the same."

"Fine."

She paused alongside Addis.

"Sorry we didn't have a chance to talk more, Nick. I'm still hoping you change your mind, maybe come with us to the show tonight."

"Good luck," he said.

As she left the room, an armed guard appeared at the door. He spoke to Margaret, and she turned toward Lancette.

"Dear, you have a visitor. Sent by your employer. Please give the director my regards. I'm sure you'll be quite safe now."

Addis wondered why Margaret had not pressed them further. Was she too preoccupied with her own plans?

A man in a dark suit came into the room. His jacket was unbuttoned and an empty holster was visible. CIA security, Lancette thought. You could always tell. Then she realized that she had seen him before.

"Ms. Lancette?" he asked.

The accident outside headquarters—this was the same guy. He showed no sign of recognition.

"The director would like to see you, Ms. Lancette. I'm supposed to bring you to his office."

"Let me get my things," she said.

"Right away," he added.

"Nick," she said, "show me where you put my purse."

"Sure," Addis replied. He said good-bye to O'Connor and Whalen.

"It was good seeing you back home," Whalen said. "Hope we're done with all that."

Are you playing with me, Flip? Which ''all that'' do you mean? Donny Lee Mondreau? Blue Ridge?

The CIA man followed Addis and Lancette to the study. "I'll be right out," Lancette said to the security officer. She closed the door before he could respond.

"That was a crock of shit," she whispered to Addis. "The white supremacy stuff."

"How do you know?" he asked, keeping his voice low.

"There's something I didn't tell you or Clarence. I got involved in all this because one of our in-house shrinks told me he thought he once treated this guy—I guess it's Dawkins—for alcoholism. Had the same tattoo as the assassin. So there's an Agency connection. When the shrink tried to put paper into the system reporting that, the memo was kicked back. He was then conveniently detailed overseas. To Africa. And I kind of met Dawkins. At that bar. I have to tell you, he did not come across as one of these fuck-'em-all white racist kooks. He seemed pissed at the guy who killed Hanover, not a brother-in-arms. And I just don't think this guy Lopez is your typical Aryan. I mean, he runs a gay bar. There's a fair amount of bullshit flying around."

"That's a news flash," Addis said. "Did you see that memo?"

The security official knocked.

"We should be going, Ms. Lancette," he said from behind the door. "And Director Wenner said I shouldn't leave your side."

She shouted that she would be right there.

"No," she said to Addis. "But—"

The security man opened the door.

"Ms. Lancette," he said.

Lancette looked at Addis.

Damn, I can feel your eyes all the way, deep in my chest.

She took a step in his direction. A kiss, he thought. On the cheek. Perhaps a squeeze of a hand.

Then she turned toward the man in the doorway.

"Thank you for your assistance, Mr. Addis," she said. "I'm sure I was overreacting. But it was nice of you to help."

"You're welcome," he said. "Give my regards to the director."

He wondered how many hours would pass before he'd see her.

As Addis was about to leave Blair House, Lem Jordan stopped him.

"J-J-Jack heard you w-w-w-ere here."

"I'll go say hello," Addis said. "Are you ready for the show tonight?"

"Su-supose so. D-d-on't you think she should do it?"

"I'm not so sure, Lem. It's like she's holding on too much. Like she's holding on to an anchor, and you don't know if she's going to get it out of the water so she can move ahead or if the anchor is going to pull her in."

"You c-c-can always cut an anchor."

"I guess so."

"Once I went on this b-boat with my d-d-dad in the G-G-ulf. Before he went to Arkadelphia to b-b-be with this woman who had a k-k-kennel. And we had this dog. Guess he g-g-ot it from her. A m-m-mutt. We had him on the b-boat that he b-b-borrowed from a guy he knew. And we g-got lost out in the G-Gulf. So he d-d-decided to just stop and figure things out. Look at the m-m-maps. He t-t-told me to throw the anchor over. I didn't have to really throw it. It was hooked up to a line. You just p-p-pulled a lever and then pushed it off. So I pulled the lever and went to the side to p-p-push it off. And that damn d-d-og ran across the line and his leg got c-c-c-caught. I didn't see it, and the an-ch-chor dropped and the dog got p-p-pulled through the hole and right into the water. I heard a crunch as he went by me. Saw him get sucked down. There was b-b-blood on the side of the boat. I yelled to my dad. He came over. He c-c-cussed me out. Said I gotta learn how to clean up m-m-messes I make. He p-p-pulled up the anchor. The dog was still in the line. His leg was g-g-going the wrong way. His head was knocked in. His eyes were open. My dad told me to b-b-bring him in."

Jordan was looking past Addis, at an empty vase.

"I did and put him on the d-d-deck. He wasn't really moving. But he was breathing. So my dad gave me this stick and told me to finish what I had started. To be God-sure he was d-d-dead. And then I had to p-p-put him in a bag and bring him b-b-back with us, show everybody the m-m-mess I made and give him a proper burial. So I did. Had to show him to my brother and sisters and my mother. And he made me bury him in this lot down our street. He said, 'N-n-ow everyday when you walk by, you can remember what happens when you screw up.' But in the m-m-middle of the night, I got up and dug him up, put all the dirt back, and carried him to this park a mile away. I buried him there. Under a tree. I didn't want to be walking by him every day. . . . So that's how I know about anchor lines."

Addis was wondering what to say. Before he could reply, Jordan changed the subject.

"And, you know, she'd do more than M-m-mumfries any-w-w-way."

Jordan stopped himself.

"Y-you should go see J-Jack," he said and walked off.

Addis found Jack's room. The boy was in his wheelchair, sitting by a table. On the television, a man was talking about an affair he had with his wife's sister.

"I know what she's going to do," Jack said.

"Are you okay with that?" Addis asked.

"Guess so. She's mad about Dad not being here. And she doesn't like him much."

"Mumfries?"

"Yeah." Using the remote, Jack aimlessly changed channels. "She was looking at him on television, when he was talking about meeting with these teachers—"

"The historians?" Addis interrupted.

"Yeah, them. And she started crying again. Said he reminded her of my grandfather."

Jack pushed his wheelchair next to a table and picked up a baseball magazine.

"See what I've been trying to do?"

Reading, Addis thought. The brain damage that Jack had suffered in the car crash had inhibited his ability to read.

"That's good."

"Lem gave me this"—he held out the magazine—"but he didn't bring me anything from New Orleans."

"He probably was busy with his mother."

"He always brings me back something."

"Maybe he forgot. There's a lot for him to do."

"Are you coming tonight?"

Addis knew what he meant: the television studio. She was bringing Jack? Perhaps this was Carey's idea.

"I don't think so."

Jack flipped a few pages of the magazine.

"You still going to come around?" he asked, his face in the magazine.

"Yes, I will."

"Why?" Jack asked.

"To see you," Addis said.

Jack almost smiled.

38

"Turn it up, please," Lancette said to the security officer.

They were a mile from the entrance to CIA headquarters. He ignored her request. She leaned over and increased the volume on the radio.

"So last night I hear noises. But I afraid to go downstairs to see. I wait and I hear nothing. Then I hear it again. So I call police."

It was a woman's voice, thickly accented, high in pitch.

"And when police come, I go downstairs, and we go together. There, we see, window is broken. I open the door for police, and they look. They tell me, nobody here. So I go, I go upstairs. Then this morning—I get up at six, there is bang, bang at door. There is men. They say they from government. They say they want to go to downstairs apartment. I open door for them. I do that. And they look everywhere. They look in closet, they look in drawer, they look under bed. Then they ask me many, many questions about Mr. Dawkins. I ask why they want to know. They don't say. They say it's *in-vest-a-ga-tion*. Then I know why."

"You realized that Mr. Dawkins was a suspect in a conspiracy to kill President Hanover?" a male voice asked.

"I knew it was because of the President Hanover."

"And you're saying there was a break-in at his apartment before the federal agents appeared."

"Window is broken," she said.

"What can you tell us about Mr. Dawkins?"

"He is quiet—"

The security officer turned off the radio. He picked up the car phone, dialed a number, and reported he was at the front gate.

Dickhead, she thought, showing he could do what he wanted. It was O/S modus operandi all the way. She remembered when she was an analyst. Anytime a security officer visited the branch, there was more fear than if a Russian had strolled into the section. They relished finding a safe open at the wrong time, or a classified document in the wrong pile. They chased after the slightest infractions. A totalitarian environment for the protectors of democracy.

The car stopped at the main entrance. The driver nodded toward the door on her side.

"Guess they think you don't have to escort me all the way," she said.

The security officer did not reply. She got out of the car.

"You do remember hitting my car?" she asked. Now the Dart was ruined.

"Yes," he said. "You called the number I gave you, and everything was taken care of."

Not going to get any more conversation out of him, she thought. She walked into CIA headquarters.

In the outer office of the director's suite, Lancette stared at the photographs on the wall. They showed young Chinese men and women protesting in Tianamen Square. The photos had been taken by a student leader whom the CIA had helped escape from Beijing after the tanks were sent in. On Lancette's first trip to Wenner's office, he explained his reason for placing these photographs on the wall: They were a reminder of the good the Agency can do.

Viv Novek was on the phone, rearranging Wenner's schedule. He needed to move his appointment with the chief of the French service. He wanted to keep his promised afternoon visit to a Washington high school. (Lancette imagined the questions he would face: Did the CIA kill Kennedy? Why does the government suppress information about UFOs? Does the Agency deal drugs? Did the CIA kill Hanover?) And he wanted a full briefing from the IATF on the latest in the investigation.

Novek raced through a series of calls to reconstruct his day. Then she ordered flowers to be sent, in Wenner's name, to Dunne's hospital room.

"Just terrible, just terrible, what happened to Mr. Dunne," Novek said to Lancette. "Did you ever hear from Mr. Grayton? He was just on the phone with the director."

"Yes, we had dinner."

"And?"

"We've been busy since then."

"Yes, sorry to hear about your accident. Seems like everyone is having a run of bad luck lately."

The phone rang. Wenner was ready to see Lancette. He was at his desk, wearing half-moon reading glasses and poring over audit records. In the corner of the room, a television was tuned to CNN, with the sound off. A reporter was interviewing a Vietnamese woman. The legend on the screen read, "Arlington, Virginia."

254

Wenner did not look up from the papers.

"In your ICEMAN work to date," he asked, "have you ever come across anyone connected to us who's involved with a white supremacist group?"

"Not in this country," she said.

"In this country?"

"There was the German case. The leader of the group that burned down a housing project for immigrants. He said that when he lived in East Germany he gave information to an American businessman he knew as 'Mr. Mike.' 'Mr. Mike' was one of ours—"

"Yes, and that skinhead asshole slit his wrist before the trial. One break for us."

Wenner took off his glasses and placed them on his desk.

"How are you feeling?" he asked.

"Fine," she said.

"Would you mind telling me what's going on?"

"About what, sir?"

"You want me to be a little more precise? First, a maniac tries to run you off the road. At that particular moment, Clarence Dunne is driving by and comes to the rescue. Then you disappear for two days. Now it's not as if we can't get along without our historical exercises for a day or two. But then Mr. Dunne is shot in *unusual* circumstances, and you turn up that night with Mr. Addis at the White House. I only find this out when Mr. Grayton calls to inform me about last night's raid. Next, I gather, you spend the entire evening at the White House."

"Actually, Blair House, sir."

"Thank you, Ms. Lancette, for that correction. You would concede this is an unorthodox series of days and nights? And you would acknowledge that the head of an intelligence service might have a question or two for an employee involved in such a string of events?"

"I would, sir."

"It is time for you to speak."

He pushed the audit records to the side. There was a coffee stain on his tie.

"Yes," she said. "Yes, it is."

Shit, she thought, let's see what happens.

"There was an irregularity in an ICEMAN request regarding the Hanover assassination. A report didn't come in. The branch chief assured me the delay was due to changeover in the office. Then I was contacted by an officer in the branch who claimed that a memo he had written in response to the request had not been forwarded, that it had been . . . repressed. This officer—"

"Dr. Charlie Walters in the psychiatric office."

Lancette stopped speaking.

"We know all about Dr. Walters," Wenner said.

"What about him?" she asked.

"He was arrested in Bujumbura yesterday after he hit a street vendor with his car and nearly killed the man. The police said he was drunk at the time. He was traveling as a State doctor. So he's covered by immunity. The police released him to the embassy but they're holding on to his passport. God knows what they're going to do. Walters told one of our officers there about the report claiming he met the assassin once before."

"That's not what he told me," Lancette said.

"That's what's in the cable. I checked with his branch chief. He told me that Walters is facing two administrative actions. One for being too forward with a patient. The child of a deputy station chief recently back from Indonesia. He touched this patient"—Wenner reached for a paper on his desk and read from it—" 'in inappropriate spots, including genitalia.' In another instance, he recently returned from lunch too inebriated to perform his duties."

Hell, Lancette thought, if every employee who ever did that was booted, the Agency would be radically downsized.

"They also suspect he was helping himself to samples from the pharmacy. Which might explain the memo he wrote in response to your request. It's gibberish. Look at it."

He handed her a document and waited as she read. It was one long paragraph, single-spaced, covering two pages. Walters claimed he had once met the assassin at a bar, that this person had told him that he was part of an off-the-books hit team directed by Wenner. In the memo, Walters said that his own life was in danger, and that he would cooperate in the investigation if the administrative actions against him were dropped.

"Did he show you this document?" Wenner asked.

"No," Lancette said.

"He admitted to our officer in Burundi that he misled you."

But he hadn't, she thought. He had told her enough so she was able to find Dawkins.

"Ms. Lancette, you know what happens when you start investigating craziness. You establish a paper trail that will be misinterpreted for decades to come."

There could be no greater nightmare for him, she thought, then to have the Agency linked to another presidential assassination—especially when his name would be associated with the conspiracy. Someone had played him well. Or was he allowing himself to be played?

"So no one at IATF knows about this?" she asked.

"I've discussed it with Mr. Grayton, and we agreed that allegations deemed worthless need not be officially presented to the task force."

We agreed. She looked at Wenner's eyes. They had the same distant appearance as always, as if he were searching for smudges on the wall at the opposite end of the room. *We agreed.* He and Grayton. Never hold anything back from me, he once had told her, I can always go back to Cal Tech and teach. This job needs me more than I need it. But Walters had known where to find Dawkins. His story—the one he told her—contained more than craziness.

"Director, I don't want to challenge Mr. Grayton's and your reading of the situation." She paused.

"Then don't," he said.

"But Dr. Walters did tell me enough so I could locate Dawkins through that bar."

"I left something out. The patient he touched inappropriately was a seventeen-year-old boy. Dr. Walters is a repressed homosexual. I don't care about a person's. . . . But he lied about it on his personnel records. We just want people to be open about it, that's all. So he's been to the bar. And maybe he really did meet Dawkins there and figured out something about this conspiracy. But it doesn't matter. We cannot unleash such a noncredible source into the investigation. It will be poison. And since the owner of that bar was found with Dawkins, the investigation can target the bar. There's no need for Walters's report. It takes us nowhere we cannot already go."

Except, she thought, that this is not his real report. *We agreed.* On how much? she wondered. She felt very far from the *we.*

"If Walters was in trouble, why was he sent to Africa?" she asked.

"Budget cuts. The branch was short of qualified psychiatrists. It couldn't afford to place Walters on administrative leave."

"I see."

Wenner walked to the window. His shoes were scuffed. He gazed out at the woods surrounding the compound.

"I wish we could see the river from here," he said.

"Yes," she said. This is how they do it, she thought. Ruin and discredit a life. Walters was fucked. They were burying him.

"So you're well enough, I suppose, to return to your normal duties?" he asked. Lancette realized it was not really a question. "And I've told Mr. Grayton that you will be at his disposal in case the task force does end up needing information on the Walters matter."

"Yes, sir," she answered.

"Thank you," he said. Wenner was dismissing her.

She stood to leave. *We agreed.* That's it? she thought. And what about her? If she didn't *agree*? She opened the door to leave.

"Ms. Lancette?"

She paused at the threshold.

"I took your advice on the El Salvador business."

She had to think for a moment. He was referring to the ICEMAN case they had recently discussed: the former death squad leader who was arrested for drug smuggling and who once had been on the CIA payroll. Wenner had decided not to interfere with the prosecution.

"Thank you," she said and closed the door.

39

The U.S. Capitol
June 30

Addis flipped through the stack of compact discs in Senate Majority Leader Hugh Palmer's private hideaway office in the Capitol building. It was all reggae. The senator had never publicized his fondness for the music he first encountered as a Peace Corps volunteer in Barbados in the 1960s. He did not believe Iowa voters would appreciate his devotion to ganja music. Only in his most private spots and moments—and this windowless office was one of Washington's more private locations—did Palmer indulge.

The small television on the desk was turned to an all-news channel, with the volume muted. Video footage of Governor Wesley Pratt appeared. He was standing outside a grocery store in Florida, with several reporters questioning him. Addis turned on the sound.

"I don't care which one I run against," Pratt was saying. "But it's not time to be campaigning. We're all still mourning. I'll be going to Washington for the Christian Women's Association conference. But we're not campaigning yet. And since you asked, I don't think there's much difference there on the key issues. You know, both have said they're for this anti-Christian trade treaty with China."

He's right, Addis thought. With the President gone, would Margaret change her position? Follow her natural instincts? Or would she defend her husband's decision? Addis guessed that the China treaty was not foremost in her thoughts this week.

"Look at it. We got a country that tortures Christians—imagine being thrown into jail because you worship Jesus Christ—and we're going to treat them like an equal? I don't see why any Christian in this country would stand for that. But, we'll have time to talk about this soon."

"What do you have to say about the report on the wires that Edwin Hanover, President Hanover's brother, is supporting you?"

Addis shook his head.

"Listen, I want everybody's support. And I know he's a religious man. But where I come from, we stand with our kin. Family first. So I'm happy to pick up votes from anyone, but I don't want to be a part of anything that brings personal pain to a widow—a woman whose husband made the ultimate sacrifice for our great land. Thanks. Melinda's shouting at me from the car. I gotta go. We'll see you soon."

He's getting better, Addis thought. If he gave up the heavy Christian stuff, he'd be competitive. Thank God, Addis said to himself, for . . . God.

He changed channels and stopped when he came to a broadcast of the House of Representatives. Nine days after the assassination and congress had resumed business. A jowly congressman from Houston was in the well. He was the one, Addis recalled, who once got an intern pregnant. "I ask for unanimous consent to revise and extend my remarks," the legislator said in a booming voice. Only in Washington, Addis mused. You make a speech on the floor of the House and then you can change the transcript before it appears in the *Congressional Record*. For whatever reason. Add sentences that were never uttered. Remove words that were actually said. Reality and official reality.

Addis thought of a phrase Hanover had liked to use: *the king's truth.* Hanover had borrowed the term from the king of Saudi Arabia. In the first year of the administration, the king met with Hanover at the White House. At a subsequent press conference, a reporter asked if Hanover had agreed to help the Saudis set up an electronic surveillance post in northern Saudi Arabia. The king fielded the question. "Nothing was asked for," he answered. "Nothing was promised. Next question." He then pointed to a woman from French television.

When Hanover and the king left the East Room, Hanover thanked the king for handling the question. The two had discussed establishing such a base, which was supposed to be a secret installation. The Saudi winked at Hanover and said, "The king's truth." Hanover laughed. "Sure could use some of that sometimes," he replied. With a slim smile, the king remarked, "Comes with the job, Mr. President. Comes with the responsibility. Those with great responsibilities must be permitted to decide what it is for others to know. That may be the most difficult duty of a leader. And, here, it is indeed my truth, for I do not remember any asking or any promise. I remember only a preliminary exchange of views."

Hanover later told Addis about this conversation, and the phrase became a private joke between them. When Hanover had to respond to an inconvenient disclosure or a White House foul-up, he would look wistfully at Addis and say those three words, but never so anyone else could hear.

Addis switched the television to the Senate channel. Palmer was on the floor, trying to block legislation that would force federal workplace safety officials to provide forty-eight-hour notice to companies before they conduct on-site inspections. The measure would render safety inspections meaningless, for employers could temporarily remedy any potential violations. Again, Addis thought, his party, imperfect as it was, was at least trying to stop the other side from screwing Americans who do the hard work. Or, that is, a portion of his party was.

When Sal Conditt, Addis's successor as Palmer's chief of staff, had escorted Addis to the hideaway, he had informed Addis that Palmer did not believe he had the votes to stop the provision. There were going to be too many defections from their party.

During their walk through the Capitol, Conditt had been as gruff as always. Addis assumed he knew that Addis had advised Palmer not to hire Conditt, a fast-riser at party headquarters and a veteran of several presidential campaigns. Addis considered Conditt to be in the Hamilton Kelly category: professional political guides. These were aides who cared little for policy particulars, except in one respect: that they lead to political success. Addis knew—he was certain of it—that Palmer saw the difference between a Sal Conditt and a Nick Addis. But Addis also realized that a Conditt was tempting to a politician juggling multiple responsibilities, obligations, and desires. A Conditt made life work, the trains run. He rarely asked uncomfortable questions. Who could resist that?

Addis sat in a birchwood rocking chair and looked at the familiar pictures on the wall. Palmer marching for civil rights. Palmer marching against the war. Palmer and his wife and the movie actress, whose advances Palmer admirably had not accepted. Addis thought about the days when these hideaway offices—reserved for senior members of Congress—were occupied by the old southern bulls. When Addis first worked on the Hill, there were still porters and janitors who could pass on stories of that era. The prodigious booze sessions. The all-night poker marathons. The brawl that left one senator with one less tooth. And all the women granted individual tours of these private areas: aides, receptionists, constituents, lobbyists, interns, and prostitutes. One porter, since retired, told Addis about a janitor who once came upon a senator alone, naked and bound in his hideaway. Addis asked which legislator that had been. "I can tell a story and still keep a secret," the porter said.

Addis looked at the small refrigerator in the corner. He knew it contained only bottles of spring water.

Palmer burst into the office.

"Shit," he said. "Lost Sterling and Canton. That probably does it."

He dragged his hands through his thick, gray hair. His legs still look half-a-foot too long for the rest of his body, Addis told himself.

"Did you have commitments?" Addis asked.

"Yes, I had fucking commitments from them. But I don't have an army of cell-phone-carrying, god-damn lobbyists who give them money and tell them how to vote. You try holding this party together. Talk about a dysfunctional family. Hell, I have the widows of those poor S.O.B.s killed in that chicken factory fire in North Carolina in the gallery. And it doesn't mean diddley. Reed and Mahr wouldn't even see them when they went to their offices."

"Do you think it'd be different if he was still . . . ?"

Palmer threw his jacket on the couch and sat behind the desk. He grabbed a handful of roasted peanuts from a jar.

"Don't know, Nick," he said, as he cracked open a shell. "He would have had to push these bastards hard. And, you know, rest-in-peace and all that, but he wasn't always so good at pushing for the right things. . . . I did call Brew and asked if the White House could do something. He seemed a slight bit distracted."

"He's trying hard to hold on."

"And then I tried to get Alter to say something. As if Treasury—or he—cares. There's no corn growing there."

"And Mumfries, on his own, sure as hell won't."

Palmer sighed. "It's just not easy doing what's right. And I got to get back there soon. Sal already chewed me out for taking time to talk to you. He feels threatened whenever we spend time alone. So what do you have on your mind that you don't want to put on a telephone line?"

"It's about the assassination."

"Got briefed on the phone by Grayton. Don't much care for that one. And the commission's meeting soon. They're going give us the whole dog-and-pony show when we get together. Fucking nutcases. At least this isn't going to help Pratt, Gravitt and those yahoos who want more guns out there and who dump on big government all the time."

Palmer crunched several peanuts against the desktop.

"So what then?" he asked.

"I don't think they got it right."

Palmer did not reply at once. He peeled several nuts and ate a handful.

"What's not right, Nick?" he asked.

"The story."

"What part of the story? And how, may I ask, do *we* know this?"

Addis gathered his thoughts.

"I'm not sure about everything. Clarence Dunne was looking into this. So was this woman at the CIA. They tracked down Dawkins before anything was announced. I don't think it had anything to do with a white supremacist, antigovernment thing. And while they were doing this, the CIA woman—"

"Does she have a name?"

"Yes, it's Julia Lancette. . . . Someone tried to run her off the G.W. Parkway. And you saw what happened to Dunne—"

262

"Still unconscious in the hospital?"

"Last I heard. . . . Also, a friend of the Georgetown student killed in the Mayflower—she was hit by a car on her bicycle, hours after she told me and Clarence that she and her friend worked for a bizarre escort business."

"A what?"

"I don't know. And then the fellow who ran the service was killed, too."

"Nick, you've been working overtime."

"Senator, it just kind of happened."

"And the proof that these deaths may be connected?" Palmer asked.

"Basically, just that woman's—"

"The bicycle rider?"

"Yes, her word."

"But she was a . . . and now she's—"

"Yes," Addis said.

"And the CIA?"

"Someone inside, a psychiatrist, told Julia that he once treated a guy with the same tattoo found on the assassin. It probably was Dawkins. Which could mean the Agency's somehow connected. And they killed his report on this."

"Okay, okay," Palmer said.

He placed a row of peanuts on his desk and applied his palm to each one, breaking them open in succession.

"Nick, here's the question I have for you: Why are you telling me?"

Addis blinked. He rubbed his chin. He thought it was obvious. He began to worry.

"Well . . . you're on the presidential commission on the assassination."

"Yes, I am. But I'd have to be a damn fool to say a single syllable about the CIA being involved in the assassination unless I got something we lawyers call *evidence*. You got five thousand FBI agents chasing after every turd Morrison and Dawkins ever kicked out. Everyone's swarming over what happened to Clarence. Do you know for certain if he was out last night doing something that was part of this little *independent* investigation you two got going?"

"No, I don't."

"So I think it would be premature for me to say that the attack on poor Clarence was connected. And then there's the CIA. I dislike the pricks there as much as anyone. Except for Wenner. I like him fine, but he can't control his own gang. Like a rabbit in charge of mules. Or maybe it's the other way around. But I can't start to say boo about them. Even at one of our own meetings. I do, and it will leak. Don't you think Gravitt would

263

get a horse's boner, telling a reporter I was accusing the CIA of something like that? It's a no-brainer for him. Either I look like I'm batty, or the administration is implicated in this god-awful thing. And what else can I do? Tell Wenner. Tell Mumfries. Hell, Nick, you could do that yourself. You could hold a press conference right now on the steps of the Capitol. I'll pick up this phone here—"

Palmer lifted the receiver.

"Hello? Press gallery? Please notify everyone that Mr. Nicholai Addis, senior adviser to the President of the United States, wishes to meet with the congressional press corps in two-and-a-half minutes. . . . We can whip up a fine audience for you, Nick. But seems to me you have stories, not proof. Damn interesting stories. But I'm not going to be your storyteller."

He put the receiver down. The line rang. Palmer put the phone to his ear.

"Fuck them!" he said. "Tell them that I better not see their backsides at the next caucus meeting crying about how the transportation grant formula screws their states."

He slammed the phone.

"Lewis and Davis. Lost them, too. . . . Nick, there's something else."

He scooped up the peanut shells and dumped them in a metal garbage can.

"Haven't even told Sal this yet. But I will. . . . Kelly called last night. Asked if I was free enough of 'obligations' to talk to Sam about the future. I said I was plenty free. Sam called me twenty minutes later. Said that Rick Torrie is going to be leaving by the election. They found a lump in Suzy's breast. So Sam asked if I would consider being Secretary of State."

Addis's stomach tightened.

"He said, 'Sure, we've had our differences. And we'll have plenty more. But if you think you can work with me, let's give it a try.'"

"And you just have to declare your support. . . ."

"He did ask if we could announce this soon. Before the convention. Said he had other Cabinet changes. Wants to do them all at once—"

"And make sure that Margaret can't . . ."

"You know, Nick, I honestly don't think it's a good idea for her."

"What did she offer you, Senator?"

"Damnit, Nick, I'll never get you to call me Hugh, will I?"

"Not while you're in office."

Palmer placed his hands behind the back of the chair.

"Nothing, Nick. Nothing at all. Which was fine with me. But she didn't even say anything about Vice President. I don't think she's put any thought to it yet. Which shows she shouldn't be doing this."

"And you told Mumfries?"

"That I was honored by the invitation. That I would have to talk to Shirley about it. That I would let him know tomorrow morning."

"And you're thinking . . ."

"Look at those god-damn baboons down there."

Palmer threw a handful of peanuts at the television screen.

"They don't give a god-damn shit if somebody's husband or wife who makes minimum wage plucking feathers from a carcass gets roasted alive because a fucking supervisor bolts shut a fire door so employees can't sneak out for a smoke."

"And you're thinking . . ."

"That I'd like to leave the zoo and join the circus."

"But Mumfries. It's not like he'd be voting right on this bill."

"Better to worry about one clown than ninety-nine."

"Well, then, congratulations, Secretary-designate."

"Fuck you, Nick," he said with a laugh.

"And all those differences Mumfries mentioned?"

"One trapeze at a time."

And don't forget the mountains of elephant shit. Accepting the China trade accord. Retreating on global warming negotiations. Forcing foreign ministers of Third World countries to adopt austerity budgets in return for loans.

"Good luck, then," Addis said.

"And I know you mean it."

"I do."

There was a knock, and Conditt opened the door. "Excuse me for being the schmuck you pay me to be," he said, "but you should get back there if you want to keep a loss from turning into a massacre."

Conditt shut the door.

"You got to love him," Palmer said. He stood up and grabbed one more handful of peanuts.

"Not really," Addis said.

"Call me later if you need to. And if you find anything hard . . . take it to another commission member."

Palmer laughed and straightened his tie.

"Just kidding. If you come up with something solid, I'll be there for you. But it has to be solid. Feel free to use the phone if you need to. And help yourself." He left the office.

"Thank you, Senator," Addis said to no one. "Thank you very much."

Addis exited the rear of the Capitol and walked through the plaza. He felt the heat rising from the asphalt and looked toward the sky. No clouds today. He saw the Statue of Freedom—a woman wearing flowing draperies, her hand resting on the hilt of a sword—atop the Capitol dome. She faced east, out of the city, not toward the Mall, not toward the White

House—as if she were considering an escape from the capital city, perhaps peering toward a place of refuge in the distinctly nonfederal and dilapidated neighborhoods beyond Capitol Hill. Addis wondered why he had never noticed this before.

40

George Washington University Hospital
June 30

"I ain't never been in no hospital before," Anjean Jameson said, as the automatic doors swept shut behind him.

"No way," Willie Jameson said.

"Fuckin' word," Anjean said loudly.

Several attendants at the reception desk looked up at Anjean and his two companions. Anjean was wearing a shiny black bandana tied tightly around his head. A gold chain hung around his neck. His black nylon pullover and black nylon sweatpants rustled with each movement.

"Shut the fuck up," Starrell said in a low voice. "Act like you fuckin' know where we're going."

The three men walked past the reception desk.

"Where *are* we going?" Willie whispered to Starrell.

"Like you fuckin' know where we're going," Starrell repeated. He was wearing his wraparound sunglasses and carrying a beat-up knapsack. Willie was toting a plastic bag full of clothes.

They entered an elevator.

"What floor?" Willie asked.

"Any one, like you fuckin' know where we're going," Starrell said and punched a button.

"Like fuckin' Superfly," Anjean said.

"Man," Willie said. "He was a dealer. This trip's more like Shaft. And what you mean you ain't never been in a hospital?"

"What I said," Anjean replied.

The elevator stopped at the fourth floor, and the doors opened.

"Get out," Starrell said.

He turned right and the two brothers followed. They passed three pregnant women in hospital gowns.

"Look, man," Anjean said. "This here's for bitches about to pop." He laughed. "Don't think your man's around here, Twayne. Not unless there's something you ain't tellin' us."

Starrell said nothing. He saw a door marked *exit* and opened it. The three took the stairs up a floor. There was not much activity in the hall. Starrell spotted a men's room, and the young men entered it.

Starrell checked the stalls. No one was there. He took off the sunglasses, the sweatshirt, and the T-shirt that advertised the name of a New York fashion house. He grabbed the bag of clothes from Willie and pulled out a crumpled white dress shirt. Anjean sat on a sink, and Willie stood by the door.

"Now he puts on the disguise," Anjean said, as Starrell started changing clothes. "I-Spy shit, man!"

"You must've been in a hospital," Willie said to Anjean. "Like when momma was there."

"Nah, when we was little, they wouldn't let us come and we stayed with 'Tie Rita. And after she said I couldn't come home no more, well, I figured she don't want me visiting her at no hospital. I almost was in one night before Halloween. We was at the video store and when we came out, this black Wagoneer came by loaded, and they start shootin'. They blew out the window. Randy whipped out his piece and shot up that Wagoneer. Got the back window. Like an explosion. Then I see Mouse-man on the ground. He's cryin' like a baby. 'I'm fuckin' wet,' he says. 'I'm fuckin' wet.' So Randy gets his Jeep and we put Mouse-man in it. Randy's shoutin,' 'I'll fuck you up you get blood on my Jeep.' Mouse-man keeps cryin', 'I'm wet, I'm wet.' We kick it to D.C. General. And Mouse-man gets real quiet. And when we slide to at the hospital, Randy says, just put him by the . . . what you call it?"

"The curb?" Willie said.

Starrell was doing the buttons on the white shirt.

"Yeah, the curb. And I say, 'We got to bring him inside.' Randy says, 'Don't think like a bitch. We blew those niggers away. They'll be lookin' for us. Leave him there, they'll find him.' Couldn't say that ain't so, right? So that's it. Right by the door. But not inside."

Starrell stared at Anjean.

"He died, right?"

"Sure did. But he was almost stiff when he got there. His blood was on E. So made no diff, man."

Starrell took a blue tie with red stripes out of the bag and looped it around his collar.

"You know how to do this, Willie?" he asked.

Willie helped Starrell with the tie.

"But I bet you've been in a hospital," Willie said to his brother.

"Bet what, man?"

"You have to send momma some flowers."

"She don't want zip from me."

"You think she don't want zip because that's what she says. But that don't make it what she really wants."

"Yeah, and what you putting up?" Anjean asked.

"Next time you want to hide something in the house I won't tell you to bounce yourself the fuck off."

"You got it," Anjean said.

Willie straightened the tie.

"Stay here for five," Starrell said. "Then go wait outside."

"How you going to find him?" Willie asked.

"I'll find him. And don't be calling any attention to your black asses. Okay?"

Neither brother said anything. Starrell put his face in front of Anjean.

"I said, okay?" Starrell said.

"Yeah, right. Why you asking me?"

"Okay, Twayne," Willie said. "But maybe we'll go check out the flowers downstairs 'cause An is going to be in the market."

"Unh-unh," Anjean protested.

" 'Cause he was in a hospital. He sure was. He was born in a hospital." Willie laughed.

Starrell picked up the backpack and smiled. As he opened the door, he heard Anjean mutter, "Oh fuck that shit."

Starrell stood in a hallway on the sixth floor and placed his hands over his face. He thought about the book of drawings done by Willie and Anjean's brother, Marco. He thought about the way Marco had been found: at least a dozen bullet wounds, half of them in the face. And his mother kept wailing about having an open casket at the funeral. At the church, she tried to open the lid, crying, "Just wanna see my baby boy." Willie had to pull her away.

He pictured his cousin Barry all laid out. And how his uncle said nothing that long day. And Tamika's brother Wendell. Buried with his basketball card collection. Tamika and her mother never knew that Wendell had been collecting for the Stillman Crew. They had a rule: No collectors over thirteen years old. Wendell was twelve-years, ten-and-a-half months old when a bullet exploded his heart. Shit, everyone knew the Stillman Crew was pushing too far into the wrong hoods. If Wendell had asked, Starrell would have told him to quit. But what's a kid supposed to know?

At least the face was left, so Tamika and her mother could kiss, kiss, kiss it before the reverend placed his hands on their shoulders and said, "It's time."

He imagined the baby—maybe a boy—growing inside Tamika. Those little hands. What he would do if any fucker tried to cause that baby harm. But how could he make sure that this baby would not end up in a Sunday suit in a box in the ground? Shit, why wouldn't Tamika let him be the father of this baby he would protect forever?

He removed his hands from his face. He felt the wetness sliding away from his eyes.

Shit, he thought, it's not that hard to cry.

A nurse was standing nearby. She was pretty: big eyes and caramel skin. "Can I help?" she asked.

"Yeah," Starrell said. He tried a sob. "I was looking for my uncle. They told me downstairs where he is. But"—he wiped a tear—"I wasn't really listening. . . . He's Clarence Dunne. You know, the—"

"Oh, yes," she interrupted. "Of course. Come with me."

She gently put her hand against his back and guided him to an elevator.

"I'll show you," she said. "My name's Cynthia."

Starrell tasted the saltiness at the corner of his mouth.

"T-Thomas," he said.

They rode up two floors, and the nurse escorted him through a hallway. She paused outside a room with a closed glass door. Starrell saw a black woman in a blue dress, and two black men wearing ties and jackets. A bearded white man in a white coat was talking to them.

"Your aunt and cousins," the nurse said. "You want to tell them you're . . . ?" She took a step toward the door.

"No," Starrell said. "Not when they is . . . they're talking to the doctor. That's okay. Maybe I should just look in on Uncle Clarence, if I can."

"Let's go see," Cynthia said.

Down the hall, a uniformed police officer was sitting in a chair outside a room. A nurse came out. Cynthia asked if Dunne could receive a visitor.

"Still unconscious," the nurse said.

"It's his nephew," Cynthia said.

The police officer looked at Starrell, who rubbed his eyes and tried to ignore the stare. Just be like one of those Chevy Chase oreos, he told himself. They don't fuckin' freak when a cop checks them out.

"For a minute," the nurse said.

Cynthia opened the door. The officer held up his hand. "Wait a sec."

Starrell felt a tremor in his legs. He looked for the nearest exit. His muscles tightened; he was ready to sprint those thirty yards, ready to start pumping . . . in a moment.

Chill, he said to himself. Chill, chill, chill.

"Need to check his bag," the policeman said.

"No problem . . . sir," Starrell said. He swung the backpack off his shoulder, opened it, and held it out for the policeman. The officer pawed through it, saying the contents aloud: "letters, papers, brochures, more papers, more papers." This could be fuckin' it, Starrell said silently. He looks at this shit. Fuckin' didn't think of this.

Starrell breathed through his nose. Chill, man, he repeated to himself.

"Okay," the policeman said.

Cynthia and Starrell entered the room.

"I'll be back in a couple of minutes," she said. She smiled at him and closed the door.

Dunne was connected to various machines. A tube ran from the bandages on his neck. A catheter was stuck into his arm. An assortment of electronic devices were at one side of the bed. His skin color was yellowish, his eyes closed.

Starrell approached Dunne slowly. The air smelled funny, he thought. He felt a nervous sweat pouring out of his body.

"Mr. Dunne," he said.

Shit, he thought, what if the guard could hear?

"Clarence?" he said. "Uncle Clarence?"

Dunne didn't move. Starrell sat down in a chair. He leaned over Dunne and placed his mouth near Dunne's ear. He could hear the hiss of oxygen flowing through a tube.

"It's me. It's me, Starrell. Twayne."

He pulled back and looked at Dunne. Nothing.

"Fuckin' come on, man," he said in a low voice. "I got all this shit here"—he patted the backpack—"from that house. Remember, man, we were in the car, talking. You were telling me all that shit. All that shit you wrote down in that notebook. Said like, someone else should know this shit. And right now the only someone else is my black ass. And you said that this whacked-out guy lived with this gook woman and that his bud shot up Hanover and that you wanted to check out the place, you know?"

Dunne's mouth moved. His eyes flickered open, then closed.

"Come on. We busted in there. Not much there. Man, a mountain of empties. Some nasty-ass magazines with freaky motorcycle bitches. It stunk, man. But we Hoovered the place. Found this bag with all this shit in it. Letters. Newspaper shit. C'mon, wake up. I can't park my ass here all day."

Starrell glanced toward the door. He took Dunne's hand from underneath the covers and put it on the bag.

"What the fuck do we do with this? You tell me."

Dunne's eyes opened. His lips parted. A phlegmy croaking came out.

271

"Fuck," Starrell said. "You can't say nothing. Shit, this sucks. I should get myself out of here."

Dunne moved his hand off the backpack and placed it on top of Starrell's hand. His grip was weak.

"Can't sit around here and hold hands."

Dunne's eyes glared at him. With much effort, he shook his head. Then he tapped Starrell's hand once. He paused. He tapped it twice. He paused. He tapped it three times. He stopped and blinked hard at Starrell. Then he tapped it four times. Then five. Then six. He blinked hard again.

"Shit, what do you want man?" Starrell asked. "Just fuckin' tell me."

Dunne's finger poked Starrell's palm seven times, then eight, then nine. He blinked. He then tapped once and grunted at the same time, making a short "ah" sound. He grimaced with the pain.

"Come on, fuckin' say something."

Dunne tapped and grunted once more, wincing.

"Yeah, yeah, yeah. I'm thinkin', thinkin'."

Dunne lifted his finger to start again.

"A . . . B . . . C . . . " Starrell said.

Dunne blinked his eyes fast several times.

"Okay, okay, alphabet city."

Dunne tapped out one, then four, then three—

The door opened. Starrell jumped back. Margaret Hanover and the black woman in the blue dress—Dunne's wife—entered. In the hallway behind them was a crowd of people: the doctor, Dunne's sons, several nurses, men in dark suits, and the policeman. The door swung shut.

Starrell stood up.

"Who the hell are you?" Alma Dunne asked.

Oh shit, he thought. Oh—

"Who let you in?" She turned toward the door.

Oh—

"I'm going to see about this."

Starrell held out his hands, palms up.

"Praise, Jesus!" he shouted, drawing out the words. "Praise the Lord!"

What do all those Jesus-nuts shout on television? he asked himself.

"Look at him." He pointed to Dunne. "Oh, the Lord heals the sick and the afflicted. His power saves. See for yourself."

Alma Dunne saw that her husband's eyes were open. She rushed past Starrell to Dunne's side and grabbed his hand.

"Oh, honey," she said. "Oh, honey, Clarence, Clarence. Oh, Clarence." She stroked his face.

Starrell moved past Margaret Hanover, zipping up the bag.

"Praise the Lord," he said to her. "Praise him and the power of prayer and our hospital"—damn, what's the word?—"ministry. I've been praying over him. Yes, ma'am, I have. Eugene Carver, of Christ Healing Ministry."

He stopped and held out his hand. She took it and stared at him, not knowing what to say.

"A pleasure," he said. "Praise Jesus."

"Thank you," Margaret replied.

Starrell opened the door and pushed through the clutch of family, security personnel, and hospital employees. "Who's that?" he heard someone say. "His nephew, right?" another voice said. "He's not a nephew," a different voice replied. Starrell kept walking and emerged from the crowd.

"Hey, you, wait a minute."

Starrell broke into a sprint. The backpack slapped against him. His feet pounded the tile; he stretched out his gait. He heard someone—maybe two people—running behind him. Only dead men look back, he told himself. There were more shouts. He heard the voices, but did not listen to the words. Pump it, pump it, pump it, he said to himself.

He grabbed the metal door handle. He yanked it open and leaped down the first flight of stairs. He landed, reached for the railing and flew around the turn. He heard the door slam open behind him and more shouts. He gained his footing, took two quick steps, and jumped again. He caught the railing, turned himself, and passed the door to the seventh floor.

Concentrate on the feet, he said to himself. Concentrate. Jump, grab, turn, two steps. Then again. And again. He heard the grunts and groans of the people chasing him. He couldn't tell if they were gaining. He wondered if they had guns. Jump, grab, turn, two steps. "Concentrate"—he said it aloud. "Concentrate."

He went by the third floor. Shit, he thought, the men in suits outside the hospital room—Secret Service. Must be a whole posse at the hospital. If not for Dunne, then for Margaret Hanover. They all got those radio things in their ears. They're probably waiting for him at the bottom floor. God damnit.

Starrell pulled open the door to the second floor. He looked both ways: no men in suits. He ran to the right. He felt the blood speeding through his body. His legs kept pumping. Like a fucking machine, he told himself. He brushed by two orderlies and an old man using a walker. He thought he heard the door to the stairwell bang open. There was more yelling. Don't look back, he told himself. Only suckers do.

He turned a corner. Another long corridor. Shit, shit, shit, he said to himself. How the fuck do I get out? He ran its length and entered another stairwell. The basement, he thought. Maybe a parking garage. Keep on going down. He jumped the first flight. Hit the landing. Jumped the next flight.

"Fuck!" he shouted. A metal gate blocked access to the stairs leading to the lower levels. "To get to the parking levels," a sign read, "use the stairwell at the western end of the corridor." He pulled on the gate. It was locked. He heard the door to the second floor slam open. He burst into the hallway and ran.

He raced by visitors and patients. He shoved aside two children holding flowers. He thought he was running toward the entrance. But he had lost his sense of direction. He couldn't feel his legs. Just blast by those Secret Service dudes, he told himself. Like through the backfield. The motherfuckers are right around the corner. Fuckin' party time, Starrell said to himself.

He rounded the corner and saw the front entrance to the hospital. And six suits between him and the door. They were coming his way. There were shouts behind him.

I am fucked, he thought. Super-fucked. He remembered a coach from a long time ago: Keep that C of G low, 'cause, you ain't going down, if you're already down. Starrell lowered his head and tried to find more strength in his legs.

Then the world exploded. There was a crash. Glass was flying. Several suits dropped to the ground. An ambulance had driven right through the front doors and into the lobby. An alarm went off. A siren started up. People were screaming. The ambulance skidded toward the reception desk. Nurses were running to get out of its path.

Starrell looked up. Willie was in the ambulance, waving at him from the passenger side and shouting something. Starrell spotted two suits coming toward him, but other people were in the way. He pushed bodies aside and leaped over one of the suits on the floor.

He could hear Willie's voice. "Move it, man! Move it!"

There was one more suit. Starrell saw a gun. He heard several shots. He saw the suit go down. He wondered if he was too pumped to feel a bullet. He then noticed Anjean leaning over Willie, holding a gun.

"Fuckin' shit," Starrell said and sprinted toward the ambulance.

He jumped on the running board. Willie grabbed his arm.

"Hold the fuck on!" Anjean screamed.

The ambulance accelerated backward and out of the lobby. Pieces of glass fell on Starrell. The ambulance skipped over a step and crashed into a car in the driveway.

"Blow, Anjean, blow!" Willie shouted.

Starrell heard more shots. They hit the ambulance. He saw a suit with a gun at the entranceway. The same one he had jumped over? Good, he's not dead, Starrell thought, but let's get the fuck out of here.

Anjean threw the ambulance into gear and punched the accelerator. The rear of the ambulance fishtailed and struck another car. Starrell nearly fell off. The backpack slid off his shoulder. He held on to the strap. Willie's grip tightened on him. More shots hit the ambulance.

Anjean had room on Pennsylvania Avenue and sped through a light.

"Whooo-fuckin'-eeee!" he shouted. "This is vicious!"

"You're fuckin' crazy!" Starrell yelled.

"Crazy enough to save your skanky ass," Anjean shouted. "We flipped the script, man!" He waved his gun outside the window and fired a shot into the air.

"Quit that shit, Anjean!" Willie screamed at him.

Starrell looked back toward the hospital. No cars were chasing them.

"Ain't going to be nobody back there," Willie said to him. "Not right away. We saw them all run into the hospital. Figured it had something to do with you. They left their cars. So. . . ."

He held up a knife and smiled. The ambulance hit a pothole, and Starrell's feet flew off the running board. Willie pulled him close to the vehicle, and Starrell regained his footing.

"Fuckin' D.C," Starrell muttered.

"You know what I learned today?" Anjean shouted.

Willie and Starrell waited for the answer.

"They don't use the fuckin' Club on ambulances." He laughed and turned right on Twenty-first Street, through a red light, the tires screeching.

"Pull over," Starrell yelled at Anjean. "Now."

"Man, I'm Luke-fuckin'-Skywalker!" Anjean yelled.

"Now!" Starrell insisted. He looked at Willie, and Willie pulled on the wheel. The ambulance jerked to the right. Anjean hit the brakes.

"What the fuck's wrong with you?" Anjean screamed at Willie.

Starrell stepped off the running board. His body was shaking.

"Three niggers in an ambulance ain't goin' nowhere fast," he said. "We foot it back to Willie's. Separately. Walk to a Metro. And then we meet back there."

The two brothers nodded and got out of the ambulance.

"And take off the headpiece and glasses," Starrell said to Anjean. "Try to look different, okay? Now book."

A group of college students was staring at them. "Hey, ain't you ever seen the D.C. summer jobs program at work?" Starrell said to the crowd. Sirens sounded several blocks away.

"Bust it," Starrell said to the brothers. They jogged off. Starrell sprinted down an alley. As he ran, he told himself that he had to tell Tamika what he had been up to, show her what sort of man he could be. He felt the knapsack slap against his back. Shit, he thought, all that and I still don't know what the fuck to do.

41

The White House
June 30

When you have nowhere to go, there's the office. That's what Addis thought, as he walked by the armed guards at the entrance to the West Wing. He passed Ann Herson, Hanover's personal secretary. She was carrying a cardboard box. "D-day," she whispered, without breaking her stride. Outside the press office, Ken Byrd was talking to a scheduling aide. His eyes were tired, his shirt wrinkled.

"Only lost two," Byrd said to Addis. "Both pretty junior. Margaret's going to need more than them. But it's been a bitch getting ready for Chicago. Kelly hasn't put out the schedule yet. And the big babies"—he meant the White House correspondents—"are screaming. 'When's he arriving at the convention? Will he be watching Margaret tonight? Is he offering Cabinet posts to build support? Is he trying to push her speech to the second night? Is it true he asked her to be his running mate?' Yeah, right. Watch for them to come on out holding hands."

"You'll do fine. Just keep 'em fed."

"With what?"

"Empty calories, like always."

Byrd let the remark slip by.

"You know what's weird?" Byrd asked.

"Not anymore."

"It's been a day, and there hasn't been anything more on that story about Mumfries and Katie. You hear anything?"

"No, but I'm not on the A-list these days."

"The reporter who called yesterday, all hot to get a photo of them, never called back. And no one else is asking about it. These stories always leak before they come out. But, so far, nothing. It's like . . ."

"Like what?" Addis asked.

"Like . . . I don't know."

"Maybe it's been taken care of."

"By who?"

"Someone above our paygrade. . . . Which tab was it?"

"The *Weekly Express*. The one that ran the pictures of that black kid. Said he was Bob's son and a hooker was his mother. Remember that?"

The one owned by the millionaire who also owns Hynes-Pierce's paper. Now that makes sense. Give up a one-week boost in circulation to protect Mumfries . . . and the China treaty. Business is business.

"I'm not a religious man," Addis said. "But there's something to the proposition that everything happens for a reason, especially when it's nothing."

"You know, Nick." Byrd leaned close to Addis. "This elliptical, who-the-fuck-cares bullshit is getting old fast. Thanks so damn much."

Byrd walked away.

"For me, too," Addis muttered.

Several memos had been dropped on Addis's desk. A notice about a credit union screwup. A memo from security: Do not leave automobiles in the lot overnight without informing the guards in the booth. The office of administration had sent out a reminder about not using White House phones for long-distance personal calls.

He turned on his computer and checked his phone messages. Lancette had not tried to reach him. He had received more than a dozen calls regarding events in Chicago. Would he be available to appear at a party fund-raiser at the Chicago Museum of Art? A policy forum sponsored by two health care corporations and an insurance company? Two restaurants—presumably trendy establishments—wanted to know if he would be requiring reservations. There was a message from a Mrs. Gunn—he did not recognize the name—who had called and asked if he had a private fax number. She left a pager number. There were more invitations: A reception for union activists. A cruise on Lake Erie for donors from Los Angeles. An event at Wrigley Field—including batting practice—for contributors to the party's senatorial campaigns. A charity run for a disease he had never heard of.

Silence means no, Addis told himself. He deleted the messages from his computer.

"Nice of you to drop by."

Addis sighed; the voice behind him belonged to Kelly.

"If you're not too busy. . . ."

Addis pushed himself out of his chair.

Hamilton Kelly led Addis to McGreer's office. He said nothing along the way. McGreer was not in the room.

"Please," Kelly said. "Close the door behind you."

Kelly sat behind McGreer's desk. Addis took a chair in front of the desk. Kelly pushed aside photos of McGreer's wife and daughters. His shirt collar was too small, squeezing a fleshy neck. He picked up a legal pad and recited from it.

"Twenty-one, fifty, June 29. Signed into Blair House. Eight-thirty-nine, June 30, signed out. . . . A nice evening with the widow Hanover as she prepares to challenge a sitting president for the nomination of his party. Others present include M. T. O'Connor, Flip Whalen—making one of his rare visits to our city—and Dan Carey."

Addis wondered how much he should explain.

"And one Ms. Julia Lancette of the CIA," Kelly went on. "If I am not mistaken, just days ago you told the President of the United States that you considered yourself one of his loyal employees."

"It was a place to go after hearing about Clarence."

Kelly puffed out his cheeks. That facial tic is not going to look good on the talk shows, Addis thought.

"You're lucky you caught me in a good mood. I have your new assignment. When we head out to Chicago tomorrow, you'll be there with me. Always in the room next door. So we can dispatch you on one important task after another. If I have to address the caucus of women state legislators, you write the remarks. If the mayor is upset because he gets five minutes not six-and-a-half from the podium, you hold his hand, and tell him how much we fucking love him. . . . You know, it's a good thing you convinced Hanover to cut the convention back a day. Makes it harder for outside momentum to build."

Not here, not now.

"Sure," Addis said.

That old chestnut: Keep your friends close and your enemies closer. You've watched too many movies.

"Let me ask you something," Addis said.

"Shoot."

"Somebody in the White House keeps records of all the outgoing phone calls of White House personnel," Addis said. "Right?"

"I believe so."

"And who has access to these records?"

"I'm not sure I'm familiar with the entire list. Why?"

Because I fucking want to know how a third-rate scumbag reporter discovered I was making calls to Louisiana.

"Got curious when I was reading the memo on personal phone calls.

I mean, if someone wanted to get serious about it, they could go over the individual records."

"That's fascinating, Nick. Really. We'll detail you to administrative services after the convention."

Addis could discern no clues in Kelly's expression.

"There's an eight o'clock meeting later on logistics. There's an eight-thirty tomorrow morning on scheduling. Chicago staff will be departing in the evening tomorrow. The President's arrival in Chicago is still being planned. He's going to make one or two stops before he gets there. I'll let you know when the details are finalized."

"Thank you."

"He'll get there on the Second. Give an opening address that night. A remembrance of Bob. Short, no politics."

Yeah, right.

"And spend the Third and the Fourth in Chicago."

Promising, promising.

"Okay," Kelly went on, "be here at eight. And have a draft of remarks he might make tomorrow at the stops on his way to Chicago."

A yank on the leash, Addis thought.

"Yes," he said.

"You're so good at that grand-moment stuff."

Another yank.

The corners of Kelly's mouth turned slightly upward. He had an oily smile, Addis thought.

"Then we're done here," Kelly said and picked up the phone.

"Karen," he said into the receiver, "who's that pain-in-the-ass in San Francisco, head of the northern state caucus, who said she'd rather vote for Pratt than us? Get me her number. But first call Frank in Sacramento and ask what might make her wheels spin."

The air was moist and heavy. Summer suited Washington, Addis thought, as he walked out the Pennsylvania Avenue gate. It smothered a city with clogged arteries. He put on sunglasses and passed through the concrete barriers that now sat in the middle of the street. The illusion of security, he told himself. Did they have to be so damn ugly? Why not a moat, filled with large carp? A gift from the Japanese people, perhaps. Or every lobbyist and lawyer-fixer in town could chip in. A lily pad each.

He crossed 17th Street to the sidewalk coffee stand.

"Cherry Coke?" the vendor asked.

"You know it."

Addis had made Tommy Corman's street-corner business famous. In the first year of the Hanover administration, Addis came by most after-

279

noons. Soon, people started waiting for him at the stand: job-seekers, trade association representatives, administration officials who had not been invited to an important meeting, tourists, and gawkers. The Secretary of Labor once staked out the stand when he could not get in to see Hanover. Please give this memo to the President, he had urged Addis. It had been written on plain paper, no letterhead. Addis had to stop his regular visits to the coffee stand.

"Sorry to hear about Dunne," Corman said. He brushed the green-dyed dreadlocks from in front of his face. Corman had dropped out of MIT, gone white-Rastafarian. "He came by sometimes. No cream, three sugars. It's a bitch. . . . Hey, tell me, what's going to happen with Margaret and the new President? That's wild, man." He handed Addis the drink.

"Sure is," Addis said. He paid Corman. "Business okay?"

"Yeah, you know, the suits leave in the summer. But Middle America drops by. You wouldn't believe how many people still don't know their espresso from their cappuccino. But it's not so bad. This waiter I know at the Mayflower told me that people are calling there and asking for the room where they found that reporter and that girl. And on the radio, they said skinheads were using razor blades to carve the word *HAPPY* on themselves. It's a sick world, man."

Addis took the drink and thanked Corman.

"Haile Selassie, man. Peace."

Addis headed back toward the White House. As he waited for the light to change, he half-noticed a man in a white suit next to him.

"May I share something with you?" the man asked. It was Evan Hynes-Pierce.

"Not today," Addis said. He took care not to look directly at the reporter. The light changed, and they crossed the street.

"A bit of news, that's all," Hynes-Pierce said.

Addis felt a piece of paper being slipped into his jacket pocket.

"Read it at your convenience," Hynes-Pierce said. "It's a strange coincidence. I'm sure you'll find it interesting. We can talk after you've had the opportunity to digest. You'll see, matters have become more serious."

Addis glanced at Hynes-Pierce. His usual smirk was not present. There was anger in the reporter's eyes.

"You people are . . ." Hynes-Pierce grasped for the right word. "Thugs."

The Englishman turned up 17th Street.

From his pocket, Addis pulled out a short wire service report: "Accountant Found Dead; Apparent Suicide Once Worked for Hanovers." He read the item. That morning, a homeless man found Harris Griffith dangling against the rear of the building that housed his office. He was dead.

His feet were four feet above the ground. The rope around his neck was tied to a radiator in his office.

Addis's shirt was getting sticky. Instead of returning through the northern gate, he entered the Old Executive Office Building. He hurried down a hallway. A memory struck him: It was from the first month of the administration. He and O'Connor were in this corridor. They passed a men's room. You know what someone told me? she had asked. This is where what's-his-name peed right before he approved the Watergate break-in. They laughed the laugh of winners.

Shit, get the fuck away from me.

Addis took a flight of steps to the basement. He found the office he wanted: Computer Services. A young woman was sitting at a desk. Her face glowed when she saw him.

"Do you have backups of computer phone messages?" he asked.

"We're supposed to," she said. "Ever since we lost that lawsuit. You should see all the work we have to do to keep track of everything. . . . Do you want to? I could show you our big boys in the back. They're really something." She stood up.

"No, thank you. But could you do me a favor?"

"Anything," she said.

"And I'm curious," he added, "if you retrieve something that's been lost, is there a computer record that the material has been retrieved?"

"Depends."

"On what?"

"On whether I want to leave a trace of the search. You're supposed to, and that's what automatically happens. But there are ways around it. . . . Sure you don't want to see the computers in the back?"

"Okay," he said. "But I only have a minute or two."

"Won't take long." She smiled again. "My name is Amy."

Addis stood at a pay phone inside the Washington Connection, a restaurant across the street from the OEOB. He dialed a series of numbers. Then he looked at the pay phone and punched in another set. Addis hung up and waited.

An old woman, who was walking with a cane, asked to use the telephone. Addis explained he was expecting a return call.

"I have to call about a doctor's appointment," she said.

"Please," he replied. "Just a minute. It's important."

"Don't they give you people cell phones?"

And they can monitor their use. Now, fuck off, please.

"Yes they do. But we're not supposed to use them for every call."

"So, this isn't official business?" she asked, her tone more defiant.

281

Probably a phone call that will go down in history, lady.

"Official, in a way," he said.

She limped away, grumbling. He watched as she approached the hostess and began complaining. The hostess handed her a cellular phone. Addis envisioned an item in the gossip column tomorrow: White House aide refused to allow a cripple to call her doctor during a medical emergency. Half the items in that column were fed to it by restaurant employees.

The phone rang, and Addis grabbed the receiver. There was silence on the other end.

"You know who this is?" he asked.

"Yes, hon, and you know who this is?"

"I think so. I am sorry about—"

"Forget it, hon. . . . Can't say I'm all broken up. Don't know exactly how to feel. But I know one little thing: I don't want to get mixed up any more in his shit. Glad you figured out my little code: Mrs. Gunn and the New Orleans area code. Didn't want to leave my name. This stuff freaks me out."

"What happened?" Addis asked.

"I don't know. But he came by the house two days ago. Was nervous. I thought he was on something. Said he was trying to get himself out of trouble. I tried to calm him down. . . . Well, one thing goes to another, you know. . . . And, well, just and . . . it was like it used to be. . . . Then he gets up. And I'm half-asleep. I hear sounds. I get up and peek down the hallways and see him taping this envelope to the inside of the grandfather clock. He loved that clock. Bought it in England when he was meeting some Arabs. Once said I could have everything in the whole goddamn house if he got the clock. I said, forget it, I want the clock. I didn't, but. . . . I ran back to bed, so he wouldn't know I saw anything. He took off. And you know what? He went through my purse. Took two hundred dollars and my credit cards. Like I wasn't going to cancel the shit out of them? What a creep. Guess I shouldn't say that now. . . ."

"And the envelope?"

"Papers. Financial stuff. About the you-know-who's. Today, his fucking lawyer called me and asked if he left anything with me. I said, 'Fuck off, scumbag.' You know, he hit on me after our last hearing. I just know he wanted those papers. Like he could still do something with them."

"And what are you going to do with them?"

"Send them to you. I don't want them."

"Just like that?"

"Why not?" she said. "Don't you want them?"

There's no deal. Fucking amazing.

"Certainly."

"I'll fax them to you now."

Not to the White House, he decided. He told her to wait and placed the receiver on the shelf. He asked the hostess if the restaurant had a fax machine. It was broken. The hostess gave Addis the fax number for a copy shop around the corner.

Shit, Addis thought, that's taking a risk. But there's no choice.

Addis hurried back to the phone. He recited the number for her.

"And send it to Dana Cummings," he said.

"Who's that?"

"An intern in the White House. It's better that my name not—"

"Sure, hon. You have everything covered, don't you?"

"Occasionally."

"Well, here it comes. Enjoy. 'Cause after I fax this to you, I'm trashing it. I don't want it. It'll be history. Just like Harris."

"Thanks—" He tried to recall her first name.

She hung up.

"Tracy," he said.

At the copy shop, a young man with a shaved head and a pierced lip said he could not release the papers to Addis.

"The fax is not in your name," he sneered. "I can only give it to you if your name is the name on the cover sheet. Store policy."

"There's a mistake. I work at the White House. The sender must have put the name of the intern on it."

"I *know* where you work. But this is store policy. Even more than that, it's chain policy. Some dweeb in St. Paul sends us memos on this stuff. You want me to challenge national policy, man?"

The manager came over. Addis explained the situation. The manager shook his head.

"Get the stuff," he ordered the employee. The young man shuffled off.

"I hope she kicks butt in Chicago," the manager said.

Addis smiled, and the manager waited for him to say more. When Addis did not, he said, "I sure as hell do." Addis nodded. He ignored the manager's look of disappointment.

"I'll check on him," the manager said and went to the back.

The counter clerk returned with two dozen pages. Addis paid for them.

"Interesting stuff," the clerk said. "Let's hope St. Paul doesn't find out about this."

You're just fucking with me.

"Thanks for your help," Addis said.

His office was stuffy and hot. The air conditioning was not working well; the door was shut. The documents faxed to him were spread out across his desk. They detailed several real estate transactions. Their meaning was explained in an unsigned, undated memo that Addis presumed had been written by Harris Griffith. That note told the same story that Hynes-Pierce had disclosed to Addis in New Orleans—with more facts.

A parcel in the area known as Blue Ridge, had been signed over from one limited partnership to another. For the four partners in the first group, there was a document connecting each to Chasie Mason. Five months after they had bought the land for $27,000, their partnership signed over the property to the Elva Partnership. Two of the three men in that enterprise were executives in a Baton Rouge law firm that represented various Mason businesses. Three months after that, the Hanovers bought the land for $20,000. Addis held a copy of the purchase agreement in his hand. It was signed by Bob and Margaret. A year-and-a-half later, they sold the land to a development firm for $153,000. The corporate secretary for the development firm was the owner of a construction company that had subcontracted for Mason's construction business on several state projects. The batch included a one-page consulting agreement between Griffith and an entity called First State Holding Company. It called for Griffith to provide unidentified services on a "periodic basis" for a "per-project fee." The vice president of First State, according to a page from a legal deposition, was a corporate officer of the development firm that had bought the land from the Hanovers *and* an investor in a dog track, of which Chasie Mason controlled the majority interest. First State, then, had been part of the seemingly endless Chasie Mason daisy chain. The consulting agreement meant that Griffith, when he was the Hanover's accountant, had been on Chasie's payroll. That made him an all-too credible source.

Addis checked the dates of the transactions. The deal began shortly after Jack was born.

No reasonable person, he thought, could avoid the obvious conclusion. The papers were clear. Except on one point: what Bob and Margaret Hanover had known about it. Hynes-Pierce had unearthed a damn good story. Now Griffith was dead—one more body—and Addis had what might be the only set of documents that proved the story. For a moment, he felt like calling Hynes-Pierce and offering him the whole god-damn file. Sleaze to sleaze, he said to himself. Get all of it off my desk. Over and done with. But the urge passed.

He went to the suite next to his office. He ran the pages through the copier and returned to his office. He put one set in a manila envelope, another in the folder with the records he already possessed on the land deal. He scribbled "Pension Reform" on the tab of the folder. The Blue Ridge assignment was done.

284

But, he wondered, whose land had it been before all this? That piece was missing. He picked up the phone, dialed directory assistance in Rapides Parish, and asked for the parish clerk's number. He called and was transferred.

"Office of Records," a woman said.

"Hello. I'm calling from St. Louis, and I'm interested in checking who was on the deed for a certain property in the parish"

"Yes?" There was a long pause.

"Are you there?" Addis asked.

"Well, you only said you're interested. What's that supposed to mean to me?"

"Can you help me with that?"

"Maybe. But you have to ask."

Shit. Another pain in the ass.

"I thought I was asking, ma'am. Can you please look up some records for me? I have an address. It's—"

"You have the property identification number? You got to have the property identification number." She sounded like an older woman.

"Okay."

"And how far back do you want to go?"

"Fifteen, twenty years."

Addis shuffled through the records.

"Is this going to take all day?" she asked. "You know, we don't have to take phone requests."

"I'm looking."

"Maybe you should call back. The office is shutting early. We got the funeral for the chief processor."

"Wait a moment. I'll get the number."

"I got to go. Try back tomorrow."

"Hey," Addis said, as he kept searching, "you a Cougars fan?"

"Sure am. My cousin's grandson is on the team this year. How do you know about them? All the way in St. Louis?"

Heard a bunch of old farts talking about them.

"Read about them in a sports magazine. They sound like a great team." He found the number.

"Best in the state two years now. They're gonna do it again."

"That's what I saw."

"So do you have the property identification number?" The edge in her voice was gone.

"Think so."

Addis read her the string of digits, and she went off to check. He looked at his computer screen and called up his phone messages. Still nothing from Lancette. The clerk returned to the phone.

"Got it," she said.

She started to read through the file, which was in reverse-chronological order: There was the development firm that purchased the land from the Hanovers, the Hanovers themselves—"Now that's interesting," she said—the Elva Partnership, and the one before that.

On the computer screen, the list of phone messages changed. A new message appeared: Julia Lancette was holding for him.

"And then there was—"

"Can I put you on hold a moment?" Addis asked.

"Honey, they're all waiting for me. If you're too busy . . ."

"No, no, sorry." He waited for her to proceed and gazed at the screen. If Lancette tired of waiting and hung up, one of the White House operators would turn the holding-for-you message into a called-for-you message.

"Then there was Peters. Yeah, a Peters. P.E.T.E.R.S. Peters, Helen. H.E.L.E.N.—"

"Okay, Helen Peters. Thanks. I have a call on the other line; it's an emergency. I'll call back if I need more."

"But—"

Addis cut her off and picked up Lancette.

"I need a favor," she said.

He heard street noises coming across the line.

"Yes," he said, and shoved the file underneath others stored in the bottom drawer of his desk.

"I haven't said what it is."

"Yes," he repeated. "Yes."

42

Georgetown
June 30

"This is all wrong," Lancette said, as she got into Addis's Honda.

"Hello," he said.

Let's just drive out of town. Follow the old canal to West Virginia. Find a bed-and-breakfast. Stay there a few weeks. And then drive again—anywhere, as long as it's in the direction of away.

"They have it all tied up, answers for everything. They're good. Whoever they are. But there's one thing. If we can find it, they'll have a hard time keeping everything packaged."

Addis pulled away from the curb. He caught a glimpse of an older woman wearing a scruffy raincoat and lying in front of a trendy clothing store. Propped up next to her were cardboard slabs bearing her psychotic scrawl. He had read the signs before: "The U.S. Government Killed My Son! I KNOW it, and they KNOW it!" *How do people like that survive?* he wondered.

"Where are we going?" he asked.

"The Kennedy-Warren," she said.

"And what's there?"

The car rumbled across cobblestones.

"A piece of paper . . . I hope."

He looked at her and registered the exact color of her green eyes.

"I'm just doing my job," she added.

"And today that is . . . ?"

"Connecting this Max Bridge—what are they calling him now? Matthew Levon Morrison, right?—to people who would rather not be connected to him."

"That would change things," Addis said.

So would the fax he had received. He considered telling her about it, perhaps ask her advice on what to do with these records. But would she

287

think he was forever mired in a dilemma? One chunk of secret history at a time, he said to himself.

"Will this evidence tell us why it happened?" he asked.

"Probably not. Maybe blow-back from an op. I don't know. But you should hear the crap the director was giving me today."

"And the tough part is you don't know if he's on the wrong side or just wrong."

"That's right." She looked at him. Addis felt himself yearning.

"I've seen that," he said. "In Washington, it's not that unusual."

"With Wenner, it is. . . . Or it was."

"When I first went to work for Palmer, he told me, 'In this town, everybody takes a dive once in a while. You have to, if you want to get anything done. So don't be too disappointed when I take mine.' "

"That's a record-setting level of self-awareness for Washington," Lancette said with a laugh. "Did he take many?"

"Not many. But some."

"And were you disappointed?"

"Every time. But I understood."

"Maybe that's the problem," she said. "We understand too much."

They drove past large Victorian homes with wide porches. Mike Finn lives on this street, Addis thought. It would be nice to make $300,000 a year.

"I was thinking about that story you told me," Lancette said. "About Donny Lee Mondreau. And this is going to sound pretentious, but it made me think of a passage in Dante's *Inferno*. But don't think I'm an intellectual. When I was in college, me and my friend Beth used to memorize lines from the great books. We wanted to impress smart guys like you."

"I'm sure it worked."

"Actually, no. College was a lonely time."

"Hard to believe."

"Believe it. . . . So we opened Shakespeare to random pages and looked until we found passages we liked. We wrote them down on index cards. Flashcards for snobs-to-be. Did the same with existentialists, Walt Whitman, Kierkegaard, whatever. I forgot most of them. But there's this line from Dante; it goes something like: 'The more someone is perfect, the more he sees the good and the bad.' "

Good, you're thinking about me.

"I'm not sure I get the connection," he said.

A soccer ball bounced in front of the car, and Addis hit the brakes. Two young girls ran into the street. He looked in his rearview mirror. The sedan behind him had enough room to brake. He waited for the girls to retrieve the ball and then resumed driving.

"Glad somebody's watching the road," Lancette said. "I've had enough car trouble this week. . . . Anyway, the connection? I'm not sure either. Maybe it's a way of saying, don't beat yourself up too much, because at least you're decent enough to see something may be wrong."

"I'll take that as a compliment."

"As you should," she said.

"And what came out of your honesty-in-reporting exercise? The Serbs you wanted to help—"

"Got screwed over. They were almost real democrats. But there were mucho irregularities with their finances—some corruption involving a German coal concession and the number-two man—and they couldn't organize a tea party, let alone a political party."

"And?"

"Eventually, the information about their deficiencies made it into the pipeline—"

"Thanks to you," Addis interrupted.

"Yes, thanks to me. And the all-knowing mandarins at State and the NSC got spooked and decided not to help them out."

"Then?"

"Nothing. They fell apart. Internal bickering. Not such a big deal. But if we had helped. . . . Well, it probably would have gotten screwed up another one of ten thousand different ways. But you never know."

"That's just it," he said. "You never do."

Addis found a parking space on Connecticut Avenue, across from the Kennedy-Warren. It was one of the larger complexes in town. Built in the early 1930s, the art-deco building was a reminder of Washington's grander days. Addis pictured society couples arriving for a dance at its ballroom. He imagined the excitement that filled the halls when the building was home to dozens of New Dealers busy rescuing the country, or, later on, when it housed the young go-getters of the Kennedy days. Now it was simply a place where yuppie lawyers, career bureaucrats, retired Foreign Service officers, and blue-haired widows lived. It had been years since Washington had a theme.

"What are we doing here?" Addis asked, as they entered the building.

"Follow me," she said.

Anywhere.

Lancette approached the porter at the front desk. He was an older black man, sitting hunched over, his face in the sports section. Addis stood a few feet behind her.

"Hi, we're from the White House," she said. "On official business. This is where Dr. Charlie Walters lives, correct?"

He put down the paper. "Yes, ma'am."

"He's on assignment for the administration in Africa," she said. "And we need access to his apartment and storage area. He asked me to retrieve some clothes and books. His assignment's been extended."

"Ma'am, we're not permitted to let strangers into people's apartments. Not unless the resident tells us first."

"Well, this is unexpected," she said. "Is the building manager here?"

"No, his little girl got sick. Real bad. A virus in her brain. So he's at the hospital. Maybe he could let you in later."

"Mister—"

"James, you can call me James." He had a large growth on the side of his neck. Lancette made certain not to stare at it.

"James, you're in charge, then?" she asked.

"Suppose you could say that."

"Well, we don't have much time. And I'd hate to have to call the hospital to get the building manager back here. But we have a flight going out tonight, and we promised Dr. Walters we'd send this material right away. He told me what to get. Look, here's the cable he sent."

She handed a piece of paper to the porter. Two janitors were standing inside the front door. They were arguing in Spanish. Addis's Spanish was lousy, but he picked up a few words. They were fighting over whose turn it was to clean the dog shit from the front sidewalk.

"You see," Lancette was saying, "we know where to look. And he said we should ask for Mr. Reynolds—I guess he's the building manager, right?—and tell him it was okay to check his apartment and storage area."

"Well, you know, we got this policy," he said, as he read the cable.

Addis figured it was his turn to step in. James had not yet noticed him. He stepped up to the desk. The porter recognized him, and it showed.

"James," Addis said, "I'm Nick Addis. It's important. We don't have a lot of time. Dr. Walters is doing some important work for us."

"Yes, sir, I'm sure of it," James said. "You sure it's okay?"

"James, the President knows we're here. Want me to get him on the phone, so you can speak to him?"

"Oh, no, no . . . I suppose it'll be okay. You just got to show me what you take, alright? Cause I can't leave the desk."

"That'll be fine," Addis said.

"Can I keep this?" He held up the cable. "To show to Mr. Reynolds when he gets back."

"I'm sorry, you can't," Lancette said gently. "See these markings." She pointed to a string of letters and numbers at the top of the page. "That's sensitive communications code. We can't let that out. I shouldn't have even let you look at this. But we can trust you, right?"

"Yes, ma'am. You know, I was in the Navy. Served on a sub out of

San Diego. Back in 'sixty-three. We had nukes. Worked in the kitchen. But got all those security talks. I wrote my momma and couldn't say where we were."

God bless the national security state, Lancette told herself. "So then you'll understand. Thanks, James."

He reached under the desk and handed her a key. "It's for the apartment. He's in two-seventeen. And it's also for the storage area down on the second basement floor. Same key. You got to go way back and then turn right. Okay?"

They nodded their heads.

"And you're going to come back and show me what you're taking? Maybe leave a note for Mr. Reynolds, okay?"

"We will," Lancette said.

"The President thanks you," Addis said.

Lancette and Addis walked down a carpeted and poorly lit hall. The smell of cleaning solvent was strong.

"You're a very good liar," he said.

"Must be something in the water at Langley."

"You cooked up that cable on your own?"

"Yeah."

"And the building manager? You knew he was gone?"

"I called, got his name, and was told he was tending to a family medical emergency."

"And I was the insurance."

"A first-rate policy. Hope you don't mind being used."

Not by you.

"This is very impressive," he said.

"We call it tradecraft."

"Sounds like you're making furniture or pottery."

"Just tapping the devious child within."

She opened the door to the apartment and flipped on the light. Nothing in the living room seemed unusual. Two walls were lined with bookshelves. On another, three framed Ansel Adams posters were hanging. A book on Native Americans was on the coffee table.

The two walked through the apartment. There were a few dishes in the sink. Addis ran a fingers across the top of a stereo speaker and then brushed the dust off his hand. The bed in the bedroom was unmade.

"Let's find a few sweaters," she said and began looking through a closet.

"Let me ask you, why would he need sweaters in Africa?"

"In the mountains, on the high plains, it gets cold at night."

"I know you had to say he needed something," Addis said, "but couldn't he buy sweaters over there?"

Lancette tossed two sweaters to Addis. "He's hyper-allergic. He can only wear sweaters made with organic fibers and natural dye. And over there, you can never tell."

"That's good," Addis said. "Good tradecraft."

"Now rip the labels out of the sweater and flush them down the toilet," she told him. "Good tradecraft is the work of an obsessive, anal, compulsive mind that would otherwise drive you crazy—an Agency instructor once told me that."

"So I'm learning." He walked to the bathroom.

Lancette searched the back of the closet and pulled out a box full of University of Michigan memorabilia.

"What are you looking for?" Addis asked.

"I don't see it. Let's go downstairs."

They left the bedroom and headed toward the door.

"Wait a second," Addis said.

"What?" she asked.

He was staring at the bookshelves.

"Something's wrong," he said. "Hold on." He wiped the front edge of one of the shelves with his fingertips and showed his hand to her.

"No dust," he said. "Clean. Dust on top of the speakers. No dust on any of the shelves." He pulled out several books. "So—"

"Either he has a spotty cleaning lady or somebody went through all his books, maybe looking for something stuck between the pages. We're not the first. Great minds think alike. Let's check downstairs and then get out of here."

The journal about his work for the prison system, she thought; it wasn't in the closet. Shit, someone had been here.

Lancette tried the lightswitch in the storage room. It didn't work.

"We'll have to keep the door open," she said. "For light."

There was a slight puddle of water that had formed beneath a pipe that ran across the ceiling of the dark room. The air was musty. The room was full of plastic crates. Most were packed with books, a few contained clothes. One was full of videotapes.

"Think they missed all this?" he asked.

"Could be. They would have had to have known about it."

Addis picked through a box; none of the videotapes were marked. Porn, he guessed. More secrets.

"And overlooked something so obvious?" he asked.

"I've been in this world a little while, and I still ask, how good are they or, I guess I should say, we? Like could anyone I've met in this line of work have pulled off something like the Kennedy assassination and have it never come out? I think the real secret is, we're not that good. But every once in a while, they make a rabbit jump out of a hat—an invisible rabbit no one can see. Except those who are screwed by it. They overthrow a government. They raise a submarine from the ocean floor. They steal a document on the negotiating strategy of a European trade ministry. They get a foreign newspaper to print what they want printed. They deliver arms to secret soldiers in a jungle in fucking nowhere, using money Congress thinks is going to buy another satellite. So how good are they? I don't know. It's not inconceivable that the same bunch that installs a bug in the Chinese consulate in Paris could miss a storage room. Never forget one thing: We're more of a government bureaucracy than anyone thinks."

"Thanks for the lecture," he said. "Don't you think we should . . . ?"

She went back to the crates. She had to hold the material toward the middle of the room to catch the light coming from the hallway. One crate contained shoeboxes stuffed with photos and letters. Another had papers from college and medical school. One file contained typewritten pages of poetry. High school? she wondered. College? More recently?

This is like doing an autopsy, she thought.

Lancette searched a container stuffed with old newspapers and magazines. Beneath all this were two composition books bound together by a rubberband. Neither had any markings on the cover. She opened the first book. The page read: "Security briefing. Man—mid-50s. One arm. East European accent." These were Walters's CIA journals.

"They really are not all that good," she said softly.

She held the book upside down and shook it. Nothing. She did the same with the other book. A folded piece of paper fell to the floor.

"Not that good at all," she said louder.

Addis turned around. She read the paper: a copy of Walters's one-page ICEMAN report. On CIA letterhead. Signed by Walters. Initialed by Dr. Blum's secretary. She looked at the last entries in the second composition book. "Meeting with J. L.," one read. A subsequent note said, "More questions about memo."

The memo *and* supporting records, Lancette thought.

"Let's get out of here," she said.

The light in the hallway went off. The room turned black.

"Shit," she said and stood still.

"Now what?" Addis asked. He could barely see her. A low red glow from an exit sign down the hallway trickled into the storage room. A fire door slammed. Opening or closing? Addis wondered. They heard footsteps on the concrete floor.

"Close the door," he said.

A flashlight beam hit the opened door. Lancette pushed it shut and turned the bolt.

"Damnit," she whispered to him. "The key's in the lock."

"Good tradecraft," he said.

"Fuck you," she said.

"Sorry." He dug through boxes.

"What are you doing?" She sounded scared.

"Looking for anything hard or sharp."

Lancette reached into her handbag.

"Pocket knife," she whispered. "From an old boyfriend."

"Most women carry pepper spray."

Addis heard the click of a blade. The flashlight beam passed by the crack beneath the door. Lancette stepped to the side of the door.

"Just fucking books," Addis complained. He found a heavy hardback with sharp edges and stepped delicately to the back of the storage area.

The keys jiggled. The lock moved. The bolt turned. The door opened.

"Who's—"

A man entered the room. The flashlight was pointed at the floor. Lancette raised her arm, the knife in her hand. She held her breath. She picked a spot on his neck.

The flashlight beam hit Addis on the face. He lifted the book. The beam reflected off the book's shiny jacket. He saw the man's face. He noticed the knife blade. It was moving.

"Wait!" he shouted at Lancette.

The man turned to see her; the flashlight illuminated the knife. He jumped back.

"Dios mio!" he shouted.

"Julia, no!" Addis said.

She stopped her swing.

"It's okay. He's a janitor."

Lancette studied the man in the dim light of the exit sign. He was young, Hispanic. He wore a work uniform. She lowered her arm.

The janitor stared at her. "What the Jesus you doin' here?" he asked.

"We were looking for something for Dr. Walters," Addis explained. "And when the light in the hallway went out, I guess we got frightened."

"Man, you crazy," he said, as he checked out Lancette. "I was trying to help." He shined the light on his shirt, on which was embroidered the words "Kennedy-Warren" and his name, Tico. Addis recognized him from the lobby.

"See?" the janitor said.

"Sorry," Addis said. "There was no light in this room, either." He heard Lancette breathing.

"I was coming in from the garage," Tico explained. "And I saw the light was off. Both lights were off in the hall, at the same time. . . . You wait here while I fix it up?"

"No, that's okay," Addis said. "We were finishing. Can you show us out?"

"Okay. It's way dark down here."

At the front desk, Addis and Lancette showed James the sweaters. The composition books and the memo were stuffed in Lancette's handbag.

"That's it?" the porter asked.

"Yeah," Lancette said. "We couldn't find the books he wanted. There were too many boxes to go through."

"Doctors like reading, I guess," James said. "Did that other guy find you?"

"Other guy?" Lancette asked.

"Guess not. Tall guy. Had on sunglasses. Boney face."

"Yeah," Lancette said. "That would be Steve. I didn't expect him to meet us here. But you told him where we were?"

"Yes, ma'am."

"Well, I guess he decided to wait outside. Thanks, James."

"Glad to. Am I going to read about Dr. Walters in the papers?"

"You know, James," she said. "I really don't know."

Lancette and Addis left the building. It was getting dark.

"There's no Steve?" Addis asked.

"No," she said.

Addis checked the street before they crossed. Were any cars about to come screeching toward them? The trees next to the Kennedy-Warren grounds—could they provide cover to a shooter? In the evening light, he could only discern the outline of the greenery. And the sedan behind them earlier when he had braked for the soccer ball—what was its make? He couldn't remember. They walked across the avenue and got in the car.

"I'd like you to know what we found," he said. "But, first, I think we should drive."

"Yes, I think so," she replied.

He noticed she was holding on to the grip above the door handle.

How long would it take to set a car bomb? she wondered.

"Nick—"

He turned the ignition. The car started.

"Yes?"

"Oh . . . where are we going?"

He glanced at his watch. The meeting at the White House was going to start soon. Plans for Chicago, for Mumfries's triumph—or so they hoped—over the widow Hanover.

"To eat," he said. He steered the car into the stream of traffic. Lancette was silent for the entire ride. She cradled her handbag in her arms.

43

Havana Village
June 30

Rolando showed Addis and Lancette to the same table where they had sat the previous night. Addis ordered two shots and two beers. Rolando bowed and withdrew.

"This is eating?" Lancette said. She wiped her brow with a napkin. "Sometimes I wish I smoked."

"So, tell me, what is it?"

She took the memo out of her bag. Addis saw the CIA emblem on the top. The memo was exactly as Walters had described it to Lancette: Walters's response to her ICEMAN request. She paged through Walters's journals and found the entries that corresponded to his treatment of the anonymous covert operator with the tattoo identical to the one found on Hanover's assassin.

The drinks came. Addis raised the shot. Let's try not to be afraid, he thought. She lifted her shotglass. Neither offered a toast. They drank and then reached for the beer. He ordered another round.

Lancette explained the documents. "They prove two things. First, the CIA is linked to a person with the same tattoo. Second, someone tried to contain this piece of information. Everything beyond that is speculation."

"But speculation that can get people killed," Addis said.

His White House pager sounded. People at adjoining tables looked toward him. Addis reached into his coat pocket and shut it off. He assumed it was Kelly.

"So where do we take the facts and speculation?" Lancette asked.

"Palmer? He's on the commission. He said he might be willing to raise questions if we had hard evidence."

"And he takes dives."

Addis could not tell if that was a question or a declaration.

"It has to be someone," he said. "Who do you trust? Not Wenner. How do we know who's on the ride and who's off?"

"We're definitely off. . . . A reporter?" she asked.

"And wait for them to figure it all out—and then screw it up? I don't know. We'll be damn exposed in the meantime." There was a trace of beer beneath her lips. He wanted to wipe it gently with his hand. "And I'm worrying more about our safety with each day."

"Clarence?" she asked.

"I checked before I left the White House. He's still in bad shape. Can't talk. They're letting only the family in. And they're really tight after the disturbance today. Some kid got into the room and then took off in a stolen ambulance. He didn't do anything to Clarence. No one knows what he was up to."

"A black guy?"

"Yeah. Why?"

"Just curious."

The drinks arrived. Without saying anything, they downed the shots and chased the whiskey with Mexican beer.

"How many more do you intend to order?" she asked.

"No more than necessary."

Lancette tapped her beer bottle lightly against the table. She started to speak and stopped. She jerked her head toward the far end of the bar. A man was standing by himself. He was wearing khakis, a black T-shirt, and a long tan raincoat. "Would you call that boney?" she asked.

The man scanned the room, but he did not look directly at Addis and Lancette. He then left the bar. Lancette realized she was sitting by a window that overlooked an alley. She took back the ICEMAN memo and placed it in her bag with the composition books.

"I think we should go," she said. "We're very well lit here."

"To where?"

"Now. Get up and move out of this position."

She stood and stepped toward the bar. She wedged herself between two groups of young women at the bar. He squeezed next to her.

"And the reason I became a travel agent," a woman with bright red hair was telling a woman in a short fake leopard-skin dress, "was that I just hate the fucking airlines. I'd do anything to screw them. It's like—"

"A crusade?" the woman in the leopard-skin dress said.

"Yeah. On the nose."

"Is there another way out," Lancette whispered to him, "other than the front?"

"Probably a basement door that goes to the alley."

"If he's working with others, one could still be in here."

Addis looked all around the crowded restaurant. Latino toughs, young professionals, boisterous Cubanos. He saw several candidates. Rolando passed by.

"What's wrong?" he asked. "The table's no good?"

"Muy bueno," Addis said. "But we need a favor."

He spoke so low that Lancette could not hear him. Rolando whispered back. Then Addis said something else.

"No problem," Rolando replied, louder than necessary. "You go dance."

Addis grabbed Lancette by the hand. "Let's go," he said. "Upstairs. Dancing." He placed an arm around her.

"What are you doing?" she asked.

He stared straight into her eyes. "Upstairs."

Rolando led them to the stairs. There was a disco on the floor above. They could hear the salsa music.

"I'll keep the food hot for you," Rolando said. "Have a dance. It will be ready for you when you come back." He was still talking loudly.

They entered the dancing area. It was long and narrow, lined with cheap wood paneling. A mirror ball hung from the ceiling. The beat of the music banged loudly. Several men stood by the bar. They each wore gold chains and shiny shirts that showed off hairy chests. The dance floor was full.

Addis took her hand again. Don't ignore how it feels, he told himself. He guided her through the dancers, to the back of the room, and through a door that led to a storage area that held cartons of beer, wine, and rum. He closed the door. He moved six cases of beer that were stacked against a wall. Behind them was a dumbwaiter.

"You're fucking kidding," she said.

They heard the compartment moving in the wall. Then it stopped. Addis opened the door to the dumbwaiter.

"Get in," he said.

Lancette shook her head.

"It can handle the weight. This is how they bring the booze up here. Rolando has his two nephews in the basement running the thing. The parking kid is bringing the car around to the back. Get in."

"This is nuts," she said.

"We'll discuss other options later," Addis said. He put his hand on her shoulder. She pulled away. "Nuts," she repeated. She took a breath and let it out slowly: "Okay."

Lancette squeezed into the dumbwaiter and crouched on her knees. Her bag was between her legs. The floor was moist. The air was dusty. She coughed. Her hair fell in front of her face. "I feel like a jack-in-the-box," she said.

Addis tapped on the floor. "See you down below," he said and shut the door. He heard her descend. He kept his eye on the door to the storage area. He listened to the music. The dumbwaiter came back, and he crawled in. It was a tight fit. He had to bend one leg and tuck it under his chin. He folded the other leg beneath his butt. He ducked his head and felt a spasm in his neck. He closed the door, pounded on the floor, and was lowered smoothly to the basement. The nephews helped him out. Lancette stood there. Her blouse was covered with grime.

"I'd be dazed if we had the time," she said.

Addis thanked the young men, and rushed to the back door. He opened it. The Honda was there. The engine was running. The parking attendant was standing next to the car. Lancette came up behind Addis.

"Shit," he said. "It's pointed in the wrong direction. I don't want to drive by the front. . . . Damnit . . . let's go."

They ran out of the basement and to the car.

"You can back out," Lancette said, as they climbed in.

Headlights—high beams—lit up the inside of the car from behind. The rear way was blocked. Addis had no choice. He threw his car into gear and punched the accelerator. "Put on your seat belt," he said to her.

He sped out of the alley and turned right and then made a quick left. He kept his speed up as he went downhill. "My house," he said, halfway down the street. "On the left. Is Eric in the window?"

"Can't tell." Lancette was struggling with the seat belt.

"It sticks," Addis said. "Force it in."

Shit, he thought, my driving glasses.

He ignored the one-way sign at the bottom of the street, made a right—the tires screeched—and went through a red light. A motorcyclist swerved to miss him and nearly collided with a bus. The Honda skidded across the road. He gripped the wheel tightly and turned left on to the Duke Ellington Bridge.

"Where to?" he asked.

"Wherever you want," she said. "How about some place real quiet."

Yes, yes, yes.

He checked the rearview mirror. A Trailblazer was running a red light at the end of the bridge.

"Shit," he said. "Hold on."

Addis made the first turn he could. A hard right. Lancette was thrown to the left. Her bag flew out of her hand and landed on the floor. The Honda banged over a series of potholes.

"I bet he's pretty good at this car-chase stuff," he said.

"They usually are," Lancette replied.

The street ended. Two quick rights. He was heading toward the parkway. He saw no car in his rearview mirror. A minivan was stopped at a stop sign at the entrance to the parkway. Addis leaned on the horn and cut to the left of the minivan. He hit the brakes. The Honda skipped up on the curb and passed the minivan.

"You're clear!" Lancette yelled.

He pressed the accelerator, and the car jumped on to the parkway, ahead of the minivan. Addis dodged a station wagon entering from another ramp. He straddled the two lanes. Behind them, several horns sounded.

"New idea," he said.

"What?"

"A police station. Let's find one. What are they going to do? Blast into a police house? We can call whoever we want from there."

"Okay," she said. She was holding on to the armrest.

"What's the nearest one?"

"I don't know," she said. But she once had memorized the location of the precinct houses. The closest, she realized, were V Street and Idaho Avenue. V Street was nearer but that meant going through congested Dupont Circle. Their pursuer might have the chance to catch up. Idaho Avenue offered them a clearer run.

"Idaho Avenue," she said. "Get off at the next exit."

The parkway curved sharply. Addis tried to maintain speed. He was gaining on a convertible in the left lane. He flashed his high beams. He looked in the mirror. The Trailblazer had caught up to them. The driver's arm was extended out the window. He held a gun. Addis grabbed Lancette by the shoulder and pulled her down.

"Stay there," he said.

With his right hand, he reached into his coat pocket and grabbed his cell phone. He held it out to her.

"Call nine-one-one."

"And ask for what?"

"I don't know. Just call."

He sped up. He felt the centrifugal force drawing the Honda into the oncoming lanes. More speed, he thought and pulled the steering wheel further to the right. He pumped the horn.

"Come on!" he shouted at the convertible. "Come on!"

Lancette opened the phone. She pressed the power switch. Nothing. "It won't go on," she said.

Fuck, it hasn't been charged.

Addis took the phone from her and tossed it on to the backseat. She reached over and dug her fingers into his thigh. She looked behind them.

"Getting closer," she said, keeping her voice steady.

"Move over!" he yelled at the car in front of them.

The convertible shifted to the right lane, and Addis sped by it. The convertible's driver, a woman with a blond mane, gave him the finger.

The gun, he thought, the one Dunne had given him.

"There's a gun in the glove compartment," he told Lancette.

"I've never used one before. Have you?"

"Not in any of the training they gave you?"

"No," she said. "But I can tell you how to kill someone's career with bureaucratic reports."

"Get it any way."

She tried the compartment. It wouldn't open. "It's locked," she said.

"Damnit, you need the ignition key."

Two cars ahead were driving side-by-side at the same speed. Addis realized he was about to be boxed in. In the rearview mirror, he saw the Trailblazer trying to pass the convertible. But the woman wouldn't let him by. Her car straddled the two lanes. A flash exploded from the muzzle of the gun. The convertible veered to the right, jumped the curb, and headed down the bank of Rock Creek.

"Oh fuck," Lancette said. "Did he . . . ?"

"I think he just shot out her tire," Addis said. But he had not been able to tell.

Addis flashed his high beams and pressed the horn.

"The turn's coming up," Lancette said.

"I know. I know."

The cars in front were still side-by-side. Addis brought the Honda to a few feet within a hatchback in the left lane. The car in the right lane, a large sedan, slowed and dropped back. Addis began to shift lanes.

"Right around this bend," she said.

"Yeah, yeah—"

The hatchback started changing lanes and was about to collide with the Honda. "Fuck!" Addis yelled. He pumped the brakes and swerved to the left to get around the hatchback. "Fucking idiot!" He accelerated to pass the hatchback. The Trailblazer was fifty yards behind.

"Right here!" Lancette shouted.

Addis looked to the right. The hatchback was next to him, and close behind it was the sedan. He couldn't shift lanes. He raced past the exit.

"Damn," Lancette murmured.

Addis passed the hatchback and jumped into the right lane. In the side-view mirror, he saw the headlights of the Trailblazer. There were no cars ahead. But the road was bending slightly to the left, providing the driver of the Trailblazer a better angle on the Honda. Addis guided the Honda as far to the right as possible. The tires kicked up gravel from the shoulder. To his left, he saw asphalt illuminated by the lights of the Trailblazer.

"After the overpass, take the sharp right," Lancette said. "It's Pennsylvania Avenue. We can head toward the White House."

Yeah, blow by all the squad cars, concrete barriers, and patrols, and crash the gate, right into the West Wing. Sorry, Kelly, I'm a little late.

"Sure," he said.

The Trailblazer's driver had a straight line to the Honda. But he would have to shoot across his windshield. Addis wondered if the driver was left-handed.

"You're going to have to slow down to make it," she said.

A shot hit the front fender of the Honda and blew out the electrical connection to the left headlight.

"I don't think so," Addis said.

The Honda passed beneath Pennsylvania Avenue. Addis saw the ramp to the right. He took his foot off the accelerator and yanked the wheel. He felt the car pulling against him.

"It's not . . ."

The car flew across the ramp. He was losing control. He thought he heard a shot. The car jumped the curb and slid over a grassy incline. Was a tire gone? "Hold on!" he yelled.

Lancette shouted something. He couldn't make out the words. The Honda was heading toward a metal post. He tried turning to the right. The wheels caught the cobblestones of the footpath leading to the C&O Canal. The car cleared the post and bounced across the cobblestones—toward the canal.

Addis saw the lock. He saw the dark water. He pounded the brakes. He gripped the wheel tightly, locked his elbows, and braced himself. Then they went over the edge, and they were in the air.

The car slammed against the water. Addis felt the impact in his lower back. He heard metal scraping against stone. His side of the car was flush against the wall of the lock. As the car began to sink, it tilted toward the left, pulling Addis toward the door. He heard pops and hisses. The interior lights and the remaining headlight went out.

"Julia!"

She was slumped forward. There was a bloody gash on the side of her head. Addis grabbed her by the shoulder. She was unconscious. He realized that his feet were becoming wet—and that the water was rising.

There was no room for him to open his door. He tried the window. Nothing moved. The electrical system was out.

"Julia! Wake up."

The nose of the car dropped forward, into the water. His ankles were wet. He shook her. Her eyes were shut. Her body was limp.

Think, think, Addis told himself. He remembered something from Driver Ed, a million years ago. The ponderous voice of the filmstrip narrator: *Even in shallow water, water pressure will pin a door shut.* He leaned across her for the door handle. *Turn and push—and be ready for the water to pour in.*

The handle turned. He pushed against the water. The door opened several inches. Water rushed into the car. Then the door stopped. It was stuck against a mound of silt.

"Oh shit!" he shouted.

He pressed his feet against the driver-side door and placed his hands on the passenger-side door. He tried to stretch out his body and push the passenger-side door open further. It would not move. Water was lapping over the seats. He pulled the door shut. But it would not close all the way. Branches and muck had clogged the latch. Water streamed into the car.

He propped Lancette in her seat. He shook her. He yelled at her. She did not wake. Pink streaks ran down her face. Was she breathing? Shit, he couldn't tell. The base of the windshield was below the water's surface. The car was descending. *How deep is the lock? How much time?*

He raised his feet above the dashboard and kicked at the windshield. His feet slid across it. He tried again. He could not get a solid shot at it.

"Damnit! Damnit! God damnit!"

Sinking. The water was higher on the windshield.

"The fucking gun!"

He snatched the key out of the ignition and unlocked the glove compartment. He grabbed the pistol. With his free hand, he searched for the bullets. He pushed aside repair bills and unpaid parking tickets. He felt metal and pulled out two bullets.

"Come on, Julia. Please. I'll shoot out the window. Yeah, more water, I know. But it will be a way out. And it will be so much easier if you can get yourself out. I'll do it, if you can't. But, come on, please—"

The car lurched forward. The bullets fell from his hand. Into the water inside the car. He reached into the glove compartment and found another round. He started to place a bullet in the chamber, and the Honda dropped a foot. His head slammed into the windshield, and Addis bobbled the gun and the bullet. Both disappeared into the brackish water.

"Jesus!"

Halfway up the windshield. The water had reached Lancette's breasts. She was leaning against the passenger door.

"Somebody fucking help us!" he screamed.

He looked out the back window. It was partly covered by water. In the yellow, refracted glow of a streetlight, someone was walking toward the canal. Addis could make out a form. The silhouette came to the edge.

Thirty feet, twenty feet away. The driver of the Trailblazer or someone else? he thought. Fuck.

"Come on!" Addis shouted at the figure. "Please!"

The person did not move. Addis leaned over the front seat and crawled into the back. He pounded on the rear window.

"Do something! Do fucking something!"

Halfway up the back window.

Addis pulled Lancette's head back by the hair to keep her mouth above the water in the car. He hit the back window again.

"Don't stand there! Get some fucking help!"

The figure raised an arm and pointed it at the back window.

Oh fuck me!

Addis ducked. The glass cracked into a crazy spiderweb. But the window held in place. He lifted his head. Water poured through the bullet hole. The figure was still there. Addis dropped his head again, reaching back to keep Lancette upright. Another shot hit the window, and it gave way. Water collided against Addis. He lost hold of Lancette. The Honda's descent quickened. Addis pushed his face toward the roof. He took in a deep breath. The water was at his chin.

He turned around. Lancette's mouth was below the water level. He took one more breath, expanding his lungs to the point where there was pain. He dropped below the water, and undid her seat belt, and grabbed her by the shoulders. He tugged, and she lifted off the seat. But she was caught on something. Addis placed his hands in her armpits and heaved. She moved only inches. He tried again. Nothing.

There was no air in the car. Addis's chest began to tighten. He clawed at the spot where he thought she might be caught. He grabbed her left arm and pulled as hard as he could.

Get out, a voice said. Get out, so you can breathe.

Julia! he screamed silently. Julia!

Get out. Get out.

He could not get her free. His chest was exploding. He let go and pushed his way through the remains of the rear window. He swam a stroke or two to the surface. He looked at where the figure had stood. No one was there. He gulped air, shouted for help, and dove back beneath the surface.

He could see little. He felt his way back into the car. He cut his hand and face against shards of glass. He grasped Lancette and tried once more. He could not get her out of the car.

In less than a minute, the words returned: *Get out, get out.*

He went back to the surface, yelled again, and swam back to the submerged car. He did this several times. At one point, he heard a siren. Then

305

he saw flashing lights and headlights illuminating the lock. On his last dive, beams of light pierced the water. He could see Lancette's hair floating, the long strands flowing upward, moving with the water. As if part of her were still alive.

44

Bennington Gardens
June 30

Starrell sat at the dining area table and sifted through letters, pages of assorted writings, and newspaper clips.

"What's a 'psyop'?" he asked.

Willie and Anjean Jameson were on the couch in their mother's apartment, waiting for the television news.

"That badass with one eye," Anjean said.

"Fool," Willie snorted. "It's a combo: 'psychological' and 'operation'—"

There was a knock on the door. The three went quiet. Starrell gathered the papers into a pile. Willie stepped gently to the door. Anjean moved to far corner of the room. Another round of pounding. Their mother coughed loudly in her bedroom. Willie slipped on the chain lock.

"Who is it?" he shouted through the door.

The door vibrated with a slam. Willie jumped back.

"Open the door!" a woman yelled.

It was Tamika Timmons. Willie let her in. She was wearing jeans and loose, blue Snoopy sweatshirt that did not hide her pregnancy. Her hair was braided into corn rows. She strode past Willie.

"Yo, whatsup, Tamika?" Anjean said. "Heard your uncle came back from Lorton with the beetle. Man, that's a bitch. Bad blood."

She ignored him and turned toward Starrell.

"I knew you'd be here," she said. "You go do this to me." She used both hands to point to her stomach. "Then you ain't nowhere. And then I hear you got some money. And where's it going?"

"Hey, you told me you were DIY. Told me to drag my ass out of your life." He stood up, and she hit him in the chest with both hands.

"That was when you were just hanging out doing nothing. And I don't want my baby to be part of nothing."

"Slap her back, Twayne," Anjean said gleefully.

"Shut the fuck up," Starrell told him.

"I ain't never let no woman push me like that," Anjean mumbled.

Starrell turned to her. "Baby, I was trying to do it straight-up, workin' for my unc. But you said bug out. So I did."

"Like I meant that. I want to see what you'd do for me."

"Baby, I'm doing a lot."

"Yeah, right. That's why I got to come looking for you."

"That's right. Tamika," Willie said. "Lissen to—"

Timmons pivoted and stuck a finger an inch from Willie's nose. "Wh said I came here to hear your skinny behind making noise?" She turne back to Starrell. "So what you been doing then?"

He pulled out a chair for her.

"Sit down, baby," he said. "It's wild shit."

"Yo, Double-T, your homey's a desperado," Anjean said, with a mis chievous smile.

Timmons glowered at Starrell. He sat down next to her and tried t take her hand. She drew it back.

"An OG alright," Anjean said.

"Damn, let's hear it," she said with a sigh.

When Starrell was done explaining, Timmons was silent for a momen "That all true?" she then asked.

"Sure is."

"Why would this Dunne guy tell you all that?"

"Like I said, he called his boss, the dude in charge of all the money—"

"That's the Secretary of the Treasury," Willie interrupted.

"And he says to him that he's got all this stuff that shows there's some thing funny with the assassination," Starrell said. "And this dude—"

"His name's Louis Alter," Willie said. "It's on every—"

"No more nigger-Einstein," Starrell barked at Willie. Then he contin ued his story: "He says to Dunne he don't want him out there doing wha he ain't supposed to be doing. Dunne's all burnt up, says all this guy care about is a fuckin' Chinese deal."

Starrell shot a harsh glance at Willie.

"I ain't sayin' anything," Willie said. "But I know."

"He has to lay this on somebody, and that's me."

"Let me look at those letters," Timmons said.

She grabbed them from Starrell and began reading. "And this is th guy who shot—"

"That's right," Starrell said.

"So now," she said, "what are you going to do?"

"Don't know. Dunne tried to tell me something. But he didn't finish One-four-three. That's A-D-C. But what's that mean?"

"Shuddup, man," Anjean interrupted. "Here comes the news."

"I know what that means," Timmons said.

"Not now," Anjean said.

"What?" Starrell said.

"He never finished."

"Shit, I know that," Starrell replied.

"No," she said, "like he never finished the last letter."

The newscast began with footage of a car being lifted out of the Georgetown canal. A photograph of Addis appeared.

"Could be him," she said.

". . . The police are not providing any information at the moment. And the White House has yet to issue any statement. Mr. Addis is believed to still be at the Second District station house." A live shot showed the police building. It panned to reveal news crews maintaining a stakeout. ". . . There is no word yet on whether he is being held on any charges. One source reports that Addis has been tested to determine the amount of alcohol in his blood. But there is no information on the results of the test."

The spot cut to footage of a body on a gurney and covered by a white sheet. ". . . The women's identity has not yet been revealed. According to witnesses at the canal, she was white and had light colored hair. Apparently, Addis did try to . . ."

"God-damn," Starrell said.

They all looked at him.

"I know who it is." He looked at Timmons. "She's the one at that cowboy-bitch bar. I stopped that guy from messin' her up. Oh fuck." He shook his head.

"Maybe it ain't, baby," she said.

"Maybe. But I know. Dunne. Then her. I know it."

". . . The news of the accident is likely to overshadow Margaret Hanover's announcement of her plans for her political future. . . ."

"So Dunne was talking about this guy?" Willie said. There was stock footage of Addis walking with Hanover. "What do we do?"

Wesley Pratt and Representative Wynn Gravitt, both in formal wear, stood in front of a Washington hotel. A reporter held a microphone before them. "It's like this White House is cursed," Gravitt said. "You have to wonder. You really do." Pratt interrupted him: "My prayers go out to the lady's family—whoever she is—and I wish Mr. Addis all the best. He's a dedicated public servant. There'll be time down the pike for asking questions." Pratt placed his hand on Gravitt's arm. "Thank you for the chance to express our concern for the family and Mr. Addis."

"Oh, man," Starrell said.

"Fuck this," Anjean complained. "Where are we?"

A reporter was interviewing a white woman with silver hair in the Chicago airport. "This can't be good for Margaret," the woman was saying. "It takes attention away from her tonight." The reporter asked a question. "Yeah," the woman answered, "I've been leaning toward her—and I think most of the delegates from northern California have—but we'll see. I doubt this accident—and I hope Nick is okay—will affect the convention."

"So this Dunne guy," Timmons asked, "wanted you to take what you got to this guy who busted up his car and maybe got that girl killed?"

"How we're going to get to him now?" Willie asked.

"Okay, okay, now you all shut the fuck up," Anjean said. "They're coming to us."

Next to the news anchor was a screen legend: "Mayhem at Med Center." The show cut to footage of broken glass in the lobby of the hospital, and then to the abandoned ambulance roped off by yellow police tape. Anjean bounced on the couch: "Man, they ain't showin' those tires we cut. That would embarrass their asses."

A police sketch of the "young mystery man" who visited Dunne's room barely resembled Starrell.

"Don't look like you, suge," she said.

Anjean threw a cushion at him: "You the mystery man." He laughed and slapped his knee. "A damn ugly mystery man."

". . . Fortunately, there were no serious injuries. . . ." That was what Starrell had been waiting to hear. The segment ended, and commercials began.

"We should have been first," Anjean complained.

Starrell dragged his chair next to Timmons. "Sorry, baby," he said lowly. She ran a finger down his cheek. Anjean was about to speak, but Willie raised a fist, and Anjean closed his mouth.

"Me, too, baby," she said and kissed him on the cheek. "Was she nice?"

"I guess so. I don't know."

"So now you got to have a plan."

"Sure. Like how we're gonna get this"—he held up some of the pages—"to a guy cribbed by the police, when they want me? And even if he's out, like I just call the White House and say we got this package for him?"

"Fuckin' no way," Anjean said. He leaped off the couch. "Man, we sell this shit to somebody. I didn't save your black ass for nothing, man."

"Who we're going to sell it to?" Willie asked.

"Shit, I don't know. There's all these motherfuckers on television or at magazines that pay jumbo-size for this kind of shit."

Starrell stood in front of Anjean. He stared hard at the man. "Ain't happenin' that way, Anjean."

"Man, who says you make the call?" Anjean waved his hands. "Who the fuck found the asshole's joint? Willie did on his computer? How much that thing cost you, bro?"

Willie didn't reply.

"And who B&E'd it? I did. And then we got you black butt out of that hospital. What do you owe a nigger who ain't done nothing for you? Or for no black man. He's just guardin' Big Whitey. And then he comes to you, when he ain't got no game. Man, you don't know what he's playin'. But you know one thing: you got this." Anjean jerked his head at Timmons's stomach. "Don't you think you owe it? Get a stash for little Twayne? Man, how you know that if you hand this shit to some other player he ain't gonna do with it like you should. It's like this: Keep it in the community. Man, us. Why don't you ask your lady what she wants?"

Starrell turned toward Timmons. She didn't say anything.

"Bro's got a point," Willie said. "Now I ain't saying I agree with it. But it's a point to consider."

"Fuckin' damn righteous point," Anjean said. "And Twayne should consider it fast." He patted the side of his pants. "Fast."

"Oh, come on, Anj," Willie said. He took a step toward his brother.

"Hold up," Anjean said. He pulled a Glock from his pocket.

"Shit," Willie said. "Not here."

"Willie, you know we're talkin' dino-dollars. Fuck, man, imagine the load. Not just for me. For all of us. Right, Tamika? Tell 'em, bitch."

She shook her head.

Starrell moved toward Anjean.

"This ain't the way we're doing this," he said.

Anjean pointed the gun at him. "Don't do it, Twayne."

"That thing ain't gonna make any decisions here. No way." Starrell took another step forward.

"I said don't." Anjean extended his arm. The gun was a foot from Starrell's face.

"No way," Starrell said. He reached for the gun. He kept his eyes focused on Anjean's. Anjean returned the stare. His finger hugged the trigger.

A shot sounded. It came from behind Anjean. The bullet shattered a lamp across the room. Anjean spun around to face the spot from where the shot had come. Starrell grabbed Anjean's gun and pulled hard. Both men fell to the ground. The gun in Anjean's hand slammed against the wood floor, crushing his knuckles.

"Fuckin' shit!" Anjean screamed in pain.

"Let go!" Starrell shouted.

Both men looked toward the doorway to the bedroom. Willie and Anjean's mother was standing in the threshold. She wore a red bathrobe with large fuzzy buttons and purple, plastic slippers. She held a small pistol.

"Stop it, you boys!" she yelled. She waved the gun at them. Her arm was wobbly.

"Momma!" Willie shouted. Timmons jumped out of her chair. Starrell and Anjean stopped fighting to stare at the heavyset sick woman.

"I told you Anjean Jameson, you're not welcomed in this house," his mother said. "I told you not to come back 'til you repent upon your evil ways. I told you." Sweat was on Cass Jameson's face.

Anjean let go of the gun. Starrell pulled it away and jumped up. Anjean stayed on the ground.

"Momma, put that gun down," Willie said.

"Not 'til that sinner is gone," she said.

"C'mon Mrs. Jameson," Timmons said. She walked slowly toward the woman. "C'mon." Anjean looked at his mother. He began laughing. He held his stomach. He rolled over on his back and laughed.

"Man, a real motherfucker," he said between guffaws. "Get it Willie?" He looked at his brother. "Our momma's a real motherfucker."

Cass Jameson had the gun aimed at her son. Her glasses were crooked. Timmons drew closer to her.

"Where'd you get the popgun?" Anjean asked. "Inside some Cracker Jacks shit?"

"When Mrs. Ellis in 4B was robbed and raped, I said none of you sinners is going to do that to me. I'd shoot you in Jesus's holy name first. And send you on to his glory."

Anjean got to his knees. "Yeah, like someone would want to rape your old black ass."

"Anjean!" Timmons yelled at him.

"That's alright, Tamika," Mrs. Jameson said. "He's just black trash. Just so happened he came out of me. Just like someone's gonna come out of you. But just 'cause someone comes out of you don't make them a part of you forever. Otherwise we'd all be dead from grieving."

Anjean got up off the floor. He saw Starrell draw tense.

"Don't worry," Anjean said to him. "I ain't that stupid." He straightened the bandana on his head and pulled down his shirt. "Got my own business to get to." He nodded toward his mother. "You keep practicin'. Maybe you'll get me next time."

"Momma," Willie said. "Let him stay. He's helping Twayne and me."

"He knows the rules," Mrs. Jameson said. She kept the gun on Anjean.

"There ain't no room in that church for me," Anjean said. "So, see you bro'. Twayne, we'll be running together real soon. Keep the piece. Ain't the only one I got." His gaze shifted to Timmons. "Girl, tell him to talk to his brains."

Anjean left the apartment. Timmons put her arm around Mrs. Jameson and led her to the bedroom. Starrell felt himself shaking.

When Timmons returned to the front room, Willie and Starrell were at the table. "She won't let go of that damn gun," she said. "But I got her to bed."

"Man, I ain't never going to forget that," Willie said.

Timmons placed a hand on Starrell's shoulder.

"So what you gonna do, baby?" she asked.

"I dunno. Take all this down to the White House and say, 'Let me see that white boy'?"

"No, you got to get someone else to call for you," Timmons said.

"Yeah, like his personal attorney," Willie sneered.

"Someone who knows him already," Timmons said.

"Who's that?" Starrell asked.

"I know who."

Willie snickered at her.

" 'Cause I read the papers, too," she shot back at him.

"So who?" Starrell asked.

"Tell me you love me," she said, "and I'll tell you who."

45

Through an inside window in the interrogation room, Addis could see Margaret Hanover on a television by the sergeant's desk. Then there was footage from the canal; next, a live shot from outside the station. Addis sat alone in the room. He was wrapped in a blanket. His clothes were wet. He listened to the air conditioner hum. He considered asking someone to shut it off.

A detective entered the room. He said that Addis was not under arrest but that Addis still had the right to an attorney. He asked if he could pose a few questions to Addis. Unofficial. No notes. No tape recorder.

"Go ahead," Addis told him.

"Who was the woman?"

Addis said her name.

"Does she have relatives in the area?"

Addis said he thought her family lived nearby. Hadn't she said something about staying at her parents'? he thought to himself. He wasn't sure.

"Where did she work?"

"The CIA." The detective paused. "An analyst," Addis explained.

Shit, I've blown her cover. It's going to be on the front page tomorrow. . . .

"And what was the nature of your relationship?"

"Friends."

"Know her long?"

"Not really."

"And, Mr. Addis, what happened?"

After I came into the possession of information indicating the Hanovers were involved in a shady land deal, Ms. Lancette and I discovered that the CIA was tied to the murder of the President of the United States. Then a maniac working for god-knows-who tried to kill us. He had to settle for one out of two.

"I'm not really sure," Addis said. He explained that a crazy man in a Trailblazer drove up alongside the car and started waving a gun. Addis

314

tried to outrun him but he could not. There was a gunshot. One, maybe more. He lost control when he tried to get off the parkway.

"And the gun in the car?"

Yes, Clarence Dunne had put it in the glove compartment after the assassination. It probably was registered to Mr. Dunne. Addis had tried to use it to shoot out a window.

"It wasn't fired."

Yes, he had dropped it in the water.

"But the back window was shot out."

Yes.

"By whom?"

Addis didn't know. A blurry figure. He could not say if it was the driver of the Trailblazer.

"And your visit to the Kennedy-Warren? We were called by a resident there who saw you in the lobby with a woman. Was it Ms. Lancette?"

Addis explained that Lancette was trying to get something for a friend, and that he had been helping her.

"Who was her friend?"

Addis didn't know.

"Anything else you can tell us now that might be of help?"

No, he didn't think so.

The detective informed him that the White House was sending someone over. He asked if Addis wanted to make a phone call. "Not now," Addis said.

"We recorded your alcohol as .09," the detective said.

Addis said nothing.

"That's as close as you can get."

As close as you can get. Addis absorbed the words without responding. He closed his eyes and saw her in the water.

The detective left the room. Addis looked out at the television. More footage of the canal. A gurney. A white sheet. He felt cold. There was water in his ear.

Brewster McGreer pushed the door open. He wore a denim shirt and shorts. He stopped a foot shy of Addis and stood there.

"You alright?"

"Think so," Addis said.

McGreer sat on the edge of the table.

"You need anything? They offer you coffee or something?"

"That's okay."

Addis waited for the real questions.

"You call your folks?"

315

"Not yet."

McGreer drummed his fingers on the tabletop. He took a long breath.

"Okay, Nick, what the fuck happened? Who is she? What does she do for them? What are you up to? Why did Dunne give you a gun? Is this connected to what happened to him?"

Addis told him what he had told the detective.

"Bullshit, Nick," McGreer said. "But let's get the fuck out of here."

"They said I could go?"

"Yes. I told them that you'd be available for questioning whenever they want. You're fortunate there's another D.C. budget crisis. The fucking mayor called me when I was coming over here. Asked if he could be of any help. I said, 'Thanks.' He made fucking sure to let me know that they were listing you at .09. Like maybe it was fucking .095, and—lucky day—they were rounding off down, not up. He probably thinks he'll pull another $100 million out of our next budget."

Addis shrugged.

"Come on," McGreer said. He helped Addis up.

"Need to see a doctor?" he asked. "Have him look at those scratches."

"No. . . . Where are we going?"

"Stephanie said I should bring you home."

"I'd like to go to my place."

"No fucking way. The fucking vultures will be swarming there."

He led Addis out of the room. Water squished in Addis's shoes. He kept the blanket draped over his shoulders. Cops were staring at him. The detective appeared and asked how he could reach Addis in the morning. McGreer gave the detective his own direct number. McGreer's cell phone went off. He answered it and stepped aside.

"Did you find her parents?" Addis asked the detective.

"Yes. We sent two officers over. They'll have to make the official identification."

The morgue. Washed-out skin. Empty eyes. Blue lips. Then he remembered: the memo and the composition books.

"Did you find her handbag?"

"Not that I know of."

"She had some composition books in her bag."

"I'll look at the report again. But nothing was recovered. . . . What's in the books?"

"I'm not sure. Some writings. Her family might like to have them, if they're not ruined. . . . And I had a manila folder. Some odds and ends. Financial records. Nothing important."

"No."

All gone. No surprise there.

"But we're going to empty the lock in the morning," the detective said, "and do a daylight search."

McGreer returned, and a policewoman guided Addis and McGreer to the side entrance. McGreer had parked his car near the door. There were no reporters. They got into the Volvo station wagon.

"That was Kelly on the phone," McGreer said. "First thing, he said: 'Does this fuck us at all?' I told him, I didn't know. And that you were fucking telling some fucking story. He said: 'Seven-thirty-in-the-morning meeting.' Didn't even ask how you were. You know what he fucking said next?"

Addis shook his head.

" 'Christ, he really screwed Margaret royally.' He sounded happy."

McGreer's pager went off, and he looked at the number. "Dan Carey," he said. He dug into his pocket and pulled out the cell phone. He tossed it on Addis's lap and started the car.

"I've got fucking nothing to say to him," McGreer said. "Call you folks . . . First, watch this."

McGreer drove out of the parking lot. The television lights illuminated the car. Police officers scurried to keep the camera crews and reporters out of the path of the Volvo. Shit, Addis thought, we're going to have a parade. As McGreer steered the station wagon on to Idaho Avenue, four squad cars, their lights flashing, moved to block the road behind the Volvo. The journalists could not follow. Addis heard horns blaring.

"I did ask the mayor for one favor," McGreer said. He looked in the rearview mirror. "The fuckers did a good job."

Addis dialed his parents. They had been called by several friends. They had been watching the news. He assured them he was fine, that he did not have to see a doctor. The woman? She was a new friend. No, he didn't quite understand why it had happened. Maybe the guy was just a loon.

"Even a loon," his father said, "has his reasons."

Addis promised to call them in the morning and hung up. Neither he nor McGreer said much during the ride to Falls Church. When they were getting off the Beltway, McGreer asked Addis if he was warm enough. Addis nodded. He felt the hot, humid air against his face—McGreer had not turned on the air conditioner—and a chill inside him.

"Nick, who are you going to tell the truth to?" McGreer asked.

Fuck if I know.

Addis did not reply.

"Okay, then. I'm sure Stephanie has some hot milk or something like that for you. So you'll get some rest tonight. And we'll fucking deal with this in the morning."

"How's Clarence?" Addis asked.

317

"In and out," McGreer said. "Can't talk. Fucking doctors say it's going to be a day or two before he's stable. All that fucking excitement today probably didn't help. The police haven't been able to ask him much. We still don't know what he was doing the fuck there. It's just like—"

McGreer didn't finish the thought. Addis could guess: . . . *we don't know what the fuck you were doing in the canal.*

"But he asked for you today."

"He did?"

"That's what I was told. But the doctors say no visitors except family."

Addis stared straight at the moving spot where the headlight beam struck the ground. He was silent.

"Wonder why he asked for you."

Addis watched the light rush across the road.

"Of all people. . . . Not that you wouldn't be on my fucking mind if I was fucking fighting for my life."

Addis said nothing.

"But it did strike me as somewhat fucking odd. Doesn't it strike you as fucking odd, Nick? The same man who gave you a gun for god-knows-fucking-what is calling out your name from his near-fucking-deathbed."

McGreer steered the car on to his street, and they both saw two news vans in front of his California-style home. He drove past them, and harsh lights illuminated the car. McGreer pushed a button and the garage door opened; he pulled the Volvo in and pressed the button again.

His wife, Stephanie, was waiting at the door to the garage. She was wearing an oversized Tulane T-shirt and gym shorts. She held a bathrobe. She hugged Addis and led him to the kitchen. She had made hot cocoa. She picked up a piece of paper from the counter. Nine reporters had called so far, she said. So had Alter, Wenner, O'Connor, Palmer, and others. Ken Byrd had phoned to ask about the press statement. The White House was receiving queries from around the world. The lead question: Who's the woman? McGreer picked up the phone to call the police. He wanted those vans gone.

"And Jake Grayton," Stephanie McGreer said. "He's on his way over."

McGreer was on the phone with Byrd when Grayton rang the bell. Stephanie let him in. The news vans were gone.

"Nice porch," he said.

She brought Grayton into the living room. Addis was in the bathrobe and sitting in a rocking chair. He was looking at the photographs of sad-eyed, brown-skinned children hanging on the wall, shots Stephanie had taken while traveling in Central America.

"Doing okay, Nick?" Grayton asked. His hair always looks perfect,

Addis thought. Straight back. Nothing out of place. Grayton did not take off his jacket. His tie was not loosened.

"Yeah."

"Mind if we talk?"

"Sure."

Grayton looked at Stephanie. He was dismissing her. She headed toward the kitchen, from where a series of loud "fucks" was flowing.

"In here?" Grayton asked.

"Where else?"

"It's cooling down. On the porch?"

He imagined what would be Lancette's response: *one car, driving slowly. . . .*

"I'm fine here."

Grayton sat on the leather couch. "Looks like Guatemala," he said, nodding toward the photographs. "Been there. Didn't have the chance to take snapshots."

Addis crossed his arms. He resisted the urge to comment on Grayton's remark. Grayton put his hands on his knees.

"Sorry about Julia, Nick. Very sorry. What were you two doing?"

That was quick.

"Doing?"

"Yes. You went with her to the Kennedy-Warren. You visited the apartment and storage area of a Dr. Charlie Walters. I assume you were there at her initiative. Why?"

You mean, "What do I know?"

"She said she needed something for work."

"What?"

"She didn't say. She said she would know it when she saw it."

"And you were merely her . . . escort?"

"She said it might make it easier if I came along. It was a favor."

"And?"

"She showed the guy at the front desk some paper—I think it was a cable—and said she needed to get into her friend's apartment, to find something for him. She thought if I were there, then . . .'"

"She would be believed?"

"They'd be more inclined to help, I suppose."

"And you went along with this unorthodox request because . . . ?"

"What do you think?" Addis replied.

Grayton lifted a small silver dish that was on the coffee table. He turned it around in one hand.

"Did she take anything out of the apartment?"

"Some sweaters."

"Why?"

"I'm not sure. Said she was going to send them to her friend."

"And from downstairs?"

This is what you want to know. If I know. Can't lie too much. That would show you I'm in on it. And, anyway, someone's got the memo already.

"Two notebooks, I think. It was dark."

Shit, I told the detective they were hers.

"And what was in these notebooks."

Shit. Shit. Shit. Let's hope there won't be full and complete coordination between the police and the FBI.

"I don't know."

"She didn't say?"

"No, she didn't."

"You didn't ask? Weren't curious?"

"Well, I thought it would be better if I didn't."

"Plausible deniability."

"I suppose."

"And you were a bit struck by her?"

Addis did not answer.

"She didn't explain her interest in Dr. Walters?" Grayton asked.

"Sorry, no. Don't you know?"

Turn it on him.

"We're not sure."

Addis gripped the arms of the rocking chair.

"And that's supposed to be good enough?"

Raise your voice. . . .

"How do I know we weren't shot at and chased off the road and she . . . because of what she was doing at the Kennedy-Warren?"

That's it. . . .

"Maybe she's dead because of something she was doing for her job? Don't you think her family should know? Was someone after those books? Or the fucking sweaters? Why don't *you* tell me what the fuck's happening? Or should I tell the police that they ought to be looking for . . ."

Muff the name. . . .

"This Dr. Charles Whoever? Should I?"

"It's interesting that you haven't already," Grayton said.

"I thought I'd talk to Wenner first."

"Why?"

"Just in case. . . ."

"There was some trouble? So have you called him?"

"Not yet." And before Grayton could ask why not, Addis answered the question: "Stephanie said you were on the way over."

"Well, frankly, I don't know what she was up to. I'm going to talk to

Director Wenner, and we'll piece it together. Maybe those notebooks will turn up."

Sure.

"I'll keep you posted," Grayton continued. "I think your instincts were sound—about checking with Wenner. I'm sure he'll thank you. . . . By the way, when did you and she first—"

Stephanie McGreer looked into the room. "M. T.'s on the phone," she said to Addis. "You can take it in the den."

She stared at Grayton and led Addis away. More "fucks" were coming out of the kitchen. Addis sat at the desk and picked up the phone. Stephanie left the room. He didn't say anything at first.

"Nick, hello. Is that you? . . . Nick?"

"Hello."

"How are—"

"Fine."

"And she's . . ."

O'Connor had to know.

It was on the fucking news.

"Where are you?" Addis asked.

"Back at Blair House."

"Who's there?"

"Margaret. She told me to tell you that if you need any help—"

"Thank her for me. And who else?"

"The usual. Jack. Whalen's here. You know."

"And Dan?"

"Yes." A stretch of silence passed.

"Jack's really upset," O'Connor said. "He wanted to talk to you. But Margaret put him to bed."

"Where's Lem?"

"I don't know. Haven't seen him in a while. It's been a busy night. . . ."

"He didn't go to the studio?"

"No."

"And the show went okay?"

"Considering."

"Sorry about that."

"You sure you're alright?" O'Connor asked. "Anything I can do? Want me to come over?"

"What's planned for tomorrow?"

He picked up a piece of yellow construction paper that was on the desk. Stripes of red and blue paint ran across the page. Sparkles were in the paint. "I love Daddy," was written on the bottom.

"Mainly, the Children's Aid Fund lunch. It's at the Mayflower."

Shit. . . . Where he had stayed?

"And she's okay with that?" Addis asked.

"They asked if she wanted the venue changed. She said no. And then, on to Chicago in the evening. . . . Nick, what happened tonight?"

"I'm not sure. Let's talk about it later, okay?"

"Is there . . . anything Margaret needs to know?"

"She ask you to ask that?"

"No."

Of course not.

"Dan asked you, right?" Addis said.

"Nick, with Clarence and everything else, we just thought—"

"And with Harris Griffith, a dead accountant—"

She said nothing.

"I'll see you tomorrow," Addis said. "Somewhere. Washington is a small town."

"Then, I guess . . . Well, good night, Nick."

"Yeah."

He hung up the phone and returned to the living room. Stephanie was on the couch. McGreer was at the window, peering out at the street. Grayton was gone. "He said to tell you good-bye," Stephanie said. "That he'd talk to you in the morning."

"I'm sure there'll be a lot of that," Addis said.

"Come on," she said. "I'll show you to your room."

When they were in the guest room, Addis faced McGreer's wife. "Why is he sticking with Mumfries?" he asked.

"And not helping Margaret. . . ."

After being associated with the Hanovers, as a fund-raiser, adviser, or friend, ever since their law school days.

Addis did not say anything.

"He really likes it," Stephanie explained. "Really does. More than he thought. . . ." She looked into the room. "The bed is made. There are towels. If you need anything, just . . ."

He doesn't think Margaret can do it, and he won't take a risk for her. It's Stephanie who feels the shame. Damn, never ask a wife why her husband is a shit.

"I'll be fine," he said.

Addis lay in bed. It was less than a day since he had slept inches from her and had breathed the air that had brushed against her skin. How could he describe the smell? Sweet? Warming? He could not find the accurate word.

What had she died for? Nothing would give her death meaning. During the past weeks, he had floated down the path that led to the canal . . .

Hands and arms moving smoothly with the current. A billowing blouse.

. . . while Julia had consciously, conscientiously pursued a course that ended in the water and muck. He needed to push aside the numbness, the shock. Nothing he could do would compensate. But there would be choices to make, Addis thought. Tomorrow. And they would have meaning.

So, then, who knew? Knowledge was responsibility, he told himself. Grayton had been aware of what she was doing. And Wenner? Addis always had thought well of Wenner. Would he wittingly smother the truth about a presidential assassination? What about Kelly? Would Grayton tell him, warn him of a flap of historic proportion? If Kelly knew, would he tell Mumfries? Had the current President been informed that the assassin of Bob Hanover could be tied to the CIA, a government agency over which Mumfries once had oversight authority?

And what was there to do? Could he go to Palmer? He was left with nothing. No water-logged memo. Nothing. Just a story she told him and . . .

The light cut through the water. A head bobbed.

Addis tried to recall the Dante passage she had quoted to him.

He closed his eyes: her hair floating.

He opened them: the ceiling.

He felt cold. Water ran from his eyes.

The more you see the good, the more you see the bad? It was something like that.

46

The White House
July 1

Sprinkles from a doughnut clung to Hamilton Kelly's face. He was pacing inside McGreer's office. Addis noticed a shaving cut on his cheek. Brew McGreer, Mike Finn, and Ken Byrd were in chairs. Addis was alone on the couch.

"It's simple," Kelly said. "You get a lawyer. One of those shit-storm specialists. I'll call one for you. And we put out a statement that says we've given you a few days of leave, you're cooperating with the investigation, you don't know why this maniac came after you. And that you and she were. . . . What did you say, Ken?"

"Social acquaintances," Byrd said.

"Yeah," Kelly continued.

"And he expresses sorrow to her family," Byrd added.

"Sure. And cool your heels for a few days. No Chicago. Then when the cops are done, you'll make yourself available to the press."

Why don't I scream right now? None of this is about Julia. What's to be done for her?

Kelly ceased his pacing. He wiped at the sprinkles. Byrd cleared his throat. "What is it?" Kelly asked, not hiding his irritation.

"You know, I was listening to the radio on the way in," Byrd said. "People were giving their own cockamamie theories. Some said this had to have something to do with the assassination. And that it took the government so long to figure out who the killer was. How could that be possible? There has to be something more. And who would know? The CIA. And then a presidential aide is nearly killed with an ex-CIA agent—"

"Analyst," Kelly said. "Not an agent. She studied reports. Damnit, if our own press secretary can't get that right—"

"Well, I don't think it means a fucking difference to anybody out there," McGreer interrupted. "She was CIA. Front group or not. So all this fucking shit is going to keep growing like fucking kudzu. Especially if Nick holes up. We all know the fucking rules. These guys are going be in a frenzy until we give them Nick. So it'd be fucking smarter to do it sooner than later. Get him out there. Sacrifice the first day of the convention. A press conference. A group interview with a few of them. Whatever. It'll step all over tomorrow. But we still got the next two days. Besides, what do the fucking delegate counters say? Margaret needs the clean shot in Chicago. Not us. But we do anything that looks like we're fucking hiding something, we'll get hosed."

Finn nodded his head. Byrd said he agreed, too. Addis knew that McGreer had the right read—that is if Addis could be trusted before a media audience.

"I talked to the President," Kelly said.

Addis knew what was coming. He, too, often had used that phrase.

"And he agrees this should be put off for a few days."

Kelly knows. He knows why this happened. Why she's dead. And they want me quiet. Don't scream. Don't shout. Keep your shit together. Go along. For her. Find out, for her.

"So where do I cool my heels?" Addis asked.

"Not at home, obviously," Kelly said. "We'll find a place in town. And we can have security to keep people away. Grayton says it's no problem. The life of a White House official was threatened. It's an appropriate use of official resources."

"Sure," Addis said. "I'm sorry I never got that speech language to you last night. Should I work on that?"

Sound pathetic.

"I'd kinda like to keep busy," Addis said.

"No, it's done," Kelly said. "Let's find a lawyer. Have him come here. You stick around until then. Take it easy."

"Okay," Addis said. "But if I can be of any help—"

"We'll let you know," Kelly interrupted. "Now, I've got to plan a convention. At one it's the Cabinet meeting send-off. Then at two, it's wheels-up. First to Columbus, Ohio."

The wife of the governor of Ohio had gone to college with Margaret. She would be there with her husband to greet the President. A nice slap, Addis thought.

"Then Nashville," Kelly said. "An airport rally."

Everyone knew the South, except for Louisiana, was going to be difficult territory for Margaret, Addis told himself.

"And then California for the night," Kelly continued. "Announce we've squeezed out a few more dollars for cops for the cities." He rubbed his bald pate. "Too bad, Nick, you won't be with us."

325

Addis entered his office and went straight to the bottom drawer of his desk. The file was gone. The one marked "Pension Reform." The file that held the other copy of the Blue Ridge records. The phone rang. Addis ignored it and left the office.

Automatic pilot. Automatic pilot.

The door to Computer Services was locked. Addis waited in the basement hallway of the OEOB. Ten minutes later, Amy arrived. She was surprised to see him.

"I thought . . . you . . . How are . . . ?" she sputtered.

"Thanks for the concern," he said. "Can you look something up for me? Again."

"Sure," she said too quickly. Then, Addis saw, she started thinking, Should I be doing this?

"It would mean a lot to me," he said, widening his sad eyes.

I'm such a shit.

She opened the door. "What can I do for you?" she said.

"The WAVE records from last night," he said. "For the West Wing. After nine. Who came and went."

"Okay." She tried to smile, but she was nervous. "You don't have to wait around here. I'll come by your office, okay? That's what I'll do."

"Thanks."

Addis was at his desk, looking through the phone book, when Ken Byrd opened the door without knocking.

"They're showing the canal being dredged on CNN," he said.

"Pass," Addis said.

Shit, if my stomach tightens any more, I'm going to keel over.

"They said that according to police sources you were concerned about some papers you had with you."

"I asked about some personal financial stuff."

"Okay. . . . You know you've got Kelly freaked out on this."

Addis decided not to be reassuring.

"Anyway, Kelly called Vic Parmenter, the lawyer, and he's coming over later. Says if the police want to talk, tell them you have to talk to him first."

"Fine," Addis said.

Byrd looked at the opened telephone book.

"Just trying to get a number for her family."

Now get the hell out.

Addis found the number and closed the book.

"And we'll have to say something about Parmenter coming. I'll take care of that," Byrd said. He was rocking on the balls of his feet. "Something like, 'Mr. Addis cooperated fully with the police last night. He merely wanted to speak to a lawyer before making any public—no we won't say 'public.' This is better: 'He merely wanted to speak to a lawyer so he would understand his rights as he fully cooperates with the investigation.' Sound okay to you?"

Who the fuck cares? Can't I just pick up the phone, dial a number, and hear her voice?

"Sure," he said. "Whatever you think best."

"Good," Byrd replied. "Guess we're done for now."

On his way out, Byrd passed Amy from Computer Services. Addis could tell he was curious why she was here.

"Got it," she said and handed an envelope to Addis. He removed the printout and examined it.

"Thanks," he said to her, without lifting his head.

"You're welcome," she said.

Addis heard the disappointment. He looked at her. "I owe you one," he said. "Or two. Maybe when things calm down I can make it up to you."

The corners of her mouth lifted.

"Yes," she said.

His eyes returned to the paper. He found what he was looking for on the log. "Thank you," he said.

"I thought you might want . . ." She handed him a can of Coke.

"That's kind of you." He rolled his chair next to the mini-refrigerator and opened the door. It was empty. "See," he said. "I'm out." He placed the can in the refrigerator and rolled back to the desk. "I'll have it later."

"Well if you need . . ."

"Okay."

"Uh, good luck," she said as she left.

He put the log to the side of his desk and stared at the phone number for Lancette's family. What could he tell her parents without withholding information or lying? he asked himself. But they deserved to know. He closed the phone book and tossed it on a bookshelf.

Not yet, he thought. Not just yet.

47

K and 17th Streets
July 1

Anjean Jameson stood on the street corner and watched an Asian man selling sunglasses. Korean, he thought. And the guy at the next booth— Korean, too. Another Korean next to him. And they all were peddling shit. These weren't DKNY sunglasses. Or Tommy. Or Ray-Ban. You don't get shit like that for nine dollars. Not even if some G.B.'ers do a warehouse. The words on the frame don't mean nothing. They must crank this shit out somewhere. Maybe in Korea, wherever that was. But one thing he told himself he knew was that you don't get nothing for almost-nothing. Either you pay the man and get it real. Like his T-land specs. One-seventy-five, in Georgetown. He dished it out. Two Bennies. The sales clerk couldn't even look at him. Like his money was no good. But she held out her hand, didn't she? Palm up. 'Cause green is green. . . . Or you take it. You want, you take. That's the other way. So you give it to the man or you take it from the man. You don't pay no change to some squinty Korean chink who smiles at you, holds up a mirror to your ugly-ass face, and says, "Lookgood, lookgood." But he had one fool after another. Office creeps crawling to work. Twelve dollars for a Calvin Klein. Man, who believes that bullshit? People are fucking stupid.

Jameson fixed his gaze on the entrance to an office building across the street and pushed his sunglasses tight against the bridge of his nose. Motherfucker, he said to himself. Can't fucking believe I'm sweating my ass off in the god-damn a.m. That sucker's not right. It ain't. I could have taken steel for that shit. I could've been busted at the chink's house. Man, why are there so many fucking gooks every-fucking-where? I fucking hate this shit.

He wiped his brow with his sleeve. He felt the moisture beneath the silk bandana wrapped around his head. No fucking way, he thought. He should have listened to me. Showed respect. He could have entertained what I was trying to say. Man, just entertain it. Consider the damn prop-osition.

The Korean peddler looked at him. He was in between customers.

Like I can't fucking stand here, Korean chink-man, Jameson thought. Brothers made this country, when your sorry-ass was in a rice paddy somewhere.

The Korean turned toward a customer.

You worry how to rip the fools, Jameson silently said to the Korean.

Starrell came out of the office building. A white woman was with him. They walked down K Street.

Good, Jameson thought. They ain't taking no cab. Man, even in Choc-olate City, a nigger can't get a cab. Fucking Africans, man. Don't even speak English.

He crossed the street and followed the pair.

48

The White House
July 1

Addis was at his desk, bouncing a pencil against a yellow pad—no notes, he told himself—and considering options: try Palmer again, visit Dunne in the hospital, locate the CIA shrink, go to the *Post*.

He felt water, cold water, moving up his leg.

He saw her face, eyes closed.

He held his breath. He squeezed his eyes shut. He pressed his feet against the floor. His lungs began to hurt. He grabbed the arms of the chair. His body started to writhe. The pain moved to his throat.

One more second, one more second . . .

He saw her face and gasped for air. There were tears on his cheeks.

A Secret Service officer knocked and entered the office. He wiped his face with his hand.

"Excuse me, sir." It was one of the few women officers. "A Ms. Holly Rudd at the Seventeenth Street entrance says you're expecting her. But you didn't answer the call from the desk."

She was the redheaded officer, one of the first to reach Hanover in the briefing room. Addis recalled that her head had looked like an explosion flash in the color photographs on the newsmagazine covers.

The officer noticed that Addis had disconnected the line to his phone. "Ms. Rudd was adamant that someone look for you. One of the officers at the desk did recognize her. From a photograph in the paper. So . . . hope you don't mind."

"No, that's fine," Addis said.

"Shall I have someone escort her here?"

"No, I'll go. Get some air."

Rudd was sitting on the wooden bench by the guard's desk, her hair pulled back. She stood as Addis passed through the security turnstiles.

"How are you?" she asked.

"I wasn't hurt," he said.

"Good. I didn't want to disturb you, but—"

"Let's go outside." He knew people—the guards, the employees coming and going, the visitors waiting to be cleared into the White House—were watching, listening for a clue that could be fed into the city's gossip machine. Rudd must have realized that by merely trying to see him she could be in the newspapers tomorrow.

"Okay," she said. "There's somebody I want you to meet."

Your boyfriend? What else can happen now?

They walked two blocks before either said anything.

"Not hurt at all?" she asked.

"No," he said.

Haven't we already covered that?

The people they passed on the sidewalk gawked at him. A red-faced man wearing shorts and a U.S.A. T-shirt handed a young child to a woman with frosted hair and grabbed his videocamera. Addis maintained his thousand-mile stare. How much could the fellow get for the footage? Enough to cover this family vacation? I don't mind, Addis told himself. Today, he was selling newspapers and drawing people to TV shows and radio programs. Helping the economy, he thought. So was Julia Lancette.

"Was she special?" Rudd asked.

"She would have been," he replied.

"I wish I could say more than 'I'm sorry,' but . . ."

"Yes." He acknowledged the sentiment without helping.

She guided Addis into a sandwich shop, and they walked to the back. A young black man, wearing a white shirt and a blue tie, was sitting at a table. She introduced him to Twayne Starrell. He looked uncomfortable. His eyes were. . . . Addis could not decide. Hard? Edgy? Mean? He was not a lawyer, not a student, not a congressional aide, not a reporter. A canvas knapsack was on his lap.

"A messenger from Clarence Dunne," Rudd said.

Starrell placed the knapsack on the table.

"What's in it?" Addis asked.

"I don't know," Rudd said. "But he"—she nodded toward Starrell—"insisted I—"

Addis raised an eyebrow; Starrell frowned at the show of suspicion.

"Requested, and politely so," she corrected herself, "that I arrange for you two to meet." She explained she had received a call from a woman who claimed she had papers that Dunne had wanted to get to Addis.

"Tamika," Starrell said. "Tamika Timmons."

Timmons, Rudd told Addis, had followed Addis's social life in the newspapers and tabloids. She had seen an item about Addis's recent tri[p] to New Orleans with Rudd.

"She don't forget nothing," Starrell remarked. "Makes it hard."

"I'll bet," Addis said. He and Rudd sat down.

Rudd continued the explanation. Timmons remembered the name [of] Rudd's law firm and called it this morning. She told the receptionist th[at] she was with the Secret Service and needed to speak with Rudd imme[-] diately.

"She watches lots of old TV shows," Starrell said. "With detectives an[d] all that."

When Rudd came to the phone, Timmons confessed the ruse and sai[d] she had a friend who had been working with Dunne. She told Rudd abo[ut] her friend's visit to the Gauntlet bar, about her friend's rescue of a lad[y] from the CIA, about her friend's conversation with Dunne in the car.

Julia had not told him everything, Addis thought. Not about this rescu[e] at the bar. Not about Starrell. Had that been oversight or prudence? Mi[s-] trust or the natural reticence of her profession? Dunne, too, had not men[-] tioned Starrell to Addis.

I've been compartmentalized. By him and by her.

"You?" Addis asked. "The friend?"

Starrell almost smiled. "Man, you looked right at me, at that burne[d] up diner. I was in the car. Guess you don't remember."

"Guess not."

Timmons, Rudd went on, also told her about the notes Dunne ha[d] taken during his conversation with the man from the Gauntlet, about th[e] break-in at the house in Arlington, about Starrell's visit to the hospital.

The man from the Gauntlet? That must be Dawkins. The man whom Grayt[e] *said was Morrison's accomplice. Dunne had found Dawkins before he was kill[ed]* *in the raid. More proof Julia was right. The Agency was hooked into this.*

Starrell peered around the room. Students—even in the summer. The[y] kept looking at his table. He wondered if any had seen him the day befo[re] when they ditched the ambulance.

Timmons had told Rudd the knapsack contained papers that Dunn[e] wanted Addis to see. She asked Rudd for help.

"But," Rudd told Addis, "she said that I couldn't see what was in th[e] bag. Only you could."

Starrell sat erect. He watched Addis absorb the information. He al[so] kept an eye on the students. Was anyone heading to the phone? No w[ay] anyone would recognize him from that sketch. His lips were not as bi[g,] his face not as square.

"And all this is true?" Addis asked Starrell.

"Yes—" He thought about saying "sir," but did not.

"And does anyone else know what Clarence was up to?"

"Don't think so." Starrell saw Dunne in the car. A bullet passing through the neck. The red spray.

"There was this one thing," Starrell added. "Mr. Dunne was flicked. Said he had tried to talk to somebody."

"Who?" Addis asked.

"His boss. Said all he fuckin' cared about was some Chinese shit."

That made sense to Addis: Dunne went to the Treasury Secretary, and Alter wasn't interested. Just like Palmer wasn't interested.

"May I?" Addis said and pointed to the bag.

"Yup," Starrell said. He slid it across the table. "The notebook's there, too."

Addis unzipped the knapsack. Rudd moved her chair so she could gain a better view. The notebook was on top. The writing was neat and tight—the product of an organized mind—distinctive enough to determine if it belonged to Dunne. That lessened the odds someone was running a hoax. He skimmed the pages.

Action team formed. Deep cover. Outside CIA.
Terr. targets. Hong Kong, Germany, Mid East.
inc. assassination

An undercover government hit team? Addis wondered. Is that what Dunne's notes meant?

Tangiers car blast.
3 dead/3 left; T. L.
Disbanded. No-trace pensions.
DCI/some in Cong. knew.

Addis remembered an explosion in Tangiers that had killed a dozen—or more?—civilians, including three American aid workers. Shit, the same event? Had these Americans been killed by . . . a U.S. operation?

Mattie to Raymond
One mting/Crystal City.
Man on TV in charge?/JG?

J. G.? Jake Grayton? Did Dunne suspect that Grayton had run this outfit? Had pulled together a small squad to assassinate suspected terrorists? Addis thought about the timing. The Tangiers blast had occurred during the administration of Hanover's predecessor. Before Wenner was DCI. When Mumfries chaired the Senate intelligence committee. "3 left." Who did that refer to? "Mattie" must be Matthew Levon Morrison, the man identified as Hanover's killer. Was he part of this team? With Dawk ins? That made two. Who or what was "T. L."? Shit, think of a worse nightmare. A presidential assassin from a covert government hit squad Had he taken his government-provided skills and used them against Han over? . . . And why?

No wonder Grayton was freaked. Kelly, too. Fuck, had Mumfrie been in on the creation of this god-damn off-the-books outfit? Signed of on an operation that eventually led to the murder of a President This couldn't be. No, it couldn't. And who was the third? Where the hel was he?

A bad movie. A fucking bad movie. Who could believe such shit really happens It sure gives the fuckers plenty of reason to kill. But why kill Hanover?

Addis looked up from the notebook.

"And the rest of the stuff was in the bag when you found it a Dawkins's apartment?" Addis asked Starrell.

Starrell nodded. "We didn't know what to look for. Just scope around. Looked like evidence or somethin'. Took it and booked."

"We?"

"Had two buds helping. Shit, I thought Dunne was deader than dick So I ain't goin' to be walkin' into no crook without backup."

"That's okay," Addis said. "I just want to know who knows what."

"Don't worry about no others," Starrell said.

Addis removed the other papers from the knapsack. Xeroxed article about the Tangiers explosion. Stories about the Hanovers, mainly profile from the presidential campaign. One headline read, "The Hanover Leg end: More Truth Than Not." There were three passports in differen names. Each photograph was the same: close enough to Morrison. A pass book for a numbered bank account in Geneva. Photographs cut out o magazines of the presidential briefing room. An article about the bar tender at the Mayflower; the name of Brady Sandlin, the reporter Mor rison had impersonated, was circled. Pages of handwritten notes on grapl paper. The writing was small, difficult to read. Phrases, not sentence: "Cleared money." "Semtech source burned." "Bird-man at the emb. "Car dealer bribe." An envelope of travelers' checks—several thousan dollars—with signatures matching the name on one of the passport: There were pages torn out of *Soldier of Fortune* magazine. Four bottles c pills, the labels in German. A short newspaper death notice: "Reginal Morrison, Alexandria"—

Louisiana? Alexandria, Louisiana? That would be too fucking a coincidence

—"72-years-old, pneumonia." Farmer. Electrician. Husband of Hele Alice Morrison, deceased. It was dated seven weeks before the assassi nation. And letters, handwritten in a wobbly scrawl. The top of the fir: page of each letter had been torn to remove the name of the addresse

The bottom of the last pages were similarly torn so Addis could find no signature.

Addis read one:

Went to Mother's grave yesterday. Been long time now. She never got used to being in that home. Doctors say I'm pretty sick. Maybe you can make it back, tho' I dont know if you get these letters at that address you gave me. One thing I guess you got a rite to know. You know how we lost the spread at Blue Ridge. Sold it stupid 'cause they told us a judge was going to swipe it for iminet domain. There's more than that. Some years on—when we was living at Uncle Pete's—I heard from this real estate guy how the Ridge was sold again to Govnor Hanover and then sold again to some other folks. . . .

Blue Ridge? At the Mayflower, he had checked in under the name of Max Bridge. B-ridge. Was that the message?

. . . And the Govnor made like a prince. So when I hear this, I was ready to be beat. Should have been ours. So I tried to see the govnor to complain. Drove to Baton Rouge. Guess I caused a stir at the office there. This lady won't let me see him or no one else. Then this fellar comes to pull me out of there. He's rough at first. But he asks me to explain why I'm so agitated. I tell him I see what's been done and it ain't fair. So he says that he'll take a look and get on back to me. Talks like your momma did. I ain't no fool so I say what if you don't. He writes down his telephone number for me. And a week later he comes by Uncle Pete's. Says what's done is done and all that. But says some folks want to make it up. Big folks, he says. This is when you got your troubles at training. So I tell him you punched out this sergeant and they going to bust you out. He says, he'll talk to the big folks. A week later you called me to say your on to something big and secret and all's OK. So I figured they done kept their word. So I don't fuss no more about what's been done. Cause maybe I figured it's a good thing cause it got you something. But if things ain't turn out good, then I don't know what. Anyhow, I hope you ain't got no twitches yet. Your momma fought them for a long time. She always prayed and smiled, and made everybody feel good. Just like her name. And the docs always said they may pass you. I am praying for you. More for you than for me.

Addis let the page drop on the tapletop. He stared at the wall. A Redkins calendar.

This can't be. It's not a bad movie. It's a bad joke. The worst fucking joke of all time. The worst in the fucking history of the U.S. and the entire fucking universe. Who could believe this? This guy's—he's like Oswald—every-fucking-where. Worse than Oswald. Not the biggest damn coincidence ever. The two biggest. One on top of another. Son of the hick ripped off by Chasie Mason to help the Hanovers, and, then, to keep that deal quiet, he's bounced to some scum squad of government assassins. And then he . . .

Addis's heart pounded. Might he be reading this wrong? The Blue Ridge property had been owned by a Helen Peters. He looked again at the death notice. Helen A. Morrison had been the wife. Two Helens. Could they be the same? Had Matthew Morrison's mother once been Helen Peters?

". . . and made everybody feel good. Just like her name."

Or Helen *A.* Peters? Addis had cut short his phone conversation with the clerk in the Rapides Parish records office. Had there been a middle name? One that began with an *A*? Helen A. Peters? Initials: H. A. P. That's damn close to *HAPPY.*

"Oh fuck," Addis said.

"What is it?" Rudd asked.

"Nothing," Addis replied. "And everything. Every fucking thing."

336

49

Connecticut Avenue
July 1

Addis and Starrell pushed through the lunchtime pedestrians. Addis didn't care about the surprised looks. Screw it. He was the clown of the day. The media object of the moment. Stories around the clock on cable. The canal footage repeated over and over. Endless demands from journalists for comments. Television reporters interviewing his neighbors. Ever see this woman before? Uninformed speculation from pundits. Jim, what does this mean for the convention? Well, Bob, it could mean a great deal, but we won't know until all the facts are in. Lawyers trading theories on talk shows. Journalists chasing after anyone who knew her. Nothing unraked, nothing untouched, nothing left alone.

Oh shit, her family.

He pondered what he had read in the sandwich shop. He was still wondering if there were any other ways to interpret it. Matthew Morrison's mother—nickname Happy?—had owned the land before the Elva partnership acquired it and sold it to the Hanovers. And that line about twitching: "I hope you ain't got the twitches yet." What did that mean? He shook his head. Just like clearing an Etch-a-Sketch, he thought.

"So how did you get involved in all this?" he asked Starrell.

"Mr. Dunne asked me to."

"And you volunteered?"

"No. He cashed me."

Two attorneys from the White House counsel's office were standing at a corner. Addis nodded at them and kept walking.

"So what do you want for this?" Addis shook the knapsack.

"Nothing."

"Nothing?"

"Why not?"

A bearded man in a suit stepped in front of Addis and forced him to stop. "Gabe Hershberg, Mr. Addis. *L.A. Times.* Got a minute?" He was pulling a notepad from his pocket.

"No." Addis tried to pass the reporter. The man moved to block Addis.

"Just one or two questions, please."

Starrell grabbed the journalist, spun him around, and pushed him into the street. A cab braked to avoid striking the reporter.

"Thanks," Addis said to Starrell.

"Fuck you!" the reporter yelled.

Addis resumed walking, Starrell by his side. Neither responded to the shouting: "Fuck the fuck you!"

"So I was asking," Addis said. "Why don't you want anything out of this?"

"NYFB," Starrell replied before he thought about the answer.

"That's a new one on me, but I can guess."

Starrell cleared his throat. "Just trying to prove something," he said.

"To who?" Addis asked.

"Just trying."

Addis entered the revolving door to the Mayflower Hotel, and Starrell followed. He tried not to think the obvious: It all began here. With two people shot dead when they walked into a room floors above. But that was wrong. It had started somewhere else. Where? He could not say for sure. At the spot where Matthew Morrison's father first learned his family had been shafted so the Hanovers could pocket $130,000? In the dining room of the director's suite at CIA headquarters, where the director—now dead—had said to himself (or to Grayton, or to Mumfries), We need to kill a few people, on the sly, to ease our foreign policy woes? In the office where Chasie Mason first cooked up the land deal? Was it in the Louisiana town where the hospital collapsed, killing a bunch of kids, in a tragedy that confirmed the charges being made by a nobody law professor running for state attorney general? Or in the boarding school dorm room where late on cold Vermont nights Margaret Mason listened to her room-mate rave about a young man from back home—and Margaret decided she would find him?

The chain was long; it was twisted. He envisioned it shaped like a string of DNA. The code for life . . . and it led to Julia Lancette dead in a canal. And his place on it? How responsible had he been for Hanover's election to the presidency? In the large three-ring binders of Nick Addis clippings maintained by his parents, there were articles—by the best political reporters in the nation—that credited him with providing decisive advice during the first presidential campaign.

As a family of arguing Germans walked by, he recalled one particular piece of counsel: Fly back to the state for the execution of Donny L.

ondreau, the mentally retarded convicted murderer. Why? Hanover
d asked. To be there and accept full responsibility, Addis had argued
ring the conference call, in which M. T. O'Connor had urged Hanover
keep his distance. What had Hanover desired? He had wanted it both
ays: to be seen in favor of the death penalty—a compulsory position
r a southern politician—but not be so close to a practice that Addis
sumed he did not actually favor. You can't run away, Addis had told
m. Voters will consider you a politician afraid of your own stands. You
n't be for killing murderers and scumbags, if you're not willing to *be*
re for the killing. Hanover followed Addis's recommendation. And he
on the nomination. Because of the episode? Probably not. But who
uld say?

And . . . there was something else. Less obvious. The Honduras busi-
ss of a few years earlier, when Addis had leaked to the *Post* that the CIA
d been funding those drug-dealing generals in Central America. Had
umfries and the CIA director taken their antiterrorism hit squad—Mor-
on's squad—so deep, kept it secret from the agency and most of Con-
ess, because they had been so embarrassed by this particular leak? The
ak had been the right thing to do, Addis was sure. Senator Palmer, his
ss, had practically ordered him to slip the information to the press. Addis
membered: Palmer leaning back in his leather chair, feet on the desk,
oes off: "Wish somebody'd go public. Nick, some things don't have any
ght being hid." The fact that the revelation would injure Mumfries, a
lmer rival—that had not been Addis's motivation. Or Palmer's. He knew
at. He was sure. Right? There had been no other options. No other
annels. Right?

One long curving piece of DNA. A Möbius strip.

"Now what?" Starrell asked.

Addis looked at him.

"You just standing there. Like you're buggin.' People are lookin'. Over
ere"—Starrell moved his eyes—"suits."

Two Secret Service agents on the other side of the lobby were watching
em. They were part of Margaret's security detail. One was talking into
e microphone attached to his lapel. Reporting Addis's presence to some-
ne? The one talking looked familiar to Starrell. Was he the man Starrell
aped over during his dash to the ambulance yesterday? Shit, Starrell
d to himself, hope he ain't recognizing me.

"Plan, man?" Starrell asked.

"No thanks."

Starrell did not know what to say.

"Okay," Addis said. "You take this." He handed Starrell the knapsack.
Wait for me over there." He pointed to a couch in the lobby. "Anything

happens, you take that bag back to Holly." She was waiting for Addis's call in her office. Addis pictured her leaving the sandwich shop. "Nick," she had said, "I'm glad to help." He knew she was—and that he only needed a certain sort of help from her now.

"And then you get all this to Clarence," he said to Starrell. "But, this time, try not to destroy a hospital."

"Anything happens, like what?" Starrell clutched the bag.

"If I knew . . . Just wait. In thirty minutes, take off."

"Think I'm going to stick out here?"

"Today, don't ask me about sticking out." Addis headed toward the front desk. He saw the clerk's eyes flare with recognition.

"Hope you don't mind." Addis strode behind the front desk and into the back office. He moved quickly through several rooms. He found the door to a hallway used by the hotel's employees. Work in Washington long enough, he told himself, and you learn the hotels inside and out. He passed waiters carrying dishes from the main ballroom. He pushed against the swinging doors.

Margaret Hanover was illuminated. She stood at the center of the dais the target of piercing television lights. She was . . . glowing, Addis thought. In the crowded, darkened room, every face turned to the one reflecting the white beams. The words barely registered with Addis "National security means many things . . . How do we treat our most tangible and important asset? . . . One in five live in poverty . . . Our most precious resources . . . When last year I was named Children's Friend of the Year, I . . ."

Addis looked around the ballroom. He saw M. T. O'Connor in a corner Dan Carey was next to her, holding a rolled-up report in his hand. Numbers, numbers, numbers. Flip Whalen was a few feet to their side. Jack in his wheelchair, was facing the side wall, not the dais. Addis walked the perimeter of the room.

"A crusade that is above any election . . . There is no more solemn duty . . . For years I sat on the board . . . When I was in a village in India. . . . I remember what my grandmother—we called her 'Memmie'—once said . . ."

O'Connor stepped away from Carey when she saw Addis approaching

"Nick," she asked in a whisper. "What are—"

"Is Lem around?" He kept his voice low.

"He went upstairs to check out a suite Margaret's going to use afterward."

Fund-raising calls, Addis thought. Can't use the phones at Blair House for that.

"What, what do you want with Lem?" she asked.

"Need to ask him about a security matter."

She waited for a more detailed explanation.

"Hear anything about Harris Griffith's death?" he asked.

She brought her hands together by her stomach. "Been busy today."

"What room?"

She glanced toward Margaret.

"M. T., what room?"

"Six-oh-four. . . . Nick, are you—"

"Don't ask. Please. I'm tired of being asked that."

"You look, you look . . ."

"Like what?" Addis asked. He was curious. What was showing on his face.

"I don't know," she answered. "But then . . ."

But then I watched someone die. And then learned. . . .

Carey and Whalen came over.

"How ya holding up?" Carey asked.

"Sorry to hear, Nick," Whalen said. "Any further word on—"

"Fine . . . and no," Addis replied. "Excuse me."

"Can we talk before we leave for Chicago?" O'Connor asked. Why were her eyes moist? Addis wondered.

"Whatever," he said and walked off.

O'Connor watched as Addis paused by Jack. He leaned close to the boy and said a few words.

"There are millions of children who will suffer—who will be denied access to government health care, nutrition, and education programs—if we allow the views of our opponents to prevail," Margaret was saying. "As we celebrate our birth as a nation, even in these tragic, dark days, let us pledge, as a way to commemorate the honor of my husband, that we will . . ."

The maid was leaving, and she let Addis into the suite. He passed through an anteroom and into a sitting room with two sofas and a desk. No one was there. The door to the bedroom was ajar. He peered inside: empty. He turned back to the sitting room and then heard a noise behind him, a click.

"Don't m-m-m-move." It was Lem Jordan.

Addis stood still, keeping his back toward Jordan.

"It's me. Nick."

"How d-d-did you get in?"

"The maid."

"God-d-d-damn m-m-maid. T-t-took three calls."

Addis slowly faced Jordan. Margaret's bodyguard did not lower the gun in his hand.

341

"Margaret likes hot c-c-c-compresses after she speaks. Smaller towels. We n-n-needed smaller towels. Took three calls to get them."

Addis wondered what sort of gun it was. He knew nothing about weapons. He could not even identify the gun that Dunne had placed in the glove compartment, the gun that he had dropped, the gun that he had watched sink into the muddy night water of the canal.

"What do you w-w-want?" Jordan asked.

"To talk, Lem. You can put the gun down, can't you?"

"About what?"

"Things."

" 'Things' can mean lots of d-d-d-ifferent th-things."

"Guess that's right. I'm going to take a seat, okay?" Addis sat on a sofa. Jordan let his arm drop. He did not holster the gun.

"So what things?" he asked.

Addis reached into the inside pocket of his jacket and pulled out two pieces of paper. He held one up.

"White House log. You were in the West Wing after I . . . after we were chased off the parkway."

"Y-y-yeah?"

"Lem, can you tell me why you were there?"

"Picking up a b-b-box of books. And some stuff for J-j-jack."

"At"—Addis looked at the page—"9:47 at night."

"G-g-go ask the Marine at the d-d-desk. He saw me with the box."

"At 10:38. Almost an hour to pick up a box."

"Guess I spoke to a few guys."

"I saw you last night, Lem. I saw you standing there. At the canal."
I think it was you. But let's see.

Jordan said nothing. The gun remained in his hand.

"Then afterward someone took a file from my office."
Show me something, dammit.

Jordan's expression did not change. He stared at Addis.

"Blue Ridge records. Some from Tracy Griffith, the wife of Harris Griffith. You know who he is—or was?"
Can he keep this up? He's not denying anything.

Jordan did not blink.

"Did you kill Harris Griffith, Lem?"

His mouth was tight. Addis stood up. The hand holding the gun clenched.

"Did you, Lem? Because he wanted to blackmail Margaret?"

Jordan shifted his feet.

"Who knows? Does Margaret?"

Jordan bit his lower lip.
Come on, Lem. Jesus, come on.

342

"Does M. T. know? Did she tell you about Griffith? Did she or Margaret end you to New Orleans?"

Please, don't let it be M. T. Please.

Jordan's free hand was balled into a fist.

Shit, he won't give anything up.

"Just scare him, right? I'm guessing. That was the plan? But he wouldn't care. And I know that lawyer of his—Joe Mik—fucking asshole . . . So ou . . . you."

Addis held up the White House log.

Proof leads to more proof. Someone must have seen him near my office. What about fingerprints? Would there be any?

"But why last night, Lem? Why did you try to—"

"I saved you!" Jordan shouted.

He raised the gun and pointed it at Addis's chest.

"I saved you," Jordan repeated. "I s-s-saved you."

Addis felt Jordan's spittle on his face. He didn't wipe it off.

"You shot out the window—"

"To save you!" The arm that held the gun jerked. It looked as if Jordan vanted to throw the pistol at Addis. "To save you! You!" Jordan hit his high with his fist. "And, and . . . her."

"But you weren't in the Trailblazer?"

Jordan shook his head.

"But you were following us, too. That it?"

There was no answer on Jordan's face.

"Why?"

Jordan's face was red.

"Put the gun down. Please, Lem. And tell me why."

Jordan's lips were tight.

"Somehow you knew," Addis said. "You knew I was looking at the 3lue Ridge deal and that . . ."

Addis recalled the day before when Jordan had told him the story about the time he accidentally killed a dog on a boat. "You knew there vas a connection, didn't you? Blue Ridge and the assassination. That if someone got past the official bullshit on the assassination, it would track)ack to that deal. You didn't want that. And you heard Julia and me alking at Blair House."

Addis thought about the morning they had been at Blair House.

"No, no . . . Jesus, you saw her shake her head at me when we were ll watching Grayton making the announcement about Morrison and)awkins. Was that it? One gesture. Enough to keep an eye on us. That vas damn smart of you. You knew about Morrison's son. You remem->ered Matthew Morrison. You made the connection. Only you . . . Look, .em."

Addis held out another piece of paper.

"A letter from Morrison's father. He spoke to someone in the governor's office. Someone who took care of things. And who helped his son hook up with a—I don't know—some sort of squad. Out-of-channels, off-the-reservation, undercover."

Addis could read nothing in Jordan's eye. They were pebbles floating on his pie-pan face. A fireplug with a pie-pan face: Addis always had been proud to have conjured up that description of Jordan.

"Reginald Morrison was screwed by Chasie who was helping Bob and Margaret make a shitload of money," Addis continued. "Then he found out, raised a stink, and someone in the governor's office fixed it up. Got his boy, who was booted from the Marines, the job of a lifetime."

A steel-cold pie-pan.

"That someone," Addis said. "You, Lem. You did that, right?"

"Talks like your momma did"—that's what the letter said.

"To help the Hanovers, right? Just to help."

The arm with the gun trembled.

"It's like a sick joke, Lem, isn't it? Like a stupid script somebody wrote. Somebody who doesn't really know us. Doesn't really know you. But they made us do all these things. Lem? All these things. They never told us what it would mean, right Lem?"

The arm stopped shaking. Jordan held it stiff.

"G-g-give me that," Jordan said, referring to the letter.

"It's a copy, Lem." Addis and Starrell had stopped at a copy shop on the way to the hotel.

"Give me the god-damn letter!"

"Other people have seen it, Lem. They have the original."

Jordan's eyes stopped shifting. Addis could see the inside of the barrel. He thought of a small piece of metal. A pill. Flying through the space between here and there.

"Lem, you can't. You can't. You know that. I know it, too."

"I d-d-d-don't know, Nick . . . It's not—"

"Yes, you do. You do know, Lem. This isn't part of it."

Fuck, hasn't it been ten minutes?

"I d-d-don't. I d-d-don't."

Jordan's eyes were watering.

"I s-s-saved you. You shouldn't have come. You shouldn't have."

"Yes, thank you, Lem. Thank you very much for last night. Just like you saved Margaret in Cincinnati. Now, can we try to figure everything out together—"

"N-n-no," Jordan interrupted. "Sorry, Nick. Sorry." He blinked tears from his eyes.

God-damn, this is it. And it's not even going to help him. They'll find him

omewhere—a wreck, or a corpse with one bullet wound, self-inflicted in the head.
should tell him about the knapsack. There's too much evidence, he can't stop it
*y—

"S-s-sorry, I'm . . ."

Addis took a deep breath, felt his lungs expand. Like last night. Like
right before leaving the air for the water.

A bang sounded by the entrance to the living room. Addis and Jordan
turned toward it and saw Jack entering the room, with the wheelchair
scraping against the doorjamb. His eyes were wide and wet. He held a
cardkey in his hand. He rolled a few feet, then stopped.

"Told Bruno I had to go empty out," Jack said. He patted the plastic
container that held the waste his body produced. "But, uh, he's in the
hallway."

"Thanks for coming," Addis said.

"You asked me to," Jack said. "And I did. Ten minutes, like you said."

"You heard some of that?" Addis asked.

Jack nodded weakly.

Wish I didn't have to do this.

The boy faced Jordan but said nothing. Jordan's arm was limp, the gun
pointing at the floor.

"Lem, who chased us off the road?" Addis asked.

Jordan stared out the window. "Don't know. Never saw enough of
him."

"How did you get Morrison's son into that unit? How could you do
that?"

Jordan gazed nervously about the room, as if he felt exposed and
couldn't decide in which direction to move.

"Lem," Addis said, "I don't know what to say. I—"

"Once we were at a funeral," Jack interrupted. He paused and swal-
owed. "My great aunt or somebody. And this man comes up to me, says
he's my grandpa, and if I ever need something I should just tell Lem, and
Lem would let him know. And, like, I would get it. Said he was sorry for
something . . ."

*Shit, Harris Griffith and now Lem. Chasie, that S.O.B., had it wired. Margaret
had chosen Bob over him, and still her father was doing what he could for his
daughter and grandson.*

"Were you being paid by Chasie?" Addis asked Jordan. "To keep
Chasie in the know, smooth things out? Help him look after them?"

*Chasie and the Mumfries's family had done business together. Had Lem gone
to Chasie with the Morrison problem? The kid was in trouble with the Marines,
so Chasie called a friend in Washington? Mumfries? And . . . Morrison ends up a
trained assassin?*

Addis recalled his ride with Mumfries the day Hanover was shot. In

345

the back of the limousine. The two of them. On the way to the White House. "Nick, I can't tell you how much I really helped them—both of them." That's what Mumfries had said.

Or had Mumfries been thinking about the time his family's newspaper sat on the story that Bob was drinking the night of the accident?

"Did you tell Bob or Margaret about Morrison and his son, about going to Chasie for help? No, you couldn't have. You probably didn't even know how Chasie fixed it. And she didn't know either, did she? She only knew about the land deal. Or suspected. Or didn't know, but does now. What secrets to keep, Lem."

Jordan looked at Addis and was silent.

Addis kneeled next to Jack. "Thanks for the help."

"Was Lem going to—"

"No," Addis said. "He's just upset about things. That's all."

"You sure?"

"Yeah, we'll go to an Orioles game soon, okay?" Addis picked up the page from the White House log. He tucked it and the Morrison letter into his jacket pocket.

"Bye, Lem," he said.

Margaret Hanover strode into the room. Behind her were O'Connor, Carey, Whalen, the head of the Children's Aid Fund, and several Secret Service officers.

"What's all this?" she asked, her eyes on Jordan's gun.

"Had to go," Jack said.

She caressed his head, stroked his hair. "That's fine, sweetie. And Nick?"

"Just talking with Lem," Addis said. "And just leaving."

There's so much I have to tell Julia.

He brushed past Margaret and whispered to her, "About Blue Ridge. About Chasie. About Griffith. And about . . ." He moved through the crowd and felt a hand on his shoulder. He thought it belonged to Carey. But he did not acknowledge it. His eyes met O'Connor's. He shook his head and kept walking. He left the suite and headed to the elevator. Someone called his name from behind. It was Margaret.

50

Mayflower Hotel
July 1

It's like I got a monster bag of radioactive kryptonite shit, Starrell thought to himself, as he sat in the lobby. All these people going by, all these SSers, they don't know clue one.

He kept talking to himself: They ain't the man. I got it. This stuff could blow some big-asses apart. The big bang.

He didn't know how. But he figured it could. People were dead because of it. Clarence Dunne, too—almost. This White House guy was acting like a god-damn ghost because of it. All in this bag. On this couch. Next to Twayne Marcus Starrell. And Tamika knew he was doing something big.

Starrell watched everybody. The tourists with whiny kids. The hotel people trotting by without smiling at him. The Secret Service agents who checked him out. This white shirt of his—this funeral shirt—smelled, but he was getting his money out of it. Keep observing, he told himself. For what? Fuck if he knew. But there was nothing else to do. So just watch.

Two of the four Secret Service agents started to move. The others were cocking their heads, listening to the earpieces. Shit's happening. Just keep on waiting, he said silently. The ghost-geek told him to wait thirty minutes.

A man came through the revolving doors. The first thing he looked at were the Secret Service men near the entrance. His eyes were slits, tightly focused. Like he's zooming bitches, Starrell thought. The officers were talking to each other and did not immediately notice the man. He was wearing a long raincoat, black sneakers—like a basketball ref wears—and portable headphones. But when he stood still nothing moved. No finger-tapping or body-swaying. He was like stone. What music was he listening to? The man scanned the room and then his eyes popped open. Like he's changing his whole look, Starrell thought, and now he's a gee-whiz gumby-head. The man headed toward the bar.

347

"If I worked for the suits, I'd follow a crazy-ass like that," Starrell said to no one.

Anjean Jameson sat down on the couch. Starrell, occupied with the man in the raincoat, had not noticed him entering the hotel. The knapsack was between them.

"Hey, bro-man," Jameson said, flashing a malicious smile.

Starrell saw the Secret Service men staring at them.

"Ain't the time, Anjean."

Starrell pulled the bag closer, and Jameson grasped one of the straps.

"I got nine reasons why its fuckin' perfect Miller time—and each one is a millimeter." He patted the lump in his nylon sweatpants.

"Anjean—"

"Don't make me go crazy bad on you," he said. "I tried to be a reasonable black man, but you—"

"Shit, we got fed-boys all over. This ain't no place for you to make a dumb-ass move."

Jameson gazed across the lobby. "They couldn't catch me yesterday. They can't today."

"This ain't yesterday."

"Where's your white-boy partner?"

"He's coming."

"And the deal?"

"Ain't no deal, Anj."

"Gotta be something for me, Twayne. And Willie. Our family keeps your ass safe, and we don't get shit. Man's gotta look out for family."

"Anj, let me play it out, and when we got it all straight, we'll figure something, okay?"

"Can't feed no family on promises. How 'bout this: I hold on to this for a while"—he pulled on the strap—"and you tell him to call me up?"

"Fuckit, Anjean, you're a real—"

The two Secret Service officers were leaving their positions. Jameson pulled the gun out of his pocket and pushed the barrel into Starrell's thigh.

"A real player," he said. "And you know I'll do it. Especially now that those faggots are gone."

The man in the raincoat came out of the bar. He was following the Secret Service men, keeping his distance.

"Listen up, motherfucker," Starrell said. "Shit's happening right the fuck now. You listen to me and I'll make sure you—"

Jameson pushed the gun harder against Starrell.

"No, lover-man, here's the tune: I'm going to get up. You let go of the fuckin' bag. Or else that'll be fuckin' it for Twayne. Got it? Here I go . . .'"

As the elevator door closed, Margaret Hanover stepped in. The lift began descending, and Addis could hear the protests of the Secret Service officers trying to stop her from getting on the elevator without them. She had wanted to be alone with him.

Margaret stood in front of him, her back to the door.

"What do you know? Or *think* you know?" she asked.

"Probably less than there is to know."

She said nothing and waited for another reply. He looked at the illuminated numbers above the door.

Six, five . . .

"Okay," Addis said, "something like this: Blue Ridge was a setup, orchestrated by your father. The son of the couple who were fleeced was the one who killed your husband. This isn't about white supremacists. This is more than a self-mutilating antigovernment nut with a gun. You created him—"

Margaret tried to interrupt, but Addis kept talking.

"Maybe not you directly. I can't say. But all the bullshit wheeling-and-dealing down there and then all the bullshit wheeling-and-dealing up here. He was a monster of two worlds. And a shitload of people are dead because of . . . Of what?"

Margaret took a long breath.

Five, four . . . And what about Donny Lee Mondreau and the asshole who said he had committed that murder? And did you really connive to meet Bob when he was at Harvard? And Julia. What about Julia? Did you send me to New Orleans just to see what could be found out about the Blue Ridge deal? And then sent Lem to do the real work? Sorry, six floors is not enough to cover it all.

"Nick, you hold a tremendous amount of power. You're dangerous. You are. You can decide . . . Despite what you think of . . . this, you have a responsibility. What you do will affect not just us, you and me, but millions, whose lives can be made easier or harder by the decisions we make here . . ."

Four, three . . . She's not even asking about the assassination. She only cares about—

"You know what will happen if Mumfries wins? Who will gain and who will be fucked . . ."

He was startled by her use of the word.

"You want to put them in charge? You and I have worked too damn hard to . . . My father and others—perhaps Lem—made mistakes. I have. So did Bob, whom we both loved . . ."

Three, two . . .

"Don't forget. We don't always have the luxury of being self-righteous. Sometimes when we judge, others pay the costs . . ."

Two, one.

"Here we are." The doors began to open. "Think," she said to him, "about the others. This is not about me."

"That's for damn sure. . . . You know, I think it's about me."

She stepped out of the elevator. Four Secret Service officers quickly surrounded her. One began chastising her for not allowing the officers to descend with her. Behind them, Addis saw a man in a raincoat brandishing a gun, pointing it at him.

"Fuck, Anjean, that white guy's about to drop someone. You got rocks, you come with me."

Starrell yanked the bag from Jameson and headed after the man in the raincoat. Jameson jumped up and pointed the gun at Starrell. Someone screamed at its sight. Starrell ran a few steps. He spotted Margaret in front of the elevator. The Secret Service officers were focused on her. They had not yet seen the man in the raincoat—or the gun in his hand.

"Shoot his ass, Anj!" Starrell shouted and dropped to the floor.

As the man in the raincoat pulled the trigger, a bullet tore into the back of his head.

Addis heard something slam into the back of the elevator. Then he realized a rush of air had passed by his left ear. He watched the man in the raincoat fall.

The Secret Service officers pushed Margaret Hanover to the ground and drew their weapons.

Anjean Jameson stood in the lobby, his arm held high, his gun dangling on his finger. He saw the officers aiming their weapons at him. People were running. He heard shouts. He raised his other hand over his head.

Twayne Starrell, on his hands and knees, scurried over to Jameson. "You play it right," Starrell said in a low voice. "Say you're just here looking for a bud, and you get to be a god-damn hero."

Starrell jumped to his feet and bolted toward the front door, the backpack slapping against him. Too many people were trying to move through the opening. He shoved aside two elderly women carrying large shopping bags. They fell to the ground. Others tripped over them. Someone was yelling at him from behind, ordering him to stop. He sprinted through the door and turned right on Connecticut Avenue.

Too much running, he told himself. Yesterday, today, too fuckin much. He cut right on M Street. He stretched each pace. Why was he running? He knew—just knew—that the White House geek didn't wan to be explaining everything in the middle of a god-damn hotel lobby. And with all the shit pulled, he was not going to hand over the bag with this kryptonite—Dunne's gold—to just any G-man. At the intersection of 17th Street, he ran straight into the road, dodged a delivery van, and kept going. Two blocks later he slowed and glanced behind. No one was there.

Addis stood over the man in the raincoat. The lower half of his face—his bony face—was gone. His eyes were open. A Secret Service agent had pulled back a flap of his coat. Addis could see that his headphones were attached to a radio receiver. He bent closer. Through the speakers of the headphones he could hear Secret Service communications.

Julia. Julia.

Her hair had looked alive. Dancing.

He thought about kicking the corpse. In the face—what remained of it—and sending pieces of gristle and blood flying through the lobby of the Mayflower.

One of the Secret Service detail asked Addis to step back. Other officers were standing tightly around Margaret. Another group had pulled a young black man to the side. He was handcuffed and they were questioning him. Police officers were filling up the lobby.

The Secret Service man asked if Addis needed any medical attention. Addis shook his head. The officer was young. The skin on his cheeks was red and irritated.

"First the President, then his wife," the agent said. He looked at the corpse. "But not this time, dirtbag." He turned to Addis. "Fifth week on the job." He then shooed away several hotel guests who were trying to take photographs of the dead man.

A white-haired man in a turtleneck snapped a shot of Addis. He felt the flash against his face and shut his eyes. When he opened them, he saw the young Secret Service officer pushing the tourist back. The elderly man was wearing a large button on his shirt. It read: "Pratt's for God. Pratt for President."

"Bless you," the tourist said to Addis, over the shoulder of the Secret Service man.

Addis looked toward Margaret. She was staring at him and tucking strands of hair into place. She mouthed one word at him: "See?" Did he think that the man in the raincoat had come for her? That her cause was so strong she was targeted for assassination? Addis decided not to ask.

The young Secret Service agent was demanding the tourist hand over the film. Addis stood by himself. No one had told Addis he could not leave, so he headed out the door.

51

The White House
July 1

"We were told to notify Mr. Grayton and Mr. Kelly immediately if you showed up." The uniformed guard at the Pennsylvania Avenue gate had an apologetic expression on his face.

"So notify them," Addis said.

"I think they'd probably want me to have you wait here."

"Did they order you to detain me on sight?"

The guard shook his head.

"Then tell them I am heading toward an unscheduled meeting with the President."

Several limousines, towncars, and sports utility vehicles—all obligatory dark blue, all with dark windows—lined the driveway that led to the front portico. Camera crews and technicians were hustling across the compound. Correspondents were filing live remotes. Like the old days, Addis thought. The security restrictions had been eased to facilitate media coverage of the President's departure. Of course.

Media uber alles, he said to himself. Besides, Grayton was aware that no threat existed. Not now. They all were dead. All the remnants of the covert action unit—Grayton's unit?—were dead. They had been trained, at taxpayer expense, to kill foreign enemies. Then they came home. And one had . . . Addis recalled a line from the letter. *I hope you ain't got no twitches yet.* And what else had the father written to his son? That the governor's aide *talks like your momma did.* What did this say about the man who had killed Hanover? His mother stuttered. His father worried he might develop "twitches."

Shit, Addis thought, Huntington's disease? He knew the symptoms. He remembered accompanying his own father to see a specialist on Huntington's years ago when his father was writing the Woody Guthrie book. Jerking movements. Speech problems. Mental deterioration. The child of a parent with Huntington's has a fifty-fifty chance. They wait years for that first "twitch." Had Matthew Morrison felt a "spasm" and realized what lay ahead? Pissed-off, cheated, little to lose—the classic profile.

Two reporters spotted Addis and rushed toward him. One of Byrd's assistants cut them off. Addis was off-limits. Not right before the big send-off. The assistant press secretary stood in front of the reporters, while Addis headed toward the West Wing.

"You can decide." Margaret had said that to him. She had not revealed what she knew. Not about the deal. Not about Griffith's death. Had she approved Chasie's scheme for her family? Been in on the planning? Realized that her father had maneuvered Matthew Morrison's family off their land? Was Addis right to assume Jordan had been dispatched to New Orleans to tend to Griffith? Or had Jordan done this on his own, as a gift to Margaret?

"What do you know?" she had asked him. That was the question for her.

But, then, did it matter if she knew all the details, all the history? Allison Meade was dead. So was Gillian Silva. That reporter, too. And the guy who ran that bizarre escort service. What did the adult services ads in the alternative weekly call it? "Private viewings," didn't they? Some CIA shrink was in deep shit in Africa. And, and . . . Damnit, was it better to try to remember what Julia Lancette had looked like, felt like, smelled like . . . or better to let it go?

"She knows." That's what Morrison had said. Was that what he meant? A guess on his part, or a wish? Did it matter what Margaret knew?

Not to the dead.

But it *should* matter—particularly to Margaret. In her name *or* at her hand—was there any difference? What had been done had been done for her. The deal-rigging. The fixing. The god-knows-what. For her and for Bob Hanover. Had the sheriff of Opelousas been one of those who had been of help to the Hanovers? Or had a lying psychopath had the decency to commit suicide and save the judicial system a few bucks?

"This is not about me." Margaret's eyes had searched for acknowledgment—for agreement—from Addis in the elevator. Yes, it was about more.

Pink trails on her face.

Hands floating as the water reached her breasts.

"You can decide."

He certainly could. Margaret or Mumfries.

He walked past a Marine in the lobby of the West Wing. Cabinet members milled in the waiting area. Labor talked to Health and Human Services. Defense huddled with Education. Alter and Wenner were on a couch

353

talking, waiting for the meaningless, photo-op predeparture Cabinet meeting. Everyone stared at Addis when he entered. He walked toward the couch. Wenner got up; Alter remained seated, his hands folded atop his wooden cane.

"What happened at the Mayflower?" Wenner asked.

"Everyone's fine," Addis answered. "Margaret's fine."

"But it was close?" Alter asked.

"Yes," Addis said.

"We're going to have to turn this damn city into an armed camp," Alter said.

No, just stop the games.

"And he's dead?" Wenner asked.

"As dead as Bob Hanover," Addis said.

"Good," Alter blurted out. He then smiled weakly. "Though it would have been preferable to have taken him alive. For questioning and all that."

"If anyone was curious," Addis said.

Alter and Wenner exchanged glances.

"About Ms. Lancette—" Wenner began to ask.

"She worked with you directly?" Addis interrupted.

"She was a good officer, and I promise we're—"

"Fuck you, director," Addis said. "And fuck you, Mr. Secretary."

Wenner's eyes widened. Alter stared at his wing-tip shoes. Other Cabinet officials shied away. Addis straightened his tie.

"Excuse me," he said. "I have to see a man about a dog."

Grayton and Kelly intercepted Addis in the anteroom outside the Oval Office. "Whoa, cowboy," Grayton said and placed a heavy hand on Addis's shoulder.

"Got to go," Kelly said into his cellular phone. He snapped it shut and slipped it into the pocket of his jacket.

Addis ignored them and looked at Mumfries's startled secretary: "Please tell the President that I need to speak to him for a minute."

Grayton stiffened his arm and held Addis in place. Kelly shook his head at the secretary. Two Secret Service officers at the door to the Oval Office stepped forward.

"Sorry, Nick, the President is busy," Grayton said.

"I think he'd want to see me," Addis replied.

"Now's not a good time; he's occupied with more pressing matters," Kelly said. His thin lips barely moved when he spoke.

Addis pushed Grayton's arm away. He turned toward Kelly.

"Actually, Ham, now's the most appropriate time ever."
Grayton positioned himself inches in front of Addis.

"And *now* is *not* going to happen," Grayton said.

Protecting yourselves? Protecting him? One and the same?
Would talking to Mumfries change anything? Addis had pondered that question as he had walked past the Roosevelt Room, where aides and media technicians were preparing, where Brew McGreer was barking at underlings—fucking this, fucking that—as a flustered Ken Byrd looked on.

There were two possibilities: Mumfries was an honest sleazeball, or he was a dishonest sleazeball. Maybe he didn't know that the plan to run an off-the-books hit team had led to the murder of Bob Hanover. Or perhaps he was aware of the ripples and now was encouraging Grayton—depending on Grayton—to run cleanup. Or maybe this was a Kelly and Grayton operation, with Kelly following Washington rules and keeping the bad news from his boss. Was it crazy to give Mumfries a chance to explain? To give Mumfries the opportunity to claim that he was merely a run-of-the-mill shitbag pol, not a murderous conspirator? If so, what then? Only Margaret would have to pay?

"You can decide." But how much did he want to decide? To determine who would be the next President of the United States?

"I noticed you're not beefing up security here after the attack at the Mayflower," Addis said to Grayton. "Someone takes a shot at Margaret and you're not sweating. . . . Think the President might be concerned about that? Or do you have reason to believe that the threat has been . . . neutralized?"

"What the fuck do you want, Nick?" Kelly asked with a sneer.

"Not to deal."

Grayton jabbed a finger into Addis's sternum. Addis jumped back with the pain. Grayton moved close to him. Addis breathed in his cologne.

"Let's keep it simple," Grayton said so only Addis could hear. "You turn and leave now, and you have a nice life ahead. Sure, there's shit to deal with. But that's what lawyers are for. And you got the best. You'll get through it. Then you have book deals, TV appearances, job offers. Fuck, go teach at some overpriced college and grab all the peach-bottomed coeds you can find. Hop a flight to California, buy a convertible, and score in Hollywood. Yeah, L.A. bimbos. Or, be a master-of-the-universe at some investment house. But you push now, with your stories, *her* unconfirmed speculation, and . . ."

Do you know about the backpack?
"And what?" Addis asked. "One big happy game of make-believe?"
Grayton squinted at Addis and said nothing for a few seconds.

The sound of a decision being made.

"No, thank you," Addis said. "I'd like to see what happens here when all the bullshit runs out."

Grayton nodded at the Secret Service men. They moved closer to Addis.

Shit, they're not going to let me leave, Addis thought.

Grayton looked at Kelly, and Mumfries's chief of staff entered the conversation. "Nick," he said. "We got a call from Metro. Unofficial, you know. Did some lab tests. Turns out—well, it's just preliminary—Julia Lancette was all coked up—"

Fucking perfect.

Addis grabbed Kelly by the collar of his jacket. "You fuckers—"

He started shaking Kelly, who struggled to break free. The two tussled, and Addis pulled Kelly closer. The Secret Service men looked at Grayton, awaiting an order. Addis tightened his hold on Kelly. Grayton slid his arms between the two and pushed Addis back. Addis breathed hard and stared at Grayton. He held his right hand inside his jacket, as if he were clutching his side.

"Nick Addis the tough guy—that was not very characteristic," Grayton said.

Addis said nothing. He dropped his arms to his side. Don't move too much, he told himself.

"Yeah," Kelly said, straightening his tie, "they found traces in her blood. So there are people thinking, like, maybe, she could've gotten out of the car, if it weren't for that. Since you two were seen at this club before the incident, well then, maybe, somehow, you might be . . . I don't know, responsible or something. I'm no lawyer, but there's manslaughter. I know that. And other things when drugs are involved. Now, as I said, this is all unofficial. We just got a heads-up. From friends on the force. So, maybe . . . And, damn, Nick, think how shitty her folks are going to feel. That maybe, maybe, if it weren't for that shit, she might have . . . well, you know."

What god-damn assholes. Can they pull off some stunt like this? Who the fuck knows?

"And," Grayton added. "That other lady friend of yours. The lawyer. On-again, off-again. One of the partners in her firm has been backdooring funds between a prominent union and your party. Right, Ham?"

Kelly shrugged: "It's too bad some of our people get so wrapped up in winning."

"The Bureau's been looking into this," Grayton said. "There's a union informant telling stories. And the agent handling him—well, he's not certain if the informant has mentioned a Ms. Holly Rudd. There have been

356

iours of interrogation. But he's going to ask the informant about her. Sometimes asking the right question at the right time jogs a memory."

"A memory," Kelly repeated.

"Dead or alive, reputations do matter, Nick," Grayton said. "Don't hey? In the end, that's all one has, isn't it?"

You fuckheads give me no choice. And you don't know it.

"Henry, see Mr. Addis back to his office," Grayton said to one of the Secret Service men. He kept his hand on Addis's arm. "We'll talk more ifter the President leaves."

The door to the Oval Office opened, and Mumfries walked out. He was reading a document. "Mrs. Dee, can you explain where—"

He looked up at the people gathered outside his office.

"Holding a meeting?" he asked. "Nick, is Margaret okay? You were here, right?"

"Yes, Mr. President—"

"Didn't even come close," Grayton interrupted. He squeezed Addis's arm.

"Good," Mumfries said. "It's turning into a god-damn free-fire zone."

"Mr. President," Addis said quickly, "could I speak to you a minute?"

Mumfries looked at Kelly. His expression asked, what's this about? 'Don't think there's time, sir," Kelly said to Mumfries. "The networks will carry the send-off, but they asked that we don't go too far into the slots for the soaps."

"Later, then, Nick." He returned to the document and headed back toward the Oval Office.

"But—"

Addis felt a jab. He looked down. Grayton had drawn a gun and shoved the barrel into Addis's side. Because Grayton had moved closer toward Addis, no one else could see it.

No fucking way. Here in the White House? In front of the President? You're not that stupid.

Then Addis realized Grayton was no fool. In the time that Addis had processed Grayton's threat, Mumfries had entered his office and shut the door. Grayton returned the gun to the holster inside his jacket. He stepped away from Addis.

"It does distract," Grayton said. He turned to the Secret Service agent: "Henry . . ."

The burly officer took Addis by the arm. Grayton whispered into the Secret Service man's ear.

"Sorry, sir," the officer said to Addis and led him away.

Addis stood by his desk. The door to the office was closed. Henry was standing guard at the other side of the door. Addis took Kelly's cell phone—the one he had pickpocketed during their struggle—out of his inside jacket pocket. He stared at the phone on the desk. Monitored or dead, he thought. The smart move would be for them to keep it alive to see whom he called. He picked up the handset: no dial tone. Addis flipped open the cell phone and punched the buttons.

Please, Ham, don't need to make a call. Not now.

"It's me." He spoke in a low tone. "Is he there? . . . Good. And he's got it? . . . Keep him there. I'm going to have someone come by. . . . You'll know. It'll be a surprise. Show him what's in the bag. Point out Clarence's notebook. Make copies. Lots of copies. Give him the originals. . . . Yes, the originals. He'll need them to make people believe him. And hide the other copies everywhere. Around your office. Give them to friends. To strangers. . . . Can't get into it now, got to go. . . . Yeah, yeah, I'm okay. Thanks for asking. And thanks for helping more than you had to. I'll explain everything real soon. Everything. Promise."

He pulled a directory of Washington reporters from his shelf and found the right page. He dialed the number.

Be there. Be there. Be there. . . .

"Hulloh." It was that unctuous British accent. "Hynes-Pierce here."

"Evan, listen good. This is Nick Addis. I am about to make your life. Pulitzer. Money. Fame. A movie with god-knows-who playing you. This is it: The Blue Ridge deal is just part of it. There's more. It runs into the assassination. Check out who owned the land first. See if her nickname was Happy. . . . Yes, *that* Happy. . . . Anyway, there are documents. And they're all yours. . . . No, this isn't some fucking joke. . . . Yes, this is an exclusive but only for one day. You don't get the story out in tomorrow's edition, and it's everyone's: CNN, the networks, the wires, you name it. . . . You better put it all out, no games with your publisher—or you're going to look like an ass afterward. . . . Yeah, yeah, the Blue Ridge deal *and* the assassination. . . . Don't have time to go over it. I will vouch for the accuracy of the documents. . . . But there's one other thing: Julia Lancette, the woman I was with last night, was trying to find out the truth, and that's why she was killed. She never really got it all. But she tried. . . ."

Water covering her lips.

"She did. Came close, came . . . Quote me on that if you want, but I can't get into it now. . . . And here's some advice: Don't call anyone for comment—not the White House, not Margaret, not anyone—until your story's set and you're in a safe place. . . . Yes, a safe place. . . . How the hell should I know where one is? I'm just telling you to be careful. . . .

Why you? I'm not sure. You want a simple explanation: You have the background. But do me one favor—don't ask again."

He gave Hynes-Pierce the address of Rudd's office.

"I'll try to meet you there. But start without me. In return, I want you to answer one question, okay? . . . Later on, but you'll have to answer it, okay? . . . Trust me, for this, it's not too much to ask. . . . You'll see. You will. Good-bye."

He hit the "end" button. Addis turned toward the door. How long did he have? No one had barged in yet. He found the phone number he had scribbled on his calendar.

"Mrs. Lancette, this is Nick Addis. . . . I'm sorry I didn't call sooner. . . . There's a few things I think you should know. . . ."

When he finished, he asked for the funeral information. He then turned off the cell phone and placed it on the desk. He noticed a sealed manila envelope with no markings on it. He opened the envelope. Inside was a set of the documents that Tracy Griffith had faxed to him. He examined the inside of the envelope and found a folded-up note. It was written in red Magic Marker on plain white paper.

My cuz's boyfriend is an intern in the White House, so I think he can get this to you. I heard on the radio that papers were missing from your car. Must be heavy shit time, and figured these might be them. Fuck the State!

At the end of the note was a capital *A* enclosed within a circle. Anarchy, Addis thought. The kid at the copy shop. The little shit had kept a set for himself. "Fuckin' A," Addis muttered. All that's missing is the ICEMAN report—what Julia Lancette had gone looking for.

He placed the papers back in the envelope. He hiked up a pant's leg, wrapped the envelope around his leg, and taped it in place. He then pulled the pant's leg over the envelope.

Addis turned on the television. The Roosevelt Room was crowded: Cabinet members, congressional leaders, including Senator Hugh Palmer. The message was clear: Mumfries is the favored, Margaret a far-shot. The President was talking. Addis kept the sound off. Grayton and Kelly were standing behind Mumfries. It seemed as if Kelly was patting the side of his jacket. Was he looking for the cell phone?

Addis called the Associated Press news desk and said that he would be holding a press conference outside the West Wing as soon as the President departs.

"What's the subject?" the desk editor asked.

"I'm announcing my resignation."

"Why?"

"Personal reasons."

He noted that if he were late for the press conference, the servic should contact Jake Grayton, deputy director of the FBI, and ask abou Addis's whereabouts. "At the moment, it seems, Mr. Grayton is attempt ing to detain me in my office."

He called CNN and several newspapers and newsmagazines.

The President was now standing. People around him were clapping.

Addis wondered if this cell phone stored the numbers he had jus called. He reached into the small refrigerator for the can of Coke that Am from Computer Services had brought him earlier. From one of the boxes—

At least, I won't have to unpack

—he grabbed the oversized commemorative beer stein he had receive during the Berlin trip and poured the soda into the glass.

The President was leaving the Roosevelt Room. CNN switched to shot of the helicopter on the White House lawn.

Addis turned on the cell phone. He dropped it into the stein. The sod fizzled and hissed.

"*Ca-runk,*" he said, recalling the term Kelly had used. Tossing arma dillos to alligators.

He sat at his desk and realized this was the last time he would be i this office. Was there anything he wanted to keep? Next to him was th box containing the framed photographs he had not yet placed on th walls. A picture of him and Hanover riding in Jackson, Wyoming. A sho of him, O'Connor, and McGreer hugging in celebration on election night Playing chess with Margaret on Air Force One. Standing two rows behin the Hanovers at the inaugural swearing-in at the Capitol. Being burne in effigy in front of the White House by members of a political cult wh had accused him of masterminding a convoluted conspiracy, the detail of which Addis had never understood.

Mumfries and his family were boarding the helicopter. The Presiden waved to the crowd. Sally Mumfries threw kisses.

"*You can decide.*" And he had. But had he played it right? For the bes results? The fairest for all concerned? And for the country, too?

Close enough for government work, he said to himself.

He returned the photographs to the box. No, he thought, he didn' need any of these. But he picked up the framed postcard from LaTeenal Williams, one of the few students he had managed to reach and affect s long ago. She went on to college, social work school, and then hard worl on hard turf in the Bronx. He hoped she was still out there setting o ripples in the right direction. "Thank you," it read.

This I'll keep.

He waited for the door to open.

52

Bethesda, Maryland
November 3

n the night darkness, Addis walked carefully along the stone steps that
:d to the front of the tree-surrounded colonial. He rang the bell, and Alma
unne came to the door.

"Oh, I forgot to turn on the outside lights," she apologized. "I keep
orgetting."

"That's okay."

She took his hand and pulled him into the house. "What have you
een doing with yourself?" she asked, a touch of hesitation in her voice.

"Reading Dante," he replied.

"Oh," she said, not knowing how she should respond.

Why be a shit?

"Actually, I was out of town. At a wedding."

"That must have been nice."

*No, it was painful. But not as bad as I thought it would be. Holly looked great.
ut she's gone and that's okay. You don't get over things. You learn to live with
iem.*

"Yes, it was lovely."

*Especially when a law professor said he had written a law review article on
ie trial of Donny Lee Mondreau and asked if he could send it to me. I said, no.
Jot right now.*

"Clarence has been looking forward to seeing you. He's in the den."

he guided Addis to the room.

Dunne sat in a pale-green easy chair. Addis noticed a folded-up wheel-
hair in the corner. The television was on.

"Come on in," Dunne said. His voice was raspy. His mouth drooped.
Vhen Addis took Dunne's hand, Dunne squeezed hard and held the grip.

"Not too bad," Dunne said.

"Not at all," Addis said.

Alma excused herself.

"How are you?" Addis asked. He tried not to look at the television.

"Better than some," Dunne said. He swallowed hard after finishin the sentence. "Still scarred," he explained. "The cords."

Addis waited as he swallowed again.

"But moaning don't help. . . . Working hard. Phys-i-cal ther-a-py. V cal ther-a-py." He pronounced the words mockingly.

"No men-tal ther-a-py?" Addis asked.

Dunne started to laugh. Then phlegm caught in his throat. He grimace as he cleared it and spit the saliva into a tissue.

"Don't make me laugh," Dunne said. He dropped the Kleenex into wastebasket.

"Promise," Addis said.

Dunne pointed to the rocking chair next to him and Addis sat dowr Senator Hugh Palmer was on the television screen. Family, friends, ar aides huddled behind him, as he addressed a crowd.

"Want to hear?" Dunne asked.

"It's history, right?"

Dunne pushed a button on the remote.

". . . It was a long, a hard, and an uphill fight. Not for a moment w I regret returning to the Senate. And we will be back. Our values hav not been spurned. We shall continue to serve them and rebuild for th future. We are loyal to our cause: a just, productive America, where pro perity, tolerance, and opportunity reign for all. Where the political syste is not ruled by those who exploit it to selfishly advance their own advar tage. Where a child can grow up knowing his future is determined b what is in his heart and his head, not the surroundings into which he— or she—is born. Where our nation is as strong as it is diverse. Come ar other day, we will triumph."

The audience applauded and yelled his name. People held signs bea ing the year of the next presidential election.

"We will!" Palmer shouted. "We will!"

"There you have it," an anchor said, "an early concession speech tha was no surprise. On an election day that broke records for low voter turr out—"

Dunne silenced the television.

"Been getting on?" Dunne asked.

"Shit, Clarence, how can I complain when you're—" Addis caugl himself. "I'm sorry, I'm really—"

Dunne waved a hand at him: "Stop it."

"I suppose I'm doing alright. But sometimes I feel there's not muc left of me, after the hearings, the grand juries, you know."

On the screen, the network was recapping the previous months. There as the front page with Hynes-Pierce's story and footage of the press onference where the reporter had displayed the documents supporting s scoop.

Addis looked away from the set. In his mind, he saw the reporter in e bar. It was days after Hynes-Pierce had broken the story, the chaos of e Chicago convention was done. In the afternoon. No other customers ere present. They exchanged greetings, and Hynes-Pierce quickly got to e point: "And your question, it is?"

"Who first put you on the Blue Ridge story?"

"That would be revealing a source."

"Yes, I know."

"And you know that's against the rules."

"And I know you're going to tell me."

Addis waited for him.

"I doubt you will believe me."

"I think I will."

Hynes-Pierce ordered a gin and tonic.

"Your friend Sal Conditt, chief of staff to your other friend, Senator ugh Palmer."

Addis tried to hide his surprise.

"Why?"

"At first, I couldn't really say. Nor could I fathom why he would have ıy information on said transaction. But you don't look at what's behind leak now, do you? Not in this town. If we did, all us hacks would be on e dole."

"But . . ."

"Then Mr. Conditt shared the phone numbers of calls you had made Louisiana, and I concluded that he was fronting for colleagues of yours Casa Blanca and that Señor Kelly was conducting this orchestra. Mum-ies may well have have been in a position of familiarity with certain crets of Margaret's clan. And is there anything Mumfries knows that is ot shared with his very own Sancho Panza?"

Hynes-Pierce paused, as if to permit Addis to absorb the information.

"Now, with Governor Pratt the likely but unelectable opponent, the umfries band could take a cut at President Hanover and not have to orry about losing the White House. Merely hobble him. After all, would decade-old land matter mean so much? As you know, it's a tradition in is town: Presidents leak disparaging information on their seconds so as seem grander in comparison; the number twos do the same to their asters to cause their own value to be enhanced. But the leaks, of course, e supposed to be pinpricks, not on-the-nose punches. In this case, I would wager that operation occurred at what you call the staff level between Mr. Kelly and Mr. Conditt, with their respective barons out the proverbial loop."

Hynes-Pierce sipped his gin and tonic. A drop ran down the side of his mouth toward his chin. He caught it with his tongue.

"Did you know that the two once resided together in a group house Indeed. Out of curiosity, I did poke about. This was when they were both young, enthusiastic, fresh-faced Capitol Hill interns. In any event, credit Mr. Kelly for possessing the good sense to find an unlikely pathway for the information. If he had dangled it before me himself I might have chosen to write about internal White House plotting against the President And why would Mr. Conditt play along? For old times' sake, perhaps, a favor to his friend. To stick you? It's a possibility. One should never underestimate the psychological motive in this repressed Southern town You might be interested to know that a colleague of mine informed me that he had heard that Conditt, prior to the tragedy, had been under consideration for a senior position within Vice President Mumfries' office. any event, I long ago ceased attempting to discern motives in this city What counts is what counts. . . . Sorry, truly, if all this adds one more disappointment to your stock."

The reporter paid for the drink and left. Addis remained in the bar and traced another chain. Because Kelly and Conditt had introduced the story to Hynes-Pierce, Addis had been placed on the Blue Ridge trail; because he had investigated, he had pieced together the bizarre story that brought down . . .

The network was now airing video from the Chicago convention: Margaret's arrival. Mumfries's initial refusal to answer questions about Hynes-Pierce's story. Margaret's teary-eyed withdrawal. Ken Byrd passing out written statement—on the Fourth of July—announcing that Mumfries would no longer seek the nomination. Then film from the extra day that was added to the convention, when shocked, confused, and exhausted delegates eventually selected Palmer as the party's presidential nominee

A young black woman holding a swaddled-up infant entered the room Twayne Starrell followed. Addis stood and said hello.

"My wife Tamika and my daughter," Starrell said.

"Congratulations," Addis replied.

"They're staying with us a while," Dunne said. "Gives Alma something to do other than fret over me."

The couple sat on the couch. Starrell took the sleeping baby in his arms Addis returned to the rocker.

"What's her name?" he asked.

"Vanessa," Timmons said. "After my grammie. Her middle name Clarissa."

Addis looked at Dunne, who grinned.

The network played footage from the congressional hearings: Representative Wynn Gravitt, the chair of the special joint committee, lecturing Brewster McGreer. Jake Grayton arriving at the Capitol, accompanied by a lawyer, pleading the Fifth before the panel. Hamilton Kelly being yelled at by a senator, who accused him of scheming with Grayton and forging the memo on White House security to discredit Dunne. Members of Grayton's interagency SWAT team wearing hoods to conceal their identities and testifying that Grayton had placed an outsider in charge of their group and then used the unit to follow and monitor Dunne, Lancette, and Addis.

Dunne squeezed the arms of the chair. I led them to Gillian Silva, he thought—for the thousandth time. Grayton was watching me from the first. He realized that anyone investigating on their own posed a threat.

The masked figures on television were explaining that they had identified and located Raymond DeNoefri after breaking into his office and collecting fingerprints samples. They acknowledged that they had raided the apartment and killed Dawkins and Lopez, after being informed by their new commander that intelligence proved the pair had been part of the conspiracy to assassinate Hanover. It had been the commander who found the white supremacist material beneath the bed.

The image switched to M. T. O'Connor at the witness table, denying she had told Jordan to murder Harris Griffith. Next, a gaunt, pale Flip Whalen—his wife Amelia had died three weeks earlier—claiming he knew none of the secret details of the Blue Ridge deal. Secretary of the Treasury Louis Alter appearing irritated, as legislators questioned him. Why hadn't Alter taken Dunne's suspicions more seriously? Had Grayton informed him of the problem at hand, that Dunne's probing could undermine the entire administration? Alter dismissing the speculation with indignation.

There was CIA Director Timothy Wenner announcing his resignation, maintaining he had been misled by Grayton and claiming he had been unaware that Grayton had intervened with the Agency's director of administration to suppress Charlie Walters's original ICEMAN report. Walters's attorney announcing a $35 million suit against the U.S. government, charging that the CIA's Office of Security, at Grayton's behest, had sent him off to Africa and then had set him up.

The montage segued to Ken Byrd, the former press secretary, crying during an interview. A shot of Mike Finn, the former political director, in a luxurious office overlooking the Potomac, his cane lying on the desk. This was the cover of his just-published, bestselling memoirs, *Blind Luck*, which he secretly had been writing throughout his time at the White House.

A mug shot of Matthew Levon Morrison, the Marine washout transformed into a government killer as a political favor. A picture of his mother: Helen "Happy" Morrison. Footage from the bombing in Tangiers. A tourist's snapshot of a dead man in a hotel lobby. And an autopsy photograph showing a tattoo on the man's chest: an *M* with a dagger.

T. L., Dunne thought. Team Leader. The last survivor of the secret hit team Grayton had organized several years ago, with the knowledge of Mumfries, who then was chairing the Senate intelligence committee. The outsider whom Grayton had placed in charge of his more recent creation, the interagency SWAT unit. The man who had shot Dunne and killed Gillian Silva, Raymond DeNoefri, and Julia Lancette. All to prevent one truth of the assassination—that it had resulted in part from the excesses of the national security crowd—from becoming known.

There was video of Nick Addis taking one of the many sips of water he swallowed during three days of testifying. Next came footage of Clarence Dunne walking with Bob Hanover in the Rose Garden. Hanover had his hand on Dunne's shoulder, and Dunne was laughing.

The four adults in the room stared at the old Dunne on the screen. Dunne broke the silence: "I remember the joke. He was telling one on himself. It went something—"

Dunne coughed hard and continued speaking through the pain. "They—he and Margaret—were back in Louisiana. They passed through this small town where she, when she was a girl, had spent a summer, and they pulled over at a filling station. Turns out the owner and she had a thing that summer." Dunne spit out a gob of phlegm. "So when they leave the station, he says to her: 'Honey, if you'd stayed with that fellow today you'd be the wife of a mechanic.' She says, 'No, dear, if I'd stayed with him, today, he'd be President of the United States' . . . He liked that one. A lot."

Commercials had replaced the footage of Dunne and Hanover.

"What are you doing now?" Addis asked Starrell.

"Helping out my unc at the building, looking for a real job."

"I told him he should join the force, go to the academy," Dunne said.

"Police?" Addis asked.

"Ain't happening," Timmons said. "Too many get capped."

"Then what?" Addis asked.

"Don't know," Starrell said. "I kinda liked what I was doing with all this. Finding things, figuring things out."

"I know," Dunne said. "You and I can open up a private investigation firm. Be like something on TV. An old cripple and a young buck from the streets."

"Should just get on with the TV idea," Timmons said. "Hell, Anjean' doing a book. And he can't write." The baby was stirring; she took her daughter from Starrell. "Got some white guy, no offense to you"—Addi nodded—"doing all the damn work. You know the name they got for it? *Street Hero*. That's a joke. And they're going to be putting his picture on t. Sent him up to New York—on a plane—for a guy to take his picture." She stroked her daughter's neck, and the baby went back to sleep.

"I ain't complaining or nothing, but all he got was one lucky shot. And Twayne had to tell him what to do."

"Leave it, Tamika," Starrell said.

"And they were going to give you all that money—over a million, right?—and you don't want to do it," she said to Addis. "Why's that?"

"Tamika, hush," Starrell said.

There was a photograph of Julia Lancette on the television. It had been taken during a rafting trip. Her hair was wet. She held a paddle over her head in a triumphant pose.

Dead or alive, reputations do matter. . . . In the end, that's all one has, isn't it? Addis could hear Grayton saying those words. Addis had his, but . . .

In the photograph, she was smiling. You never found the ICEMAN report, he said to her silently. And it never turned up. But just by looking for it, you—

The network switched to a shot of Lem Jordan being led into a New Orleans police station in handcuffs. Addis thought about the autopsy report on Griffith: severe head trauma was the cause of death. Jordan had not confessed, but Addis guessed—he hoped—that a scuffle between Jordan and Griffith inadvertently had turned lethal and that a panicked Jordan then tried to make it seem a suicide. That was how Addis liked to think about it.

Next, the recap showed the house outside Baton Rouge—the gated and fenced estate where Chasie Mason had resided—where Margaret was now living with Jack in reclusion. A long-distance shot, compressed because it had been taken with a telephoto lens, with Margaret pushing Jack in his wheelchair toward the high hedges of the garden.

The image faded, and Dan Carey was on the newscast set, sitting next to the anchor. As Carey spoke, he looked confident, authoritative. He cut the air with short, deliberate strokes of his hand. A legend on the screen labeled him a "special political analyst" for the network.

"Just didn't feel like it," Addis said to Timmons. "Pretty stupid, I guess."

"Up to you," she said.

Alma returned to the room and handed her husband a glass of water. She gave Addis a Coke. A chart on the screen showed that control of the Senate had changed. Palmer, Addis thought, would no longer be majority leader.

Shit, put the truth out, and now they had all of Congress and . . .

Wesley Pratt gazed out at the crowd. His eyes were full of wonder. His wife held her hands over her mouth. He pumped a fist into the air and red, white, and blue balloons fell from the ceiling. His silver hair shimmered, reflecting the television lights.

Dunne turned on the sound. A band was playing, "You're a Grand Old Flag." The camera pulled back and showed the stage was set in front of the State Capitol in Tallahassee. A full moon was shining behind the dome. People in the crowd jumped up and down and wildly waved flags. Others held signs: "Pratt: For God and Country." Two people raised a banner that read, "John 3:16." The band slid into a country tune. The crowd roared. It was one of the hits of Pratt's recording career.

Pratt held out his hands to quiet the crowd. The cheering lessened. Then he kissed his wife on the cheek, and the din resumed.

"Sure you want to watch?" Dunne asked Addis.

"Hate to spoil all your fun."

"God-damn cracker," Timmons said.

Alma looked at her disapprovingly.

"Thank you, thank you," Pratt shouted. He introduced his wife. He hugged his children. He looked toward each side of the stage. "Where is he?" he asked. "Where is he?"

Representative Wynn Gravitt bounced on the stage, pulling his wife along. "Ladies, gentlemen," Pratt said in a booming voice, "the next Vice President of the United States, Representative Wynn Gravitt!"

The crowd kept on cheering. Gravitt waved; his wife looked terrified. Pratt threw an arm around Gravitt, and the audience shouted, "Pratt and Gravitt!" Pratt again tried to calm his supporters. The band stopped. The cheering tapered off.

"My fellow Americans," he spoke slowly, overemphasizing each syllable. The crowd roared. "My fellow Americans," he repeated. Another roar.

"Boy, I sure do love the sound of those three words. My fellow Americans, we did it. We did it. For us, our families, our children . . . and for Him."

Another swelling of noise. The network cut to two white-haired women hugging each other, crying with joy.

"We have triumphed, with His help, support, and love. And we will take this nation back. Back to traditional values of right and wrong. Faith and love. Family and responsibility. We will restore the moral foundation of a nation that has been blessed from above. We will revive the spirit of America. We will protect and take to our breasts the most innocent among us. We will make sure our children live and thrive in a culture free of dangerous and malicious content. We will take our government back and limit its ability to interfere with our families and our right to prayer. We will have church and neighborhood charity instead of bureaucratic gov-

ıment programs, low taxes and freedom instead of regulations that
other business. We will live in one nation under God."
The crowd shouted its approval. The band struck up another Pratt hit.
ove the dome, fireworks exploded. Red and green tracers descended
m the sky. The camera zoomed in on Pratt. Tears were in his eyes.
pporters in the audience were dancing.
"Some show," Dunne said.
"Crackers," Timmons sneered.
The fireworks ended. The band finished. "There, there," Pratt said. He
s again trying to quiet the crowd.
"There, there, my friends. This is a time for thanks. For all of us, a time
thanks. First and foremost"—the crowd began cheering—"and you
ɔw who is at the top of our list, let me thank God."
The audience clapped and yelled. The network showed a young, clean-
man on his knees praying.
"He's first on a long list."
He didn't say "Jesus."
Addis remembered the news report about a confidential memo sent
Gravitt's chief political consultant to Pratt. Don't use the "J-word," it
l advised. Polls showed people were more comfortable with "God."
"Then there's my wife, Ellen, and our six beautiful, little miracles:
ra, Susan, Rachel, Todd, Sarah, and Emily. My parents who are smiling
ıs tonight from the eternal kingdom. The tens of thousands of you who
ʾe me your time and faith. And, of course, my running mate and part-
ʾ, Congressman—oh excuse this country boy's mistake—that is, Vice
ʾsident-elect Wynn Gravitt."
The audience shouted, "Wynn! Wynn! Wynn!"
"This is a great night," Pratt yelled over the crowd. "A great night.
ɔok forward to working closely with Wynn Gravitt, a statesman and
isionary. No one will play a more important role in my administra-
ı."
Gravitt raised his index finger in the air. The crowd cheered him.
I do hope someone's up there.
"We have control of both houses of Congress," Pratt said. Another
r erupted. "From the Capitol to the White House—we will put into
ion our campaign of decency. And to those who have not supported
let me say: You might disagree with our views. But I promise you—
ɔod is my witness—we will implement those views honestly and fairly.
r administration will be clean and open. Free of dishonest entangle-
nts and backroom dealings. No one need ever be ashamed of our gov-
ment."
Gravitt shot a thumbs-up at someone he recognized in the crowd. He
s not listening to Pratt.

"Not one brother or sister up there," Timmons said. "These oh-decent white folks gonna give it to us."

Maybe it won't be so bad. How far can they go? There'll be congr sional elections in two years. Or . . . Damn, it's hard to stop spinning.

"So to all of you, I say, thank you," Pratt continued. "And good nig Get some rest. We got work to do."

Pratt, his family, Gravitt, and his wife grabbed hands and forme line.

"Pratt didn't thank you," Dunne said to Addis.

"An oversight, I'm sure," Addis replied.

And he didn't thank Julia.

"Guess you kinda feel responsible," Timmons said.

Starrell nudged her in the side.

"Well, don't he?" she said. She was facing her husband, but her e looked toward Addis.

The more perfect someone is, the more he sees the good and the bad.

After returning from Rudd's wedding, Addis had checked the Da quotation that Lancette once had recited for him. He discovered that had mangled the passage. So much so that he had difficulty finding it. he did locate the lines she had memorized when she was in college: "more a thing is perfect, the more it feels pleasure and likewise pain." O time, the quote had changed for her. Her version had a different mean than the original. And he preferred hers. Unintentionally she had i proved on the truth as seen by a fourteenth-century poet. Perhaps, thought, memories become what we want them to be.

"Don't he?" Timmons asked again.

"That's enough of this," Dunne said and shut off the television.

"Yes," Addis muttered, "yes." He tasted the Coke, closed his eyes, a saw a face. She looked as though she understood.